His touch felt so good, warm and gentle for such a large man. She found herself leaning into his palm. *Kiss me.* The thought whispered in her mind, but he somehow knew what she craved.

He took her mug from her hand and placed it on the table next to his as he leaned forward, his lips hovering over hers. "Just a taste. Aye?" His seductive whisper stroked over her mouth with the effect of a soft kiss. His hand slipped to the nape of her neck, drawing her closer as he deepened the caress.

Heat spread through her, warming her from the inside out. He tasted of the sea, whiskey and sweet temptation. The more she indulged, the more she wanted. The thick beat of awareness ran through her blood, making her heart beat faster. Her hands cupped his face. His five o'clock shadow barely prickled her palm.

The kiss ended if only to take a breath, but he didn't move away. His lips still hovered near hers as if to reclaim them again.

"I knew you'd be a good kisser." Her voice a hoarse whisper, laced her words like an invitation for more.

His lips slid into a seductive curve. "Did ye now?"

She nodded her head, still a little breathless.

"This was a mistake, ye know."

"It was?" She tried to move away, but he held her still.

"Shush. I only meant it was a mistake on my part to indulge with a promise of only one taste. I want so much more." His mouth covered hers again, taking her under his spell.

Praise for *MAGIC OF THE LOCH*

"This was a very good reinterpretation of the Loch Ness Monster story. The characters are very well written and the story is fast paced right from the beginning."

~Felicia Wright, ParaNormal Romance Reviews
~*~

"*MAGIC OF THE LOCH* will wrap the reader in its spell on the first page and won't let go until the end."

~Stephanie Burkhart, author
~*~

"A tale of curses, folklore and revenge, *MAGIC OF THE LOCH* is a wonderful story for paranormal romance readers. Ms. Nutt has created a sweet romance spun from a legend and delivered a suspenseful story as well."

~Catherine Bybee, USA Today bestselling author
~*~

"In a nail-biting, breathtaking read, *MAGIC OF THE LOCH* will keep you on the edge of your chair until the last page."

~Cheryl Pierson, author of Sweet Danger
~*~

"Fascinating story that hooks you from the beginning with a clever version of an old tale."

~Cathy Nickol, reviewer
~*~

"I look forward to reading the tale again and again as the bond of brothers transcends time."

~Adryanna Coleman, reviewer
~*~

"This well-written, fast-paced novel kept me reading until the wee hours of the morning. I dare you to try to put this one down!"

~Martha L. McBryar, author

Magic
of the Loch

by

Karen Michelle Nutt

Magic of the Loch

Cover Art by *Rae Monet, Inc. Design*

The Wild Rose Press, Inc.
PO Box 708
Adams Basin, NY 14410-0708
Visit us at www.thewildrosepress.com

Publishing History
First Faery Rose Edition, 2012
Print ISBN 978-1-61217-292-7
Digital ISBN 978-1-61217-293-4

Published in the United States of America

Dedication

Thank you to Greg, Kendra, Katrina and Vincent
for suffering through
when my muse demanded my attention.

~~~

And special thank you to Cathy and Stephanie
for the adventures we have
from ghost hunting to sharing a cup of tea. Hmm...
We should add a hunt for the Loch Ness Monster
to our list of things to do.
Thanks gals for your endless support.

Prologue

The Legend of Loch Ness

Alan shot from full sleep to wakefulness as the horn blared, shattering the early morning with the threat of danger. He threw back his furs, grabbed his dagger and bolted from his dwelling. His gaze swung to his brother, Hyatt rushing forward to join him in the center of the village.

"Do ye see anythin'?" Hyatt's hoarse whisper only intensified Alan's unease.

The scrape of metal resounded as the other clansmen charged out of their dwellings with weapons. From one of the huts, a baby's cries joined the horn's cry like a symphony of impending doom.

The foliage to the left rustled in protest, announcing someone's approach. Alan stood ready with his dagger raised.

Ronson burst into view, his eyes wide with anxious fear. "We must go. Now!" he shouted the warning.

Ronson stood guard with Dougal tonight, a formality they had not given up even though the clans were at peace. If Ronson stood in their midst, it meant Dougal faced the threat alone.

The unexpected blare of the horn shattered the tranquility of the night. Alan gripped Ronson's arm before he could sprint by him. "Who dares threaten us?"

"No' who. The well's cover is gone. The water spirits are angry and seekin' vengeance. Can ye no' hear it? Water pours out of the well like a river,

1

headin' straight toward us. Dougal is tryin' to stop it, but it's too late. Even if he finds the lid, he cannae secure it the way the water is ragin' out of control."

Dougal's horn was abruptly silenced as if the instrument had been ripped from his grasp. The stillness, like a hush spreading over them, proved worse than the resound warning. Even the child fell quiet.

"Dougal failed." Ronson proclamation ignited his fear again. "I must go to my wife and daughter." Ronson tore free from Alan's grip.

Wails of panic rose as Ronson's warning spread through the village like wild fire blazing out of control.

Alan leveled his gaze on Hyatt. "Spread the word that we must head for higher ground. Help Gordana and her son. I will tend to the elders."

"On my way." Hyatt hurried toward their sister's dwelling, shouting the alarm as he went.

"Take only a few meager belongins," Alan warned when he spotted some of the women trying to carry more than they could handle. "There is no' time."

Dougal's children hurried by him, but the little girl tripped and fell. Her cry halted her brother's steps and he jogged back to her.

"Get up Moira," he urged, but the little girl wouldn't budge. Alan hurried over to them. He righted the girl, planting her firmly on her feet. "No cryin'. I need ye brave. Do ye understand?"

Moira's blue eyes stared up at him. She nodded her head and sniffled.

"Good. Now take yer brother's hand and follow the others to higher ground." He looked to the boy. "Doonae stop. Do ye hear me?"

"Aye." The boy nodded and reached for his sister's hand.

"Go now." Alan turned away to help others.

He stayed to the last to make sure no one was left behind. Then he headed to the plateau, his feet sinking in the mud as the ground became saturated, making it just before the full onslaught of the water spirits' wrath.

Huddled together, they watched in horror as water poured down the mountainside in an explosion of raging waves like a greedy beast devouring everything in its wake. The watery death showed no mercy as it swept the dwellings, plants and trees away. The valley flooded into a dark pool, whitecaps glittering in the sun's light.

"Why have the gods forsaken us?" One of the women cried in a choked voice.

"It was Gordana's doin'," Ronson accused, pointing his finger at her.

Alan leveled his gaze on the guard. "What say ye aboot my sister?"

"She and her laddie were at the well yesterday. She must have forgotten to replace the lid."

Alan turned toward his sister, hoping for a denial. Instead, tears spilled down her face and guilt lit her eyes. "I dinnae mean to." Her voice choked in remorse.

"Gordana, surely—" Alan had no time to question her further. The gods finally answered the clan's clamoring of despair and grief. Druid Daly appeared before them in a streak of white light.

"Who is responsible for freein' the water spirits?" Druid Daly's gaze wavered over the clan in accusation.

Alan met his sister's gaze. Fear shone in the depths of her eyes and her hands shook. He wanted to reach for her, pull her into his embrace and tell her everything would be all right, but he couldn't. She had admitted her guilt by her own words. He could not protect her from the gods' judgment.

Hyatt stepped toward Gordana and her son, his

intent obvious. Alan couldn't let his brother make the mistake. His hand snaked out, clasping his brother's arm in a firm hold.

"Unhand me, brother." Hyatt's body tensed, readying for a fight. "Let me hasten them away before Druid Daly exacts a punishment."

Alan shook his head. "The clan willnae allow it."

His brother balled his hand into fist. "Let them try and stop me."

Alan's grip tightened. "Think this through. We cannae fight the whole clan. We must see what Druid Daly decides before we make our move. Aye? If the gods will no' show leniency, then we must strike a bargain."

Hyatt pursed his lips, but he gave a curt nod that he understood. Alan loosened his grip.

Samuel, one of the clan's elders turned toward Gordana. "We have the one responsible." He grabbed her arm, intent on dragging her forward.

His thick fingers wrapped around her upper arm with a steely grip, preventing her from turning away and fleeing. On her hip, she clutched her cherub faced, dark haired little boy. His arms wrapped around his mother's neck like a vise. Fear radiated in the depths of his blue eyes.

The people parted, clearing a path to where Druid Daly waited to judge the accused. Samuel thrust Gordana forward.

Druid Daly stood taller than most with long lean legs and arms. His hair fluttered over his shoulders in waves of white. Though he must be ancient, his face remained smooth from lines of age, but the depths of his eyes laid proof he was no innocent laddie. "What say ye?" Druid Daly demanded, his voice boomed, bringing silence to the woods.

Gordana lowered her head in shame. "My son was playin' near the fire. I feared for his life. I...must have forgotten to replace the lid over the well. I'm sorry. I'm so, so sorry."

Druid Daly remained silent for so long, the clan's murmurs stilled. Alan wondered if Druid Daly had not heard his sister's plea for forgiveness, but then the Druid's expression changed. A gasp from someone in the crowd made Gordana lift her head to look at the druid. She took a step back, but hands from behind her pushed her forward, preventing her from retreating.

Druid Daly's light blue eyes blazed with fury, making them look like shards of broken glass. "Ye forgot?" Birds flew from the safety of the trees as if they too feared the druid's wrath.

Gordana nodded her head. Her son struggled in her arms and she let him slide down to stand at her feet. The laddie hid behind the folds of her skirt.

"Do ye see where yer folly has led ye?" He pointed to the flooded valley below, not far from where they stood beneath the spruce trees.

"Can ye no' help us?" Ronson braved a step forward, brushing his long hair away from his face. "We should no' be held accountable for her mistakes. Can ye no' drain the valley so we may live as we once did?"

"Why would the gods or I be so lenient? I gave ye a gift of the everlastin' waters, but ye abused my trust. Ye were told to keep the lid secure over the well. It is the only way to keep the spirits from takin' the everlasting' waters below the surface and out of reach." His long finger pointed toward the loch, his sleeves hung from his arms, waving as the brisk wind lifted the loose material to and fro. "Yer well is beneath the surface in an underground cavern. The waters are too deep for a human to swim and survive."

"It was Gordana who did this." Ronson turned his deep-set eyes on her. "Why should we be punished for her mistake?"

5

"Why indeed," Druid Daly bit out. "Where were ye when the poor lassie needed help tendin' her young?"

Ronson opened his mouth to argue further but Druid Daly held up his hand. "No more, I say. I will no' grant ye more favors. Ye will have to make a new home and rely on yer own resources to find fresh water to drink. Ye will live yer life as other humans do."

Druid Daly ignored the gasps and sobs. "As for Gordana..."

Gordana drew her child closer against her. "I know I must pay for my sins, but I beg of ye to spare my child. He is young and has no' learned the ways of the world."

Druid Daly nodded. "Fair enough. The boy will be spared. However, Gordana, ye will pay for yer sins. The well still needs to be guarded."

"Is the well no' under water?" Ronson asked. "Ye said no human could reach it."

"Aye, but the world is forever changin'," Druid Daly told him. "There will be a time, when the well will be in danger. The oracle has said as much."

"How can we still guard it when it is underwater?" another asked.

"There is a way. Yer people are descendents from a line of shifters and now it's time to call upon the beast that lurks beneath the surface of yer existence. A creature that will embrace the watery depths of the loch."

He raised his staff, pointing it at Gordana. Magic sprung from the staff like lightning striking the earth. The people stepped back in horror and Gordana's little boy flew back as the bolt hit his mother.

Gordana screamed withering on the ground as bright energy encased her body, shifting it, changing it. Bones popped, elongated, and skin stretched, darkening to gray as an enormous creature with a long neck and tail emerged.

Druid Daly spoke again. "Ye have failed to guard the well in yer human state. Ye shall guard it in a more suitable skin."

Ronson's eyes widened in fear as he stumbled back. A woman grabbed Gordana's child less he be trampled by the monster Gordana had become.

"Ye cannae do this." Alan pushed his way through the crowd.

Druid Daly's gaze swept over the man who would dare challenge him. "And who might ye be?"

"Alan of the Glens." He bowed his head in respect before meeting the druid's gaze once more.

"Ye dare question me? I have been ordered by the gods to act in their name."

"Aye, and I respect their wishes, but Gordana needs to raise her child."

Druid Daly inhaled deeply, irritation evident in the depths of his eyes. "Is there any other who wish to challenge what the gods' bid?"

Hyatt stepped forward.

"I will stand by my brother. I am Hyatt."

They remained silent as the druid circled them. "Why would I spare Gordana when she disobeyed?"

"She is a good woman and deserves a second chance. She has a child who needs her," Alan pleaded.

Druid Daly's shoulders lifted in a shrug. "Ye are the child's uncle, are ye no'? Will you no' care for the laddie?"

Alan was losing his case. The Druid knew Hyatt and he would care for their nephew. He pursed his lips in frustration. Their love for the child would never compare to a mother's love.

Alan met the Druid's gaze and tried a different approach to win clemency for his sister. "Gordana's husband died when choppin' wood. A tree fell on

7

him, crushin' him. The curin' waters from the well were of no help in healin' a body that was crushed beyond repair. The laddie lost his father; must he lose his mother as well?"

"Hmm...the well must be guarded. Would ye both step up to take her place then?"

Alan glanced at the beast with thick gray skin, long neck and wide body, a hideous creature, but the eyes—the eyes of the beast were still Gordana's. She was his sister and he would protect her. He stood a little taller. "Aye, that I would."

"And ye?" Druid Daly looked at Hyatt.

"Aye, I will stand by my brother." He threw Alan a disgruntled look, but he would do what must be done.

"Then ye both shall be guards in her place."

"Wait," Alan stopped Druid Daly from waving his staff and unleashing magic. "There should be a chance for redemption. It is only fair since we are takin' on the accused punishment, aye?"

"Quite true," Druid Daly rubbed his chin. "Ye both shall live within the loch for half a century, but then ye will be allowed to come ashore for fifteen years, givin' ye time to seek yer soul mate. Only she will be able to break the curse and end yer confinement."

"We will be human and no' the beast." Alan wanted the terms clarified. "We will be able to search as far as needed for our soul mate, aye?"

Druid Daly shook his head. "Ye will still be chained to the loch. Ye will no' be able to resist its pull. Only during those fifteen years will ye be able to shift from beast to human and back again. If ye doonae find yer soul mate, ye will return to the loch as the beastie for another half a century." His shoulders lifted in a shrugged. "Ye'll have to bide yer time for another chance and so on through the years."

"An endless cycle," Alan murmured with grim acceptance. He looked to his brother. "Ye need no' share my fate. I will do this myself."

"I shall go where ye go, brother." He clasped Alan's shoulder.

"So be it." Druid Daly raised his staff and commanded the magic.

Chapter One

Present Day
Drumnadrochit, Scotland

Michaela Grant broke through the trees with hopes of seeing a landmark to pinpoint where the path had landed her. Douglas firs and spruce surrounded her on both sides. Moss carpeted the ground with foxglove, bluebells and other wildflowers.

Inhaling slow even breaths to lower her heart rate from the cardio workout, her gaze took in the beauty before her. In the distance, the dark murky water stood at the horizon with the lush foliage as an ornament of green. A good sign she had headed in the general direction she wanted. Reaching into her backpack, her hand latched onto her water bottle.

Feeling hot and sweaty, she took generous swallows to quench her thirst. The hike hadn't been strenuous, but her stamina had suffered in the last few months.

To the right of her, she spotted a small pier and a boat berthed at the end of a wooden boardwalk. "There's only one boat. This can't be right." Where were the other boats? Surely they couldn't all be rented this early in the morning. Then again, the streets of Drumnadrochit were buzzing with the news of recent sightings of the Loch Ness Monster. Everyone wanted to capture his or her own photo of the legendary creature.

She chewed on her lower lip as she debated turning around and heading back the way she had come. This had to be private property. There weren't any signs indicating boat rentals or tours.

She glanced behind her with a heavy heart. Her energy had dwindled and walking back seemed an impossible feat. Maybe she could see if the owner of the boat could help her out or at least let her rest for a spell.

With hopes for a reprieve, her steps took her down the small hill and toward the welcoming boardwalk. It was peaceful away from the hubbub of the Village Green with only birds and the soft lapping of the water against the pillars.

Stepping onto the wooden pier caused the boards beneath her to creak. "Hello," she announced her approach, not wanting to startle anyone.

A fierce bark greeted her from behind. Whirling around, her eyes widened in fear as she spotted a lumbering beast, masquerading as a German Shepherd, chasing a black cat. Both headed straight to where her feet stood rooted in the middle of the boardwalk. Her gaze darted in all directions in hopes of escape, but the narrow pier left very little room to maneuver out the way. The cat flew by brushing against her legs seconds before the dog charged after it.

Michaela tried to sidestep, but the dog's large body bumped against her, causing her to lose her balance. She let out a yelp. Her arms reached out in desperation to grab some invisible rope and stop her fall into the icy waters below.

Strong hands came out of nowhere, yanking her back and steadying her. "Easy now, I got ye, lassie." His voice was whiskey worn, deep and flavored with a Scottish brogue, indicating a local resident.

Her fingers gripped strong muscled forearms as her gaze sought out her would-be-rescuer. Her jaw dropped and she stared for a full two seconds, admiring the tall, dark and handsome Scotsman with hair glimmering like polished ebony. He had a chiseled chin and striking blue eyes fringed with thick sooty lashes. Her gaze lingered on his generous mouth. Surely, no one could be this beautiful and be real. "Thank... uh... Thank you," she stuttered, frustrated by her inability to articulate a clear sentence. Where had he come from? She could have sworn there hadn't been anyone on the dock a moment ago.

"Are ye sure ye're fine?"

She nodded but held on tighter simply because she wasn't ready to let him go.

"Then ye need to watch where ye're goin'," he snapped, his beautiful eyes narrowing and flashing with contempt.

Michaela opened her mouth in shock. The rude man had the gall to reprimand her. His dog had nearly dumped her in the loch, not the other way around. "I'll do my best." She lifted her chin and glared back at him.

"Ye're trespassin'. If ye want to schedule a tour, ye need to call ahead of time."

"I assure you I didn't mean to trespass. I took the path Mrs. O'Malley told me to—"

"Mrs. O'Malley?" he interrupted.

"Yes, I'm renting out her lovely cottage up—"

"I know where her cottage is, ye doonae need to draw me a map."

"You don't have to be so rude about it."

His blue eyes, like a flickering flame of a gas stovetop sparked with intent to burn.

What an unpleasant man. If she possessed the strength, she'd push him in the loch to cool off his hot temper. Intent on giving him an off-handed retort, her mouth opened only to clamp shut again at the sound of a deep chuckle behind her. Michaela turned her head and glared at the new arrival with the warped sense of humor.

"I'm sorry, for my brother's behavior," The man, who stood an inch or two taller than *Hot Head* next to her, announced with a meaningful glint in his eyes.

Michaela became on guard. She found herself far away from the Village Green with two men. One not too pleased for company and the other who looked at her as if she were a yummy treat.

Amusement danced in his eyes as he chuckled. "We arnae goin' to harm ye. Might I remind ye, my brother just saved ye from an unsavory dunkin'."

"I never implied—"

"Yer expression gives ye away, lassie." He reached out and gently rubbed the worry lines between her brows.

"Oh." Michaela felt a tingling where the stranger's fingers had brushed.

"I'm Hyatt MacLachlin." He held out his hand. "And the sour puss is my brother, Alan." He nodded toward *Hot Head*.

"Michaela Grant." She let the warmth of Hyatt's handshake seep through her. His glance was lazily seductive, causing her heart to thud like a drum as he took in every curve of her face.

"Hyatt." Alan's voice held a slight warning.

Hyatt took a step back, releasing his hold and taking the magnetic pull with him. She shook her head at the absurdity of her thinking. *Magnetic pull? Yeah, right.*

Rapid barks and hiss snapped her out of her trance. She looked at Alan. "I believe your dog is trying to devour a cat. You might want to call him off." She pointed toward the German Shepherd who barked and paced by the boat as the cat purposely walked along the boat's railing as if to say, *Come and get me if you dare.*

Hyatt laughed. "That's just Elvis and Priscilla."

Michaela arched a brow. "Elvis and Priscilla?

You're joking. That's their names?" She then noticed the name of the boat painted in blue script, *The Hound Dog*.

Hyatt lifted his broad shoulders in a shrug. "Ye have to speak to the owner." He motioned to Alan.

Michaela stared at Alan with his scowl of displeasure marring his handsome face. She chose to ignore his obvious wish for her to be gone from his sight. "You wouldn't happen to be an Elvis fan by chance?"

"Isnae everyone?" he growled and turned his attention to his pets. "Elvis stop yer racket." Surprisingly with this one command, the dog fell silent and sat down on his haunches. Priscilla sat on the ledge preening herself, oblivious to her near death experience. "There," he said turning to give Michaela his full attention. "They'll behave now."

"That's amazing."

He shrugged with indifference. "Ye only have to ask."

Hyatt drew her attention again. "I see ye have a backpack. Ye must be out for a day of adventure, aye? Are ye lookin' to try yer luck at catchin' sight of auld Nessie?"

A rush of warmth flooded her face. "Well...I...Yes," she said with an exaggerated sigh. "Guilty as charged. What can I say? I'm a tourist."

"No need to apologize." Hyatt beamed. "Drumnadrochit relies on tourism to survive."

Alan harrumphed.

Her gaze shifted to Alan once again. His massive shoulders filled the seafarer's sweater, his chest tapering nicely down to a tight waist and slim hips. He stood at least six two with sinfully thick strands of black hair. Her hands twitched with the urge to run her fingers through that hair to find out if it was as soft as it looked.

He cleared his throat as if to draw her attention.

Her gaze shifted to his sensuous face, direct and challenging in its appeal. The narrowing of his eyes lay witness to how much he disliked her presence.

"My brother has a boat as ye can see," Hyatt continued, ignoring Alan's deepening frown. "We could take ye out on the loch for a closer look."

Michaela hesitated. The dock didn't look like the regular pickup for tourists and she didn't know these two men. They could be crazed lunatics and she was a stranger to the country, where no one would miss her. At home, her boyfriend, Blake... Well she supposed ex-boyfriend now, was the only one who knew she'd taken this trip. Since they broke up weeks ago, he wouldn't check on her whereabouts anytime soon.

Her gaze lingered on Alan's intense scowl. He'd probably sooner toss her in the loch than drive her around it. Her body would never be discovered in its seemingly bottomless depths.

She worried her lower lip, hating that she hesitated. *You wanted to take a tour of the loch. Isn't that why you're here?* She reminded herself.

Hyatt must have sensed her fear. His brows drew together in an agonized expression as if he was hurt by her uncertainty of him. He reached out and lightly fingered a loose tendril of hair on her cheek. "Doonae be afraid, Michaela." His gaze touched her, so full of life and unquenchable warmth, begging her to trust him.

What did she have to lose really? Her days were numbered as it was. She turned thirty-two last month and most likely wouldn't see her thirty-third birthday. Every second counted. Isn't that why she quit her job at the hospital in Newport, made out her will, and checked on her life insurance? When her inevitable fate claimed her, her appointed executive would find everything in order. Now was her time to enjoy the days she had left to the fullest.

15

No regrets. Her annoying little voice insisted.

She could think of worse things to do than spend a day with two gorgeous looking Scotsman. "I would love a closer look...of the loch that is," she stumbled to clarify.

"Of course." Hyatt's lips twitched, threatening to smile.

"But Mrs. O'Malley told me to—"

"Mrs. O'Malley?" Hyatt questioned in the same surprised display as his brother.

"Yes, I'm renting a cottage from her."

"Weel, is that no' splendid." Hyatt's mouth spread into a full smile. "Mrs. O'Malley is a friend of ours. If she sent ye walkin' in this direction, it's more than likely she meant for ye to find us."

That seemed plausible. She had pointed out the path for her to take and *The Hound Dog* seemed to be the only boat in sight. "How much will this tour cost?" She had limited funds and wanted to stretch out her money for as long as possible.

"Dooncha know it? It's the second Tuesday of the month and tours are half the price to the first beautiful lassie we come across." Hyatt offered his arm.

She knew he lied. His brother Alan looked like he would bust an artery by the way he clenched his teeth and how the little vein at his temple throbbed.

She chose to ignore Alan and concentrated on the friendlier brother with the dark chestnut colored hair and blue-green eyes that sparkled when he smiled. "I'd be a fool to let an opportunity like that slip by." She took a step toward him and looped her arm through his.

"Aah, 'tis fate that brought ye to us, Michaela. Aye?"

Chapter Two

Alan wanted to throttle his brother. They didn't do private tours and they most definitely didn't offer their services for near to free. *Damn, Mrs. O'Malley's interferin' ways. Who does she think she is, sendin' a woman to them as if they needed to be bothered?* He should tell the Yank to go back where she came from, putting a stop to his brother's flirting.

He would have done so from the start, but all coherent thoughts had left him the moment his hands touched the woman's arms. Her scent struck him like an electric current, jolting him.

Then his gaze shifted, focusing on her auburn hair streaked with gold strands, to her eyes the color of moss in the early morning, and finally centering on her wide and lush lips.

Awareness filled his every pore and it took all his self-control to rein it in. His snappy retort had been harsh, but better he hurt her feelings than exploit her mouth for all its worth. If he'd lost control, she'd have willingly jumped into the loch to distance herself from him.

When his blood pressure finally returned to normal, a new sensation hit him—the urge to heal.

As they walked toward the boat, his gaze traveled over the length of Michaela's slim shape. Diligent exercise would keep her slim, but his senses told him that something else had caused her body to become fragile.

Look away and forget her, MacLachlin. He warned himself. *No good will come from this. Even if ye wanted to help her, ye cannae save her.*

He readied the boat for departure, while Hyatt entertained Michaela with stories about the Loch Ness Monster and other such nonsense. Hyatt's bold laugh grated on his nerves, but he was hard pressed to tell him to bugger off.

Once he released the boat from its tether and maneuvered it free from the dock, his gaze wavered back to Michaela as if some invisible line reeled him in. What could be the connection? It wasn't entirely his need to heal. He didn't know her, yet his body yearned to hold her. Hell, he wanted to kiss her—taste her. *St. Bride in heaven*, he swore under his breath. It had been too long since he had a woman beneath him, but it wasn't just *any* woman he wanted. He yearned for Michaela Grant.

The wind had kissed her skin pink and excitement danced in her eyes as she searched for the legendary creature. Would she be thrilled if she actually caught sight of the beast? Probably not. She would be no different from the rest. Humans were fascinated with the unknown, but faced with the reality they ran screaming in fear.

Why did Michaela Grant travel so far from home? He would have thought she'd want to be close to family now. Most humans clung to familiarity when their lives neared its end. They didn't set out on new adventures. Maybe she didn't realize how close she danced with eternal sleep.

As if she sensed his thoughts, her eyes shifted and her gaze latched onto him. Her strong chin lifted in defiance, as if she meant to tell him to back off. His lips twitched. Illness had weakened her body, but not her spirit. Aye, the fool lassie knew her time was limited. Scotland would be the final chapter in her book of life and it had him curious. Of all places in the world, why did she settle for Drumnadrochit?

"Where do ye live in the States, lovely lassie," Hyatt sat down next to her on the bench, draping his arm around her shoulders.

Alan clutched the wheel tighter, not liking his brother's bold advances.

Michaela's cheeks flamed a deep red. Such a beautiful woman and not one who flaunted it like a calling card.

"I'm from California."

"Aah Disneyland." Hyatt nodded.

"Yes." She smiled. "I don't live too far from the *happiest place on earth*."

"Now, why is that I wonder—*the happiest place on earth*—when ye could have all this." Hyatt swept his hand around him. "Ye have the beauty of nature and water a plenty."

She gave Hyatt a polite nod.

As Hyatt and Michaela conversed, Alan familiarized himself with Michaela's subtle expressions. The slight tilt of her head when enthralled with a story, a curve of her lips when amused, but her last expression had him puzzled. She blinked her eyes as if a piece of lint irritated them. Something had changed and not for the good. Her pallor turned ashen and her fingertips sought her temple with a quick massage.

Aah, she did well, forcing the headache not to take hold. If she hadn't rubbed the side of her head, he would have missed her discomfort.

He slowed the boat not caring they were in the middle of the loch. The wind had picked up, causing the water to lap hard against the hull and the boat swayed back and forth.

"Why are we stoppin' here?" Hyatt asked as he turned toward him.

Alan ignored the question. He walked over to the cooler and took out a water bottle. He knew Michaela watched him, her eyes wary to his every move. He couldn't blame her for her apprehension. He didn't exactly welcome her with open arms.

Karen Michelle Nutt

And ye should keep her at arm's distance, his conscience warned him again.

All caution went unheeded as his steps brought him closer to her.

"Will ye mind the boat for a spell?" he asked Hyatt, not leaving room for him to refuse.

Hyatt lifted his brows but said nothing as he relinquished his seat.

Alan sat down next to Michaela and handed her the bottle. "I thought ye could use a drink. Bein' out on the loch with the sun and wind, ye can become quite parched." Her eyes narrowed with suspicion before turning her attention to read the label on the bottle. "It's only water." he assured her.

"Thank you," she said with a brief nod. Strands of her hair slid over her right shoulder like beams of gold and red light.

He waited for her to take the first swallow before he spoke again. "Now, close yer eyes, Michaela."

"Excuse me?" Her voice rose with her suspicion.

He refused to give up, keeping his voice calm and smooth so not to frighten her. "Close yer eyes. I can help with the discomfort."

She looked ready to snub his help. He couldn't blame her. His ill-mannered display when they first met, gave her no reason to trust him. Her gaze wavered to Hyatt as if silently asking him to help her.

His back teeth ground together, but he managed to keep his voice calm. "Please," Alan implored, drawing her attention back to him.

She licked her lips, chapped from the wind. Her gaze met his and held.

"It's okay, I'll no' harm ye. I only mean to help."

Finally, she gave him a quick nod.

"Close yer eyes then. It'll make it easier."

He gently placed his fingertips on both sides of

her head, massaging the temples in a circular motion with his thumbs. He chanted words, sending a vibration of warmth through his hands. Michaela leaned her head back as she absorbed the heat. The lines on her forehead smoothed away, leaving her brow relaxed and unmarred by pain.

Her eyes snapped open in amazement, her gaze traveling over his face before locking onto his eyes. She raised her hand to grip his forearm. "What did you do?" she asked, her eyes brimming with tears of gratitude.

"Do ye feel better then?"

She nodded. "Your hands are like magic." A tear slid down her face.

Without a thought, his thumb wiped away the tear with a light caress. "Doonae cry, Michaela."

"You don't understand. Nothing has worked. No amount of medication has helped once the migraines take hold."

"I'm glad I have given ye some comfort then. It's the least I could do since I was bein' so boorish with ye earlier. Will ye accept my apology, then?" He flashed a smile. The one he knew the lassies found difficult to ignore. Hyatt wasn't the only one who could charm his way around a woman.

"Yes, yes of course." She returned the gesture, her mouth tilted into a smile. She possessed a wide full mouth made for kissing. He leaned forward and her lips parted in invitation as if she too wanted his lips pressed against hers. Surely one taste wouldn't hurt.

Behind him, Hyatt cleared his throat, slapping him back to reality and making him realize the foolish mistake he was about to make. He dropped his hands to his side and tore his gaze away from Michaela. He glanced at Hyatt and frowned, not caring for his brother's smirk. Without a backward glance to Michaela, he stood and made his way over

21

to Hyatt. "I'll take over now."

"Ye never fail to amaze me, Alan. Ye used the *well* water," Hyatt whispered the last part. His brother actually looked worried.

Good, Alan thought. It was about time Hyatt knew what it felt like. Night after night, he lay awake worried about what trouble his brother would manage to wreck upon the village.

Alan didn't meet his brother's gaze but glanced at Michaela. The human race was so fragile. Healthy and free one moment until death began to rear its ugly head, threatening to take it all away. It wasn't much, but he would grant Michaela a reprieve from her troubles for at least today.

"Where are we going?" Michaela asked as she sipped from the water bottle and looked over the edge of the boat.

"This is where most sightins have taken place." Alan pointed toward the distant shore. "Ye might want to take out yer camera."

"Would you mind telling me about the loch?" she asked as she dug in her backpack.

"Weel, where to begin." Alan tapped his chin. "Loch Ness is one of the largest deep freshwater lochs in the Scottish Highlands. It extends approximately thirty-seven kilometers, or as ye Yanks like to say, twenty-three miles southwest of Inverness. If you look to yer left a wee bit, ye'll see the Castle Urquhart."

She glanced up and looked toward the castle before snapping a picture with her pocket-sized digital camera.

"All that remains is the upper bailey, part of the five story tower house and the section of its fortifyin' wall. It's a mere ruin now, but it once stood strong on the rocky promontory, towerin' over Loch Ness."

"At one time, it must have been breathtaking."

"Aye, indeed it was."

Her gaze riveted to his and her perfect ruddy brows arched. "You say it as though you know firsthand."

Alan lifted his shoulders in a shrug. "If ye live in these parts long enough, the past and the present begin to merge together as one. Aye?"

Her gaze absorbed the wonderment around her, making her green eyes shimmer with warmth. Alan's brows lifted in surprise. The woman understood perfectly what he meant.

Her lips curved. "If you don't mind me asking, do you both believe Nessie is real?"

Alan briefly met Hyatt's gaze before answering her. "I suppose, we do. People need to believe in somethin' or else what's the use in livin'. Ey?"

She laughed with her mouth and eyes, transforming her face into pure sunlight that warmed him from the inside out. Dear gods, what pull did this woman have on him?

"Have you seen her?" she asked truly curious.

"And what makes ye so sure the creature is a lassie?" Hyatt piped up.

"So true. Maybe all these years, the pictures are of Nester and not of Nessie."

Hyatt wrinkled his nose in disgust. "Doesnae have the same ring to it, does it now?"

She chuckled. "No, it doesn't." She looked toward the castle again. "I'll have to take a tour of Castle Urquhart, while I'm here."

"Oh aye," Hyatt agreed. "Ye doonae want to miss its grandness."

"I'm takin' the boat out this way tomorrow." Alan heard himself say.

Both Michaela and Hyatt's gaze riveted to him.

This should have been a big clue to keep his mouth shut, but it seemed his tongue had a mind of its own. "I could give ye a lift."

Michaela's fair skin flushed pink. "Uh... thank

23

you. I…" Her words trailed off making him think she was searching for a way to say, *no thanks.*

He shrugged as if he didn't care, but his damn heart pounded hard against his ribcage proving him a liar. "Ye can let me know. I'll be goin' no matter what." This gave her a way out if she wanted it, while leaving the invitation open.

"Thank you." Her sweet smile was for him only and he found his lips curving in response.

When she turned away, his gaze caught sight of his brother staring at him in disbelief. Well, he was little surprised at himself, too.

Michaela snapped a few pictures of the castle with her pocket size camera. Her interest was genuine. Now if she would look at him with the same passion, he'd know she felt the pull as he did.

Chapter Three

By the time Alan brought the boat around, the morning slipped away to late afternoon though Michaela found it difficult to tell with the sun still high in the sky. Summer days were long in Drumnadrochit with the sunset after ten or so in the evening. They lucked out. The threatening clouds of the early morning passed them by, leaving the sky a clear blue, but the wind still blew strong.

Hyatt helped Michaela out of the boat, holding her longer than necessary. His lips curved into a wicked smile while his eyes sparkled mischievously. "So Michaela from the States, what do ye have planned for the rest of the day? If ye doonae mind me askin'."

She thought she'd be exhausted from her outing and would need to head back to the cottage to take a nap, but she felt fine—wonderful in fact. "I don't know."

"How aboot I take ye to lunch. I know a place where ye'll have a crackin' fun time with Scottish home cooked meals and array of whiskey to take yer breath away."

Michaela chuckled. "I don't know about the whiskey, and I should probably—" Her stomach growled, drowning out her protest. Why not go with him. She was here to have fun, not spend time in her cottage. "I wouldn't mind a warm cooked meal."

"Splendid."

"Hyatt, I would like a word with ye, please." Alan interrupted with a stern frown.

Michaela pointed over her shoulder as she took

a step back. "I'll wait for you at the end of the pier."

"Sure, darlin'." Hyatt winked.

Hyatt liked to flirt, Michaela thought, but his flirtatious overtures were harmless enough. He'd make no advances unless she offered.

From the end of the boardwalk, Michaela watched both men. They were different in looks as well as personality. Hyatt possessed dark chestnut colored hair and a roguish attitude, while Alan's hair looked like polished ebony and his personality bordered on brooding.

Alan's stance spoke volumes, too. His feet stood apart in a military fashion and his arms folded across his chest clearly indicating his far from pleased attitude with his brother. They were obviously arguing. Maybe about her, but she didn't understand why Alan would be against her having lunch with his brother. What could be the harm? Unless... Was there a wife waiting at home for Hyatt? She didn't remember seeing a ring on his finger, but sometimes that didn't mean anything. However, instinct told her something else troubled Alan, only she couldn't put her finger on it.

She let out a long sigh. Too bad Alan didn't ask her to lunch. Of the two brothers, Alan drew her attention, made her heart beat a little faster when his eyes fastened on her. Wouldn't it figure she'd fall for the one with an attitude, but he did have a sensitive side to him. He came to her rescue when one of her headaches had begun to take hold.

Those hands had felt warm against her temples as if energy passed through his fingertips to penetrate her skin and alleviate the throbbing inside her head.

Afterward, when their gazes met and held, she thought he would kiss her. He had leaned forward, but at the last moment he turned away. The funny thing was she wanted to feel his lips against hers.

"What a crazy thought." Her gaze landed on Alan as he argued with his brother. He stood tall, fierce and too handsome for his own good. Even now, she wondered what a kiss from Alan would feel like.

****

"Do ye mind tellin' me what ye're doin'?" Anger narrowed Alan's eyes and stiffened his jaw as he clenched his teeth.

"What?" Hyatt shrugged. "Ye volunteered to take her to see the castle tomorrow. Why cannae I ask her to join me for lunch?"

"I shouldnae have offered." Alan shook his head, still wondering why he had the impulse to offer his services in the first place. "It's best no' to get too close. Ye know this and yet ye continue to do as ye please no' worrin' of the consequences."

"And what aboot ye? Ye sat next to her all nice as ye please, givin' her water and rubbin' her temples. What was all that aboot anyway?"

Alan flinched, hating that Hyatt pointed out his folly. "She was in pain. Surely ye saw her discomfort."

"Ye say doonae interfere. Doonae change what is meant to be. Arenae these yer words?"

"I gave her comfort for the day. Nothin' more."

"Fine. Ye gave comfort. All I'm goin' to do is feed her. If ye hadnae noticed, she's nothin' but skin and bones. So for once, will ye feck off?"

Hyatt turned to leave, but Alan's hand snaked out to stop him. "Doonae hurt her, Hyatt."

"What? Like ye hurt Mary MacGregor, ye mean? Is that what yer sayin'?"

Alan recoiled, making Hyatt realize how his words stung.

"Alan, I dinnae mean it. Ye were there for Mary when she—"

Alan held up his hand to halt his words. Mary had died fifty years ago. There was no fixing what

27

was already done. He may have helped her for a while, but in the end..."Ye're right." He pursed his lips together. "I have no room to talk, but learn from my follies and doonae make the same mistake. That's all I be askin'."

****

Michaela watched both brothers stride down the boardwalk, Alan's frown deepened as he continued past her without a word.

"What was that all about?" Michaela asked Hyatt, pointing with her thumb toward Alan's retreating back.

"Nothin' Alan can be...aah..."

"Intense," she offered, looking up at Hyatt with a grin.

"Aye, I couldnae of have said it better myself."

"He didn't appear too pleased."

"Ye should see him when he's in a snit." Before she could comment, Hyatt wrapped his arm around her shoulders. "Come now, darlin', lunch is waitin'. Fiddler's Luck is one of our historic buildin's and dooncha know they won the *CAMRA Highlands* and *Islands Pub of the Year* award. Several times in fact."

Michaela could only assume the award was an accomplishment worthy of praise by the way Hyatt's eyes gleamed with approval. "Good to know."

"Oh aye, so it is."

Chapter Four

Fiddler's Luck sat at one end of the Village Green and not far from the Pelican Pedestrian Crossing. Music played in the background and everyone from tourist to locals came in to relax.

The place proved larger than Michaela first thought with its high ceiling and the strategic seating arrangements. The booths were made of fine dark wood and could seat a party of four. The round tables ranged from seating five or six to a cozy table for two.

The wood bar, located at the center wall stood as the focal point of the place. Waitresses disappeared through the doors to the right and strode back out again, carrying trays of freshly cooked meals.

In the back portion of the room, separated by two wood pillars decorated with vines were a number of tall pub-tables for cozy conversations and shared drinks. They were arranged to face the dartboards on the far wall.

Hyatt led her to the back of the pub, snagging the last table available. "Can I buy ye a drink? Whiskey?" Hyatt offered.

"Just coffee, please."

"Comin' right up." He headed to the bar and leaned over to grab two mugs from the shelf then he snagged a pot of coffee from a passing server, giving her a smile that dazzled her into giggles.

Michaela shook her head, but found her lips curving, too.

"Coffee, milady" He did the honors of pouring the dark liquid into the cups. Steam billowed up, sending the rich aroma straight to her nostrils. Her mouth watered at the prospect of the first taste. She sipped and sighed with pleasure. "Perfect."

"Is that right." He looked skeptical as he sipped his own brew. "Ah weel, it's warm anyway." Hyatt nodded his head toward the dartboard. "Do ye want to try yer hand in a game?" His full lips tilted into a mischievous grin and he wagged his eyebrows for an added effect.

"Sure." Michaela couldn't help liking Hyatt; his rich laughter proved contagious. He strode back to the bar, leaned over and pulled open a drawer to confiscate the darts.

"Hyatt," the bartender called to him from the other end. "Ye can ask politely for those. If ye doonae mind."

"Now George, I'm only helpin' ye out."

The bartender shook his head. "A little less help would be appreciated."

Hyatt waved him off with a grin and headed back. Women ogled him and he winked or blew a kiss as his gaze wavered over them with an appreciative eye. Oh, this man broke hearts.

"Are ye enjoyin' yer stay here?" Hyatt made casual conversation.

"I am. I needed this vacation."

Dart in his hand, he paused and looked at her, but before he could ask her why, a deep rich voice did the honors.

"Why is that I wonder?"

Michaela's heart stuttered and started again at the sound of Alan's voice. Turning in her seat, she met his gaze. The man had an uncanny knack of appearing out of nowhere.

"Why did ye need a vacation?" he asked again, obviously thinking she hadn't heard him the first time.

She cleared her throat and willed her heart to

slow. Surely Alan could hear the 'thu-thump, thu-thump'. It pounded loudly in her ears. "Back home, things had become... Um...unbearable."

His eyes narrowed, giving his almond shaped eyes more of a slant. "Ye packed up and ran away from what exactly?"

"I didn't run away," she defended herself.

His dark brows rose high on his forehead. The expression all but called her a liar.

"Okay, I ran away and I'm glad I did. No one was pleased with me and I didn't want—" She looked away. She didn't have to explain her reasons, revealing too much would only put her in the same predicament she'd been in at home. Blake had looked at her with pity and the thought of people doing the same here would be too much to endure.

"It was boyfriend trouble, aye?" Hyatt leaned on the table.

Boyfriend? Ex-boyfriend since they hadn't parted on good terms. Her head shook in denial, hoping to end the questioning.

She foolishly believed her last conversation with Blake had been hidden away, but the ugly truth of it crept up on her like a bad dream to remind her.

"You must have the operation." Blake paced her apartment, running his hand through his sun-streaked hair in nervous frustration. "The surgeon said—"

"I don't care what Dr. Fitzgerald said. I've been down this road before and I won't do it again. What's the point, anyway?"

"What's the point?" Blake whirled on her. "You sit there and wonder why you should bother?" He went to her and knelt down on one knee. He gripped her shoulders, shaking her as if this would make her listen. "I don't want you to die, dammit. Don't you know that?"

"We all die, Blake. I'm sorry my time is limited,

but I have no choice."

"You do have a choice. You just refuse to take it."

Michaela cupped Blake's face in her hands. "The prognosis isn't good. Even if I have the operation, I could die or become a slobbering fool in a hospital bed."

"There's a chance you'll be all right. Did you forget that possibility?"

"Blake, you weren't with me six years ago when I went through the first operation. It nearly killed me. I did it because the prognosis was in my favor. There was hope I would pull through. No one dreamt the aneurysm would return, but it did. My mother died from one. So did her mother. It's hereditary. They only caught the first one because I had the MRI done. This time, there isn't much hope because of where it's lodged in my brain. It's over, Blake." She closed her eyes, wishing Blake would let this go.

"Listen, Michaela, what if I could guarantee—"

"I want to take a trip," she interrupted him.

"A trip?" Blake's voice rose. "I'm talking about saving your life and you want to take a vacation."

"Yes. I want to go to Scotland. I thought I had more time to plan the vacation, save more money, but it's now or never." Her gaze locked onto his. "Come with me, Blake. Didn't you tell me you have relatives there?"

"Yes, an aunt in Foyers, but I haven't spoken to her in years."

"It doesn't matter. Let's call the airlines today and book a flight."

Blake pulled away from her, shaking his head. "I can't do this. I won't watch you throw your life away."

"I'm not throwing it away. I'm living it."

****

"Michaela?"

Alan's voice blinked her back to reality. "Sorry."

She chuckled nervously. "I spaced out for a moment."

"Ye look like ye remembered an unpleasant experience."

She gave him a half smile, surprised at his uncanny ability to read her. "Memories of home. No one wanted me to take this vacation." She didn't have family. She was an only child and her mother and father were both gone. Her girlfriends were supportive until Blake forced his opinion on them. After awhile, she stopped answering the phone.

He tilted his head, studying her with those unusual blue eyes. "But ye came anyway."

"Yes, I had to." She met his gaze the electricity of it blazing through her. "Drumnadrochit called to me." She shook her head, wondering why the strange comment slipped out of her mouth, but it was true. She could have picked anywhere in Scotland, but this town is where she wanted to be. Here, she didn't have to paint on a cheerful face and act like everything was okay.

At home, the stress of pretending had worn thin. Blake's refusal to let her go made her resent him. They'd only dated for nine months and maybe the relationship would have flourished into more, but time robbed them of the chance. Blake cared about her, but not enough for him to let her go. "I suppose that sounds silly to you."

"A callin' is never silly." Alan's large hand covered hers.

The heat of his touch and the impact of his gaze made Michaela believe he truly did understood.

"Hey, are we goin' to play or what?" Hyatt's voice broke the moment. Alan removed his hand, taking the warmth with him.

"Ye wannae give it a gander auld man?" Hyatt laughed and slapped Alan on the back.

Michaela had the feeling Alan was about to refuse and she didn't want him to leave just yet. "No, he's chicken," she said, challenging him.

Hyatt hooted with laughter. "Ye goin' to let a lassie call ye chicken?"

Alan's eyelids closed and opened with a slow deliberate blink of irritation, but he stood. She held out her hand, offering him a dart. He yanked it from her, determination stamped on his face. "Stand aside." He looked down at her with his eyes flickering to a darker shade of blue. "Let me show ye how it's done."

Michaela waved her hand in front of her. "Be my guest."

He rolled his shoulders back and took a deep breath before he raised his hand. His dart flew straight, hitting just inside the ridge of the bull's eye. He looked back at her with a smug smile.

Michaela pushed up her sleeves and picked up a dart. She almost let the dart fly, but Alan's words halted her.

"Do ye always stick out yer tongue when ye're concentratin'?"

She looked at him. "Excuse me?"

His mouth curved. "Yer wee tongue, it slips out when ye focus." His index finger pointed at her mouth.

"Does not." She glanced at Hyatt to back her up and was sorely disappointed.

"Afraid it does, lassie." Hyatt sighed.

Michaela pursed her lips together and turned with a swift movement and let the dart fly.

"Dead center," Hyatt cried out with a laugh. He picked Michaela up and swung her around.

"Put the young lassie down before ye break her," Alan reprimanded, but he wore a grin himself. On her feet again, he bowed to her. "Weel done, weel done."

Michaela chuckled, but her smile slid away to confusion when her gaze caught sight of a blonde woman near the front entrance of the pub. Her heated gaze narrowed in on them—first to Hyatt then to Alan before the blonde's gaze shifted to her. Blondie's nostrils flared as if she disliked Michaela on the spot. She could be a disgruntled girlfriend perhaps, but whose—Alan's or Hyatt's?

Blondie's strides were long and purposeful, heading right toward them. Oh goody, Michaela groaned inwardly. A confrontation, she couldn't wait.

Chapter Five

"Alan, Hyatt," the woman announced the names as an accusation.

"Kait, I aboot gave up hope ye'd be joinin' us today," Hyatt piped up. "We have another chair here. We already ordered, but I'm sure George willnae mind puttin' together another house special."

Michaela would bet Hyatt could smooth talk a woman with a few words, but it was his damn sexy smile that would make them melt. She watched Kait, waiting to see if her suspicions were correct.

The woman smoothed her hair behind her ear and her lips twitched. Yeah, the *thawing cycle* had already begun. "I'd like that," she said. Then her hand feathered over the darts arranged—for the moment—harmless on the table. "I'll go next, if ye're fixin' to play another round."

Michaela wondered how wise it would be to let the woman have a weapon, but Alan didn't notice the danger. "Go ahead. Give it yer best shot," he told her.

Her slim hips sashayed back and forth before making her move. "Who's yer new friend, Alan?" Kait asked as her dart attacked the board with a thud.

"Michaela's from the States," he offered. "Michaela, let me introduce Kait MacDonald."

Kait turned to face Michaela. Her gaze narrowed in on her before sizing her up with a slide down then up again. "A Yank, huh?" That bit of news obviously pleased her for her smile widened, showing her dimples and transforming her frosty expression into one of warmth and welcome. "Ye willnae be with us long then."

"Only a few weeks." Michaela's lips twitched, but she managed not to smile. Kait obviously didn't think her a threat now and could relax.

Kait threw another dart where it smacked near the dead center. She clapped her hands together. "Let's see ye beat that one, laddies." Her gaze landed on the tabletop and she clicked her tongue with a shake of her head. "Oh come on now, where are yer manners? Ye dinnae give the lassie a proper drink. She needs George's fine whiskey."

"No, I'm fine really," Michaela raised her hands in protest, but Kait persisted, whirling around to head for the bar. Her swift actions had her plowing into a young man. His beer splashed down the front of his polo shirt and onto the paper he was holding.

"Oh so sorry, I am. I dinnae see ye." Kait grabbed a few napkins from the table to wipe his shirt.

"It's all right," the young man laughed. His speech indicated a tourist. No rolling of the r's a dead giveaway. "I wasn't looking where I was going. I was studying the map the girls gave me." He held up a torn paper from a notebook page and glanced back toward the bar where two young women, one blonde and the other dark stood smiling at him with an appreciative glint. He smiled back with a wave before he looked back at Kait. "If I could have a napkin to wipe my directions off before the ink runs, I'd appreciate it."

"Oh aye." Kait handed him the remaining napkins on the table.

"May I?" He motioned to the tabletop and placed the paper down.

Alan moved the coffee mugs aside to make more room. "I'm Alan and that's my brother Hyatt." He nodded toward his brother. "This is Michaela and the lassie who honored ye with a wee bath is Kait."

Kait stuck out her tongue, but smiled broadly when the young man turned back to look at her again.

"I'm Steven Corbin."

"Ah, another Yank," Hyatt piped in. "We're surrounded, brother." He slapped Alan on the back with a chuckle.

Steven studied Michaela. "Let me guess. You're the Yank, right?"

She chuckled. "What gave it away? I'm a California girl."

His broad mouth slid into a smile, revealing his straight white teeth. "Arizona." They shook hands. He was nice looking, mid-twenties with dark hair and brown eyes. No wonder the young women at the bar kept staring at him as if he were eye-candy.

"I was aboot to buy us a round," Kait said. "Would ye like to join us, Steven from Arizona?"

Hyatt snagged a chair from the table next to them before Steven could refuse. "Where are our manners? For sure he'll be joinin' us. See if George willnae give ye a bottle, hey?" He winked at Kait. "Seein' how ye dated him, he might be more obliged to give in to ye."

"That was a long time ago, Hyatt. Doonae bring up ancient history." She whirled away, her blonde hair flying behind her. Her strides took her over to the bar without incident. Michaela watched as she snagged cups and a bottle after sweet talking George with just a few words. She leaned over the bar to give him a quick kiss on the cheek then headed back to the table with her prize.

If Michaela didn't know better, she'd say George still had a thing for Kait with the way the color rose in his neck and flushed his cheeks. When George caught sight of Michaela staring at him, he quickly turned away.

"A dram for all of us and a toast for good days. Slàinte." Kait raised her cup, making eye contact with Michaela in challenge.

Michaela knew she shouldn't indulge. Mixing pain meds and alcohol wasn't wise. Her eyebrows drew together in a frown as she remembered. *I haven't taken any meds today.*

"Ye doonae have to drink it," Alan told her.

Kait rolled her eyes. "Ye only live once."

Michaela met Kait's gaze with a determined nod. "You are so right." She raised her shot glass with a salute then threw back her head and drained the contents. The liquid burned all the way down, but damn it felt good to let loose.

"No' bad for a Yank." Kait nodded with approval.

"Hey," Steven protested.

Kait draped her arm around Steven's shoulders. "Now, I wasnae referrin' to ye, now was I? Are ye up for another then?"

All five of them played darts, enjoying each other's company and sharing a meal. George's special consisted of breaded salmon, almond green beans and warm bread slathered with butter.

Steven and Kait argued who was up next to throw darts, but Michaela didn't really care. While they figured it out, she wandered over to the framed photographs lining the walls in a grand tribute of days-gone-by.

In the late eighteen hundreds, Fiddler's Luck had once been The Macabe Hotel. There were a few photos of the hotel in its heyday.

In another photo, the year 1955 printed in gold, stood bright against the black and white print. In the photo, the place was crowded with people as if it were a party. The women wore skirts and blouses, while others wore cute sweaters with pearl buttons. The men had their hair slicked back and were wearing suits and ties. An era long past, but preserved forever.

"That was openin' day for Fiddler's Luck." Alan moved beside her. His right arm brushed against her, his body so near she could smell the sea salt and the spicy scent that was all him.

God, he smelled good. She turned to look at him.

"How's the head?" He looked at her with concern. "Anymore headaches?" His hand brushed her hair over her shoulder, his touch a featherlike caress.

"No headache." But her heart picked up a few extra beats whenever he drew near, but she kept the phenomenon to herself.

"Hmm." He took a step closer, his hand on her waist. The dark centers of his eyes dilated until she thought she would melt into them. Again she had the distinct feeling he wanted to kiss her, but fate didn't seem to be on their side.

"Alan," Kait whined, drawing his attention back to her with a deep sigh.

"What is it, Kait?"

Darn the woman for interrupting.

"Steven willnae join me in another dram."

"Enough's, enough." Steven held up his hands with a chuckle. "I'm seeing two of you, Kait."

"Only two?" She put her hands on her hips. "My da says if ye're standin' then ye're no' bladdered."

"All good and maybe true, but I need a clear head tomorrow when I head out on my hike."

"We'll be missin' ye." She held onto his arm, but he slipped out of her clutches.

"I'm sure you'll manage. Night everyone."

Hyatt nodded. "Come back tomorrow if ye dare."

Steven laughed and waved. "I might just do that." His brown eyes were bright from drink, but not too far gone it seemed. He headed out the door without swaying on his feet.

"Oh bugger," Kait stomped her foot. She turned

toward Alan, her gaze latching onto him in lazy appraisal. She sauntered over to him, not caring he'd been talking to Michaela. She threw her arms around his neck, draping her body over him as if she were a blanket. Alan gave Michaela an apologetic shrug, as he did his best to keep Kait's hands from fondling him.

Michaela found herself perturbed with Alan. Why didn't he just tell her to leave him alone?

"Oh Alan, ye see how..." Kait purred, leaning close, her mouth near his ear as if to tell him a secret or nibble on it. Michaela wasn't sure which. She strained to hear what Kait whispered to Alan, but only a few words floated back her way.

"...loch... cool breeze..."

The sporadic words may not make sense alone, but the way the woman rubbed her body against Alan like a cat in heat clearly indicated what her intentions were. Michaela shouldn't care, but she did and if she didn't stop clenching her teeth, she'd end up breaking a tooth.

Kait slipped her hand into her pant pocket and retrieved what appeared to be a folded piece of paper.

She shoved it into Alan's hand. He tried to give it back with a shake of his head, but the woman wouldn't have it.

"Ye must read it later, when no one else is around." She placed her finger over his mouth to silence him. A small chirrup sound escaped her lips in a form of a hiccup, causing her to break into a stream of giggles. "Oh no, it's trouble." She pointed over his shoulder.

"What?" Alan turned to follow Kait's line of vision. His brows furrowed and he removed Kait's arms from around his neck.

Michaela turned her head, too. An older man with a narrowed-eyed-glare pushed his way in and headed in their direction. Strands of gray overtook the dark hair he must have once possessed as a young man and lines of age marked his weathered face. Within seconds, his determined strides led him to their table. His hands balled at his side as if he readied himself for a fight.

"Ethan, ye doonae want to make a scene," Hyatt warned, materializing next to Alan, giving Michaela the distinct feeling confrontations were a common occurrence with the MacLachlin brothers.

"My quarrel isnae wi' ye Hyatt MacLachlin. It's wi' yer brother." His brogue was thick and hard to understand, but the tone could not be mistaken as anything other than hostile.

"Still the same, I'll be askin' ye to back down." Hyatt kept his voice even, but his hands also curled into fists.

Alan placed a restraining hand on Hyatt's arm, but spoke to Ethan. "We can speak later, ye ken?"

The sheriff and an officer were seated at a table near them, their meals forgotten for the moment. Sensing a confrontation, the sheriff pushed back his chair and strolled over for a closer look. He possessed bright red hair, height to compensate for his thick waist and a no nonsense attitude. "Ye need to go home, Ethan." He encouraged with a leveled-eyed look.

"Ye tell him, Sheriff Comyn," Kait cheered on.

"Pipe down Kait," a wiry, dark haired officer joined the melee.

Kait turned with a sneer. "Is that an order, Officer Jonas Wiley? Do ye want to frisk me and take me in?" Her tone indicated bad history between the two.

"Keep yer trap shut." His eyes narrowed, his features a mask of contempt.

Kait flinched in response and backed away to stand behind Alan again.

Michaela's brows rose. Oh yeah, definitely bad history.

Ethan didn't look like he cared if the sheriff hauled him off to jail. His face turned a molten red and he raised his fists.

"Damon?" The sheriff waved to a dark haired youth sitting at a table with friends. "Why doonae ye take yer grandda home."

The youth pushed back his chair, but Ethan waved him away. "I'm no' goin' anywhere."

"That's enough, Ethan MacGregor," Alan's voice boomed and silence hit the room all at once. All eyes riveted to Ethan and the MacLachlin brothers, the air thick with anticipation.

Ethan's gaze riveted on Alan again, his mouth opening with what looked like a nasty retort, but then his lips smoothed and pressed together into a fine line.

"We'll talk, but no' here where others can be hurt." Alan's smooth voice washed over Ethan like a wave.

Michaela looked around the room, wondering if anyone caught how Alan calmed Ethan, his voice like the low hum of a melody.

She frowned. What power did Alan possess? Could he hypnotize people and animals with his voice? She couldn't dismiss how earlier today he had demanded his German Shepherd to stop harassing the cat. Had Alan hypnotized her on the boat, too? He touched her temples and his unusual blue eyes locked with hers as he spoke. Her pain eased and disappeared without her having to take the meds she had stashed in her backpack. It was as if the sound of his voice hypnotized them all into compliance.

Intrigued more than frightened at the prospect of Alan possessing the ability to use mind control, she sat down in the nearest seat to see how the scene played out.

Ethan's stance changed. His clenched fists relaxed and his eyes lost its blaze of heat. The man shrugged his shoulders back. "Fair enough," he spat, wagging a finger at Alan. "It isnae over though. Ye ken? I will have my word wi' ye." He turned on his heels, pushing his way out of the pub in the same fashion he'd arrived. His grandson, Damon returned to his table where his friends waited for him. The low purr of conversation started up again and the tension evaporated.

The sheriff nodded toward Alan and headed out of the pub, too. Perhaps he planned to follow Ethan home to ensure he wouldn't cause more trouble. Officer Wiley strolled over to the bar, taking a seat at the far end.

Michaela looked to Hyatt then to Alan with a quirked brow. What had Alan done to cause Ethan to hate him so much? Whatever the reason, Hyatt knew the secret and would have his brother's back.

"Ye should have punched him in the nose." Kait jabbed with her right in imitation.

"I doonae go around punchin' auld men."

Good to know. Points for Alan. Michaela thought.

"Ethan's had it comin' a long time now," Kait insisted.

"Ye had a wee too much to drink, Kait," Alan told her. "Ye best go home now and sleep it off."

"I was aboot to order another round." She took a step and teetered on her feet.

Alan took hold of her arm to stop her from falling. She yanked free. "Piss off." She turned away, but Alan called her back with just his words.

"Kait, ye need to go home."

She stood facing him, still as a statue as if the sound of his voice soothed her into obedience. He'd done the same thing with Ethan and his dog. Hell, she supposed he'd done it to her as well.

"I'm gettin' right bladdered, arenae I?" Kait's chuckle gave way to another hiccup. Her hands motioned in a downward motion. "Okay, okay, I'll go, but..." She leaned forward and kissed the side of Alan's mouth. "Doonae forget." She turned away without saying goodbye to anyone else.

Good, she was leaving. The woman irked Michaela. Hanging all over Alan as if she owned him.

Taken back by the sudden surge of jealousy, she shifted in her seat uncomfortable with her reaction to a man she didn't know.

Alan turned his full attention on her with intent evident in his eyes as he strode over and pulled up a chair. Hyatt had already stationed himself at another table of all women, who buzzed around him like bees to honey. The pub may be filled with people, but in all other sense, Alan and she were alone with no one close enough to hear their conversation.

"Um...shouldn't you drive your girlfriend home?" She waved her thumb toward Kait, who sauntered out the door.

"Kait and I are only friends. No need to worry, she lives nearby." The corners of his mouth twitched. "Besides she'd take my head clean off if I held her hand all the way home."

Hyatt's boisterous laugh drew Michaela's attention. She smiled when he waved and blew her a kiss.

"I should warn ye." Alan leaned forward in his seat. His beautiful blue-eyed gaze proved a distraction and made it difficult to follow his words.

"About what?" She concentrated on his mouth, but this didn't help matters. His lips were thick and full with a wicked way of curving into a smile. The slow roll in her stomach and the tripping of her pulse made her finally realize why women fanned themselves when faced with an attractive man.

"My brother is fickle. His snoggin' means no more than a friendly hello."

She blinked forcing herself to concentrate on his words and not how she'd like him to kiss her. "I hate to sound all American here, but what is snogging?"

His luscious lips twitched again. "Kissin', suckin' face, I believe ye Yanks call it."

She cleared her throat, hoping he didn't possess the ability to read minds, too. "Got it. You're trying to warn me Hyatt's a player."

"He loves the beautiful lassies, but he never commits to one. Ye ken?"

She smiled. "I've known Hyatt's type before and believe me I didn't mistake his flirting for anything other than his friendly way of saying hello, but I appreciate the warning."

He took a deep breath and released it with what she thought was relief.

Sitting back in her seat, her gaze wavered over him with curiosity. He possessed strong bold features, beautiful eyes, and a killer body that the sweater and jeans did nothing to hide. He made it known Kait wasn't his girlfriend, but did he have his eye on someone else? "How about you? Do you have a special woman in your life or are you more like your brother than you let on?"

"No special lassie for me. This time I'll wait for my soul mate."

Soul mate? What a curious statement. "This time? Has some woman spurned your good intentions before?"

His chuckle rumbled deep in his chest, but humor didn't light his eyes. "No, but some relationships arenae meant to be." His hand gripped his mug on the table. Raising it to his lips, he took a generous sip before leveling his gaze on her once more. "And ye? How come ye made this holiday by yerself? Do ye no' have a man waitin' for ye back home?"

"Like you said, some relationships aren't meant to be." She frowned as the realization hit her like a sledgehammer. Her time was up. There would be no more dating, no more relationships... damn, no more sex for that matter. Unfortunately, her libido didn't listen to her brain. Her gaze slid over the man in front of her and her mind went wild with thoughts of running her hands beneath his sweater and over his hard abs. She wondered if he had a trail of dark hair leading down below the waistline of his jeans to where—"Jesus." The word slipped out beneath her breath.

"What is it?" Alan's brows furrowed.

"Umm...nothing." She squirmed in her seat. She was glad he couldn't read minds. Wouldn't he be shocked if he knew she fantasized about having free rein over his body? She cleared her throat.

Her gaze locked onto his again. He may be a brooding man, but he was still a man regardless of his claim of waiting for a *soul mate*. She couldn't imagine him waiting to have sex with his one true love, but she had a hunch casual sex didn't fit his persona either. "Do you truly believe there's a soul mate waiting for you?"

"I need to hope. I take it ye never been in love."

"Of course I have, but the relationships didn't last."

His lips curved into a ghost of a smile. Obviously, she amused him in some way and the thought rankled her. "Listen, Alan—"

He didn't wait for her to finish. "There was somethin' missin' in these relationships of yers." His voice held a note of curiosity. He truly wanted to know, not to make fun of her, but to understand.

"Exactly."

"Then ye dinnae find yer soul mate."

Perhaps he had a point. "Okay, if there is such a thing as soul mates, how would you know you'd found yours?"

"I would feel the magic."

Michaela lifted her brows. Was this guy for real? Who talked like that? Hell, who believed such nonsense? "You aren't serious."

His gaze touched hers and within the depths of his eyes laid the truth, the longing, the pain and wisdom of a much older man. She blinked and looked away confused.

"Is there no one waitin' for ye at home then?" Alan asked again.

Blake, she thought, but that wasn't true. He wanted to fix her, make her better, but it wasn't the same as loving her. In all fairness, she didn't love him either, at least not in the earth shattering way Alan described.

"Ah, ye have a husband and five wee bairns waitin' for ye."

She smiled. "No. Not exactly... I mean there's someone, not a husband or kids or anything."

"A mate?"

"If you mean boyfriend, I suppose."

The dark wings of his eyebrows arched. "Why do ye seem so unsure?"

"We ended things. Let's just say we didn't see eye to eye and I didn't have the luxury of time to help him understand."

Alan was silent for a moment. His prolonged stare of compassion and understanding sent a rush of desire coiling through her.

She fidgeted in her seat. Trying to shake the uncanny attraction she felt for this man. She refocused the conversation on him. "So why was Ethan so angry with you?"

His eyelids lowered, but not before she realized

her question wounded him in some way.

"I'm sorry, I shouldn't have pried."

His finger traced the rim of his glass. "When ye have lived as long as I have ye'll understand that sometimes ye try to do what's right, but it isnae always for the best."

"You act like you're ancient. You couldn't be more than thirty something. Not much older than I am."

"Ye'd be surprised. I've aged weel." His lips were sensual temptations as they curved into a smile.

Michaela let out a short laugh and shook her head. "Well good for you." Her hand reached for her glass. She should really switch her choice of drink to coffee, but that would require her walking to the bar. She didn't want take a chance of Alan finding interest elsewhere. The man intrigued her on so many levels and curiosity pushed her to find out why. "You aren't as grumpy as you put on, are you?"

His lips turned down, losing their humor. "Of course, I am."

"No, you're not." She tilted her head to the side as she analyzed him. Then it hit her. "You distance yourself because you're afraid you'll care too much."

It was his time to squirm in his seat. "Ye had too much to drink."

"No, I don't think so. I recognize the look."

"How so?"

She opened her mouth to explain but closed it again. "Never mind." She wanted to find out more about him, but somehow Alan kept turning the conversation back to her.

He placed his mug down and leaned forward, gently taking a hold of her chin and making her look at him. "How do ye recognize the look?"

His touch felt so good, warm and gentle for such a large man. She found herself leaning into his palm. *Kiss me.* The thought whispered in her mind, but he somehow knew what she craved.

He took her mug from her hand and placed it on the table next to his as he leaned forward, his lips hovering over hers. "Just a taste. Aye?" His seductive whisper stroked over her mouth with the effect of a soft kiss. His hand slipped to the nape of her neck, drawing her closer as he deepened the caress.

Heat spread through her, warming her from the inside out. He tasted of the sea, whiskey and sweet temptation. The more she indulged, the more she wanted. The thick beat of awareness ran through her blood, making her heart beat faster. Her hands cupped his face. His five o'clock shadow barely prickled her palm.

The kiss ended if only to take a breath, but he didn't move away. His lips still hovered near hers as if to reclaim them again.

"I knew you'd be a good kisser." Her voice a hoarse whisper, laced her words like an invitation for more.

His lips slid into a seductive curve. "Did ye now?"

She nodded her head, still a little breathless.

"This was a mistake, ye know."

"It was?" She tried to move away, but he held her still.

"Shush. I only meant it was a mistake on my part to indulge with a promise of only one taste. I want so much more." His mouth covered hers again, taking her under his spell. She didn't want to stop either, but they couldn't continue to kiss or snog as he called it right here in the pub. Not when she felt herself losing control. She moved her mouth to the side and inhaled deeply as she rested her cheek against his. "I should go soon. It's getting late."

His fingers slid through her hair, letting the stands slide out of his grip. "Let me walk ye back to the cottage."

Alan proved a smooth talker with his claims he wanted to find a soul mate, while warning her about his brother being the player. Alan's touch set off a longing inside of her, but she couldn't allow herself the luxury of an affair for numerous reasons.

She leaned back and met his gaze. The dark heat there told her he wanted more than a kiss, but brief dalliances weren't her style and she had no intentions of changing her moral standards now. "I don't think—"

He placed a finger over her mouth, silencing her words. "I'll just make sure ye arrive back safe. No more. I'm a patient man. We'll take this at yer pace."

Call her crazy, but she believed him. "I don't know if I can give you what you need." His lips twitched and she realized what she said. Her cheeks felt hot and she knew her skin had flamed crimson. "What I meant to say is I'm only here for a few weeks. I'm not one for a quick dalliance even if you're a good kisser."

This won her a full smile. "Like I said, we'll take whatever this is at yer pace. I'll no' rush ye."

She pursed her lips together actually contemplating spending time with him. "My terms?"

He nodded.

"Then I think it best I walk back to the cottage by myself." Only because she didn't trust herself to stay true to her words.

Disappointment briefly flashed in his eyes, but he didn't press her. "Then I wish ye a good evenin'."

"The same to you." She rose to her feet and turned to leave.

"Michaela?"

"Hmm?" She turned to find him right behind her. So close she could take one step and be in his embrace. Longing spread through her veins, but she stuffed her hands into her jean pockets, hoping to keep her resolve not to become involved.

"My offer still stands. I'm takin' the boat over to Castle Urquhart tomorrow. I would be honored if ye would accompany me."

"I..." she shook her head, ready to tell him no.

"Doonae say anythin' now," he interrupted her. "Think aboot it. Ye can ring me if ye like to go. Mrs. O'Malley has my number." He leaned toward her and kissed her cheek. "May yer dreams all be sweet, Michaela Grant."

It took her a few seconds to realize he had walked away. She was in real trouble here. If she wasn't dying, if she wasn't going back home... "There are too many *ifs* to make this work," she murmured under her breath. Her gaze lingered on Alan's tall frame for a moment longer as he sauntered toward his brother. With a long sigh of regret, she turned and walked out the door.

Chapter Six

Kait sat with her legs crossed, facing the end of the pier where she could see the moon's reflection on the loch's surface. *The Hound Dog* stood to the right of her, tied off and waiting to be boarded again. The water lapped against the hull with a slow rhythmic resonance.

She'd wandered down to the MacLachlins' pier numerous times with Hyatt. They would contemplate the wonders of the universe or drown away their troubles with a bottle of wine. She could use a quick drink now. The effects of the alcohol she'd consumed at Fiddler's Luck earlier were wearing off and her mouth felt thick and dry.

At twenty-eight, she thought she'd be married by now or at the very least engaged, but Drumnadrochit had limited prospects. George Fallon tried to make her happy. The sex was good but George always had one eye looking out for the next pretty lassie to wander into Fiddler's Luck.

Officer Jonas Wiley had been promising, but he had too many secrets and his control always seemed on the verge of snapping.

Maybe she should try her luck in Edinburgh. Her cousin rang monthly to brag about her fine time at the clubs.

She sighed heavily as she thought about the Maclachlin brothers. She'd like to convince one of them to settle down. Hyatt was good if she was looking for a crackin' good time, but Alan proved more serious and levelheaded. He could show a girl a fine night, but he kept most folks at a distance. Of course, she did love a challenge.

Her gaze took in the horizon. The sky had darkened to a hazy blue of night, indicating it to be about eleven or so. What was keeping Alan?

Jealousy spurred her into requesting this meeting out here away from the other patrons at Fiddler's Luck. "Ye should have just told him what ye know. Instead he's probably sittin' cozy-like with the Yank."

She'd seen how Alan's gaze lingered a moment longer than deemed necessary on Michaela Grant. Not that she could blame him. Her reddish locks and fine boned features probably drew many men to her side, but it hadn't been only her looks that held Alan's attention. His laughter had given him away. He fancied her, but he must realize Michaela would eventually go home to the States. Perhaps her leaving was what he liked the most. She shook her head. Long distance romances never worked.

"Alan, what's keepin' ye man?" She stood and paced the boardwalk.

The fog had rolled in, a thick layer of mist, giving the loch an eerie presence like a live entity ready to swallow her. She hugged her sweater closer around her. Surely, Alan had read the note she'd slipped him by now and wouldn't be long.

A flat sound tickled her ears like someone had scraped a saucepan with a spoon. Spooked, she halted her steps, trying to make out where the noise had come from. A loud splash toward the end of the pier had her swiveling around to stare into the shifting fog. The little hairs on the back of her neck and on her arms rose in warning, sensing someone watched her, but all she could see was the swirling ghostlike mist.

Something brushed against her leg, making her jump with a shriek. A black fur-ball went flying over her and onto the boat railing. "Priscilla, ye mangy cat, I ought to skin ye alive." Her relief proved short lived when another splash disturbed the shadowy depths of the loch.

"Who's there?" Her voice shook. As the low clouds shifted, she saw a movement in the water, but the mist swallowed the vision. "Alan?" Of course, it was Alan. She desperately tried to convince herself. No one else would chance the waters like Alan did. "Crazy fool." He's bound to freeze his privates off this late at night. "Alan?"

"Come closer." His voice was a hoarse whisper, but the fog and the sound of the water lapping against the pillars may have caused the effect.

"Why are ye takin' a swim at this hour?" Any hour would be fool hearty to her. The water was friggin' cold. She took a step toward the end of the pier. Alan liked the water and swam in it no matter the weather. She didn't know how he could stand it. "Ye'll catch yer death. Why dooncha ye come out and I'll warm ye," she teased. She wasn't a fool. Alan had no designs for her, but a woman had the right to fantasize.

The MacLachlins had owned this piece of land forever, but the house had stood empty for years. Then Alan and Hyatt showed up six months ago to claim their inheritance. Not many eligible men lived in Drumnadrochit, but unfortunately the MacLachlin brothers didn't seem interested in settling down with one woman.

Her gaze wavered over the water, but the shifting fog made it difficult to see, then a movement in the water caught her attention—something large. Her relief that Alan had spoken to her, quickly turned to fear. Something wasn't right.

"Alan, this isnae funny." Her words were spiced with uneasiness and irritation, but she didn't care.

A chuckle of amusement echoed and she whirled around trying to locate the source.

"If ye doonae show yerself, then I'm leavin' and ye can be damned for yer foolishness."

Silence more sinister than the laughter hung like a warning, but Kait couldn't bring her feet to move. This had been a mistake. What if the person out there wasn't Alan, but... Her eyes widened in fear. "St. Bride in heaven." Something large swam fast in a straight line toward her, the water rippling in waves to the side of the massive hulk. *Run.* Her mind screamed. Her feet took a step back, but it was already too late.

A dark shadow rose out of the water, large and foreboding. A scream clawed at her throat, but was choked back as she was yanked her off her feet and dragged beneath the murky water.

Chapter Seven

Alan shifted from the large smooth skinned creature into his human form at the shores end, and away from prying eyes. Some thought the beastie resembled the plesiosaurs of long ago, while others were convinced it looked like a kelpie or water horse described in legends. The beastie was a bit of both, he supposed.

He stuffed his hands in his pockets thankful his clothes remained dry and undisturbed. The magic of the shift allowed the two worlds of existence to remain separate. The movies always portrayed shifters having to strip down naked before changing.

Not that he didn't enjoy swimming bare arse, but thank the gods there was no truth to it. It would be hell of an inconvenience to try and find clothes every time he shifted to human form.

He strolled the short distance from the water to where *Kilmore Cemetery* stood. Most of the headstones were ancient, but the one he looked for would be newer than the centuries old Celtic crosses. His eyesight was that of the preternatural world, where the waters of the loch could be darker than a moonless night, he could see perfectly without light even in human form. He passed stones weathered with time looking for the one he sought.

It stood in the last row near the wooden fence. The name was deeply etched into the stone. Weather had darkened the words and dates, giving the final testament to what had happened. "Aah Mary, gone near half a decade now." Ethan claimed she drowned herself, but Mrs. O'Malley told him it had been a boating accident.

"I thought I'd see ye again." A long sigh of remembrance brought him back to the last day they were together.

Mary placed her hand on the side of Alan's face. "I wish ye dinnae have to go. Why cannae I be the one for ye?"

When he first met Mary her hair was the color of gold, but fifteen years later, gray marred its luster.

"Mary, I wish it were so. Believe me when I say I truly care for ye. I willnae go denyin' it, but there's no connection that wills away the enchantment. I feel the pull of the waters."

For a moment his gaze drifted to the loch with longing. As much as he wished to break the curse, he couldn't will himself to stay on the land. He was tethered to the waters with a short chain. Like clockwork, fifteen years gone and the chain retracted, pulling him back to the water's depths. "I cannae deny my destiny."

Tears pooled in her eyes. "I knew, but I had to ask. All these years I've known ye and not a line on yer face, while mine has aged with creases at my eyes. I'm younger than ye by seven years. 'Tis the magic you speak of, isnae it? Ye are much older."

Alan nodded.

"I'm sorry, Alan. I'm sorry I couldnae be what ye seek." She let her hand fall away. "When ye come back, I'll be an auld woman and ye'll look as ye do now."

"Ye'll still be my Mary."

She looked at him with a ghost of a smile. "Ye are the sweetest man I've ever known, but yer more than a man, arenae ye?"

He hesitated, but he could never lie to her. She'd always been a good friend more so than a lover. "Aye, but I wish I were no' the creature that beckons me back to the water's depths. I am cursed, Mary.

Remember that when I am forced to leave."

She shook her head. "Doonae say such things."

"Tis true. I've lived centuries. Only my soul mate, the one heart that beats as mine does, can break the enchantment. Until then, I am forced to endure. I will leave ye. No' my choice, but the curse laid upon me." He took her hand. "Ye understand this, Mary. Please tell me ye'll forgive me for leavin' ye."

"Dear Alan, there is no' forgivin' ye. Ye have given me so much. Ye gave my Ethan yer name when his father would no' bother to claim his son. Ye took care of us these past years. I knew it wasnae for love, but because ye have a carin' heart." Tears slid down her cheeks, but she made no move to brush them away. "I will miss ye always, but I know ye must go. I bid ye goodbye, Alan. Doonae fash yerself aboot Ethan and me. We will get by."

At the time, he hadn't realized her goodbye meant forever and Ethan... "He's a bitter man now, Mary. He blames me for ye dyin' so young, but I'll try to make him understand why I couldnae stay. I know ye would want me to try and I will." He placed the wildflower he'd been holding on top of her gravestone. "I'll try, Mary. I promise ye that. I owe ye that much."

Chapter Eight

"Where did ye go off to?" Hyatt asked the moment Alan walked in the door.

"I'm surprised yer home early to notice." Alan leaned down to pet Elvis, who was wagging his tail with gusto. He headed to the kitchen to give Elvis a doggy treat and open a can for Priscilla, who meowed to be fed.

"No' exactly the answer to my question." Hyatt followed him. He leaned against the doorframe. "Ye werenae with the young pretty Yank were ye?" he teased.

"Nay, and the lassie is off limits to ye. She has enough to worry aboot without ye sniffin' around."

"What aboot ye? Ye were sittin' cozy like next to her?"

"Makin' conversation is all."

"Bugger that. Ye're keen on her."

"She'll be goin' home soon. I have nay plans to see her again."

"So ye say, do ye?" Hyatt walked over to the answering machine and pushed the button.

"Hello, Alan," Michaela's voice rang through.

Alan's heart skipped a beat at the sound of her voice.

"I spoke to Mrs. O'Malley and she gave me your number. I've changed my mind. If you're still planning to go over to Urquhart Castle, I'd love to go with you."

Hyatt pushed the button again and smiled. "Ye have to love Mrs. O'Malley, the interferrin' auld bat. Ye asked the darlin' Michaela Grant to go with ye on an outin' of sorts. I thought she turned ye down on the boat, but I guess ye persuaded her into changin' her mind. No' keen on her, hey? No' seein' her again, hmmm." He chuckled and burst into an Elvis song to goad him further.

"Stop, ye're slaughterin' one of Elvis' best songs." Alan tried to ignore him with no luck. "And I'm no fool when it comes to fallin' in love. No' as if this is anythin' of the sort."

Hyatt sang louder.

"I'm sure the King just rolled over in his grave."

"Just warnin' ye, brother. Enjoy her. She's a lovely woman, but be careful. Ye know what happened the last time ye tried to save a lassie."

"And yer way around the lassies is so much better." He tossed Elvis a doggie biscuit. The dog's teeth flashed and the biscuit disappeared into the dark recesses of his mouth. He lopped over to his pillow by the fireplace and began devouring the treat.

"Aye. I only play for a time and with a lassie that has her heart set on another."

"Hence the endless fights ye find yerself in." Alan grumbled as he opened the can of *salmon delight* for Priscilla.

Hyatt lifted his shoulders in a shrug. "I see it as I do the laddies a favor."

"How so?" Emptying the cat food into a bowl, he placed it on the floor in front of Priscilla, who purred and rubbed against his leg in appreciation.

"They win the lassie in the end, dooncha know. Makes them appreciate what they have."

Alan shook his head. "Ye're an eejit, Hyatt."

Hyatt's laughter followed him as he headed for his room, cringing at his brother's warped sense of humor. He closed the door behind him, hoping for some peace.

He couldn't deny that some force drew him to

Michaela. After all these centuries, could she be the one? He kicked off his shoes, leaving them where they fell. If so, it would be bloody cruel of the gods that his soul mate was destined to die soon.

Michaela hadn't wanted to see him again. He sensed her withdraw at the pub before she bolted for the door, but then she rang him tonight. Had she felt the connection as he did? Had it scared her, making her back away or had something else sent her skittering away like a frightened rabbit?

His long limbs spread out on the bed. With his hands behind his head, he stared at the wood beam ceiling above him. As much as he wanted to be human, he missed the nights outside with the stars shining overhead and the water lapping against his body like a caress. Nothing could compare except... "Michaela," he rolled the name off the tip of his tongue and smiled. Dark auburn tresses with lighter strands that reflected light. Her sweet lips meant for kissing.

He rolled over on his side and reached for the phone to ring Michaela and tell her what time to expect him. Who would've of thought he'd fall for a Yank.

Chapter Nine

"What am I doing?" Michaela looked at herself in the mirror hanging above the dresser. "I shouldn't go." Alan MacLachlin would be trouble. His life appeared complicated with Kait pursuing him with a vengeance and Ethan's delusional accusations couldn't be ignored either. "Why did I call Alan and tell him I would go?" She shook her head, knowing perfectly well why she'd called him.

On her way home last night, Mrs. O'Malley waved her down before she could escape inside the cottage. She'd just come from the pub and still felt a little out of sorts. She'd run away. When had she ever done something so silly? She wasn't a coward and she didn't fear Alan. She'd fled because she didn't trust herself.

"Did ye find the Maclachlin brothers?" Mrs. O'Malley was a woman in her sixties, if the fine lines on her face and the gray strands in her hair were any indication of her age. Her stride though was the quick and sure step of a much younger woman.

Michaela forced a smile to touch her lips. "Yes, thank you. They were very nice. They gave me a grand tour of the loch."

"Splendid, splendid." Her eyes lit up like a Christmas tree.

Michaela frowned wishing she'd never stepped foot inside their boat. She should have taken one of the crowded impersonal tours.

"Why the long face?" Mrs. O'Malley's hands took hers in a warm embrace. "The laddies behaved themselves, dinnae they?"

"What? Oh yes, they were very kind."

"Then what's troublin' ye? Ye can tell me. I've got a good ear, ye know."

Surprisingly, Michaela found herself opening up to the woman with ease. "Alan at first didn't seem pleased I was around. He was angry that Hyatt asked me to lunch, but then—"

"Go on lassie, it's best no' to keep things bottled up."

She sighed, giving in and telling the old woman the rest. "Alan showed up at the pub and played darts with us. He was... well, very nice." She left out the part about where he kissed her.

Mrs. O'Malley's lips curved and she nodded her head. "Ye're a bonny lassie. It sounds like Alan came to his senses and realized the gem ye are, but ye doonae seem pleased that he did."

"No, no, I am glad." Then she realized what Mrs. O'Malley had said. "Gem?" she waved her hand to dismiss such an idea. "I mean...I like Alan...Hyatt, too."

"What is troublin' ye then?"

"Alan asked me to go with him to Urquhart Castle." She couldn't spend a day with him.

"Sounds like a grand outin' to me. Enchantin' place if ever there was one."

"I told him, no."

"Harrumph." The sound rose from the back of Mrs. O'Malley's throat, indicating her disbelief.

Michaela noticed Scots possessed this ability to say a lot without speaking a word. She wondered if she could learn the effect as well.

"He's a good man if ye were worried aboot bein' alone with him."

"That's not it."

"Ye have a sweetheart at home?"

"No."

"Then go." Mrs. O'Malley nudged her in

encouragement. "It's just a day excursion. It doesnae have to be more. Aye?"

"I don't believe in quick affairs. I don't want to lead him on that I do."

Her blue eyes softened. "Alan is auld fashion in that sense. He willnae expect more than yer willin' to give."

"Even if I wanted more, my time is limited...here...You know I'll have to go home." The excuses sounded shallow to her ears.

"All the more reason no' to waste what time ye have left. Ey?"

The woman sure did know what words to say to ease her trepidation. Was this another Scottish trait?

"Here." Mrs. O'Malley dug in her handbag for a paper and pen. With a few quick scrawls, she handed her the slip of paper. "Alan's phone number. Ring him and tell him ye'll join him after all. I promise ye, ye willnae regret it."

So she'd called and left a message, afraid she'd chicken out if she didn't do it as soon as she entered her room. He called her back and told her to be ready by nine.

Her nerves were on end at the prospect of seeing Alan. She'd like to kiss him again... would like him to kiss her back. Michaela closed her eyes and chuckled. "What's the harm in kissing?" He said she could take things at her own pace.

She opened her eyes and looked at her reflection again. Her fingers clasped the silver zipper on her windbreaker and slid it halfway up, leaving her white Henley showing.

She left her long hair down and put on the green knitted beanie, she'd crocheted herself last year. Reaching for her backpack, she didn't realizing it was unzipped and the contents spilled onto the floor. "Oh, no." She knelt down. Her hand gripped the pill bottle ready to toss it into the backpack, but she hesitated.

She hadn't needed her pain meds since...Her brows furrowed. "Since my boat trip on the loch." She felt wonderful—better than she had in months. She would like to leave the bottle behind, but there was no need to tempt fate and decided to keep the pills on hand. She didn't want anything to ruin her day with Alan and a migraine would definitely put a damper on the outing. With everything secured inside, she zipped the backpack shut and stood.

Catching her reflection in the mirror caused her to pause. Her cheeks were flushed with color not the pasty white of a few days ago. If only it could last. If only she could feel this way until the end. She swallowed the lump in her throat. "Enjoy life, now Michaela, worry about living today. Isn't that why you're here?" If she kept reminding herself perhaps she'd believe the words.

The knock on her door startled her. "Be calm." But her heart continued to pick up speed. She strode to the door and threw it opened. Her gaze took in the tall Scotsman all at once. He wore Khaki pants and battered low-heeled boots. His dark hair, overly long and sinfully thick, framed the planes of his face and brushed the collar of his navy blue, long sleeved shirt. The color looked good on him, making his blue eyes look like they were splashed with a tinge of smoky gray. Those eyes focused on her and she felt the intimate slide of his gaze down to her toes and back up again. His mouth curved into a pleased smile. "Ye look lovely, Michaela."

God, she loved the way he said her name like a caress. "Thank you. You're beautiful... I mean you look great, too."

His smile broadened. "I thank ye for the compliment. Are ye ready to go then?"

She nodded only because she didn't trust herself not to blurt out something else embarrassing.

Chapter Ten

Alan helped Michaela aboard *The Hound Dog* before he untied the boat from the dock. He started it up and headed out toward the center of the loch, giving them a view of both sides of the rugged land.

He questioned his motives of why he wanted to spend more time with Michaela Grant. He should have walked away, but for some damn reason he decided not to listen to good sense. Perhaps his foolhardy pursuit was motivated by the fact Michaela had a limited time on this realm. He wouldn't be able to hurt her. She'd slip away before he had to return to the loch.

But what if she's yer soul mate?

He watched her enjoy the warmth of the sun. Her chin titled upward, her eyes closed and a whisper of a smile curved her lips. The dark smudges under her eyes weren't so pronounced this morning and the color in her cheeks gave her a healthy glow. *The magic of the well water worked.*

He shouldn't have given it to her. Druid Daly forbade them to offer the well water to humans. Humans lost the privilege the water offered when Gordana left the well uncovered. However, when the lines of pain creased Michaela's brow, the urge to help her grew too strong to ignore. He would surely pay for his folly, but he had eternity to deal with the wrath of the gods. Michaela only had months.

"What changed yer mind aboot comin' with me today?" Curiosity danced in his head all night of the possibilities. Did she sense the link between them? Or did she simply want to see the castle?

She turned her gaze on him and his heart caught at the sight of her smile. "Life's too short not to see as much as you can. I'm here in Scotland and you offered." Her slim shoulder rose and fell in shrug, but her words meant more than she let on.

A human's life was short...painfully so. How many times had he witnessed the passing of a loved one? It never became easier. "So it was merely good timin' on my part, ey? I thought perhaps it was my charmin' personality that convinced ye to join me." Her lips curved again—lips tinged a dark pink, full and kissable. Gods, he wanted to kiss her again.

"I haven't quite figured you out, but I like a good mystery and I'm determined to unravel what makes you tick."

He chuckled. "Tread lightly, ye may no' like what ye find."

"You don't scare me."

He lifted his brows. He did scare her. He saw the fluttering truth of the fact before she could shield it behind half closed lids, but she proved braver than she looked. She wanted to know him, but he doubted she'd like what she'd uncovered.

"Oh look." She pointed. An otter floated by, lifting its head to stare before swimming away. "I love it out here with the wind blowing in my face." She inhaled deeply. "I can smell pine trees and something else wafting in the air."

"Raspberry canes, perhaps?"

She chuckled. "Maybe if I knew what they smelled like."

He maneuvered *The Hound Dog* toward land, sending a wake of v-shape wings behind them, rippling the peat-laden water. "We're almost there." Not that she needed to be reminded. She could see the ruins, beckoning them to come ashore. He steered the boat toward the short pier and tied off *The Hound Dog* at the end. The water lapped against the sides and the cool breeze rose off the water, curling around them like whispering icy fingers.

Michaela zipped her jacket to her chin in a quick gesture. "I've never been inside a real castle," she told him, excitement dancing in her moss colored eyes.

"Ye're in for a treat then." His attention wandered again to her generous lips curved in anticipation. He vowed by the end of the day, he'd kiss her again. Well and good this time.

He gripped her arm just above the elbow and helped her onto the shore.

Michaela snapped pictures of the grounds as they hiked their way to Urquhart Castle's tower, which stood high, like a stone guard over the loch.

The way Michaela viewed the vivid landscape on the opposite shore, and how she described the scent of the pine trees and the wonders of the loch had him seeing his home in a fresh new light.

Her beautiful auburn strands glimmered gold and red in the sunlight. He loved the way her perfect mouth curved into a smile when he unfolded the history of the place. The woman awakened something he hadn't felt in centuries. Her scent tantalized his senses, reminding him of lavender and heather. Her presence alone pulled at his heartstrings, but when her gaze drifted over to him, his body heated with each lingering visual caress.

He knew with certainty she felt the connection, too. Her eyes warmed with desire, the pupils swelling over the sea of green. She claimed life was too short, but would she allow what simmered between them to flourish into more?

He edged closer inhaling the clean fragrant smell of her hair and skin. It had been too long since he courted a woman. He wanted to kiss her, make love to her, but he'd promised she could take this at her own pace. "Michaela?" She leaned into him as the enchantment surrounded them, shielding them from the real world. His fingers gently tipped her chin up. Green moss eyes stared back with anticipation. She wouldn't stop him if he kissed her. She wanted this as much as he did. With a groan beneath his breath, he settled his mouth on hers.

"Would ye look at that? It's Nessie!"

Both Michaela and Alan pulled away, the magic disappearing, snapping them back to reality. Being drenched with cold loch water couldn't have done a better job.

Their gazes followed where the man in the dark blue jacket pointed. The cold water below was once the main route through the Great Glen of the Highlands and the strategic location at the very top of the tower gave them a view of the loch on three sides. They spotted the huge beast to the right of where they stood, lifting its head as if posing for a picture before it dove beneath the murky waters again.

"Bullocks! That eejit!" Alan blurted out without thinking then looked at Michaela who stared at him with one ruddy arched brow raised in question. No time to explain even if he had the notion to do so.

The crowd charged forward anxious to photograph the legendary beast and not caring whom they pushed and shoved to manage the feat.

A burly man plowed into Michaela. Her cry of alarm panicked Alan into swift motion. He pulled her against him, wrapping his arms around her as he prevented her from falling and being trampled. He led her away to the other side of the rampart, already calculating how he'd murder his brother for his stupidity. In front of fifty or more witnesses, the lack-wit, frolicked in the loch as if he didn't have a care in the world.

"I have to go," he announced.

"What is it, Alan? Why?" She looked up at him breathless and frightened, her small hands holding onto him for dear life.

"I have to find Hyatt."

"Hyatt?" She frowned and he smoothed the worry lines at her brow with a quick kiss.

"There's so much I wish to tell ye, but I cannae right now." He took her arm and led her away from the buzzing crowd.

Chapter Eleven

The boat ride back had been painfully strained, but it couldn't be helped. After he saw Michaela safely to her cottage door, Alan went in search of Hyatt. Not finding his smug face at Fiddler's Luck, he headed home to see if he returned there.

Hyatt lounged lazily on the couch with a beer in his hand and Elvis snuggled at his feet on the other end.

"Are ye a complete fool?"

"Good day to ye too, Alan" He tipped an imaginary hat.

"What was that stunt out on the loch today in broad daylight no less. We're to keep men from flockin' to the loch no' to send them chargin' with a wish to search its depths. I excused yer stunt the other day, but this..."

Hyatt sat up now and Elvis leapt to the floor, his tail wagging. "What are ye witterin' aboot?" Hyatt demanded to know.

"Where were you this afternoon?"

"If ye must know, I've been here all day nursin' a wicked headache. And what's this aboot the other day. The sightin' wasnae of me. I thought it was ye."

Alan froze as his brother's words sunk in. "If neither of us have betrayed the beastie side of our existence then what was out their impersonatin' us?"

Hyatt shook his head. "A hoax I would say. A good one if it went and fooled ye into thinkin' it true."

Alan wanted to believe someone had been clever enough to pull elaborate stunts, but if so to what purpose? An uneasy feeling spread through him and he couldn't ignore the warning. Be it a hoax or not, he needed to find out the reasoning behind it.

"How was yer date with the pretty Yank?" Hyatt asked, oblivious to what this prankster could do to their lives.

Leave it to his brother not to have a care in the world. Their lives could be exposed, but he worried about his love life. "It wasnae a date."

"Is that so? Did ye want to kiss her, 'cause if ye say no, I know ye're lyin'. Remember, I witnessed ye snoggin' her at Fiddler's Luck."

He closed his eyes with a long deliberate blink, forcing himself to remain calm. "Her lips are temptin', aye, but it would be a mistake to start somethin' with her."

Hyatt stared at him over the rim of his beer bottle, making his own assessments. "Ye like her." He sat up straighter. "Ye like her a lot."

"Arenae ye the romantic. Ye like her. Ye like her a lot," he mimicked.

"Ah sure make fun, but I have been with ye centuries and know when ye fancy a lassie more than another."

"I like her enough to know I should stay clear. I have no wish to cause her more heartache."

"More? What say ye?"

"She isnae weel if ye dinnae pick up on the fact."

"I knew somethin' was off kilter. Ye're sayin' her days are limited then," he stated with a tinge of remorse.

Hyatt didn't have the raw talent to pick up when someone's life neared an end. At least not like Alan could. Hyatt sensed a change, but he couldn't pinpoint what the disturbance indicated.

"Ye know ye cannae change what's meant to be," Hyatt gently reminded him.

"Ye're the last one who needs to remind me." He

turned to leave.

"Where are ye headin'?"

"To Fiddler's Luck. We have a problem. The prankster could prove troublesome and we need to find out who it is and stop him before it's too late."

"I'll go with ye then."

Chapter Twelve

He trudged away from the water, shifting back to his human form. "The people will turn on ye and hunt ye down like the animals ye are." A smile curved his lips. "I have a plan for the beasties of Loch Ness. I cannae wait to see how it will all play out." He inhaled taking in the water-sprayed air. "I can smell death." He clapped his hand in delight as the plot took root in his demented mind. He would destroy what the MacLachlins held dear. He would watch them suffer before he ended their existence. They deserved no less. He wanted them gone. Alan most of all.

They didn't realize the force they were dealing with, but they would soon. He couldn't wait to see their stunned faces when he slit their throats and let their life's blood stain the shores of the loch. They were abominations that needed to be destroyed. The people of Drumnadrochit would thank him later for his bravery and regard him as a savior.

The chuckle welled up inside of him until he couldn't contain it a moment longer. The rumble barely resembled laughter with the wheezing cough that vibrated from his chest.

Humans were so gullible, he thought. Put on a show and they come back with a tale of a lifetime. All he did was resurrect Nessie and stories flew as if a famous novelist had written the story. One tale had the beastie ripping off the head of sailor. Another claimed it captured a fair maiden and dragged her beneath the loch's depths. His personal favorite had to be where Nessie caught fish thrown to her as if she were a performing seal.

The tourists and the people of Drumnadrochit were easily fooled since everyone wanted to believe in something made of legends. Only he knew monsters really did exist. He was one in his own right, but the two who made their home here interested him. They pretended to be human. That alone didn't bother him in the least, but when they decided to make claims on the women folk, he had to put a stop to it. There were rules in the preternatural world and the MacLachlins had broken a major one. He'd make them pay for trying to infringe on his territory. They deserved no less for the misery they caused.

He trudged up the path to the cabin nestled within the trees, far away from prying eyes. The old homestead proved perfect. He didn't want someone coming across what he did before it could all play out.

He slipped the key into the lock and opened the door. The smell of fresh paint hit his nostrils. He painted the walls beige a few months ago, but the newness still linger. The living room was cozy in its own right with tan chairs and a striped couch facing an overly large fireplace. No pictures adorned the walls. He liked it bare. Shadows had their own kind of magic when the sun's rays shone through the windows to dance with them. Some liked the clouds and saw beauty in the heavens, but he adored the gloom, dark and foreboding alive with promise.

He strolled down the hall and unlocked the door to the extra room, decorated with thick plastic.

"I'm home," he announced as he swung the door open. A muffled cry came from the corner of the room where he had left the human tied and gagged. This one had fought with a vengeance, but in the end he was no match for him.

He shut the door behind him with a click of the

lock. "We're goin' to have so much fun you and I." As he drew near, wide eyes grew even larger. The human scooted back against the wall, as if he could hide.

He hadn't planned on taking this one, but by chance he'd come across the hiker, his backpack heavy for his long holiday. The opportunity couldn't be passed up. He needed victims to motivate the villagers into action. Steven Corbin from the States, his passport gave his name and location. He recognized him from the pub the other night, frolicking with the MacLachlins and Kait. "Kait," he spat the name like a curse. The nosey bitch never knew when to stop poking around.

"I know, I know." He spoke softly as he crouched down to eye level with his victim. "Ye're scared because ye doonae understand yer purpose here, but let me assure ye that it is of the most importance. Yer death willnae be in vain."

The human's head shook back and forth with denial.

"Sorry, but it cannae be avoided." He could kill the human quickly, but what fun would that be? He had a mission to fulfill, but it didn't mean he couldn't enjoy his work. The gag did prevent the full potential of screams, but until he tested how sound carried from the house, he couldn't take the chance that some stupid tourist on a hike would wander by and interrupt his fun. No, the wide eyes, the muffled pleas and the tears would have to suffice. "Now, now, it will only hurt for a little while."

Chapter Thirteen

Michaela took meaningful strides as she took the path over to Fiddler's Luck in hopes that Alan would eventually show up there. It seemed to be the local hangout. Alan may think he could drop her off without another thought, but he had another thing coming. He asked her out and she may have wanted to pretend it wasn't a date, but if Alan only wanted to play tour guide, kissing shouldn't be allowed.

Damn Nessie for rearing her head at the most inopportune moment. The warm pressure of Alan's mouth against hers only made her want more. He couldn't start something and think he could toss her aside without finishing it.

'You can't back it up with a future. It's a bad idea to pursue this, Grant.' Her conscience argued with her, but she decided not to listen.

She pulled on her shirt collar. God, she never thought she'd say it was hot, but sweat slid down her back even with the drizzle that had started to fall with consistency. "Hot and bothered is what you are. And where's my umbrella?" she said mumbling to herself. "Back at the cottage nice and dry." She could turn around and retrieve it, but she didn't want to chance missing Alan. "Oh, you have some explaining to do, Alan." The kisses and the reason why he thought Hyatt had something to do with the Nessie sighting. Did he and Hyatt have a scam running? It wasn't like it hadn't been done before.

In 1934, Colonel Robert Wilson, a surgeon, claimed his photo was of Nessie. Only in 1994, the truth came out. Wilson had taken a picture of a toy submarine outfitted with a sea-serpent's head.

She didn't know the MacLachlin brothers, not really. She had spent one day with Hyatt and a day and half with Alan. Her instincts told her they weren't dishonest, but they were hiding something. Curiosity wouldn't let her forget Alan's words when he saw the monster taking a leisurely swim.

As she entered Fiddler's Luck, the buzz of excitement hit her. Tourists and locals alike giving their accounts of what had been caught on their cameras. She'd been there, but hadn't snapped one picture. *In the midst of a great discovery, I failed to document it.* She'd been too mesmerized and not by the monster's appearance.

Alan's lips had distracted her. His lips were warm and inviting with a promise of more. He would have kissed her fully and she would have let him if Nessie hadn't distracted him. "Damn monster," she mumbled again under her breath. As if she didn't have enough with looming death messing with her love life, legendary monsters were now added to the mix.

She sidled up to the bar, plopping down on one of the stools, miserable with her thoughts.

The bartender gave her a quick smile. "Michaela Grant, isnae it?"

"You have a good memory."

"I have an eye for a bonny lassie." He winked and gave her a wide mouth grin. "Would ye be wantin' somethin' strong and sure like a wee dram of my finest?"

The wee dram was tempting. "I'll stick with a soda."

"Comin' right up."

Nursing an over carbonated cola, she eyed the people in the pub who were laughing and engaging in boastful chatter. Everyone had a story to tell about the loch sighting. This had been the second one this week. Surely Alan would end up here sooner or later.

As if the man finally tuned into her thoughts, he sauntered in with his brother close behind. Both men were impressive with their height and physically fit bodies, but her heart thudded in her chest for only one of them.

Alan's gaze landed on her as if sensing the same pull. She took a swig of her drink as she watched him head over to her. She let out a sigh of relief. For half a second she feared he might avoid seeing her again.

As he drew near, her heart thudded hard against her ribcage. She should have gone for the whiskey. Not that she thought alcohol was a remedy for courage, but it did mask the lack of bravery.

Hyatt nodded his hello but made a beeline over to the table where four women giggled and waved to catch his attention.

"I see you found your brother." Her head nodded in Hyatt's direction.

"Aye. Safe and sound at home it seems."

Alan didn't volunteer any more information, but his frown told her he hadn't been satisfied with the discovery.

"Hey, George," Alan looked toward the bartender, serving another customer at the other end of the bar.

George waved. "What's yer poison goin' to be, ey?"

"Beer for me when ye have a moment."

"Right up." A few seconds later, George slid a mug toward him.

Michaela didn't bother with diplomacy. "Why did you think Hyatt had something to do with the sighting in the Loch?" she blurted out in a low whisper meant for Alan's ears only.

He had the mug to his lips and paused. "Ye are

direct."

"And you're avoiding the question." His gaze took in her every feature. His blue eyes spoke of ageless beauty. An old soul, but in no way lacking in keen sharpness. He missed nothing around him.

He finally answered her with a sigh. "It's a complicated story. Ye would be best to let it go. Ye willnae like it over much."

George walked over to them with his towel draped over his shoulder. He leaned against the bar, surveying the people who flocked to his pub. "Can ye believe this blatherin' aboot the Loch Ness Monster?"

"Aye, it does have everyone buzzin'." Alan also kept his eyes on the crowd though Michaela had a feeling he searched the multitude for someone in particular.

George inhaled deeply and shook his head. "I cannae complain. A sightin's always good for business." He grabbed his towel and brushed it over the counter top. "Strange, I havenae seen Kait. She loves the gossip aboot Nessie sightin's. There's been talk she dinnae show up for work this mornin'."

With this statement, Alan turned in his seat to look at George. "Are ye sure?" Worry laced the words.

Michaela wondered why. So Kait had missed worked. With as much as she drank last night, it didn't surprise her in the least.

In the next breath, Alan stated what she had been thinking. "She was right bladdered last night." He pursed his lips together then shook his head. "But she doesnae miss work without callin' someone in to replace her for the day."

George lifted his shoulders with a quick shrug. "Only hearin' what people been sayin'. The salon's doors remained closed all day. Had Mrs. Milton in a snit. She had an appointment for a perm."

"Hmm." Alan drank with a long deliberate swig. "I'll head over to Kait's place and check on her," he volunteered, placing his mug on the bar.

"I'll go with you," Michaela offered, jumping to her feet.

His gaze lingered on her as if debating the wisdom of having her tag along. "Ye doonae have to."

"I know, but I thought perhaps you'd like some company." She had questions and she'd be damned if she let him slip away now.

One way or the other she would get to the bottom of his involvement with the Loch Ness Monster. Oh heck, she'd also like to know if he planned on kissing her again in the near future.

Suspicion arched his brows, obviously sensing their previous conversation wasn't over, but he nodded his head and gave her a smile. "Wonderful company at that. Come then, darlin' and we'll stroll over and see if Kait needs me to buy her a bottle of aspirin."

Chapter Fourteen

Alan understood why Michaela couldn't let the incident with Nessie go. He'd screwed up when he let his brother's name slip, giving her doubts of his honesty. How could she not think him involved in some elaborate prank concerning the Monster? He'd have to deal with it, but not right now. Later, when they had some privacy.

Michaela stood no taller than his chest, but her stride kept even with his, determination glinting in her eyes. More than the Nessie incident had her dander up. *Hmm, the kiss.* He told her he would let her take the lead if she wanted to start a relationship or not, but kissing her at the castle didn't exactly follow through with that promise.

He wanted more from her and he had been so close to making it a reality, but lips pressed together didn't qualify as a real caress, no matter how earth shattering the sensation had been. He wondered if Michaela would halt his intentions if he made another attempt.

"Earlier ... you know before at the castle..."

His lips curved. She was beautiful and a mind reader, too. "Ye wonderin' aboot the kiss, aye?"

She nodded. "I want to know why." She looked up at him, her eyes searching his for the truth.

Why did he feel compelled to kiss her? Now that was a question he'd been asking himself since he met her. He wished he had an answer besides the obvious. She was a beautiful lassie with lustrous auburn hair. He didn't miss the shimmering strands of gold, red and mahogany that blended into what made her beautiful tresses stand out.

Her eyes were green as moss in the early morning when the first light touched its softness. Her smile would light the depths of the loch. Physical attraction notwithstanding, he also loved the sound of her voice as she talked about her life back home and her wonderment of the loch intrigued him.

He knew in his heart she was the one he'd been waiting for, his soul mate. He tried to deny the fact, but he only had to touch her lips and the truth sang through his veins. His heart had stopped and restarted with a mere touch. What would happen if he took her in his arms and really kissed her? Made love to her?

He couldn't tell her how he felt, not yet. He didn't want to scare her off, before he had the chance to woo her properly. "Michaela, ye are a bonny lassie if ye dinnae know this. Why wouldnae I want to kiss ye?"

"You do know how to sidestep questions," she mumbled under her breath. "Pardon me for being confused. When I first met you, you didn't want me around. Then you kiss me at the pub with words that I can take this where I want it to go, but that isn't true, is it? At the castle, I saw the intent in your eyes before you pressed your lips to mine. You didn't look like a man who was willing to wait." She took a deep breath and looked at him. "My mind is still reeling from your turnaround attitude. What do you want from me, Alan? Do you want to kiss me or send me home?"

Indeed, what did he want with her? He wanted her to stay. He wanted to know everything there was to know about her. He wanted her to be his. "We're here." He pointed, hoping to buy some time before he had to answer her question.

Kait's home was a cottage style house she'd

inherited from her grandmother. Garden statues adorned the yard and garden. Kait had painted the picket fence white to show off the wild flowers that peeked in-between the slats.

Alan pushed the gate open, allowing Michaela to go first. He followed, enjoying the view of her rounded arse swaying with each step. On the porch, she turned around. Her lips parted to say something, but closed again. The color in her cheeks rose like a pretty pink sunrise. Caught, he thought. Oh well, there were worse things than admiring her backside.

Alan raised his hand to knock.

"Don't think we're through talking."

He glanced at her with a smirk before he let his hand fall against the door. "Kait, are ye in there?" he called out.

No answer.

"Maybe she's sleeping?" Michaela offered.

"Perhaps." Alan didn't think so. Something didn't sit well with him and he learned to go with his instincts. Kait loved her job. She wouldn't blow it off because of an inconvenience of a headache. She'd be nursing her throbbing head with aspirin and an icepack. His hands shaded the sides of his eyes as he peeked into the living room window. Her blue couches and an oak coffee table with glass inlays were undisturbed. To the right, he could see into her kitchen, but not a clear view. No sign of Kait as far as he could tell.

A glance at Michaela showed a worried expression creasing her brow. He wondered if he should have brought her. He wanted to investigate and she may not approve of how he went about doing it.

Too late now to second-guess his actions, he trotted down the steps and leaned down to pick up the frog prince yard decoration. He took out the spare key hidden in the secret compartment and met

Michaela's gaze.

One shapely brow lifted. "Good friends, aren't you?"

He didn't have to explain, but he found himself doing it anyway. "She lost her keys one night and told me where she kept the spare."

"I see."

"Do ye?"

"You don't owe me an explanation." Her shoulders lifted in a shrug.

"I know, but I wanted ye to know all the same. I care for Kait. I willlnae go denyin' it, but we were never meant to be together. Ye ken?"

She nodded. "Been there done that." Her features clouded and he knew she thought of home and the bloke who had disappointed her. She'd been hurt by this man. Not exactly what he meant by Kait not being the one for him. He searched for a soul mate. Kait wasn't his.

He opened his mouth to ask her what had gone wrong with her relationship, but instead pressed his lips together. This was not the time. Later, he'd question her and find out who had broken her heart.

He strode back up the steps and slipped the key in the lock, turning the knob as he went.

Michaela followed him inside and shut the door. Nothing had been moved, neat and in order as usual, but the stillness of the house unsettled him. *The absence of life.* He could smell the subtle whiff of the perfume Kait liked to wear, but it was stale, a day old at the very least. No fresh scent to indicate she'd dabbed a bit behind her ear that morning. He looked down the hall. Kait's bedroom door stood ajar.

He pushed the door open further and stood surveying the room with a keen eye. A white bedspread and matching pillows adorned the large wood-framed bed. A large stuffed bear sat in the rocking chair near the side window. Bottles of perfume and toiletries adorned her dresser—all undisturbed.

Michaela walked up beside him. "It looks like she's up and about. She made her bed."

More like she hadn't slept in it at all, he thought.

She looked at him and he knew his frown gave him away. "You don't think she slept here last night, do you?"

He shook his head.

"Would she have gone somewhere else?"

He ran his hand through his hair. "No' that I be knowin'." She slipped him a note last night, but he hadn't acted upon it. Maybe she'd set her eyes on someone else. He might believe it if the knot in his stomach wasn't making him think otherwise.

Michaela touched his arm. "What is it? What aren't you saying?"

He smoothed his frown away. There wasn't any reason to think something had happened to Kait. He didn't want to worry Michaela for no reason. "I'm sure she'll show up sooner or later." He didn't quite meet her gaze.

"Alan—"

The shattering of glass from the other room made them both jump. They stared at each other for a beat of a second. Alan placed a finger on his lips to be quiet and Michaela nodded. Alan took careful steps. If it had been Kait returning home, she wouldn't have broken a window to come in.

A quick movement caught Alan's eye. Whoever it was ran from the living room to the kitchen. He sprinted forward and slid around the corner. The back door stood ajar. He ran outside prepared to tackle the bloke, but his feet halted when the open yard stood empty. Scanning the area, no movement caught his eye. No one could move that fast unless...

He felt Michaela behind him.

"Who was it? Did you catch a glimpse of the intruder's face?"

He shook his head. "I doonae know, but I think we surprised him as much as he surprised us."

"Him? You saw a man?"

He looked back to her. No, he hadn't seen a man. He hadn't been sure if what he saw was even human—shimmering like a shadow in the sunlight—then nothing. If it hadn't been for the broken windowpane on the door, he'd think it was a trick of the light.

He couldn't tell Michaela he suspected a preternatural creature. A little white lie would have to suffice. "Aye, a kid given a dare most likely."

"Some dare. Ruining someone's property."

Alan nodded, wondering why a preternatural targeted Kait's house. Did the being have something to do with her disappearance?

Chapter Fifteen

Alan and Michaela headed back to the pub in hopes that Kait might show up there. Michaela didn't know Kait other than sharing a drink with her. For all she knew the woman took off at a moment's whim, but Alan was worried. His brow furrowed and his gaze riveted to the door each time it opened.

"I'll be but a moment. I want to ask George a few questions." He strode over to the bar. George nodded or shook his head in response to whatever Alan asked him.

Michaela leaned against the table, resting her chin in the palm of her hand. As promised, a few minutes later, Alan headed back to her, weaving between the patrons while trying not to spill the contents of the two mugs he held.

Alan moved and looked like an athlete—quick reflexes, toned muscles without an ounce of fat. Women turned to look at him as he passed and she couldn't help but stare, too. However, it was his unusual blue eyes that held her attention. Gaslight blue, they were intense with the power to make her body temperature elevate a few notches without him laying one hand on her.

What would happen if he did? Her heart shuddered expectantly as she fantasized about getting involved with him. If the way he looked at her now was any indication of how he felt, all she had to do is say the word.

It wouldn't be right, her conscience whispered back.

Alan placed their drinks down on the table, sliding one toward her. "Thought you'd might need a beer," Alan announced.

Good enough for her. She had been feeling remarkably well since she'd arrived in Scotland. Why not celebrate with alcohol? She sipped, indulging in the roast malt flavor. When she put the mug down, she met Alan's steady gaze. "You're staring."

"Aye. Ye do somethin' to me, Michaela Grant. Tell me ye feel the pull too."

She tried to protest, but her vocal chords stalled at his blunt assessment, forcing the lie to remain unvoiced. She managed to shake her head though, but he ignored her silent declaration as if he knew she didn't mean it.

"I believe we have some unfinished business."

Her gaze riveted to his again, her brows furrowing. "Unfinished business? Now?"

When he bent his head toward her, her heart raced in anticipation. He meant to kiss her and not like the sweet indulgence they partook in the other night. This kiss would prove his intentions.

Her response was as age-old as the sea. She wrapped her arms around his neck and enjoyed the breathless wonder of a caress to make her toes curl. His tongue boldly swept in pulling her under his spell...seducing her. He tasted of beer and wicked temptation and she wanted more of what his smooth mouth promised. His hand slipped to the nape of her neck, holding her close as he claimed her over and over before he tempered his caress and let her breathe.

Only when he released her, did she feel remorseful for her deceit. No one kissed like that without expecting more. She needed to tell him about her situation, but the words stayed lodged in her throat. The nearness of his lips muddled any coherent thought. Her hand centered over the warmth of his chest, gently pushing him away if only to take a deep breath and clear her thoughts.

He pulled his chair closer to hers and sat down. His gaze drifted to her lips as if he wanted to kiss her again, but he held back. Then she realized why. He made his intentions known and he wanted her to give him permission to move forward. How could she have been so selfish, throwing him a line when nothing could come of this? She should have let the incident at the castle go, but no—she had to bring it up, taunt him and he took the bait.

Her lungs filled with the scent of him as she inhaled. He smelled wonderful. Christ, it was like inhaling a special blend of a *pheromones' cologne*. She cleared her throat, hoping to keep her lustful thoughts under control. "I'm not sure where you want to go with this."

"I doonae *really* kiss a lassie without meanin' it."

She believed him. This hadn't been a kiss for curiosity or to pass the time. He was a man that did things with a purpose. There would be no going halfway. It was all or nothing. "Then in all fairness, I need to warn you."

"Warn me? Are ye goin' to tell me ye're married with bairns at home? I believe ye told me last night that wasnea the case." His lips twitched with amusement.

"I'm being serious here."

"Weel, so am I. I take it a might serious, if I am takin' another man's wife." His voice indicated he was only teasing, but she set him straight anyway.

"I'm not married."

"That's a relief." Before she could say another word, he easily lifted her off her seat and onto his lap. Startled, her arms encircled his neck for preservation. "That's better, aye?"

"Uh..." Yes, it felt wonderful to be in his arms,

but she still hadn't told him. He wouldn't want to be so friendly if he knew why she couldn't be with him.

"Ye were goin' to tell me a secret."

"Not a secret."

"A confession then."

She nodded slowly. "Yes."

"I'm a good listener."

"Alan, I..."

"Go on."

She was glad the pub was crowded. No one paid attention to what they were doing or saying for that matter. "I'm dying," she blurted it out and tried to move out of his embrace, but he held onto her. She looked up at him, meeting his tender gaze. "I'm dying," she repeated in case he hadn't heard her the first time. Instead of rejecting her, he held her tighter. He rested his forehead against hers.

"We're all dyin', Michaela, some sooner than others. Ye need to keep livin' until then or else ye might as weel bury yerself now."

She nodded and inhaled a ragged breath, willing her tears not to fall. He didn't cringe at her news of doom. She told him about the aneurysm and how an operation was out of the question. He didn't offer sympathy, but demanded her to live. She felt as if a weight had lifted from her shoulders. She could tell the angel of death to back off for now; she wasn't ready to go.

"Now, Michaela Grant do ye like me at least a wee bit?"

She couldn't help but chuckle. "I believe I do."

"Weel, I find ye quite pleasin' too." He tilted her chin up and with a lazy, sensuous movement, his mouth covered hers again. She wished the kiss would last forever.

"I wouldnae be covortin' wi' the likes of him."

Michaela broke the embrace and tried to move away, but Alan held her still.

"Ethan," Alan said calmly, but his even tone incensed the man further.

Ethan's gaze latched onto Michaela's. "Ye need to come wi' me now."

"I don't think I will." Why did this man have it out for Alan?

"It's no' safe," he warned.

"Ethan, ye will stop this," Alan demanded. It looked as though he was trying to make eye contact with Ethan, but the man refused to comply and kept his gaze locked on her.

"I ha' to warn her."

"Warn her of what exactly?" Alan snapped.

"Tha' ye will use her and leave her."

"Ethan, this is no' the time."

"When is it time? When ye leave her wi' a child?"

"Excuse me," Michaela interrupted. "Alan is just a friend." The statement sounded lame to her ears especially since she was sitting on the man's lap. Not to mention what she'd been doing before Ethan arrived.

Ethan lifted his brow. "He can be persuasive. Were ye no' snoggin' him?"

She knew the color rose in her face. She could feel the heat center on her cheeks. She opened her mouth, but what could she say? She was kissing Alan, a stranger. No, not a stranger, a man who listened to her, a man who didn't care she was dying. Was she fooling herself? Should she be more cautious?

Ethan made a snort of disgust. "Ye can ask my mother how this man loves then leaves wi'out a word...ah...but my mother's dead, isnae she?" This time he did look at Alan. "Pined for ye." His words not only accused but condemned as well.

Michaela frowned. Ethan had to be in his sixties. His mother would have to be at least in her eighties or close to it. She glanced at Alan, a man in his prime. Would he want a woman who could be his grandmother? Ethan seemed to read her mind.

"Ye're wonderin' wha' a strampin' young man as Alan would be doin' wi' my mother. He's older than ye think."

Alan let her go, sliding her back to her seat before he stood to face Ethan. "Let's take a walk ye and I and I'll..."

"I'll go nowhere wi' ye, ye fiend."

"Ethan..." Alan grabbed the older man's arm. This time Ethan met his gaze straight on.

"Nay, I willnae be silenced." He yanked his arm away and took a step back. "I've waited fifty years to confront ye, *Da*."

"Father?" Surely Ethan was delusional. Alan couldn't be his father. Michaela looked at Alan, waiting for him to refute the claim, but he remained silent, which confused her further.

"He isnae human," Ethan sneered. "He's one of the glamour folks. He shouldnae ha' been wi' my mother." He lifted his hand and pointed his index finger at Alan. "Ye left her and she pined for ye. When winter came and weather turned cold, she dinnae ha' the strength to go on."

"I'm sorry, Ethan. It pains me to know she was gone so soon after I left."

"Are ye? Ye should ha' been here. Ye should ha' saved her."

Alan remained silent, the side of his jaw pulsed, but he remained in control of this absurd conversation.

Ethan looked at Michaela again. "Come wi' me now lassie before it's too late."

Michaela shook her head. "I can't believe this."

"Nay? Look at him." He pointed. "His eyes will tell ye. Ye cannae look into his eyes wi'out feelin' his power. He will glamour ye and make ye do his biddin'."

Michaela stared at Alan and his gaze locked with hers, beseeching her not to condemn him. What was he? A magical being?

"Come wi' me, lassie," Ethan begged for the third time.

She didn't know Ethan and maybe she didn't really know Alan either. However, Alan gave her no reason to fear him. He had been kind to her. If anything, he had helped her when her headaches were severe. He could work magic, now this she could believe. He had done nothing to make her mistrust him.

Her gaze found Ethan's again. "I believe I'll stay."

Ethan stared at her dumbfounded as if he couldn't believe what he heard. He shook his head, the disgust lining his aged face into a frown and his eyes narrowing to slits. "Fine then. I did my duty and warned ye. Ye are on yer own then." His gaze narrowed on Alan's. "I'll make ye pay. If it is the last thing I do, I'll make ye pay." He whirled away, mumbling more threats as he pushed his way to the bar.

Michaela turned toward Alan, wanting answers. "What was that all about? You being his father and all."

He gave her a wan smile. "Doonae judge Ethan harshly."

Her brows lifted in unison. "He believes you're his father. Don't you find that odd?"

"Weel, aye I suppose it would seem a bit peculiar. Let's just say sometimes no' all is what it seems to be."

Chapter Sixteen

After Alan left Michaela at the cottage, safe
behind closed doors, he strolled toward home at a
leisurely pace. His thoughts plagued him with
possibilities of the future. He could have used
glamour and overrode Michaela's inhibitions with
little difficulty, but he wanted their relationship to
be what she truly desired, not because she bared her
soul to him tonight.

He frowned as he thought about Ethan's abrupt
arrival at the pub. Michaela didn't push for an
explanation to why Ethan was so bitter, but he knew
he would eventually have to tell her the truth. Not
just about Ethan, but about him and what the curse
entailed. Something he didn't look forward to doing.
The enduring link between them urged him to mate
with her and complete the bond, but he still
possessed his human emotions, too. He wanted
Michaela to want this as much as he did and
revealing he was the Loch Ness Monster probably
wouldn't endear him to her.

He wondered if the curse would be broken the
moment they bonded. He wished he had the
answers. Druid Daly had never explained the details
of breaking the enchantment. Probably because the
druid never believed he'd find his soul mate.
Truthfully, he had thought it impossible himself.
Once freed, would he be able to live his life as a
human, aging as they did? When he died, would he
be buried in the cemetery next to so many others
he'd befriended through the centuries? What would
happen to Hyatt? If the enchantment were lifted for

him, would his brother still be forced to guard the well?

"Ach. I'll go daft thinkin' of the possibilities," he mumbled and shoved his hands into his pockets.

His stroll took him over to Kait's in hopes he would find a light burning. He stood at the gate and listened. The stillness of the house told him no living soul lurked.

His finger lifted the latch to the gate, pushing it open. His steps took him to the kitchen door. His gaze wavered to the window that had been shattered. He'd spoken to Joshua Brody at Fiddler's Luck about fixing it. He could see he'd already been by. The man did a fine job. His fingers slid over the pane where a few chipped areas of paint were the only telltale signs there had been a mishap.

"Where are ye, Kait? Wherever ye are be safe." The words did nothing to comfort him. The sighting on the loch, Kait's disappearance and the break in at the house troubled him, giving him an odd feeling all three occurrences were related in some way.

Leaving Kait's house behind, he headed back to his place. Usually he enjoyed his walks through the village. Hints of heather, moss and forest shrubs all blended together into a pleasant aroma of home. All scents to comfort, but they weren't working their magic tonight. He couldn't think of anyone who would want to harm Kait, but he felt antsy as if danger lurked in the shadows ready to strike.

He shook his head. Kait was a resourceful woman. Most likely his unease had more to do with the dilemma he faced with Michaela. He had no doubt Michaela was his soul mate. As much as he wanted to give her time to accept him, he also knew time proved a threat. Each moment brought Michaela closer to the inevitable. "I am truly cursed. I have found my soul mate. Only I shall lose her to the angel of death."

He needed a plan if he was to win Michaela over. His best ideas came when he took to the water. He felt at home within the depths of the loch. There were things about the loch that others didn't understand. He knew the legends and the truths and it was his job to keep the secrets safe. The water was as much a part of him as breathing and eating were to every human soul.

With a mere thought, the magic rolled over him, changing his body into the beast that ruled the depths. He dove deeper, letting the water wash over him like a cool massage, tingling his smooth seal-like skin.

Michaela would die—soon. He sensed it, but it didn't stop him from wanting her. She wanted him too. The beating of her heart and the sweet urgency of her kiss confirmed the rest. If they could be with each other for a short time, why not take what was offered? He couldn't promise her forever, but neither could she.

So why did he hesitate?

His strokes took him to an underground cave. He resurfaced where the pocket of air enveloped the hidden cavern. He switched from beast to human as he stepped onto the cool wet surface made of limestone. The magical transformation from one reality to the other not only allowed him to keep his clothing at will, but he could carry items he needed with him.

When he and Hyatt were forced to take to the waters for fifty years, they weren't restricted from learning what passed above on land. Sometimes it took a few days, but what happened through the years became known to them as if someone had whispered large amounts of information into their brain as they hibernated.

He supposed it was similar to the way computers were updated to run efficiently. "The gods thought of everythin'," he said with sarcasm. They couldn't have their guardians of the *well* ambling around without a clue of what transpired through the ages.

But being given the information wasn't the same as living through the experiences. They only knew of the advances and the changes in speech, but not of the friends they left behind. The information updates left him wanting more, but he supposed that was part of the punishment. They lived in two worlds but were never truly a part of either.

The chamber stood about sixty meters long and about thirty-nine to forty meters high, large enough to house a beast.

Treasures of years gone by were stashed in the corners, giving the cave the look of a pirate's sanctuary. He and Hyatt had gathered items from their life and from what was tossed into the loch. It would be a historians dream, but the items were memories for them.

He headed for the stone structure in the center of the chamber. He shoved at the large wooden lid, sliding it to the side and revealing the bottomless well of fresh water. The liquid was clean and pure. "The water of life."

He dipped into the well using the ladle that had been there from the beginning of time. It still looked as if it had been molded only yesterday.

Perhaps the water kept the object from decaying, like how it stopped the natural aging of any living being.

He filled two bottles; then he took out the third. The plastic felt cool to the touch, a simple container to store the precious water.

Should he fill the third bottle? He had brought it with him for that purpose, knowing whom he would give the bottle to.

He wasn't supposed to interfere with destiny,

but what if fate had sent Michaela to him so he could save her?

Should he turn his back?

His grip tightened on the ladle and he filled the bottle, answering his own question.

Chapter Seventeen

Michaela settled in for the night, taking a book with her to bed. Alan left her at the doorstep with a quick goodnight kiss—on the cheek. Disappointment felt heavy in the pit of her stomach and she was sure he'd read the frustration in her gaze. His mouth twitched—damn him for his arrogance—as if he felt great pleasure that his peck on the cheek had annoyed her. Lucky for him, he didn't grin or she'd have lost it.

No, instead he teased her further. His hand slid down her arm like an intimate caress while his deep melodic voice vibrated with promises to see her tomorrow.

Maybe he was preoccupied thinking about Ethan and his constant harassment. The old man had to have some form of dementia to think Alan was his father. *But Alan didn't dispute Ethan's claims.* She reminded herself. "Don't be ridiculous. Of course he didn't refute the claim." If Ethan did suffer from dementia then arguing with him wouldn't help matters. Still, it was obvious Alan cared for Ethan. But it didn't seem safe for Ethan to wander around without care.

Smoothing the blankets to her waist and settling into a comfortable position on the bed with two pillows propped behind her, she opened her book to where the jeweled bookmark held her place. The story was a simple romance to pass the time away.

Normally, her preference was an edgy paranormal that kept her spellbound from beginning to end, but the newsstand at the airport didn't have her favorite author's new book and she'd already read the others.

The book she settled on sported a dark haired, blue-eyed hunk with definite promises of a steamy romance. Hmm...the description could be used for Alan. Her lips curved as she conjured Alan's image into the hero in the book. Now the story would prove exciting.

Two pages in with the heroine putting herself in danger and the hero angry that he had to save her, the vibrating buzz of her cell phone pulled her out of the story. She leaned over and picked it up from the nightstand. The name flashed with the number. "Blake."

Disappointment then irritation washed over her before she squashed both feelings down, leaving her with guilt. She should have called Blake and let him know she was all right. She chewed on her lower lip. Why should she feel guilty for not calling when he had left her? She had the right to move on and forget about him no matter how noble Blake's intentions were.

She needed a man who wanted her without needing to fix her. She wasn't broken. Damn it anyway. She had a condition, an aneurysm that would eventually take her life. It was no one's fault, just her lot in life.

She flipped the phone open. "Hello."

"Hey, babe." Hearing his voice and his endearment set her nerves on edge. He didn't want to stand by her decision, which in her mind left him no right to sweet talk her.

I can't do this, Michaela. I don't want to come home one day and find you dead. His words, not hers echoed in her head. "Blake, what do you want?" Her voice sounded harsh to her own ears.

"I..."

"What?"

"You aren't going to make this easy, are you?"

"Why should I?"

"I'm worried about you."

"I thought you made it clear you didn't want to know how I fared. Wasn't that why you stormed out of my apartment with your ultimatum?"

A tired sigh reached her ears. "Don't make this difficult, Michaela."

"Oh, I'm sorry. Did I make your life too complicated? I apologize for developing an aneurysm. How inconsiderate of me." Sarcasm laced her words and Blake heard it loud and clear.

"Okay, I deserve your wrath."

"Yes, you do." She smoothed the already unmarred blankets.

"Is it a crime that I want you to live?"

"You know what the surgeons told me, Blake. You forget. I used to work in a nursing home before I came to work at Hoag as a nurse practitioner. I've seen firsthand how this operation can go wrong. First, it could kill me. Heck, that would be a blessing compared to the horror of stroking out or living in a nursing home drooling and not aware of my surroundings."

"The artery could be repaired, too. Did you forget about that possibility?"

"The odds weren't in my favor. I'm not a gambler, Blake. It has nothing to do with your ability as a doctor or your judgment of whom you thought was the best candidate to operate on me. I've accepted my fate. Why can't you?"

"I see hope in saving you, but you won't take it."

She noticed he didn't say he loved her. He didn't say he'd stand by her and see this through. He didn't offer to wipe the drool from her lips if the surgery failed. She was only a patient to him now. "This is my choice."

"Yes." He sighed again and she could imagine

him rubbing the bridge of his nose. A habit she pinpointed as his way to relieve tension. "Are you having headaches?" he asked her. "Any loss of time or..."

"Or what? Are you asking me if I'm experiencing hallucinations?" She knew what to expect. She'd seen the x-rays and knew where the aneurysm sat, waiting in her brain like a ticking time bomb.

"You know that's a possibility."

She chuckled. She couldn't help it. Blake wanted forever with her, but he didn't care about her quality of life. She didn't need Blake hounding her to do something she didn't want to do. She had Alan, a man who didn't care if they had tomorrow. He wanted today. This she could offer.

She frowned as a thought played through her mind. What if Alan MacLachlin was only a figment of her mind? Wouldn't that beat all? God, if Alan happened to be a hallucination, she prayed sex would be part of the fantasy, too. Large hands touching, caressing and bringing alive every—

"Michaela?" Blake interrupted her musing.

"I'm here." She put her hand over her mouth, suppressing a chuckle that threatened to bubble over. She took a deep breath. "I'm fine, Blake. In fact, I've never felt better. Maybe Scotland's air has some miracle qualities we aren't aware of. I haven't taken any pain meds in two days."

"None?" He didn't sound as if he believed her.

"I told you I've been fine."

"Your condition won't miraculously take care of itself. Something is wrong, Michaela. You won't get better. Dammit, you shouldn't have risked the flight over there. When are you coming home?"

"I haven't decided. I have an open ticket."

"You're so far from—"

"Stop it, Blake. I mean it. If you have nothing better to talk to me about other than my impending doom, we're done here."

"Michaela, I just want to make sure this miraculous recovery isn't in fact a new symptom and—"

"I warned you. Goodbye." Michaela ended the call. A second later her phone buzzed, again. She didn't have to see the screen to know it was Blake. Six weeks, she hadn't heard a word from him, and now he wanted to be in her life again. No, she didn't need him hovering and analyzing her every move.

"Feeling better is not a symptom," she said stubbornly for her own benefit. She had energy again. She had an appetite that had failed her weeks before when the migraines caused her stomach to churn.

She whipped the blankets aside and swung her legs over the edge of the bed, heading for the bathroom to look in the mirror. She looked healthier. There was color in her cheeks and the dark rings under her eyes had diminished.

When had this happened? When had she felt better? She knew the answer. It was when Alan had placed his hands on her temples. She felt the energy flowing from his fingertips, pulsating through her scalp, through bone and tissue, the energy massaging the pain away. Was he a healer of some sort? She shook her head at the thought.

Healers didn't exist in the real world only in her paranormal books. "You're hoping for a miracle where there isn't one," she told herself. Her hand reached for the light switch, flipping it off before heading back to bed.

Chapter Eighteen

Hyatt slipped his arm around the pretty blonde seated next to him. Becca Polk was her name and she was fuming mad at her boyfriend, Damon Nokes. Damon was Ethan MacGregor's grandson, twenty-two, spoiled and too sure of himself. The man stood in the back corner with his buddies, laughing at how he put Becca in her place. Hyatt had every intention of teaching Damon a lesson on how to treat a woman with respect.

When he slid into the booth where Becca sat with her girlfriends, Damon happened to look their way. Hyatt slid his arm around Becca to comfort her. That wiped the condescending smile off Damon's face and caused the color in his cheeks to change from red to dark purple. Damon took a step forward with his hands balled at his side, but his friends held him back.

Hyatt's lips slid into a wide grin. He hadn't had a good brawl in a while and would be pleased to teach Damon a lesson in manners. Becca was sweet as they come, loyal and beautiful, but Damon obviously had a few screws loose and didn't know what a gem he had.

Damon stayed with his friends long enough to down his drink before he brushed them off with determination stamped on his broad features. Sauntering over with an attitude and puffed out chest, it looked like he was twitching for a fight. He snorted, rubbing his thumb on the side of his nose.

Pompous arse. Hyatt thought but continued to smile.

"That there is my girl, Hyatt."

Hyatt didn't move away from Becca. "Seems she doesnae think so."

"I'm no' with ye Damon." Becca's voice stayed true and steady, but he could feel her tremble beneath his hand. "Ye made that perfectly clear when ye were makin' fun of me with yer friends. Go back to them. I have a real man to take care of me." She leaned into Hyatt, rubbing her hand over his chest.

Hyatt knew she only wanted to make Damon jealous. The fool girl loved the eejit.

Damon sputtered for words and settled for, "I willnae stand for this."

"So doonae stand for it," she threw back.

Damon made a lunge for her, grabbing a hold of her arm.

Hyatt's hand snaked out and grabbed Damon's forearm in a tight squeeze, causing him to grimace. "I believe the lady said she dinnae want to go with ye."

Damon backed off, jerking out of Hyatt's grip, but he refused to bugger off. "Tell him, Becca. Tell him ye're with me."

"See Damon, the thing is, I'm no' with ye. Get it through yer thick skull."

His gaze landed on Hyatt, his eyes narrowed to slits. "I should kick ye this side of nowhere."

"Ye can give it a try." Hyatt stood. He towered over Damon, giving him a warning that a fight would be one sided in this case. *His side.*

Damon swallowed hard, his Adam's apple bobbing up and down. He took a step back.

Wise fellow. "Should we take this outside, Damon? I doonae want to bust up George's place."

"I…"

"Weel? What shall it be?" Hyatt's brows lifted.

Damon's friends joined him now, flanking his

sides. This gave Damon courage. Bullies always surrounded themselves with a pack. Hyatt didn't care. He could take all of them if he had to. Hell, he fancied it.

"Let's step outside." Damon's friends pounded him on his back.

Hyatt could have jumped for joy. "I'd love to."

Becca flew to her feet, her eyes wide and scared. "Damon, doonae do this."

"Ye're my girl, Becca. No one takes what's mine."

Becca looked at her boyfriend and the other ruffians itching to slam their fists into Hyatt's face. Her gaze landed on him. "Ye doonae have to fight these eejits. I'm sorry I brought ye into this mess."

Hyatt leaned down and kissed her cheek. How sweet. She worried he wouldn't come out of this unscathed. He looked at Damon. His eyes were narrowed with murderous contempt. "Bring it on." Hyatt swept his hand toward the door.

Chapter Nineteen

Alan strolled toward the pub, slowing his pace as he caught sight of the crowd gathering. He had a bad feeling. "Hyatt," he uttered a curse beneath his breath. The eejit no doubt had managed to coerce some bloke into a fight and with the unsuspected target never knowing he'd been selected for such a purpose. "Hot headed—"

"Hit him again!" someone egged on the fight.

Alan pushed his way through the crowd. Hyatt was outnumbered, but he didn't look worried if the grin and his *come-get-me* wave could be noted as proof. Damon and two of his friends, Troy Ackman and Morton Rander rushed Hyatt but he whirled around, knocking the two friends back before slamming his fist into Damon's chin. Down the fool went. Alan shook his head. They never learned.

"Damon!" Becca rushed over to him, falling on her knees beside him. "Oh, Damon, are ye all right?" Her hands lifted his head with caution, cradling and caressing his injured face.

Hyatt took a step toward her.

"Doonae come any closer Hyatt MacLachlin. Ye're a beast," Becca yelled at him.

The crowd closed in to comfort Becca. Damon moaned, coming around to the land of the living.

Hyatt's gaze landed on Alan. He shrugged as if to say the bloke had it coming. Alan never doubted Damon deserved to be taught a lesson, but why did his brother have to be the enforcer. It made things uncomfortable in the village when he pulled stunts like this.

Hyatt walked toward him with his hands in his pockets. "Did ye have a nice night, Alan?"

"I suppose a might better than yers, by the looks of it."

"Oh, I had a crackin' good time of it."

Alan rolled his eyes. "Let's go home. I have no wish to be drawn into yer fights."

"Always the lover, Alan. It's all those damn Elvis songs ye listen to."

"Let's keep the King out of this if ye doonae mind."

"Ye cannae keep from destroyin' everyone in yer path, can ye?" Both brothers whirled around to find Ethan glaring at them with contempt.

Alan sighed. "Ethan, we were goin' home."

"Aye, but no' before yer brother knocked my grandson half dead."

"He start—"

Alan placed a retraining hand on Hyatt's arm to let it go.

"We have no quarrel with ye," Alan told him.

"No quarrel? Ye come and fancy talk yer way into everyone's life, but I know ye better. I know wha' ye are. I know of the beastie that lies in wait. Where's Kait? Ey? She cared for ye and now she's missin'. Where is she?"

"Kait's missin'?" Hyatt's gaze riveted to Alan.

"Doonae play me a fool," Ethan continued. "She's gone and ye can bet yer life if any harm comes to her, I'll make it known they should sniff around yer place." Ethan turned on his heels, heading toward Damon, already berating him for fighting Hyatt.

Alan needed to deal with Ethan and soon. Ethan had become a bitter old man, but why? He had once been a sweet child full of wonder and a quick smile. Had the death of his mother turned him against the world or was something else at work here?

If only Mary hadn't died so young. If only he had

been here when she fell ill. Would he have tried to save her? He thought about the bottles of water he filled to give to Michaela. He hadn't thought twice to help her.

"Kait's missin'?" Hyatt asked again, drawing him out of his reverie.

"Aye, been gone all day."

"That's no' like her."

"Doonae ye think I know? Michaela and I went by her place—"

"Michaela and ye, is it?" He wagged his brows.

"Just listen. Kait hasnae been home all day and by the looks of it, she never made it home from Fiddler's Luck last night."

Hyatt lost his smirk. "Ye think somethin' happened to her, dooncha?"

"I hope I'm wrong, but aye. Someone was at her place. Swift as the devil himself and I couldnae follow him."

"Do ye think this has somethin' to do with the sightin' of Nessie?"

He shook his head. "I doonae know."

"The well—"

"No need to worry. I took a swim." He pulled out one of the water bottles then placed it back in his pocket. "Nothin's been disturbed."

"So what are we dealin' with? A selkie? A shape shiftin' witch?"

At first Alan thought they were dealing with a human taking a prank to the fullest, but now he couldn't dismiss the possibility they were dealing with a magical creature. Through the centuries they dealt with many such creatures, some worse than others. "We'll keep a wary eye on things. Whatever we're dealin' with, we'll take care of the problem."

"Hmm, aye we will one way or the other." Hyatt tilted his head and his eyes narrowed as he stared at Alan.

"Ye might as weel ask the question that looks to be burstin' from yer lips."

"Ye've been a might distracted lately. Are ye moonin' over the Yank?"

His lids lowered in a blink of annoyance and he took deliberate steps toward home, hoping to give himself a moment to come up with a good answer. He wasn't sure he wanted to reveal Michaela was his soul mate. It seemed appropriate to tell his mate first. "Doonae be faniciful," he finally answered. Not exactly an answer to stop Hyatt from questioning him.

"Hmm." Hyatt kept step with him. "Ye spent the day with the lassie. Ye dinnae tell me how that went."

"We had a grand time until the beastie made a splash."

"Aah, aye, but ye met up with her again at the pub. Ye sat might cozy with her and doonae think I didn't see ye snoggin' her again. It's become a habit of yers."

Alan pulled on his sweater at the collar, feeling the threads tightening around his neck. "She's a right bonny lassie and I'll thank ye no' to be spyin' on me."

"Spyin'? Ye were in a public place, might I remind ye."

"Ye handle yer love life and let me handle mine." His voice held a rough edge to it, but Hyatt didn't heed the warning.

"Ye said ye took a swim to the well and filled more water bottles. We have more than enough water to last us for months."

Alan looked at him, drawing his brows together. "We needed more."

"Is that so. The Yank—"

"Michaela," he corrected.

"Aye, Michaela. She would benefit from the

water. Aye?"

"So."

Hyatt yanked on his arm, bringing him to a halt. "Alan, ye tempt fate, givin' the lassie the water that isnae meant for her."

"What if we're wrong? What if Michaela found us so that I could help her?"

"Ye know that isnae how it works, but let's go with yer tale, aye? What happens when she goes back home and the doctors find she's cured?"

"We doonae know if she'll be cured. Once she leaves, things may go back as they were."

"Maybe, maybe no'. If she is cured, the physician's will ask questions. They'll ask her what she's been doin'. They'll go over everythin' and she'll lead them back to us."

"When did ye become so concerned with consequences?"

Hyatt shrugged. "I usually doonae have to worry. Ye do enough worryin' for the both of us, but now it seems yer sensible side's taken a holiday."

"Michaela wouldnae hurt us. I know she wouldnae."

"No' intentionally."

Alan ran his hand through his hair as he turned to look out toward the loch. The water flowed dark as the moonless night, his home when he wasn't sporting his human skin. "I think she's the one. Nay," he looked at his brother again determined to tell him the truth, "I know she is."

Hyatt's brows rose high on his forehead. "Are ye talkin' aboot yer soul mate?"

Allan nodded.

"Weel isnae that an effin' kick in the pants." He laughed and socked his brother in the arm, but then his smile slipped. "If she's the one why hasnae the curse been lifted?"

"I doonae know." The water still beckoned him

and he wouldn't hesitate to relinquish his human skin to the beastie within. "Maybe she must see for herself she belongs with me. Maybe when we bond completely the curse will be broken. I believe she feels the pull, but perhaps she doesna trust it."

"She's dyin', Alan. Humans make peace with it and doonae go around pursuin' new adventures they willnae be able to enjoy."

Alan had thought of that, too. She had informed him of her impending death, believing she had to give him a warning as if what would eventually kill her would harm him in some way.

He had to convince her it didn't matter. They could have a future—for as long as she lived. Then there was the off chance the water would cure her. Wasn't that why he'd taken the bottles and filled them?

"Ye could tell her what ye are," Hyatt offered a solution.

Alan chuckled. "Oh that would be grand, wouldnae it? She'd pack up and leave. I'd rather gain her trust first, then ease into tellin' her she's fallin' in love with the Loch Ness Monster."

"One of the Loch Ness Monsters, if ye doonae mind." Hyatt gave him a wan smile. "Once the curse is lifted, I'll be the only one."

Alan loathed the idea of leaving his brother behind. "Hyatt, I—"

He lifted his hand to quiet him. "I'll be sad to lose ye, Alan. The gods know I wouldnae know what to do without ye blusterin' aboot one thing or another. I realize I must return to the depths, but I wouldnae have it any other way. I love the waters, Alan. I like the arrangement Druid Daly put on us."

Alan sighed. "If the truth be told, I would miss the water. However, I desire a much simpler life."

Hyatt chuckled. "Aye, one with a warm and willin' woman sleepin' next to ye, I'd gather."

Chapter Twenty

It was time to set up the next portion of the plan, the shape shifter thought as he watched the last of the patrons leave Fiddler's Luck. The only ones left in the pub were the rejects. Damon, Morton and Troy. Damon's girlfriend, Becca Polk left hours ago. Stupid girl. Damon would never live up to her expectations.

"Damon, Damon, Damon... Hmm..." The twenty-something youth was Ethan MacGregor's grandson. Seemed only fitting he included the young man in his plans. "Connections. Oh aye." The shape shifter's lips slid into a grin. The MacLachlins had an ongoing feud with Ethan. Sure it was only one sided, but the authorities wouldn't care.

Tonight's events had decided who his next victim would be or should he say...victims. He hid the small chuckle behind his hand. "So much fun. Thank ye, Hyatt with my decision." Picking a fight with Damon had been lovely. All present at the pub witnessed how violent Hyatt could be and Ethan showed up to help the plan along with his accusations and threats. How nice of them to play along. "So predictable."

"We're headin' out, George," Damon called to the bartender, his posse following behind him, all rightly bladdered.

"See ye tomorrow, aye?" Morton Rander waved and stumbled into Troy Ackman nearly knocking him over.

"Hey, watch it, ye lummox." Troy shoved Morton away.

"Sorry, I tripped."

"Yeah, weel do it somewhere else." Troy's voice faded away as the door closed behind him.

No one would see them tomorrow.

What dimwits, but then their stupidity made his job in snatching the buggers easy.

Out back in the alley passage, the three decided to relieve themselves against the wall. Animals the lot of them.

"Did ye get a look at Ann Denny's tits hangin' out of the low cut top?" Troy Ackman, with tattoos and piercings, chuckled. His hand steadied his wanker as he sprayed the wall with his piss as if marking his territory.

In the shape shifter world, he'd be the first eliminated. He thought he was tough, but was too stupid to know he wasn't.

"Before or after I fondled them?" Morton snorted with laughter.

The overweight youth with spotted black and red hair most likely would have his face slapped if he even had the nerve to put his pudgy hands on Ann's breasts. *Braggards the lot of them.*

Damon's hand jerked his zipper up and faced his friends. "She let me taste them, full and firm." His wide mouth grinned.

"Get out of here." Troy had finished relieving himself and nudged Damon against the wall with a jovial push. "Taste them, ye say. And where was Becca?"

"Went home like a good little lassie. I'm a man I told her. I cannae be waitin' for her to decide to put out."

More laughter. One would think Damon was a comedian the way they laughed at his lewd remarks. Damon's dark hair was matted to his head with jell and sweat. He reeked too, needed a right dunkin' in the loch.

Soon enough. The shape shifter thought with pleasure. The temperature had dropped, giving the night air a cool breeze. Damp earth reached his nostrils. Rain later tonight to be sure. Stepping forward out of the dim lighting to face the young men, he announced his presence. "Good evening, laddies."

"What the effin' hell." Troy's elegant way for words never failed to amaze him.

"Ye scared us half to death," Damon voiced.

Morton just chuckled nervously, his pants still unzipped.

Scared them half to death... If he only realized the truth of his statement. The shape shifter grinned with the thought. "I have a surprise for ye."

"Yeah, what is it?" Damon lifted his chin.

Pompous arse wouldnae be so cocky in a moment.

The shape shifter's body contorted and lengthened into the beast. The three gaped in horror, frozen in their spots as if cemented to the concrete.

The first raindrops fell from the sky and thunder roared the moment Morton opened his mouth to scream.

Chapter Twenty-One

The rain had come down hard last night, drenching the earth. The plants and trees glistened in the sun like sparkling diamonds. A perfect morning for a walk and Alan took advantage of it. He walked through the Village Green with fond memories.

In centuries past, it once had been the heart of the village where cattle sales took place. Today, there were tourists out for a leisurely stroll, and cyclists whizzed by enjoying the morning, too.

Alan's intentions were to ask Michaela out on a proper date, with hopes nothing pressing would ruin the day. If the shape shifter resurfaced, he'd have to go after him. Loch Ness belonged to them and they'd keep it safe no matter the consequences.

Reaching his destination, he hesitated on the walkway leading to the front door. The nineteenth century cottage retained its Georgian windows along with its charm. It stood within minutes of all amenities, making it a perfect place to stay.

"It's a might early," he murmured the excuse, deciding he should swing by later. He required less sleep than humans, but to stay at home this morning and wait for a decent hour hadn't been a choice. His nerves were in a jumble. Taking to the loch hadn't been an option this morning either. He didn't want to become carried away by the feel of the water and miss Michaela starting her day.

He paced the path, looking toward the cottage every so often, hoping she'd opened the door and step outside.

"Ye should just knock on the door. It's how it's usually done."

He whirled around to find Mrs. O'Malley standing there. Her sparkling blue eyes filled with mischief.

"I should, should I?"

"Oh, aye. Ye carvin' a new path in the walkway willnae give ye a chance with the lassie, now will it?"

"It's still early. She's probably—"

"Fiddlesticks," she interrupted.

His brows rose.

"I wager Miss Grant is wonderin' why ye havnae knocked, too. Ye look a fine sight with yer dark hair all stickin' up on end and ye mumblin' like yer half crazed."

He smoothed down his hair and his gaze riveted to the cottage. Did he see the curtain fall back into place?

"Weel?" Mrs. O'Malley waited. When he didn't answer right away she clicked her tongue. "Are ye goin' to ask the poor lassie out or no'?"

His lips twitched in annoyance. Didn't the woman have better things to do than harass him? "Aye, of course I am."

"Good." Her hand patted his arm. "I dinnae think ye were a coward, Alan MacLachlin." She chuckled as she walked past him.

"Coward indeed," he grumbled under his breath as he strode forward. His fist landed heavy on the door with two raps.

Michaela opened her door dressed in blue jeans and a coffee brown T-shirt. Her reddish locks were held back from her face by two barrettes. He thought she was beautiful but then her lips curved into a smile. *Striking* proved a better word.

He hadn't realized he was frowning until his own lips curved. "Awright, Michaela?" He greeted her with the typical Scottish 'how do ye do' of the decade.

Her brows drew together then she chuckled. "Fine and you?"

"Oh aye, grand." From his coat pocket, he pulled out a water bottle and handed it to her.

"You are a strange one. Most men bring a woman flowers, but with you it's bottled water."

His shoulder lifted in a shrug. "I can bring posies next time if ye wish."

"Oh no, I didn't mean to insult you. I find it refreshing actually. Flowers are predictable. Water... Hmm...well it's unique. I like that."

He let out a breath he didn't realize he was holding. "Do ye like it enough to come out with me?"

Her gaze shifted to the sky.

"If ye're worried aboot rain, ye doonae have to fear. The skies given its best last night and willnae be troublin' us this mornin'."

"Is that so?"

"Oh aye, I'm sure of it."

She worried her lower lip, making him wonder if she might turn him away, but then she nodded. "Where are you taking me?"

His lips curved. "Somewhere special."

Her brow lifted but she didn't question him further. "Let me grab my coat."

"I'll be right here." Alan shoved his hands in his pockets. A real date and a chance to woo her. *Doonae blow it, MacLachlin*, he silently warned himself.

"I'm ready," she said shutting the door behind her.

****

Alan took *The Hound Dog* out, leaving Elvis and Priscilla at the house. Elvis ran down to the edge of the pier barking at them.

"Ye stay, Elvis and I promise ye somethin' special tonight. Good dog," he said as he maneuvered the boat away.

Elvis gave one more bark and trotted back toward the house.

"If I didn't know better, I'd swear Elvis actually understands you."

He looked at Michaela who leaned against the railing.

"Oh aye...weel, I suppose he does."

She sighed. "So where are you taking me?"

"It's a surprise. I'm sure ye'll enjoy it. Ye brought yer camera with ye, dinnae ye?"

Her hand patted the pocket of her windbreaker. "Have it right here."

"Good." He leaned over and flipped the switch on the CD player then turned toward her. "Do ye mind if I play some Elvis tunes?"

"Not at all." She came to stand by him and he put an arm around her while keeping the other on the wheel.

Otters floated in the water to the left of them without a care in the world.

"What marine life inhabits Loch Ness?"

"Seals, salmon, sea trout, brown trout and eel to name a few."

"Eel huh?"

"Oh, aye. Have ye never had jellied eel?"

"Uh...can't say that I have."

"It's to die for when sprinkled with hot chili vinegar."

She looked up at him with her cute little nose crinkled with disgust. "I'll take your word for it."

"Doonae fash yerself, I'll no' force ye to try it, but I must say ye are missin' out." He chuckled as he leaned down and kissed her, startling both of them. Her cheeks flamed pink and he grinned despite himself. "If ye like we could stop by *Monjack Castle* on the way back. They're famous for their wines and liqueurs. Their preserves arenae half bad either."

"I'd love that, yes."

He nodded. The wind blew her hair back and he couldn't resist. His hand reached out, letting the silky strands slide through his fingertips. She turned to smile up at him. This had been a good idea. He hadn't felt this happy and relaxed in a long time.

As they passed Urquhart Castle, on the northern shore his thoughts turned to when he had tried to kiss her there. The first touch of her lips had nearly sent him over the edge, but the real kiss later at the pub had plunged him straight down. He wanted to kiss her again, but later, when he had time to savor the moment.

"What are you thinking about?"

He turned to see her watching him intently. "How I want to kiss ye proper."

Her right brow rose a fraction of an inch. "You didn't have to take me out on the loch to do that."

He chuckled. "Nay, I suppose I dinnae, but I wanted to. Our last outin' dinnae fare so weel."

"I had a good time."

"Did ye now? We'll see how ye like today then, shall we?" He maneuvered the boat toward the land on the south side of the loch. "We'll be stoppin' at the village of Foyers. Are ye game for a small hike? I promise ye, the trail isnae troublesome."

"I'm game."

The village was nestled under the brooding crags of Dun Dearduil. The village had very few homes and they were all scattered deep in the woods.

Entering the Iverfarigaig Forest, the walkway led steeply down, but it wasn't a difficult trek. The twisting banks of the brook were lined with moss and wildflowers. Squirrels darted along the path in hopes of finding pine nuts and chestnuts. Up ahead, there were areas fenced off for viewpoints, allowing tourists photo opportunities.

Alan heard the rush of water long before Michaela did and knew they drew near the spot he wanted her to see. As they came through the clearing, her sigh of awe pleased him.

"Oh Alan, a waterfall, it's beautiful." She spoke above the rush of water as she lifted her camera to take a photo.

"The waterfall is aboot a hundred and forty feet; I suppose that's the right calculation in Yank terms." She threw him a disgruntled look, but smiled before she turned away to snap more photos. "The waterfall plunges into a bubbling steaming mass below where it flows into a gorge then into the Loch Ness."

"*Among the heathy hills and rugged woods...the roaring Foyers pours his mossy floods,*" she quoted.

"Ye know Robert Burns."

She snapped another picture with a chuckle. "I couldn't quote the whole poem, but I remembered it from college. I didn't quite understand the beauty of what he wrote about until now." Her head turned to look at him. Her green eyes were the color of the plants and foliage around them. "This place is special to you, isn't it?" she asked, her voice soft and sweet.

He nodded, his throat thick with emotion. He moved close to her, his hand touching her silken strands. For centuries he tried not to yearn for something he could never have, but when their gazes met, he recognized the longing in her eyes and knew it mirrored his own desires. He lowered his mouth gently to hers, savoring all the softness and heat and unspoken promises to come. He paused only to draw in a rugged breath. His hands cupped her face and his forehead rested against hers. It was difficult to hope when all his hopes had been dashed so ruthlessly before.

"Tell me. What does this place mean to you, Alan?" Her question suggested more. She sensed his sadness and the longing for a life forfeited long ago, but to tell her of it would be a mistake. Let her know him first. Trust would be the key. Without it, he would never see her again.

"The place is full of history," he told her.

"It speaks to you, doesn't it?"

"Aye." He took a ragged breath and stepped back if only to think clearly. "Near here on a lonely towerin' mountain, overlookin' Inverfarigaig there stands a fort that was built in the Iron Age. It's called Dun Dearduil. The Celts built it in 700BC to protect them from enemies."

Hyatt and he had lived there among the Celts in the gravely and grassy roundhouses where there were pens for the cattle, but he couldn't tell Michaela of his time there. She probably wouldn't believe him anyway. "Outside there were thick dry stone walls with wooden palisades on top. Ditches and banks once surrounded the outside of the fort."

"It was to keep out the enemy, wasn't it? I read about the ancient forts."

"Aye." He nodded. "Did ye know Dearduil means Deirdre?" he asked, wondering if she knew any of the Celtic legends.

She shook her head.

"Deirdre of Sorrows lived here once with the three sons of Usnach." His voice lowered to a husky note as he remembered the past.

"It must be a sad story."

"Oh aye, verra sad. Deirdre was from Ireland and fell in love with Naoise, one of the three sons of Usnach, but she was promised to the king, ye see. Naoise and Deirdre fled Ireland and came to live here for a time. The king found out where they were and promised if they returned he would forgive them." Alan had tried to warn them not to go back, but Naoise craved forgiveness and wanted to believe in a just king. "The king lied and upon their return,

124

the three sons of Usnach were killed. Deirdre loved Naoise and couldnae forgive herself for his death and for the death of his brothers. While ridin' in a wagon, she flung herself onto a rock, killin' herself."

"And that's why they call her Deirdre of Sorrows?"

"Aye, a love that wasnae meant to be." He looked toward the falls, wondering if he continued to pursue Michaela if their love would also be doomed. She was from another time, another place so different from where he had come from.

"I see why you're drawn to this place," she sighed. Her gaze took in their surroundings before landing on him. "It reminds you how Loch Ness and the land once looked—wild, beautiful and slightly mysterious."

He swallowed back the lump in his throat. With all their differences, she understood him perfectly. "Aye, that it does."

Later they hiked back to the boat and Alan helped Michaela aboard.

He maneuvered the boat away from the dock. The sun beat down on them, but the wind was cool on the water.

"You have impressive equipment on your boat." Her hand hovered over the monitor. "Is this all for the tourists or do you have an honest interest in what swims in the loch?" Her head turned, her eyes meeting his as she waited for his answer.

The boat did have all the perks: modern surveillance and safety equipment such as VHF Radio, G.P.S., color sonar, and radar. He had recently added underwater cameras and DVD equipment. "I care aboot all that goes on, in the loch and out." He didn't usually show too much to the tourist. Just enough to give them a taste, but he wanted to share his world with her. "Would ye like me to show ye what lurks in the peat riddled depths?" He wagged his brow.

Her soft chuckle warmed. "I'd be delighted."

With a nod, he took the boat full throttle, bringing it toward the center of the loch. Cutting the engines, he let the boat free float without fear of another boat coming along and running into them. With a few flips of a switch, the monitor illuminated with a picture of what lay beneath them.

Her lips curved and her eyes widened. "Omigod, how awesome is that?"

"Ye can only see what's beneath and little in front of us, mind ye." He flipped another switch and the sonar pinged alive. "This monitors the depths to two hundred and fifteen meters."

"What are the particles I see floating about?"

"Peat mostly."

He let her study the screen as he kept watch of the boats passing by.

"Look." Her hand latched onto his arm. "There's something there."

He stared at the screen, his muscles tensing. The camera showed something long, floating near toward the starboard, but then he let out a breath of relief. "It's only a log."

"Oh."

His lips twitched at her obvious disappointment. "Most make the same mistake, thinkin' a log is the beastie. With the wake of the waves liftin' the log out of the water, it is no wonder it is mistaken for somethin' more." His hand brushed her hair away from her face, tucking the wayward strand behind her ear. "What would ye do if ye saw Nessie right now? Hmm?"

"Depends how close I'm standing to the sea creature. Either I scream in delight or in terror."

He gave her a quick smile. If she knew he could shift to the Loch Ness Monster, she would fear him. His fingers traced her arm where she'd rolled up her windbreaker. Her skin felt warm and smooth beneath his touch. She looked up at him, her eyes holding such trust. A connection shimmered between them like a hot current of electricity, heating his blood. His instincts told him to take her and make her his mate, but he reined in his lustful thoughts. Michaela was human not a shape shifter. Ravishing her on the deck of his boat wouldn't endear him to her.

He settled for crushing his mouth to hers. She surprised him by kissing him back, ravishing him with lips, teeth and tongue. Leaning against the panel, his hands encircled her waist and pulled her against him, keeping her snug between his legs and not caring she'd know how much he wanted her. If the low groan from her was any indication, she wanted him, too. *Soon.* He would make her his mate soon.

****

Later that evening, Michaela sat down on her bed and looked through the pictures on her digital camera. She paused when she came to the one of Alan and smiled. His eyes the color of blue flames were framed by dark thick lashes. With all their beauty, sadness still shadowed them. "Who are you, Alan?" Other than the facts that he loved Elvis songs, the nature of the loch and his pets, she knew nothing of the man and yet each touch, each caress urged her closer and closer to him.

His aura, his strong masculine persona hooked her from the moment his hands had touched her. Was this love at first sight or in her case, at first touch?

"Don't be ridiculous, Michaela Grant. No one falls in love the moment they meet." Besides what kind of future would they have? He lived in Scotland and she in the States. "And you're dying. Let's not forget that."

She let out a sigh of frustration and fell back onto her pillow, still clasping the camera. She lifted it to look at the picture of Alan once more and dreamed about what his rough hands would feel like against her skin.

Chapter Twenty-Two

Alan knew it was late, but it didn't stop him from heading over to see Michaela. Their outing had been a success. The way she had clung to him, the scent of her arousal told him she'd enjoyed his company, too. With trying to charm her, he didn't realize until later she hadn't taken the water bottle with her. He feared without it, her health would slip and she'd be taken from him.

He'd make an excuse why he needed to see her then he would leave the water bottle and go. He frowned. What if she wouldn't let him in? What if she didn't answer the door? He pursed his lips together. She had to.

Lifting his hand, he brought it down with two rapid quick strokes.

A few seconds went by, but he could hear movement inside and knew she was still awake. Perhaps she feared who would come calling so late at night. He sometimes lost track of time. The sun had set so it had to be after ten or eleven. He knocked again. "Michaela, it's Alan." He heard the latch and the door opened halfway.

"Alan," she whispered, "What are you doing here?"

"You forgot this." He held up the bottled water. Her brows furrowed and he didn't blame her. She didn't understand the need and he was making a muck of it.

He gave her a sheepish grin. "The truth is—I wanted to see ye. I wanted to tell ye how much I care for ye." He ran his hand through his hair. He came here to give her water, not confess his love. "I'm no' doin' this proper, am I?"

She took pity on him and opened the door, standing to the side to let him enter. He didn't hesitate. Once inside, she closed the door and leaned against it. "I need to ask you something."

He nodded warily. She looked so serious as if what she needed to say would weigh heavy on if he'd ever see her again after tonight.

"Are you real?"

His brows drew together at her strange question.

"You see," she hurried to explain. "With my condition, one of the symptoms is hallucinations and you coming here tonight with the pretense of bringing me bottled water... Well, let's say it seems a little suspicious, don't you agree?"

"If I tell ye, I'm really here will ye believe me? How do ye know if yer mind just tells ye what ye want to believe?"

A tired sigh left her full lips. "So true."

Her room was spacious with dark wooden end tables and a queen size bed with the covers pulled back. She was dressed in her night garments, a light blue T-shirt and matching pants. She might have been sleeping when he knocked on the door, but her hair didn't look out of place and her eyes weren't glazed. He put the water bottle down on the table that stood near the fireplace and turned to face her. "I doonae want to go, but I'll do as ye say. Do ye want me here, Michaela?"

"Yes and no."

His brows shot up, making her chuckle.

"I want you, Alan, but I don't believe I have the right."

He took the steps that separated them and pulled her into his arms. "Ye have the right." He leaned forward and in one fluid move covered her mouth with his own. Her eyes fluttered closed and on a sigh she gave into the kiss, giving as much back as he gave, softness and heat. When he came up for air, he sought her gaze. "Do ye still believe I'm a figment of yer imagination?"

"If you are, I don't care," she whispered. Her lips were swollen from his kiss, her eyes glazed with passion. "Kiss me again, Alan."

He did with more fervor, with the need to be close to her, kissing her thoroughly and possessively, letting her know she was his. She didn't push him away. He had come here to give her the water, but once his lips touched hers, he forgot his good intentions and gave into seduction.

Her body fit to him. Her scent was like an aphrodisiac, a soft pretty fragrance that drove him wild with the want of more. "Michaela," his voice deepened with raw emotion, "I want to make love to ye, if ye are willin'?"

Her startled gaze met his, the green of her eyes brighter and clearer than usual. A light tilt of her lips, told him her thoughts echoed his. He should tell her what he was. "Michaela, I need ye to understand—"

Her hand covered his mouth. "Don't ruin the moment, Alan. I want you, too. I'm not looking for forever since I don't have forever in my future."

He took her hand and kissed her palm. "I would give ye forever, if I could."

Her eyes misted and she swallowed hard. "Tonight. Give me tonight."

How could he refuse her request? There was always tomorrow for truths. He pulled her toward him, cradling her close. His hand skimmed down her back, gathering her shirt in his hand and lifting it over her head.

High rounded breasts gleamed white and tight nipples begged for attention. Drawing his fingertips up her side, a groan of want escaped her lips and her breasts pushed against the palms of his hands. He lowered his mouth and tasted. Her hands gripped a fistful of hair and held him captive while he buried his face in her breasts, drawing one nipple at a time into his mouth.

Her breaths were shallow and her heartbeat rapid as the air shimmered around them. He picked her up and carried her to the bed with plans to take his time. He'd bring her as much pleasure as he could before he took her fully.

Her arms went around his neck and captured his mouth in a kiss that caused his head to reel. Tightening his hold on her, he was reluctant to let her go, afraid the enchantment would break if he lost contact. Her soft hands pulled at his T-shirt, obviously just as anxious to feel his skin. He kissed her forehead before releasing her.

All clothes hindering their joining were cast aside. He left a trail of kisses along the edge of her collarbone, his tongue and mouth kissing his way down to the apex of her thighs. His senses filled with her scent of lavender and heather.

He'd forgotten how good a woman could taste. Michaela tasted sweet like passion too long denied. It had been some time for her, since he could detect no scent other than hers. She arched her back as his tongue goaded her to new heights. She shuddered beneath him in rapture, her hands in his hair to keep him from stopping. When she relaxed and her heartbeat began to return to normal, he looked up to meet her half closed lids, a smile tugging her kiss-swollen lips.

"Oh my God." Her breathless voice broke with a chuckle. "I needed that."

"I'm glad to have been of assistance then." He moved beside her, his groin swollen and rigid, begging to be touched. She rolled onto her side to look at him. He inhaled deeply at the first touch of her fingertips, his member jerking in greedy expectation. God, he wanted to bury himself deep inside her and not come out until he'd gotten his fill.

She gave him as much attention as he had given her, sliding down his body, licking and tasting every part of him until he could take no more. His hands grabbed her shoulders and pulled her close before rolling over so he lay on top.

Cupping her bottom, he tilted her hips to receive him. Her hot tunnel clutched and gripped him, holding him captive within her depths. "Sweet gods above," he cried in ecstasy. He pumped and thrust, rocking his hips and she took all he gave her with no thoughts of control.

The magic rolled over him like the loch's cool waters cascading over his body as he swam. Her tremors sent him to the edge, the heady rush of blood to his groin, tumbling him over the rest of the way with pleasure.

This is what it meant to find one's soul mate. Did Michaela feel it, too? Would revealing his true nature scare her off or would the truth bring her closer to him? He rolled to the side, bringing her with him, spooning against her.

"Alan?"

"Hmm?"

She turned in his arms so that she looked at him. "This is probably going to sound corny, but I never felt like this with anyone."

His lips curved. "Nor I."

"You're just saying that."

He lifted his brows. "Ye can declare yer feelin's, but I cannae tell ye mine?"

"I'm sorry, It's..." she lowered her gaze.

"Tell me, Michaela."

The soft green gaze found his once more. "It's too much to hope that what you say is true."

133

His fingers lightly caressed the side of her face as he looked into her eyes, willing her to see his soul. "I willnae lie to ye, Michaela. I felt a connection to ye from the start."

"You were angry with me. You may have saved me from Elvis toppling me into the loch, but your eyes told me you had the urge to toss me in yourself."

"Nay, I was afraid to trust what I already knew in my heart. Ye were the one for me."

She left his arms, pulling away not just physically but mentally as well, desperate for space. Her hand grabbed her discarded pajama top on the floor and slipped it over her head, covering her body still flushed from their lovemaking. She slipped her knickers and her pajama bottoms on next as if donning armor.

He sat up with a sigh, leaning against the headboard, not bothering to dress himself. He didn't want to fight with her, but he would allow her to have her shield.

Fully clothed now, she stood at the side of the bed with her arms folded against her chest.

Let the battle begin.

"I don't believe in love at first sight. That's what you're saying, isn't it?" she threw at him.

Love at first sight was such a human observation, which more times than not usually meant lust at first sight. What he felt went so much deeper than the primitive force that begged him to touch her.

His heart would beat for her now, a partner to share his thoughts and she to share hers with him. If the gods smiled upon their union, they would build a life together in the space and time allowed them. Didn't she realize he would sacrifice his life to protect her?

"Michaela, what I feel for ye isnae superficial

and if ye'd think aboot it a moment, ye would recognize yer feelin's as somethin' more profound."

Her stance relaxed, her arms falling to her side. She looked about to accept what he said, but then her features clouded. "If what you're telling me is true, you know we don't have a future. We never had."

He gave her a curt nod. "As ye asked, I'll give ye tonight and as many nights as yer willin' to have me by yer side. Now come here. I already miss yer warmth." He opened his arms to her, waiting for her to accept his offer.

With a nod she came willingly into his embrace and he wrapped his arms around her. Resting her cheek against him, her finger traced circles over his chest. "You must be a hallucination and if you are, I don't want the vision to end."

"Nor I." With the tip of his finger he tilted her chin up, meeting her gaze before he leaned down and claimed her lips.

The crash of splintered glass pulled them apart. Michaela gasped and Alan jumped from the bed. The window had exploded with tiny shards of glass littering the carpet. He stepped with caution as he stilled the waving curtain where the breeze from outside filtered through. He expected to see a rock or some sort of instrument that would have caused such damage, but he saw nothing. He scanned the area outside for the culprit. A movement caught his eyes, huge and dark. "It cannae be." His whisper caught Michaela's ears.

"Who is it, Alan. Who did this?"

He whirled around to face her. "Stay here." He didn't have time to explain if he was going to catch the bastard. He dashed to the door.

"Alan, you can't—"

Her words didn't register until too late. He had left the warmth of the cottage without a stitch of clothing. Michaela wouldn't understand that he didn't need the binding cloth. He would have to come up with some sort of an excuse, but now wasn't the time to worry about it.

Even in his human state, he could move fast and sure without worrying about mishap. As he approached the slope that led down to the loch, he shape shifted with ease and followed the beast into the water.

He wanted to believe it was his brother playing a misguided prank. It would make things simpler then. In his heart, he knew this wasn't the case. The beast looked like the legendary sea horse of Loch Ness, but Alan knew what he chased wasn't kin. He had no doubt whoever or whatever he dealt with here had used its tail to shatter the glass. He wanted to be noticed. Alan noticed him all right. Why the beastie decided to target them, he didn't know. However, he had every intention of finding out.

The gray beast moved swiftly, streaming through the water as if it had been born to the depths. Alan knew better. There had been no other creatures like him and his brother in centuries and none that were shape shifters.

Those creatures had been reptiles that existed for a time before becoming extinct. The beast that taunted him had to be a shape shifter, one of the true bloods that could take on any shape they wished. They were known to be territorial and sometimes pranksters, causing havoc wherever they went. He would put a stop to the shape shifter's antics before they had a manhunt on their hands.

The creature headed for the surface. He followed, bursting out of the water with a roar. The creature, a cruder version of himself, faced him with its head bent. Beady eyes the color of amber stared back at him in surprise before the eyes narrowed to slits. Good. The shifter would fight him and he welcomed the challenge. Threats came in many forms and he would protect the loch and the secrets it held, from preternatural beings or humans.

However, this creature crossed the line when he decided to endanger his mate. A cold shiver of fear raced down his spine. Michaela's health wasn't all that threatened her. Her body was fragile and this creature could do more harm than the artery threatening to burst in her head.

The creature snarled and spit before it lunged at him. Alan bared his teeth and went for the neck, but the creature anticipated the move and jerked to the right, avoiding his long jagged teeth. Alan swirled in the water with grace, his movements proving his comfort in the loch.

The shifter wasn't as fluid. His movements were choppy, unnatural, revealing how the large cumbersome shape was foreign to him. Alan met his mark on its left flank, tearing flesh away.

The shifter roared in pain. Blood pooled to the surface of the water, dark and thick. The tangy smell hit his nostrils, urging the beast within him to attack. Alan lunged again, but the shifter flipped and swung his tail, slicing it like a whip against his side.

The shape shifter dove. Magic, rich and thick clogged the waters around him. *Damn it to hell and back. The shifter had changed shapes.* Alan dove anyway. Sea creatures swam in fear at the disturbance in the water. He couldn't tell where the shape shifter had gone or what shape it had taken. He cursed, knowing the shifter had outsmarted him.

With his pursuit thwarted, he headed back to shore, emerging onto the land in a fluid motion, changing from beast to man in a blink of an eye.

His side stung. Glancing down, he gingerly touched the long angry slash where the shape shifter's tail lashed against him. He would heal, but preternatural wounds took longer to mend.

His gaze wavered toward the cottage and to where Michaela waited. She would expect an explanation. Only he didn't think she'd like the answer.

Chapter Twenty-Three

Using an iron rod Michaela stoked the fire with a vengeance, bringing the flames alive in the hearth. The breeze from outside blew in through the broken glass, making her draw her bathrobe closer around her. She was inside and pretty much shielded from the outside elements, but Alan had sprinted out of the cottage naked, not one stitch of clothing on as if it was the most natural thing in the world for him to do.

What exactly did he think he would accomplish running after the culprit like a crazy man? She had debated about calling the authorities, but how would Alan explain his state of undress? He might be the one in trouble and arrested for indecent exposure.

She worried her lower lip. Alan's response to the intruder wasn't natural. She had seen the anger flash in his eyes, a murderous look that scared her.

She smoothed her hair away from her face in frustration. Great, she'd slept with a man who could quite possibly be a lunatic.

This relationship had moved too fast.

He didn't force you into bed. Her conscience reminded her.

Damn it, she was aware of the fact.

Nervous energy had her pacing the room. Alan had run out of the cottage to chase a prankster to do what to him exactly? Beat the crap out of him? Scare him to death with his obvious nutty behavior? The thing was: She didn't know if his behavior was typical or not.

"What am I doing here? What am I doing with

him?" She botched this relationship up royally. She let *I-have-only-months-to-live* attitude lead her into a rash affair.

The knock on her door made her jump.

"Michaela, may I come in?"

It was Alan, but which one stood on the other side of the door? Naked Alan, crazy Alan or Alan who had made love to her with tender caresses?

"It's freezin' out here, darlin'."

Oh she bet it was. With sigh of resignation, she opened the door for him. She needed to keep her emotions in check, but seeing him there in all his natural glory only spiked her libido a few notches. Her mind might think he was crazy, but obviously her body had another opinion.

One dark brow lifted. "Are ye goin' to let me in?"

She cleared her throat and forced her gaze to stay on his face. "Are you going to explain the stunt you just pulled?"

He hesitated but then gave her a curt nod. "Aye. I'll explain."

She moved and swept her hand to the side in a grand display. "Please, do come out of the cold then. This I have to hear."

He eyed her warily as if debating if he wanted to come in after all. The cool breeze swept in and most likely billowed up his spine. If only for warmth, his feet moved over the threshold. She closed the door and leaned against it.

Without a word Alan searched for his jeans and donned them. Pity, but she suppose if they were to talk he should be dressed. He turned toward her when he picked up his T-shirt, her gaze landing on the angry welt against the white of his skin. "What happened?"

All thoughts of being pissed vanished in a blink of an eye. She rushed over to him, but he moved away, pulling his T-shirt on and covering the wound.

"It's nothin'." His muscles flexed beneath the sleeves.

"It doesn't look like nothing."

"I'll be fine." He glanced at the fireplace then back to her. "Ye started a fire." He chose to change the subject, making her wonder why.

"Looks that way, doesn't it." Sarcasm dripped from her words but he ignored it. She crossed her arms against her chest. "Well, are you going to explain or not?"

"I lost him," he announced as if this settled everything.

She raised her brows. She highly doubted it. His side had an angry welt suggesting something sharp had cut his flesh. Did the culprit have a knife? "You lost him. That's all you have to say?"

His shoulders lifted in a shrug. "Aye, he managed to slip away."

"Do you normally go about stark naked, because where I come from you would be arrested for indecent exposure and your ass would be tossed in jail."

His lips twitched.

She gave him a hostile glare, furious that he wasn't taking this seriously. "Do you find something amusing about this?"

"Uh no... It's just that ye Yanks say ass and that's a donkey no' our bum. Arse, my arse would be tossed in—"

"Really?" she interrupted, anger sharpening her voice. "You're going to give me a lesson on what to call your behind?"

He glanced away nervously and moved closer to the fire.

She licked her lower lip, trying to quell her annoyance. "Alan, talk to me. Who was out there? Why did you chase after him?"

His gaslight colored eyes latched onto hers once more, two glowing flames framed with dark lashes, hypnotic eyes that kept her prisoner. "It isnae who was out there, but *what* was out there."

She swallowed hard and something cautioned her not to ask what he meant. She pulled out the chair from the table and sat down, her fingers tense in her lap. She didn't heed the warning. "What are you talking about?"

His mouth opened then closed as if the word of explanation evaded him.

"Was it an animal of some sort?"

"Aye, an animal."

"A clever animal if it could break a window." She didn't believe it. Why would Alan lie about it?

"Verra clever," he answered, but his response had seemed more for himself than to appease her.

He held something back, but for the life of her she couldn't understand what it could be.

"It'll be cold in here tonight," he told her as if she couldn't figure it out herself. "It would be best, if ye came home with me."

Earlier, she might have jumped at the chance, but now she wasn't so sure.

His head tilted to the side, his gaze assessing her. "Ye pause."

"What?" She looked into his eyes and saw how her hesitation had hurt him.

"I would never harm ye, Michaela." His voice flooded her senses with warmth. In her heart she knew his words were the truth.

She rubbed her temples, feeling a headache coming on with a vengeance. Too much had happened and her brain couldn't take the overload.

"Are ye okay?" His concern couldn't be missed. Even with his odd behavior, she knew he cared about her.

"It's a migraine." She rose from her seat to find her backpack, digging inside for the pill bottle. She struggled with the lid. "Dammit, open." Alan's strong hands gently covered hers. She released her hold, letting him take the medication from her, but instead of popping the lid open, he handed her a water bottle.

"Drink."

"Alan, I don't need water. I need the medication."

"Drink and ye'll feel better. Sometimes the body needs water to revive itself."

"This isn't a normal headache. This is—"

"I know what it is. Trust me, Michaela."

Unscrewing the lid with one quick turn, she took a swig, wiping her mouth with the back of her hand. "Satisfied?"

"More."

She rolled her eyes, but lifted the bottle to her lips and drank deeply. The water felt cool sliding down her throat, tingling all the way down. "Now will you give me my meds?"

"Give it a second to work."

She wanted to tell him that this wasn't working, but to her surprise the sharp pangs of the headache eased back. Her gaze riveted to his. "How? Are you some kind of magician?"

"Magician? No." His voice was calm, his gaze steady.

She glanced at the bottle, examining the contents. It looked like a normal water bottle. The liquid tasted like water, though she had to admit it was the best tasting water she ever had—smooth, pure and refreshing. Her gaze locked onto Alan's as she shook the bottle accusingly. "What's in this? Some kind of drug?"

He shook his head with a long audible breath. "It's fresh water from an underground well."

"Is that so?" her voice turned cold, not liking that he played her a fool. There had to be something more to the water than it being from an underground well. Just one more secret and they were beginning to add up.

His hand reached for hers. She tried to pull away but his gaze held hers, his eyes beseeching her to trust him. "I would never harm ye. Surely, ye know this."

Somehow she did know, but she didn't understand the reasoning behind it. "I barely know you." Her voice was a hoarse whisper. "How can I trust you?"

"Ye trusted me to make love to ye."

"That's low, damn you." Tears sprung to her eyes unexpectedly, making it hard to swallow. He was right though. She wouldn't have slept with him if she didn't see some kind of future with him—even if it was a short one. "Trust goes both ways." She needed him to be honest with her.

A thoughtful smile curved his lips and he nodded his head. "Fair enough." He leaned down and kissed her, gently, a sweet caress. This wasn't what she meant, but found she was powerless to stop him. God, help her, she wanted him. She never wanted someone so much in her life. If nothing else made sense, this did.

He pulled away and lifted her chin, forcing her to look at him. "Will ye come back to my place? I'll try to explain... what I can."

"I don't—"

He didn't let her finish. "Even with the fire blazin' the room is still chilled. It cannae be helped as long as the window is broken. Ye doonae want to fall ill."

He had a point. She couldn't afford to catch a cold. It was essential to remain healthy as long as possible. "Fine."

She gathered her belongings in silence, shoving them into her suitcase. She was aware Alan watched her with his keen eyes. She sensed he wanted to say more, but she was grateful he gave her space.

She turned toward him, her hands clutching a pair of jeans and a long sleeved T-shirt. Her heart reacted immediately to his gaze, but she wouldn't fall prey to her desires. He needed to explain a few things first and falling into his arms wouldn't give her the answers she sought. "I'll be a moment." She didn't wait for him to say anything and headed for the bathroom, closing the door behind her.

Once dressed, she reached for her hairbrush on the sink and caught sight of herself in the mirror. "God, you look like a woman who just had sex." *Great sex.* She smiled despite herself. She quickly ran her fingers through her disheveled hair, trying to put some order into the unruly strands. "There, better."

She turned off the light as she walked out of the bathroom. Alan had put on his shoes and stood with his hands shoved in his pockets. "Are ye ready?"

"One more thing." She grabbed her backpack, her gaze landing on her prescription bottle sitting on the table. Then it dawned on her that her headache had completely vanished. Her brows furrowed, wondering how water from a well managed to do what medication never could. "Magic," she said under her breath.

"Did ye say somethin'?" Alan asked.

She looked at him standing there, tall and god-like with his flawless features. His ageless blue eyes his best feature.

Blake's words came back to haunt her. *You will suffer hallucinations.*

She took a ragged breath. So be it then if her hallucinations took care of her migraines and gave her Alan MacLachlin, she'd die a happy woman. "Only that I'm ready."

He had already taken care of the fireplace, leaving no chance for the place to catch on fire from an ember. He opened the door for her. He held her suitcase in one hand and offered his other hand to her.

She sensed if she left with him, her life would change drastically, but instead of fearing the unknown, she decided to embrace it. She strolled forward and clasped his hand. His grip felt strong, firm, and all so right.

Chapter Twenty-Four

Alan opened the door to his house and flipped the switch on the wall, illuminating the room with a warm glow of welcome.

"Rrrrf ruff." His German Shepherd came bounding in from another room, skidding to a stop in front of Michaela, his tail wagging like a whip.

"Be good, Elvis," Alan warned.

Michaela leaned down and rubbed Elvis behind the ears. "He's a beautiful dog."

"He's a spoiled dog." He dropped her suitcase beside the black and white three-sectional couch with a curved center.

Michaela took in the ambience of the room decorated in early fifties style. One glance at the décor adorning one of the walls and she nearly laughed. Over the fireplace, a blue and black velvet Elvis looked down at her with his half-tilted smile. Where in the world had he found that portrait?

Next, her gaze landed on the red jukebox in the corner. She couldn't resist taking a closer look. Glancing inside, she wasn't surprised to see it held 45rpm vinyl records. Maybe later she'd ask him to play something.

"I'm goin' out back and bring in some firewood." He pointed toward the fireplace and the empty gold colored bin.

He headed toward the room off to the side, the kitchen she assumed. The backdoor opened then thudded shut, leaving her in silence...at least for a few short seconds.

"Alan, ye're back already." Hyatt's voice called

from down the hall. "I thought ye be out all night. Ye bein' with—" He stopped mid-sentence as he entered the living room in just his pajama bottoms and his hair messed up from sleep. "Uh... Michaela. I..." He scratched his head at a loss for words.

Michaela had a hunch this didn't happen often. She took pity on him and smiled, appreciating the fact that the man didn't sleep in the raw. "Someone threw a rock or something at my window back at the cottage and shattered it. Alan offered to let me crash here for the night."

"Rescuin' damsels in distress is Alan's specialty."

Michaela frowned. "What do you mean?"

"I..." He grimaced and looked away. "He's forever a gentleman is what I meant."

Michaela didn't believe him. Was Alan in the habit of saving women who needed help? She didn't want to be one of his charity cases.

"Ye were lookin' at the jukebox."

"Hmm? Uh, yes."

He strode over to the shiny red jukebox. "I'm afraid my brother's taste in music isnae the best. He hasnae entered the twenty-first century yet. He likes the rock and roll era of the sixties mostly."

"There are some greats. The Beach Boys, The Rolling Stones, The Beatles, Roy Orbinson, Buddy Holly... Elvis." She nodded toward the velvet portrait of *the King.*

"Right." He chuckled. "No wonder my brother likes ye." He looked around the room. "By the way, where is Alan?"

"He went outside to gather firewood."

Hyatt cringed. "I was supposed to do that."

Elvis barked in agreement.

"No one asked ye, ye mangy mutt," Hyatt reprimanded with a shake of his finger. His gaze then returned to her. For a long moment, he stared then pursed his lips together.

"Is there something wrong?" Michaela notice the worry lines creasing Hyatt's brow.

He shook his head. "My brother doesnae date much."

"Oh?"

"He keeps to himself."

She had gathered that much about Alan by herself.

"What I'm tryin' to say is that he doesnae take a relationship lightly."

"Are you asking me what my intentions are?" Her lips twitched but she managed not to smile. No one had ever feared she'd take advantage of a man. Especially when the man seemed quite sure of himself.

"I guess I am." Hyatt chuckled with amazement. Obviously this was new territory for him. "I love my brother and I doonae want to see him hurt."

Hyatt appeared indifferent with his meaningless flirting, but obviously there was more to the man than met the eye. "I'm not in the habit of breaking hearts."

"Ye dinnae strike me as such, but there's so much at stake here."

Her brows drew together. "What do ye mean?"

They heard the backdoor open. A second later, Alan walked in the living room, holding a pile of wood. Priscilla darted around him to leap onto the back of the sofa with a meow.

"Doonae be cruel to a heart that's true," Hyatt blurted out and looked at her.

"What?" Michaela blinked in confusion.

"That's one of Alan's favorite Elvis' songs." His gaze locked onto hers and she knew he meant to send her a message without letting Alan know. *Don't be cruel to a heart that's true.*

She gave him a quick nod and Hyatt turned

toward his brother. "I think I'll go back to bed. I need my beauty sleep." He stretched and yawned with exaggeration. "Come on Elvis. Let's leave the two lovebirds alone so they can snog each other properly."

He motioned to the dog. Elvis seemed hesitant to leave. He whined in protest, but Hyatt snapped his fingers and Elvis finally complied, trotting off toward the back room.

Alan stared after his brother as if he suspected something wasn't right but couldn't quite put his finger on it. "If Hyatt offended ye in any way, I apologize." He walked over to the fireplace and put his load down in the log holder.

"No need to apologize. We were talking about your record collection." She pointed to the jukebox.

He glanced over his shoulder. "Were ye now?" His lips curved. "By the way, *Doonae Be Cruel to a Heart That's True* isnae my favorite Elvis song."

"No. Which one is?"

His grin widened. "Perhaps I'll make ye guess."

His smile warmed her from the inside out. For a moment she forgot about his strange behavior earlier. He was a good man and his brother worried she would hurt him, but what did Hyatt mean there was more at stake here? What was at stake? Had Alan told Hyatt she was dying? Did Hyatt fear his brother couldn't handle the prospect?

Their relationship was so new. The inevitable would happen long before a more profound relationship could flourish, but Alan spoke of soul mates, even hinted back at the cottage that he loved her.

Her gaze touched him with curiosity. Who falls in love in a few days? She didn't believe in love at first sight, but she couldn't deny how easily she could fall for Alan.

That wouldn't be wise, she reminded herself.

She would eventually have to go home. Be it her savings running out or for medical reasons. It would make leaving him all the more difficult if she complicated things by falling in love.

"What's wrong?" he asked.

She rubbed her hand over her face with a quick intake of breath. Her lips curved at the ends with what she hoped resembled a smile. "I'm just tired. We need to talk, but can it wait until morning?"

"If ye wish. Do ye want me to take the sofa?" he asked.

His house, his bed and he offered to take the sofa. Her heart warmed, bringing her closer to losing it to him. No matter what drove him to run naked in the middle of the night to pursue the prankster, he was a considerate man.

She took the steps that separated them and reached for his hand. "Keep me warm tonight."

Tomorrow she'd ask questions. She wanted the magic to surround them for one night before reality reared its ugly head and ruined everything.

Chapter Twenty-Five

Mike Picquelle brushed his hair out of his eyes, feeling a little rumpled in his wrinkled shirt. He was tired as well, since his alarm blared for a wakeup call at four-thirty in the morning. "Who in the hell thought up this plan?" he muttered beneath his breath.

He shoved his hands into his jeans pocket, as he waited outside the hotel room for Diana Watson. He had two more weeks before heading back to start his fall classes at USC. His football scholarship didn't cover his entire tuition and he had to wait tables at Morelli's Diner to make ends meet.

He shouldn't have spent his savings on a trip to Scotland. His friends were all going, but the deciding factor had been Diana's decision to join them.

Diana's eyes were a deep brown and her hair was the color of the moonshine whiskey that his cousin Charlie Price used to make back home in Tennessee.

Man oh man, did the woman have a body that pushed his buttons in a very big way. The only problem that stood in his way was Mark Andrews. Tall, dark and he supposed good looking if the girls hanging around him like flies on honey was any indication.

It wasn't like he didn't possess a few good qualities himself. He had thick brown hair and his football training kept him trim and fit, but he'd rather not have the competition. Especially since Mark was one of his best friends.

He looked up when the door finally opened and

Diana slipped out, quietly shutting the door behind her so as not to wake her roommate, Coral. They weren't really going Nessie hunting like the other tourists. Mike convinced Diana over dinner last night to spend some time alone with him, away from the other members in their group.

"Did you pack the sunscreen?" Diana asked as she dug through her backpack.

"I did and I packed the lip balm, the water bottles and the trail mix you left in my room last night."

"You're a doll, Mike."

They headed down toward the pier and wasted no time in renting a motor craft from one of the boathouses for the day. The morning turned out to be pleasant with the winds mild and the sun casting some warmth.

Mike maneuvered the boat away from the other tourists, most of whom were heading toward the western shore, near Urquhart Castle where most of the sightings of the Loch Ness Monster had been reported.

He headed southwest to check out Cherry Island. It wasn't very big now since the level of the loch increased when it became a part of the Caledonian Canal.

"What's the history behind Cherry Island again?" Diana asked.

"It's a good example of a crannog, an artificial island used in medieval times. A castle stood on the island in the fifteenth century."

Diana moved closer to him. "Aah huh."

"It was probably made out of stone and oak and used as a—" His words slid away to the recess of his mind as Diana's lips covered his in a demanding kiss he couldn't ignore.

The loud blare of a boat horn broke them apart. "Sheee...it!" He swerved the boat to the left, barely missing another watercraft heading in the opposite direction. His heart nearly leapt into his throat.

Diana sat back in her seat and gazed up at him with an innocent look, but then her lips twitched. "What were you saying about the island?"

He grinned at her. "You know I completely forgot." She sidled up to him as he slowed the boat to a stop. He looked at Diana and swallowed the lump in his throat, which he would swear had been his heart the way it pounded in his ribcage, threatening to escape.

Diane wore an Angels' baseball cap with her hair pulled back in a ponytail, making her appear an innocent schoolgirl, but her deep brown eyes gave her away. Her gaze slid over him like a hungry cat ready to devour its prey. Her lips curved into a wide grin and two adorable dimples deepened the sides of her cheeks. It was no wonder he fell hard for her with a smile like that. He pulled her into his arms. He loved Diana, but he cared about Mark as well. He didn't want to jeopardize their friendship. "You know Mark has feelings for you."

She pulled away from him, resting her hand on his chest. She brushed his too-long hair out of his eyes. "I'm not in love with Mark. I've never encouraged him. You know that, don't you?"

He nodded, but something inside of him wondered. It wasn't that he didn't trust Diana, but she could be a bit of a flirt.

"I thought we left the group behind to be together. I didn't know it was so we could talk about Mark. You should have just invited him if you're so worried about his feelings." Her pretty, pink lips pouted.

"You're right." He pushed his doubts away. The water lapped against the boat, making it sway. It was a good thing neither of them were prone to seasickness.

A cold gust of wind caused a lock of hair to fall into his eyes again.

"Oh no!" Diana cried. "My hat!" Her baseball cap flew off her head, landing in the water. Diana stood, rocking the boat to one side.

"Sit down!" Mike grabbed her arm, yanking her back.

The hat floated on the surface, but in a moment, it would sink. Mike looked at Diana, her eyes a pool of misery. The hat had been her father's who passed away two years ago. He knew it meant a lot to her. He looked around and noticed the oars strapped to the side, a safety feature if the motor didn't work.

He quickly pulled one free and leaned over the side, making the boat tilt dangerously. Diana shifted, meaning to go to the other side to balance the boat, but she slipped and fell overboard with a scream. Water sloshed over the edge of the boat, drenching him in the process.

"Diana!" Mike looked in horror as he watched Diana flaying in the water, choking and spitting on the peat drenched water she swallowed. She knew how to swim, but she looked too scared to remember how. "Grab the oar." He reached out to her. Too panicked, she kept missing it and slapping water into her face in the process. "Diana calm down. I'm right here. I'm not going anywhere. Now take a hold of the oar."

"Get me out of here!" she screamed, choked and coughed as the rough swells drenched her again.

"Take a hold of the oar," he told her again and this time she grasped it. He breathed a sigh of relief and started pulling her to safety.

Diana was almost to the boat when she jerked and turned to look behind her. "Something just brushed by me."

Mike tried to keep his fear at bay. Of course he'd heard the rumors of the Loch Ness Monster sightings, but surely it was only a hoax. "It's probably a log or something," he tried to reassure Diana. "Keep hold of the oar and give me one of your hands." He leaned forward, reaching for her as she frantically splashed to reach him. Then he spotted something in the water—large, grayish in color and coming fast. Diana must have seen the horror written on his face because she stilled. She turned her head with a scream that seemed eternal.

Chapter Twenty-Six

The shape shifter walked up the wooden steps, leading to the front door. He noticed the second step from the top needed to be repaired.

The house overlooked the loch with large spruces surrounding it like a cloak of invisibility, but not for him. He could see everything from his porch.

The house had a chill to it and he grabbed a few logs and tossed them into the fireplace, adding a peat brick before lighting it with a long sulfur stick. The black poker leaning against the wall served well to stoke the blaze until it burned nice and hot.

His gaze landed on the garbage bag next to the sofa and sighed. He'd prolonged taking care of this long enough. Settling himself on the sofa, he undid the tab at the top. His nostrils flared as he drew in the fragrance of sweat, blood and fear that wafted from the filthy clothing.

"Wonderful." With reverence, he drew out the first garment, relishing in the delight as the erotic sensation of fire and ice ran up his spine. He fisted the cloth around his hand and brought it close to his nose, inhaling deeply practically tasting the mouthwatering blood that soaked the fabric.

The animal inside of him growled in appreciation. How he wished he could keep his prize, but no one must find out what he had done. "Blend in with the humans. Doonae let them know." With a quick motion he tossed the bloody clothing into the fireplace.

The flames flickered then caught hold of the fabric in a swirl of vengeance. He loved the way it licked its way around, glowing orange and red as it devoured every last remnant.

He had to be more careful. Every day the beast inside of him threatened to take over, hampering his decisions. He'd come close to being discovered at Kait's house, but he needed to find the letter he'd written her in a fit of anger. If discovered, the police department would be looking at him for her disappearance. Thank the gods it was on the kitchen counter.

The Kait fiasco was nothing compared to last night's stunt though. It had been foolish on his part. He almost let Alan MacLachlin catch him. He'd underestimated him. He'd only wanted to taunt him, let him know he'd been challenged. He hadn't expected the bastard to give chase.

He didn't know the waters of the loch as Alan did, pursuit would have ended with Alan catching him. He couldn't allow that to happen. His chuckle burst from his mouth in a choked chortle. "I outsmarted ye, dinnae I?" If he hadn't shifted when he had, Alan would have tore him to shreds. He rubbed his back where Alan's beastie teeth had sank into his flesh. It would heal in a few days.

Aye, he was smarter and he wanted Alan to suffer before he ended his miserable life. He'd go after Hyatt, too. They deserved no less. How many times had he imagined taking his fists and plummeting their arrogant faces until the fine bones cracked and pulverized until nothing was left but bloody flesh where nose, mouth and eyes had been? However, beating the MacLachlins to a bloody pulp wouldn't satisfy the hunger for revenge.

Alan had been with a woman last night. "Michaela Grant," he said the name thoughtfully. She was definitely human and Alan marked her with his seed. It didn't take a shape shifter's keen sense of smell to tell him that. Alan came after him without a stitch of clothing on. He doubted he was lounging and sipping tea with the bonny lassie. He chuckled. "What did ye think, Michaela Grant, when yer lover tore out of the cottage naked as a new bairn?" Humans were quite fickle about when a person should be clothed and when they should shed the binding cloth. Alan would have to do some fancy talking to explain his way out of that one.

The woman must be important if he risked exposing his true nature. Then a slow smile spread across his face as he realized why. "She's yer mate." That's why Alan MacLachlin had come after him with such a vengeance. All shifters were the same, once they chose their life mate. The sense to *protect-the-mate-at-all-costs* kicks in, taking over all rational forms of thought.

When newly mated, common sense didn't always play into decisions. "The sod was protectin' his mate. How utterly splendid." Victory would be so much sweeter now. He would kill the woman first. Let him suffer the loss. Grief would weaken him and make him sloppy.

"Aye, it could work." He had to think. An impulsive action would never do. Mistakes would be made if he reacted with passion and not with a well thought out plan. "Use yer brain." He could be patient—if he chose to be. For a moment he felt joy, a pleasure surfacing and teasing him for the want of more.

He glanced up at the mantel where a faded photo of a woman stared back at him. He knew joy of finding a mate, but that was a long time ago. He'd shared his blood, but her body rejected the shifter DNA. She lay fevered and delirious for weeks, revealing secrets she would have otherwise never told. Fifty years later, her last words still rankled him.

Shape shifters were told to blend in with

humans, try to act like them, but in the end the animal took over.

She was dead, but he couldn't ignore the name she called out with her last breath. It wasn't his name, the one who had cared for her and pledged his love to her. No, her last words were not his name. He'd lost control in a jealous fit and shifted, sinking his teeth into her flesh and ripping her apart until she barely resembled a human.

When sanity returned, he'd known he had to get rid of her body. Technically, if he didn't count sharing his blood, he hadn't killed her, but how would he explain her ravaged body? Luckily, her brat wasn't at the house. His grandparents had taken him home, hoping to give his mother rest.

He took her motorboat out on the loch and tossed her remains overboard, hoping they'd sink to the bottom and never be discovered. He'd left the boat running and swam ashore. The village knew she was ill. They would think in her delirium she'd taken the boat out, fell overboard and drowned.

It was a perfect set up, but a storm washed her torso ashore. On the inside collar, she'd stitched her name. Who the hell does that? She'd been missing for weeks, the body badly decomposed with no head or limbs. It could have been anyone, but there was her bloody name. Her spirit might as well have risen from the loch's depths and announced her demise.

Obviously, the state of her body proved she hadn't drowned. He'd been sloppy. He knew that now.

Some blamed her death on the Loch Ness Monster, but it was finally ruled an accident from a motorboat's blade.

His gaze focused on the photo again. His mate's lips were curved in a smile, frozen in happiness for all eternity. Tears sprung to his eyes and he turned away, inhaling deeply to stop the grief from taking hold.

He wouldn't give in to such a weakness. Not now. Not until he was finished. She didn't deserve what he had done to her. No, it was Alan who deserved his wrath. He had waited and his patience had paid off. The beastie of Loch Ness had returned.

His hand reached into the bag, pulling out another bloody item of clothing, something lacy and sheer. He tossed it into the fire. He added another and another until the bag lay empty at his feet.

His thoughts drifted as he stared into the flames. "Soon. It will all play out soon."

Chapter Twenty-Seven

The glorious first rays shone through the window at five thirty in the morning. Alan watched Michaela sleep for a long time, mesmerized by her delicate beauty. She possessed a fine straight nose sprinkled with freckles across the bridge. Her cheekbones were high, her mouth wide and well shaped. Her skin was smooth and unblemished, the color of peaches and cream. He could stare upon her beauty for a lifetime.

She stirred with a yawn and one moss colored eye peeked out beneath a dark fringed eyelid.

"Ye're awake."

"No, I'm not," she grumbled, making him smile.

"Then I shall have to kiss ye awake." He did, taking the liberty of awakening other portions of her body as well.

It was almost eight before they showered and dressed for the day.

"Alan?"

"Mmm hmm." He slipped on his boots and leaned down to tie them.

"You said you'd explain what happened last night."

He knew she wouldn't let the incident go, but still he hoped for more time. He looked up, meeting her gaze. "And I will. I promise, but no' on an empty stomach."

She lifted a brow. "Breakfast then you talk."

He stood and nodded. "Fair enough."

Grabbing a cup of coffee each, he walked Michaela back to the cottage. They spoke to Mrs.

O'Malley about the window, letting her know what had happened. Joshua Brody already confirmed he'd have the window fixed by the end of the day.

This early in the morning with so many people roaming around, Alan didn't fear that the shape shifter would return. The coward liked the shadows.

Alan promised to meet Michaela for breakfast in an hour at Fiddler's Luck. She'd forgot her hairdryer at the cottage and wanted to wash her hair. Grateful for the time, he took advantage of a swim. He made sure to dive deep and stay out of range of the tourist's cameras. With the shape shifter appearing as the Loch Ness Monster, it posed a problem to him and his brother.

They didn't need a crew of wannabe *Jacques Cousteau* trying to find out what lurked beneath the loch's waters. They had to find the bastard and end this before someone ended up hurt.

After his swim, he dried off and dressed in dark slacks and a light beige T-shirt. He fed Elvis and Priscilla, also giving them each a treat. He downed another cup of black coffee anxious to leave the house. He didn't want to be late meeting Michaela.

Fiddler's Luck served the best biscuits in town and his mouth watered in anticipation. He strolled in expecting a crowd, but the place stood nearly empty.

George came up from the back kitchen, struggling with a large box. He placed it on the bar with a grunt. He grimaced as he straightened, rubbing his back. When his gaze landed on Alan, he dropped his hand and put on a smile for greeting. "Oh Alan, dinnae hear ye come in. Good mornin', to ye. Though I'm a bit surprised ye arenae down by the loch, too."

"What are ye talkin' aboot?" He frowned.

"Dinnae ye hear? Some woman's been killed. They're sayin' that Ol' Nessie's gone on a feedin' frenzy."

Alan felt his face drain of color and a cold sweat beaded his brow. The shifter had killed.

"Are ye all right, Alan? Ye look like ye seen a ghost."

He didn't reply but turned on his heels and rushed out the door.

As Alan made his way down to the shoreline, he heard whispers from the onlookers how some college student had seen the Loch Ness Monster rip the woman apart. Another claimed there were only pieces of her body left.

Sheriff Angus Comyn, a big man with red hair was easy to spot in the crowd. He stood to the side, questioning a young man.

Comyn lived in Edinburgh on his days off and rented a room in the village during the week. He talked about uprooting his family, wife and four children to live in Drumnadrochit, but Mrs. Comyn was dragging her heels.

Comyn took notes as the witness relayed his story. The bloke looked distraught, his hands trembling as he spoke. Whatever he witnessed, it had shaken him up pretty bad.

Alan scanned the roped off area and noticed a gray tarpaulin draped over a mound. The police photographer and the forensic specialist stood by one of the police vehicles. They must have finished what they needed to do.

Alan stared at the tarpaulin. He swallowed back the bile, threatening to come up. Who was the victim? Someone he knew? A tourist?

"Alan?"

He turned to see Michaela walking toward him. Her eyes looked big and her skin paler than usual. He immediately took her into his arms, holding her tight.

"It's awful." her voice choked. "We just saw her a

few nights ago." She sniffled back tears.

Alan stiffened. "Who?"

Michaela pulled away and looked up at him, her eyebrows furrowing. "Kait."

He blanched as if she had sucker punched him.

"Oh God. You didn't know." Michaela held onto him as his world seemed to dim.

"Kait is..." He couldn't finish the question. He knew Kait had wanted him to meet her at his boat. He'd read her message, but he had thrown the note away, not wanting to lead her on. He figured she'd get the hint if he didn't show up.

He let Michaela go and turned away, rubbing both his hands over his face. What had he done? Had the shape shifter shown up instead?

Michaela came to stand next to him. "The sheriff told everyone she was hit by a watercraft, but..."

"What?" his gaze held hers.

"See the guy talking to the sheriff...Mike, I believe he said his name was. He saw something in the water."

Alan pursed his lips as his gaze drifted over to where Sheriff Comyn stood with his back turned. "Wait here," he told Michaela and strode toward the roped off crime scene. Officer Wiley was busy holding back the onlookers and didn't see him sneak across the line.

Alan had to know for sure. He had to see for himself what happened to Kait. His hand gripped the tarpaulin and lifted it.

Not prepared for the devastation done to the woman who had been alive and well a few days ago, waves of grayness washed over him and he had to close his eyes as anguish seared his heart. It was Kait—or what was left of her.

"Alan MacLachlin get away from there," Sheriff Comyn demanded as he strode over to him. Mike, who had been talking to the sheriff, was close behind. "This is a crime scene," Comyn admonished.

"Did you know her, mister?" the young man Sheriff Comyn had been questioning asked.

Alan met Mike's haunted gaze and knew what the horror of finding Kait had cost him.

"That could have been my girlfriend, Diana," he said. "She was in the water when the beast surfaced and left only a part of that woman behind."

"Now, now, Mr. Picquelle," the sheriff tried to calm Mike down. "We don't know what happened to her."

"We saw it." His voice rose loud enough for the crowd to hear. "If I hadn't pulled Diana out of the water when I did, she would have been its next meal."

"Let's take this back to my office." Sheriff Comyn led Mike away.

"We have to stop it!" Mike implored as he passed by those gathered around. "We have to go out there and hunt it down before it claims another victim."

The crowd—tourists and locals alike—were beginning to respond and Alan didn't like what he heard. A flicker of apprehension coursed through him. This could be disastrous if mass hysteria took over.

Obviously, Sheriff Comyn felt the same and stopped to address the crowd once more. "Go back to yer hotels or homes and let the authorities handle this. Wha' we doonae need is everyone goin' out on the loch half cocked."

When no one moved, he raised his voice louder. "Go now! The show's over." The sheriff motioned to Officer Wiley with a nod of his head. Wiley started ushering people away.

Alan watched as the sheriff led the distraught Mike over to where a young woman sat huddled beneath blankets. That must be his girlfriend, Diana, he thought. He'd like to question her, but one look at her haunted features and he knew she wasn't going to be able to talk to anyone for a while.

He strode toward Michaela, who waited for him behind the tape, her jacket zipped high to her throat for warmth. He draped his arm around her and led her away.

"This shouldnae have happened." He berated himself for not meeting Kait. She was out there alone when the shifter attacked her. If he had been there, she'd still be alive.

"Alan?"

He looked at Michaela, realizing she'd been talking but her words were lost to him. "I'm sorry. What did ye say?"

She placed a hand on his arm. "They're saying a sea creature did this—the Loch Ness Monster," she repeated obviously waiting for him to refute or agree with the accusation.

"It wasnae the sea creature of legend. I can guarantee it." The shape shifter wasn't all he had to worry about. Thoughts of half-crazed humans with harpoons entered his mind.

Sheriff Comyn left the college students with the doctor who had arrived on the scene a few minutes before and approached Alan. "I would like to speak to ye...both of ye, if ye will." His gaze latched onto Michaela.

"Michaela? Why?" Alan asked.

"She was with ye at Fiddler's Luck. It was the last time anyone saw Kait alive. If ye talk to yer brother ye can let him know I'll be wantin' to question him, too. I'll meet ye back at the office, aye?"

Sheriff Comyn may be asking them to come by the office, but his voice gave no room for arguments. Alan gave him a stiff nod. "We'll be there directly."

167

Chapter Twenty-Eight

Michaela sat by Alan on the long wooden bench against the wall as they waited patiently to speak to Sheriff Comyn, who apparently still hadn't arrived back from the crime scene. The office had very few pictures.

Four desks were arranged to face each other. In the far back corner was a door, which led to the back room where two cells were located. Alan had told her the police station handled mostly small disturbances, public unruliness and such. It wasn't manned for a full operation. If Kait's death was ruled a murder, most likely the Northern Constabulary in Inverness would handle the case.

Sheriff Comyn walked in looking a little frazzled with his red hair windblown and his features grim. Michaela and Alan stood and he waved them to a seat in front of his desk.

"I'm sorry to drag ye in here, but I have a few questions to ask ye." He closed his eyes, pinching the bridge on his nose as if to steal away a headache that was beginning to take root.

"I'm tryin' to retrace Kait's last steps." He leveled his gaze on both Alan and Michaela. "I know she was at Fiddler's Luck the other night."

"Aye," Alan spoke up. "Kait joined Michaela and I for a drink and a game of darts."

"I see." The sheriff looked at Michaela. "Yer visitin' us from abroad, aye?" The sheriff's speech was thickly accented. The brogue more pronounced than Alan's *rolling-r* speech.

"Yes. I'm from California."

"Aah, an American, Miss Grant. Do ye ha' yer passport on ye to verify this?"

"Yes, sir." She dug in her backpack and pulled out the book.

Comyn opened the passport. "Any relations to the Grants of Drumnadrochit?"

"Perhaps a long time ago." She shrugged.

"And ye knew Kait MacDonald, how?" He looked at her now.

"I didn't really know her," Michaela said carefully.

"But ye thought nothin' aboot sharin' a dram or two wi' her though."

"I—"

"What's this aboot?" Alan interrupted.

"I'm jus' askin' questions." Sheriff Comyn met Alan's gaze with a challenge. "We ha' a dead lassie and I want answers to how this happened."

"And ye think Michaela will be givin' ye the answers?"

"I ha' to start somewhere, now doonae I?"

"Listen," Michaela said, drawing both men's attention. "I met Kait for the first time the other night. We shared a few drinks, laughed and played darts. What happened to her is horrible and if there is anything I can do that will help you, please let me know."

Comyn stared at her for a beat of a second before nodding his head in approval. "Thank ye for yer cooperation, Miss Grant." He handed her back her passport.

"You're welcome."

Comyn turned toward Alan now, his blue eyes narrowing. "When was the last time ye saw Kait?"

"She left Fiddler's Luck aboot seven or so."

"Did she say where she was goin'?"

Alan shook his head. "She was a bit bladdered. I believe she was headed home. She said as much."

"And tha' is the last ye saw of her?"

It seemed to Michaela that the sheriff was fishing for more. What he *didn't* say spoke louder than the questions he asked.

Obviously, Alan thought so, too. His blue-lit eyes darkened as he met the sheriff's gaze. "Aye. It's the last time I saw her."

The sheriff leaned forward and slid a crumpled note across his desk to Alan. "Do ye recognize this?"

Michaela couldn't help but read the message. Her gaze riveted to Alan for an explanation. Kait planned to meet him down at his boat. So why was he kissing her if he had a thing with Kait?

"Angus," Alan purposely used the sheriff's first name. "Ye know the note is mine." He still hadn't looked at it.

"Oh aye, tha' I do. My question is if ye met her?"

"No." He sat back in his seat. "I wish I would have. Maybe we wouldnae be havin' this conversation now."

The sheriff nodded. He tapped his fingers on the desk as if he was trying to think of another question. When he couldn't, he looked away. "Tha' is all the questions I ha' for now." He stood and so did Alan and Michaela. "Miss Grant, I know ye're on holiday, but please stay put 'til we find out wha' happened to Kait. I may have a few more questions for ye." It wasn't a request but an order.

Michaela planned to stay here for another week, but that had been before she'd met Alan. It wasn't really an inconvenience, but the idea that she couldn't leave at a moment's notice didn't sit well with her.

Alan walked beside her in silence until they were a distance from the sheriff's office then he halted and turned toward her. "I have to take care of a few things. Just give me a few hours. Then we'll have our talk, aye? We'll meet at Fiddler's Luck, let's say at three." His eyes held her gaze, beseeching her to grant him a little more time.

She wanted to trust him, but he still hadn't explained last night. Now there were questions about Kait. Why did she slip him a note and why didn't he meet her? For a fleeting second, a horrible thought crossed her mind. What if he did meet her?

"Michaela?"

She met his gaze and gave him what she hoped was a smile. "Sure, at three then."

He nodded already looking toward the walkway. "Here's a bottle of water for the road." He pulled out a bottle from his jacket pocket as if performing a magic trick.

"Thanks." Her hand clasped around it, wondering what was Alan's obsession with keeping her hydrated.

He leaned forward and kissed her forehead. "Until later then." He turned and hurried off to God knew where.

"He's no' to be trusted."

Michaela turned to see Ethan MacGregor standing there. The man believed Alan slept with his eighty year old mother. A few days ago she would have brushed off the strange grudge, thinking Ethan was in the early stages of dementia, but now? Too much had happened.

First the sightings of the Loch Ness Monster, a prankster who breaks windows in the middle of the night, and Alan chasing after him butt naked or arse naked as the Scots would say. Add Kait's murder to the list and it all sounded like a bad sci-fi movie.

Come to think of it, Alan sleeping with Ethan's mother didn't sound so farfetched now. "Are you talking about Alan?" she clarified for the hell of it.

He nodded. "I warned Kait aboot him as weel, but the floozy paid no never mind and ye see where tha' left her." Ethan's breath smelled like a brewery.

It wasn't even noon yet.

Michaela didn't want to hear anymore. "I have to go." She tried to move around him, but he wouldn't allow it, stepping in front of her and blocking her way.

"Go if ye mus', but remember I warned ye. Kait isnae the only lassie tha' died because of them."

"What do you mean?"

"My mother's name was Mary MacGregor. She's buried in Kilmore Cemetery. Ask the MacLachlins aboot it. If ye been to the house, they keep a photo book in the hall cupboard. There's a photo of her in there. It's proof, ye'll see."

"Ethan?" Sheriff Comyn called as he strode toward them.

Good, Michaela thought. She didn't want to hear anymore of Ethan's fantasies about Alan and Hyatt.

Ethan turned to face the sheriff. "Wha' is troublin' ye?"

"I'd ask ye to come back to the office. I'd like a word wi' ye."

"Wha' for?"

"Aboot Kait."

He blanched at the name, but recovered quickly. "I warned her, but she paid no never mind."

"So I've heard," Sheriff Comyn agreed. His hand took a firm grip on Ethan's arm, leading him toward the office. "I'd like to hear more on wha' ye warned her aboot, aye?"

Michaela stared after them. Ethan had given her the same warning as he gave Kait. She wanted to believe Alan had nothing to do with Kait's death.

He had seemed genuinely concerned when she hadn't shown up for work, but there were things Alan had said and done that didn't add up. He thought Hyatt was involved with the Loch Ness Monster stunt. The college student, Mike claimed Nessie left Kait's body and swam away.

Alan had run after the prankster and obviously had an altercation with him. The angry welt on his side proved something happened, but he lied and said he never caught up with the culprit. If he had nothing to hide, why did he lie to her?

She needed to do a little investigating on her own. She'd start with finding out more about Mary MacGregor.

Chapter Twenty-Nine

Michaela strode into the Glen Urquhart Library with the intent to access the Internet. She passed by rows of bookshelves and tables where people sat working or reading. There were two young women huddled together at another table, engrossed in their conversation, their voices a low murmur.

The library also posed as a learning center and the establishment had what she was looking for in the back room. Her gaze took in the pine colored desks arranged strategically around the room to utilize the limited space. The large paned windows allowed natural light to filter through.

There were six computers with only one occupied by a man in his mid-late thirties. She chose the computer farthest from him so he couldn't easily see what she pulled up on the screen. Placing her backpack on the table, she took a seat.

It took a few tries before she found what she was looking for or at least what she thought Ethan had wanted her to find. Mary MacGregor, Ethan's mother wasn't an eighty-year old woman. She died *fifty* years ago.

Surely this Mary MacGregor couldn't be the woman Ethan meant for her to find. She scanned the article again. Mary MacGregor had drowned in a boating accident, survived by her son, Ethan MacGregor. She clicked out of the site and pulled up another one. The article stated that the Loch Ness Monster had attacked Mary MacGregor. "The remains were ravished beyond recognition, only the name stitched in the clothing revealed the deceased's

174

identity."

Some sort of beast ravished Kait's body, too. The coincidence spooked her and tiny hairs on her arm stood at attention.

Alan and Hyatt were most likely in their early to mid-thirties. When Mary died, neither man would have been born yet, but she couldn't dismiss Ethan's adamant claims about Alan and Hyatt being dangerous. He believed Alan was the cause of his mother's death. He'd warned her to stay away from both brothers. He'd warned Kait, too.

"He's a crazy old man," she murmured. Perhaps it was one of Alan's relatives who betrayed Mary? Ethan was confused and paranoid, is all. Her hand brushed over her face as she inhaled deeply. Her gaze landed on the article still up on her screen. "Then why do you still have doubts?" Instead of answers, she found only more questions, but even with Ethan's warnings, she honestly didn't fear Alan—or Hyatt for that matter. However, something was going on and the brothers knew what it was.

Ethan mentioned a photo album, but for the life of her, she didn't understand what old photos would prove.

She reached for her backpack and pulled out the water bottle Alan had given her. Always refreshing with a smooth taste. Turning the bottle in her hand, she examined the label. Nothing unusual jumped out at her, only the typical information found on every water bottle.

It was made of a sturdy plastic and a blue sports cap finished the product. She had to admit the water tasted like no other water she had ever had. *Well water*, Alan had told her. Where was the well? Here in Drumnadrochit?

"I feel better when I drink the water." She knew she spoke the truth, but it was crazy to think the water had some magical power to make her feel better. She was looking for a miracle where there couldn't be one.

Her condition couldn't be cured by well water. Alan seemed to think it could or maybe it was the man himself that improved her health. Maybe Alan's caresses were the cure.

The moment Alan's mouth had taken hers, she'd felt an invisible bond take hold, but his mind-blowing kisses were nothing compared to the way she felt when he made love to her.

He radiated heat and her body absorbed the warmth as if her soul craved it. She couldn't get enough of him. He proved a distraction and his kisses tended to make her forget the world around them.

She shook her head. What happened to her resolve to keep the relationship casual? "Well, that ended the moment you took him to your bed." *And kissed every inch of him while he returned the favor.*

Alan seemed to take their relationship in stride as if they had been predestined to meet.

She sipped the water and sat back in her seat with a heavy sigh. "Why did I find love now?" The questioned stunned her. Was she in love with him after she'd claimed love at first sight didn't exist? She couldn't deny the connection or how her senses were heightened when he was around her.

God, if she wasn't in love with him, she was on her way. She chewed on her lower lip. *You can't fall in love.* But what was she supposed to do—stay away from him now that he fired every nerve ending into action? "Stop being a fool." she murmured. Their time together was limited.

Everyone dies, Michaela, Alan told her.

He was right, but not today. *Not now.*

Her gaze wavered to the computer screen. With a sigh, her hand reached forward to log out, only to waver over the escape button. A photo caught her eye. Mary, young and alive sat at a booth in what looked like Fiddler's Luck. In the background, at the bar stood a man with a half-cocked smile, the lips familiar in their curve. Hitting the zoom button, the picture grew larger. Moving the curser, the man's face came to the center of the screen.

"It can't be." Her eyes widened. The dark hair was longer, but there could be no mistaking the Scottish slant of his eyes, the noble nose and all so sensual mouth. Alan MacLachlin sat at the bar, sharing a pint of beer with his brother, Hyatt.

"That's insane." The photo was taken before they were born. The men in the photo must be relatives of Alan's. She shook her head in disbelief. She might have believed Alan resembled one of his relative, but Hyatt too? "Resembled? God, they're the spitting image of the two in the photo." How was that possible?

I've aged weel. Alan's words haunted her.

"No one aged that well." She needed to talk to Alan and this time he'd tell her the truth.

Grabbing her backpack, she headed to the front of the library intent on leaving, but two college-aged women sitting at a table drew her attention.

The tall girl with straight black hair was crying streams of black mascara. The other girl, a short blonde tried to console her, but with no luck. "I cannae believe it, Ria. I told him where to hike."

"It isnae yer fault, Nell."

"Ye think it is the beastie's fault then? I doonae believe it." Her heart-wrenching sob had her friend standing and putting her arms around her.

If she hadn't heard the girl say 'beastie', she would have left them to grieve over the loss of their friend, but she had to know what happened. Had there been another attack? "I'm sorry to interrupt."

The two turned to look at her. The dark haired girl's eyes were red rimmed and swollen.

"I'm sorry for your loss." Michaela handed the girl a tissue she'd fished out of her backpack.

"Thank ye."

"Did you lose someone close to you?"

Ria answered for her. "No, we only just met him. He was on holiday and asked us where the good hikin' spots might be."

A chill ran down her spine and for the second time today, the hairs on her arm stood up. She recognized these girls. They were at Fiddler's Luck the other night, standing at the bar. They'd given Steven Corbin a map. Did they do this kind of thing often or only that night? "Who was hurt?"

"No' hurt," Nell said. "He's dead. His name was Steven Corbin."

The dark haired boy with dimples was dead. It couldn't be right. Yet the quick twist in her gut told her the girls spoke the truth. "What happened to him?"

"The Loch Ness Monster attacked him." Nell blew her nose into the tissue then wiped.

Kait's death had been broadcasted on all the stations. Nothing was said about another attack. "I haven't heard anything. Are you sure?"

"Her mum works at the hospital," Ria volunteered the information. "It's all hush hush no one wants to cause a panic. This would be the second killin'. Oh St. Bride in Heaven, maybe there's been more, but they havenae found the bodies."

There was another wail of tears from Nell.

Ria patted her friend on the back.

Another killing. Would there be more? Had there been more? "Again, I'm sorry for your loss." Michaela started to go but turned back. "Where did you say Steven Corbin had been hiking?"

Ria gave her the information with a warning not to go into the woods by herself. She didn't have any intentions to do such a thing. She wanted to know how far away the attack had been from the MacLachlins' house and where Kait's last destination had been.

Staring at the makeshift map, led her to believe it was in walking distance. She shoved the map into her pant pocket. Her cell vibrated and she looked at the screen with a groan. "Not now, Blake." She let it go to voice mail.

Chapter Thirty

Michaela still had an hour and half before she met Alan at Fiddler's Luck. She headed back to the cottage to freshen up, and think of what questions she'd fire at Alan. *Like how come you and your brother are in a photo taken fifty years ago?*

"Oo-hoo, Miss Grant."

Michaela turned to see Mrs. O'Malley coming up the walk, waving her hand in a frantic motion above her head. "Hello Mrs. O'Malley." She waited for the older woman to reach her.

"I wanted to let ye know the window's been taken care of. So sorry for the inconvenience."

"That's quite all right. It wasn't your fault. Besides, Alan was good enough to offer a place for me to stay last night."

Ms. O'Malley's gray brows arched high on her forehead. "Indeed. What a fine laddie. Ye're gettin' on with him then."

Hmm... *gettin' on with him.* Nice choice of words. "He's been... attentive." Michaela felt the warmth spread up her neck, flaming her face.

Mrs. O'Malley chuckled. "I bet he has." Her hand rested on her forearm. "Come back to my house and have a spot of tea with me. I have the pot a brewin' as we speak."

"I really—"

"Now ye arenae goin' to hurt an auld woman's feelin's are ye now?"

"Of course not, but I can only stay for a little while. I'm meeting Alan at Fiddler's Luck."

"No' a problem. We'll sip some tea while we chat

180

and ye'll be off to meet that young man of yers."

Michaela gave in. "Sure, why not?" Hot tea sounded good.

Large Georgian windows brought light into Mrs. O'Malley's living room, giving it a welcoming presence. Plush blue chairs and carved end tables made up the decor. Oil paintings of the loch brightened walls painted in rich earth tones.

"Make yerself at home lassie." Mrs. O'Malley rolled the oak teacart between the chairs. The arrangements of scones on a fine-bone porcelain plate made Michaela's mouth water.

Mrs. O'Malley handed her a scone on a plate and a cloth napkin for her lap.

"With all the buzz aboot Nessie, I thought ye'd be up and aboot tryin' to snap a picture of the beastie yerself."

"I'm not sure I'd want to be on the loch."

"And why no'." Her blue-eyed gaze locked onto her.

"Ye have heard that the monster may have attacked Kait."

She shook her head. "Oh aye, poor Kait, but she wasnae attacked by Nessie. Somethin' else hurt that poor lassie."

Michaela wondered how Mrs. O'Malley could be so sure when the authorities still didn't know what happened to Kait. "I'm a little hesitant to try my luck."

"Alan would protect ye, ye know." The tea had steeped long enough and she poured her a cup. "Do ye take cream or lemon?"

"Cream please." She wanted to laugh. Alan would protect her from the Loch Ness Monster? The woman sure had confidence in him. "He's only a man."

As Mrs. O'Malley handed her the cup, her mouth slid into a smile that spoke of secrets. "In time ye will see he's much more."

What did she mean by that? Before she could question her, she spoke again.

"Do ye know about the legend of the Loch?"

"The legend? Like there's a monster in it?"

She chuckled. "Oh aye, that's one story, but I'm speakin' of the real story."

Michaela didn't realize there was a real story. "I'm not sure."

Mrs. O'Malley poured herself a cup a tea before sitting across from her. "No' many do I'm afraid. They've forgotten." She sighed before her face lit up again. "Would ye like to hear it?"

"I'd love to." Michaela relaxed and sipped her tea, falling under the spell of Mrs. O'Malley's story. The smells of cinnamon, orange blossom and fresh cream only added to the ambience.

"Long ago, a green valley stood near the loch. A well supplied fresh water for the village's patrons, but there was somethin' more to the water. No one in the village ever fell ill or aged as fast as others would in the other nearby villages. Some believe t'was evil power at work and others believed it a gift from the gods. No' wantin' to take a chance of offendin' either side, they followed the rules. The well would supply the magic water so long as whoever used it remembered to replace the cover over it when they were through fillin' their jug."

Mrs. O'Malley sipped her tea, placing the cup back down on the matching saucer after she indulged. "One day a lassie was drawin' water from the well and heard her wee bairn cryin'. In her haste to care for the child, she forgot to place the lid back on the well. The valley began to flood, ye see. It would have continued to flood the land, but Druid Daly took pity on the village and stopped the flow of water.

"However, there was a hefty price to be paid for

his generosity." Mrs. O'Malley paused to wet her palate with a generous sip of tea or perhaps she wanted to give her story a dramatic flair.

Enthralled by the story and the woman's plight, the statement slipped out of Michaela's mouth before she could stop herself. "But it was an accident."

Mrs. O'Malley smiled over the rim of her cup. "Oh aye, but someone must pay all the same. By the gods' demands, Druid Daly cursed the family to watch over the loch and the secret it still concealed. Ye see, in a cavern below, the well still exists.

"The druid cursed two brothers, changing them into seahorses, and the laddies would forever swim the depths of the loch. Every fifty years they would be allowed to walk the earth as humans, givin' them fifteen years of freedom on land, but then they would have to return to the cavern below to stand guard. The well water would keep them youthful and strong."

"But what kind of life could that be?"

"None at all. A curse isnae for comfort, ye know."

"And there was no way to break the curse?"

Mrs. O'Malley paused but then nodded her head. "If the laddies could find their soul mate, the curse would be broken. They could live their life as a mortal again."

Michaela sighed and took the last bite of her scone. "They never found their soul mates, did they?"

"There are still sightin's, are there no'?"

An intriguing story, but why had Mrs. O'Malley felt inclined to tell her it?

Her gaze caught the site of the gold plated clock on the wall and how much time had passed. "I have to be going." She stood and so did Mrs. O'Malley. "Thank you so much for the tea and for the lovely story." She placed the teacup on the cart.

"No trouble. I enjoyed yer company." She walked

her to the door. On the porch, Michaela turned to thank her once more, but Mrs. O'Malley placed a hand on her arm, halting her words. "Always follow yer heart, dear. Happiness awaits ye there." Then she gently closed the door.

Michaela blinked in confusion. Legends... Soul mates... Follow her heart. "What was that all about?"

She turned to head back to the cottage when she caught sight of Alan and Hyatt as they headed toward the tree line where the path would lead them back to their place. *Forget about meeting Alan at Fiddler's Luck. I'll confront him now.*

They were too far ahead to call out to them. They seemed to be arguing about something by their quickened steps and angry movement of their hands. She soon fell behind, but it didn't matter. She knew where they'd end up. Hopefully, by then Hyatt would be through with Alan and she could have her turn.

Coming around the bend, she halted her steps to catch her breath. Hyatt and Alan stood on the pier. Their stances were tense, hands fisted. God, she hoped they didn't come to blows. What could they be arguing about? Even though their voices were raised, she still couldn't make out their words. There was no way to move closer without being noticed and she already felt like an intruder.

Hyatt threw up his hands in what looked like frustration. He turned and stormed off toward the forest, luckily down farther and away from where she stood.

She turned her attention back to Alan, who stood at the end of the pier, staring at the loch. He rolled his broad shoulders back as if to loosen the tension in his muscles. It was no wonder he was stressed after arguing with his brother.

She took a step from her hiding place intent on going to him, but halted when Alan began to strip.

He threw down his jacket and his T-shirt went next. She should turn away and let him have his privacy, but she couldn't seem to make her limbs move. The pull of desire made her shift her stance. God, he was an amazing specimen of masculinity that beckoned with sexual promise.

Not that she wasn't enjoying the view, but what was he doing? Someone could come along and see him in all his natural glory. What was it with him being naked in public? As if he could hear her thoughts, he dove into the water and out of sight.

She inhaled deeply as if she could feel the icy waters closing in over her head, too. He would freeze to death.

She jogged over to the pier and down the wooden boardwalk. At the edge, she scanned the shadowy depths for his lithe figure, but the waves and the peat filled depths kept him hidden from view.

A disturbance in the water to the right of her caused her to shift her gaze. "Omigod." Her feet scrambled back, farther down the walkway, but she didn't turn and run. Her eyes fastened on the rolling body of the sea creature as it magically glided through the water with powerful strokes.

The view from Urquhart Castle was nothing compared to seeing the beast a few feet away. Entranced by its beauty for a moment, she forgot Alan had dived into the water and now swam with the creature.

What if the beast attacked Alan? Maybe this is what killed Kait and the young college student down at the morgue. The authorities hadn't dismissed the fact.

They knew Kait had come down to the dock to meet with Alan. Her note told them she would. What if she fell in the water by accident and the creature attacked her. "Oh God. Alan!" she screamed, running to the edge of the pier. "Alan!"

The creature seemed to hear her and stopped, frozen beneath the surface. It's eyes locked onto her in concentration. "God in heaven." A whisper of terror shot through her as she watched it swim toward her. It couldn't come onto the pier could it? Maybe it could. They had found the college student farther inland. He'd been hiking in the woods. *Run. Get the hell out of there, Grant.*

She blindly spun away and plowed into something hard and unyielding. She fell back with a screech of surprise, but strong arms grabbed her, steadied her. She looked up to see her rescuer and thank him, but the words lodged in her throat more from confusion than panic.

The man wore a ski mask, covering his features from view. His grip around her arms tightened and she felt the first inkling of fear that the Loch Ness Monster wasn't the only predator out here.

She tried to yank free and managed one hand before the stranger whipped her around, pulling her against him in a chokehold. A scream clawed its way up her throat but before she could bellow in protest, the man covered her nose and mouth with a cloth. She struggled, but it was no use against his brute strength. She didn't know who to fear most. The man who held her captive or the beast that rose out of the water like an avenging angel, roaring in fury as it shook its head and bared its jagged, razor-sharp teeth.

Her eyes fluttered and she didn't think she could keep them open much longer. What was wrong with her? *Fight dammit!* The cloth. The man held a cloth over her nose and mouth, drugging her. The beast lunged forward while blackness as dark as the loch itself, led her down the path of unconsciousness.

Chapter Thirty-One

Fury seized control of Alan's actions when the man grabbed Michaela and held a cloth over her nose and mouth. He'd seen the threat before she had, but as the beast, he couldn't warn her.

The man stood taller than Michaela, stocky and muscular. He knew it was the shape shifter in his human form and he had gone after Michaela, drugged her by the way her body had gone limp in his arms. Had he laid in wait for her? Followed her here?

A bigger question plagued him. Why was Michaela here? They were supposed to meet at Fiddler's Luck. She would have been safe there. Damn him for not realizing she'd be in danger by association. The shifter knew Michaela was important to him and would use her to get to him.

He rose out of the water, not caring if someone saw him. Diplomacy be damned. He couldn't allow the shifter to drag her away. Fear coiled around him like a foul scent. If he failed, Michaela would die.

The shape shifter threw Michaela to the side without care for her wellbeing. Her limp body fell like a ragdoll, lying still as death. Alan roared again, lunging forward with the intent of ripping the shifter's head off. He didn't care the consequences it would bring. There were ways of disposing the body where no one would ever find it.

The shifter turned to face him. He didn't have time to shift as he dove to safety and away from Alan's sharp teeth. His body hit the wood pier and rolled away with preternatural speed.

The shifter had the gall to chuckle as if he was enjoying this. In his crouched position with his right hand on the pier and legs tucked beneath him, he made ready to spring. "I underestimated ye again, my friend," he seethed. "We'll fight no doubt, but no' today. On my terms and when I say."

What did the bastard mean on his terms? He planned to finish this now.

The shifter sprung like a panther going after its prey. He landed beside Michaela. His hands whipped out and shoved her. Her body flew through the air, landing in the water with a splash that sent waves crashing over the pier. She was unconscious, helpless...sinking to the bottom.

"Are ye goin' to let her drown?" The shifter's sinister chortle rang like a death toll. The bastard knew he'd won. Alan would have to let him escape or Michaela would drown.

Alan roared and dove into the water, going after her.

She floated downward, her arms outstretched and her legs useless in her unconscious state. Strands of her hair drifted over her face as if they were creatures trying to devour her.

Alan swooped beneath her and shifted back to his human form. His hands wrapped around her waist, keeping her firmly against him, not daring to loosen his grip for fear she'd slip away. His strokes propelled him upward, only seconds ticked by, yet it felt like time stood still, preventing him from saving the woman he loved.

The dark water lightened and then he broke the surface, drawing in air. His strokes brought him to the edge of the pier. He lifted Michaela out of the water, laying her on the boardwalk before he lifted himself up beside her. Placing his hands on her chest, he ignored the warning not to interfere with fate and used his magic.

The vibration drew out the water from her lungs. Her body convulsed and he closed his eyes concentrating, clearing the passages so she could breathe. She choked as the water spurted out of her mouth and nose. He held her head to the side, caressing the wet strands of hair away from her face. He could have lost her. She could have drowned or worse the shape shifter could have taken her to do what he had done to Kait.

If he had any doubts before he didn't now. Kait's death was no accident. The shifter had torn the poor lassie apart. "Who are ye?" he shouted, knowing the shape shifter heard him. Believing the bastard would want to know if Michaela survived, but silence greeted him.

Michaela drew in a ragged breath and coughed, drawing his attention back to her. He said a silent prayer of thanks to the gods.

She rolled onto her back and blinked up at him. "Alan?" she croaked, her voice raspy and thick. Then her eyes rolled back in her head and she passed out again.

He scooped her up into his arms with ease and headed back to the house at a jog. He had to remove her wet clothes or the effort to save her would be for naught. Her skin already felt cold as ice. As he stepped onto the porch, he could hear Elvis barking and growling as he scratched at the door. Elvis had sensed the shape shifter—the threat. For once he was glad he had left Elvis inside. The shifter would have killed him.

Opening the door, he pushed his way inside. "It's okay, boy." His tone soothed in a singsong voice, easing the tension in Elvis' stance. His bristled fur lay flat once more and his rapid barking settled down to a low whine as he followed Alan into the living room.

Alan gently placed Michaela on the sofa. He

removed her clothing and wrapped her in a blanket before starting the fire in the fireplace.

Priscilla meowed and jumped on the back of the sofa, staring down at Michaela with her gold-green eyes.

He looked down at the state of his undress. He needed to throw on some clothes before Michaela woke up with questions. He didn't want to upset her more than she already would be. They may have started an intimate relationship, but after her ordeal his parading around without clothes might put her on edge.

How could he explain what happened? Did he speak the truth or let her believe fear had caused her to imagine the incident?

No, she had to know.

Priscilla rubbed against his arm and he scratched the back of her ear. "She willnae believe me, Priscilla," he told the cat. Her purr sounded like the low hum of his boat. "She'll probably fear me." Priscilla meowed and leaned her head against his palm, demanding more attention.

"Ye have to know, Michaela." His gaze lingered over her still form. The color in her cheeks had returned and her chest rose and fell in a steady rhythm. She was his mate, but she didn't understand the importance of what that meant.

His breath came out in a tired sigh. "First things first, aye Priscilla." He rubbed behind her ears once more before heading to his bedroom to dress.

Chapter Thirty-Two

"Bloody hell!" He slammed the front door shut with such gusto the glass in the windows shuddered in reply. He ripped off the ski mask and threw it on the floor, stomping on it over and over again as he imagined it was Alan MacLachin's face. "Damn bastard for interferin' in my plans," he ranted, furious for not obtaining his prize.

His gaze landed on the pinewood lamp on the end table and his hand curled around the base wanting to crush it. Instead he hurled it against the far wall with a scream of frustration. Glass and plaster littered the hardwood floors.

He should have Michaela Grant in his grasps, having his way with her before he ripped her to shreds. "Bitch! I hope ye drowned." A part of him hoped she died, sinking to the bottom of the loch, but another part of him hoped she lived, giving him another crack at her.

He should have waited to see if MacLachlin could revive her, but fear of being almost caught had him fleeing back to his place.

He never thought MacLachlin would risk coming out of the water in his beastie form. "But ye did, dinnae ye. Luck cannae always be on yer side." The woman had been in his grasp, but he'd underestimated Alan MacLachlin for a second time.

Mates have a bond, but they are not always in-tune with each other. The bond between the human and MacLachlin was strong. How else had Alan sensed she was in danger when he had already dove beneath the water? The trollop hadn't screamed, yet

MacLachlin knew without a doubt his mate was in danger, rising out of his habitat like an avenging prick that he was.

He opened and closed his fists, trying to calm himself. He had to remain in control to finish this. "Doonae cock this up. Ye're so close to havin' yer revenge," he reminded himself.

He needed to take out his frustrations on something. With purpose, his steps took him toward his bedroom, but he paused in front of the spare room. He stood there staring at the numerous locks and bolts, his fingers hesitating over the first lock, wondering if his anger had been reined in enough to open the door.

A blind frenzy wouldn't do and his anger would only increase. He had worked long hours to remodel the spare room to his liking, boarding up the windows, sound proofing the walls before lining every inch with a thick plastic. There was no need to ruin the fine paint job he'd done with splattered blood. The room was now perfect for his plans.

His forehead rested against the door and he inhaled deeply taking in the scent of unwashed bodies, urine and...fear. His lips curved. The tangy scent of fear curled around his senses like an aphrodisiac. The heat in his veins caused his heart to speed up and desire twisted in his gut, a hunger that needed to be satisfied.

Three humans sat in the room, tied and bound— ready for the picking. He wanted to wait a day or two before he left another breadcrumb. He chuckled, "Body," he corrected himself, "hopefully leading the authorities to the MacLachlins' door."

Michaela Grant was going to be the grand prize, but first he had to nab her. With the fecked-up job he did today, Alan will keep Michaela close not wanting to risk her safety. The fury boiled in him again. His plans were ruined.

A whimper behind the door caught his attention. It was the eejit Damon Nokes, Ethan's grandson, who didn't deserve to be called a man. He pissed his pants the first time he bit him. It wasn't even a life threatening bite, no muscle had been torn and in time the wound would heal.

Unfortunately for Damon, time was not on his side. The other two were Damon's buddies who thought they were tough. Troy Ackman spiked his light hair and wore a dog collar around his neck of all things. Oh, he'd make him his bitch before he was through with him.

The other, Morton Rander, was short, overweight, with hair dyed bright red in spots as if his hair had caught the measles. Handcuffs had hung off his belt, and he thanked Morton for bringing them when he cuffed the misfit's hands behind his back.

The world was better off without these nancys mucking things up.

They had been easy marks. Out late, drinking until they were right bladdered and couldn't stand straight without the others' support. When they'd gone out the back door of Fiddler's Luck to piss against the wall, he couldn't have been more pleased.

He took them by surprise there, shifting into the beastie. High pitched screams came from their mouths and they slapped and ran into each other in confusion instead of running for their lives.

A swift swipe and he flung two of them into the wall, their heads slamming hard and knocking them out. Damon, the coward ran, leaving his comrades to their fate. He didn't get far. Grabbing him by the leg, he propelled him against the wall and he too fell silent.

There had always been a chance he might kill the pricks with the blow to the head, but luck had been on his side and the three lived—for now.

With a flick of the bolts, he swung the door open. "Which one of ye wants to play?"

His lips curved at the sound of their screams.

Chapter Thirty-Three

Michaela's eyes fluttered open to face two gold green eyes. She blinked in confusion. Where did the cat come from? She stared back and the cat opened its mouth with a lazy yawn before kneading its paws into her chest while expressing gratitude with a low vibrating purr. "Priscilla?" She was in Alan and Hyatt's house. How did she end up here?

"Ye're awake." Alan walked into the room, holding a tray with a teapot and mug on it. He placed in down on the coffee table. He leaned down and scooped Priscilla off her chest. The cat mewled in protest over losing her cozy spot.

Michaela scooted up to a sitting position, the blanket slipping down. "I'm naked." Her hand snaked out to grab the blanket, pulling it to her chin. Alan's lips twitched but he managed not to smile over her sudden sense of modesty. He'd already seen, touched and kissed every bit of her. Feeling embarrassed at this point did seem a little silly.

"Aye, yer naked." He nodded and let Priscilla go. The cat made a giant leap to the back of the couch and perched there with her paws tucked beneath her body.

Michaela frowned. "Why?"

"Ye doonae remember, then? Ye were on the pier," he coaxed.

"I... No..." A flash of memory surfaced. "Wait..." Then she did remember—all of it. "A man attacked me and the Loch Ness Monster..." Her gaze riveted to Alan's. "Oh God... It's real. It's not a hoax. I saw it up close. The beast was huge."

Alan stiffened, his expression filled with embarrassed discomfort, his color rising first in his neck and pooling at his cheeks.

She couldn't blame him. Listen to her going on about monsters. She shook her head, a whisper of fear tightening her chest. "It's happening." She hid her face in her trembling hands. *Not now, please God not now. Please grant me a little more time.*

Alan scooted her feet over so he could sit down next to her. "What's happenin'?" His warm fingers caressed her arm, obviously not understanding her distress.

She tilted her head and met his gaze. "The aneurysm is located in my brain, there's the possibility I may experience random hallucinations."

"Mmm hmm." His hand stilled before he turned to reach for the teapot. He poured the warm liquid into the mug and handed it to her.

"Thank you." She sipped cautiously, but the tea went down smooth, the warmth thawing her insides. "That's good. I didn't realize how cold I was." She indulged again.

"What do ye think ye imagined, Michaela?"

She held the cup close to her, absorbing the heat through the ceramic. "You don't have to humor me. I knew this could happen."

His hand touched her knee with a small caress. "Tell me," he coaxed. "What did ye see?"

"A man in a ski mask and...the Loch Ness Monster." She chuckled and ran her hand through her hair only to halt her action. Damp hair. "Did I fall into the loch?"

He nodded. "Ye took a wee swim. That's why ye're with no clothes. I washed them and they're dryin' in the dryer as we speak."

She didn't remember falling into the loch. "You pulled me out?"

He nodded again.

"I guess it was a good thing you were there. It was so real, Alan. The man who attacked me, his crushing grip around my waist and the beast appeared, roaring as it rose out of the water. It was so big, so dangerous, so... So beautiful."

Alan's brows arched. "Ye thought the beastie was beautiful?"

"It's my hallucination, don't ruin it." She scowled melodramatically to gain her point.

"I wouldnae dream of it. Michaela..."

The troubled expression in his eyes and the way his fingers picked imaginary lint from her blanket made her wonder if her ranting about a sea creature disturbed him.

"Werenae ye afraid?" His voice was low, hesitant, as if he feared the answer.

"At first, but then I realized she—Nessie tried to protect me."

"Mmmhmm," the Scottish sound of disbelief came with a nod. "A beastie tried to save ye? Ye believe this?"

"My hallucination, remember."

"Mmmhmm."

"Will you stop doing that?"

"Doin' what?"

He truly looked baffled. "That sound." She waved her hand in front of her. "You know... mmmhmm." It didn't sound as impressive when she did it. "It makes me think you don't believe me."

"Oh, sorry. It's just...sorry." He dropped his gaze.

"Before all this happened, I thought you stripped down naked and jumped into the water. Was that real or imagined?"

He met her gaze again. "Michaela, I need to tell ye somethin'."

"What? Did I imagine that, too?"

He shook his head. "Ye dinnae imagine any of

it."

"What?" There was no mistaking her disbelief from the pitch of her voice.

"I'm sayin' a man attacked ye and—"

"And what? The Loch Ness Monster tried to save me?"

"Aye."

The silence ticked away as she absorbed what Alan told her, but what he said couldn't be true. The Loch Ness Monster was a legend, a myth that the town kept alive to draw in tourists. "That's crazy."

"Hmm, weel." His shoulder lifted in a shrug and his face flushed red again, giving her the odd feeling he was uncomfortable with his confession.

Then it hit her. He really believed the legend to be true. "You're serious."

"Yer eyes dinnae deceive ye."

"Nessie tried to save me then?" The note of doubt rang through loud and clear, but Alan held fast to his conviction.

"Aye." He cleared his throat. "Perhaps the sea creature dinnae want to see ye hurt."

"You act as if the creature could make a rational decision. Even if it were true, why on earth would the Loch Ness Monster rise out of the water to protect *me*?"

"*He*," Alan stressed the word, "would never want harm to come to ye. He'd do whatever it took to keep ye safe." The cadence of his low Scottish burr sent an odd jolt to the pit of her belly, the passion in his conviction only intensifying her attraction.

"He?" Did Alan just call Nessie a *he*?

"Weel, aye." He licked his lips and reached for her hand. "There's more to this world than ye know. There are other... beings that exist. We usually blend in with the humans and ye would never know we were here."

"We? We as in you... What are you saying, Alan?

That you aren't human?" She chuckled, but he didn't join in on the mirth. "Oh my God, you think you aren't human?" Her hand slipped from his grasp as the idea of him not being human weaved an unsettling path through her mind.

"Doonae fear me, Michaela." His sigh and the dark shadows that filled the light blue of his eyes told her she inflicted pain by doubting him, but what did he expect? His claim couldn't be true.

She frowned and licked her lips. Her claim that the Loch Ness Monster rose out of the water didn't sound rational either. Clearing the knot in her throat, she ventured to play along and at least hear him out. She owed him that much. "If you aren't human, what are you?"

"Are ye sure ye want to know?"

"You brought it up. So, ya."

The smell of the peat and wood fire permeated the air and she looked toward the fireplace where Elvis lay curled near its warmth without a care in the world. The dog didn't mind if his master had a few screws loose as long as he was fed with an occasional scratch behind the ear.

"I'm no' delusional."

Her gaze riveted to his. "I didn't—"

"Your face gives ye away, luv."

"Oh." And she tried to clear all expression from her face. She must not have done a very good job by the way Alan shook his head.

"Let me start at the beginnin' if ye doonae mind."

She nodded for him to proceed and took another sip of her tea.

He closed his eyes briefly then gave her a nervous smile. "Last night, when I ran out of the cottage after the bloke who broke the window, I wasnae chasin' a human. I went after a shape shifter."

She peered over the rim of the mug. Then lowered it, gripping it with both hands. "A shape shifter? As in a werewolf or something?"

He shook his head. "A born shifter can take on any animal form it chooses. Some animal forms are easier to imitate than others."

"Do you think you're a shape shifter?"

He hesitated.

"Well, are you?"

"Michaela, what do ye know of legends of the loch?"

"Funny you should ask. I had an interesting conversation with Mrs. O'Malley over tea today."

His brows shot up. "What did she tell ye?"

"That two brothers were cursed and chained to Loch Ness until they found their soul mates."

Alan brushed away a strand of hair, but it stubbornly fell across his forehead the moment he took his hand away. He looked at her, the pale blue of his eyes darkening. "Did she tell ye the legend is the true story of the loch?"

"Yes, but..." Fear and excitement mingled as one. What if all she witnessed hadn't been a hallucination, but if that were true, the Loch Ness Monster existed and so did shape shifters.

Hysteria bubbled up in the back of her throat, but she managed to squelch the urge to scream her frustration. No, she couldn't believe the fantastic story no matter how much she'd like to.

Michaela narrowed her eyes. "I love stories as much as the next person, but what does the legend of Loch Ness have to do with what I saw today?"

"I'm gettin' to that."

She nodded. "Go on."

Alan looked at her with those gaslight colored eyes burning brighter. "The sea creature ye saw is real."

"No." She shook her head in denial, but Mrs.

200

O'Malley's words echoed in her thoughts, forcing her to see the truth. *Druid Daly cursed the family to watch over the loch and the secret it still concealed. Ye see, in a cavern below the well still exists. He cursed two brothers, changin' them into seahorses and the laddies would forever swim the depths of the loch.*

Two brothers, she told her—Alan and Hyatt?

Every fifty years they would be allowed to walk the earth as humans, givin' them fifteen years of freedom on land, but then they would have to return to the cavern below to stand guard.

The picture she'd seen in the library. Two men that looked like Alan and Hyatt stood in Fiddler's Luck fifty years ago, sharing a beer with friends.

The water below would keep them youthful and strong...

Was Alan trying to tell her he was the Loch Ness Monster? Was Hyatt one, too? If that was so, it would mean they were..."Cursed. The brothers were cursed," she said more to herself, but Alan answered.

"Aye."

Michaela swallowed hard. If the legend had any truth to it, the well still existed, too. "The water from the well can cure anything?"

"It keeps the body youthful, but it doesnae mend broken bones and such."

If only it were true, Michaela thought. A miracle cure with a drink of water, but this was a legend and nothing more—a fanciful tale and yet she saw the Loch Ness Monster twice, once at the castle and then again today. Alan didn't deny its existence. Maybe she hadn't imagined what she saw on the pier. "Mrs. O'Malley claimed the brothers were allowed on land for fifteen years then to the sea for fifty."

"She spoke the truth."

"Resurfacing from time to time as the Loch Ness Monster to distract the locals and tourists alike,"

Michaela retold the story for her own benefit, but Alan confirmed the truth of it.

"The well must be kept safe." His broad shoulder lifted in a shrug.

For a moment, hope surfaced making her believe in the magic of the loch, but her mind couldn't fully wrap around the possibility of it being true. Alan was just a man. Not a shape shifter and most definitely not the Loch Ness Monster.

Then it dawned on her what Alan was doing. He was trying to make her feel better, keep her calm because he feared excitement could cause the aneurysm to burst. Perhaps there had been a man trying to kidnap her, but even that sounded farfetched. Why would someone want to kidnap her? The only people she knew in Scotland were Alan and Hyatt. She didn't have enemies.

She smiled sadly. "The story is a good one. You had me going for a moment." She didn't miss the tick in his jaw as he clenched his teeth. "Alan, it's all right. I know I hallucinated the whole thing. You don't have to protect me from the truth."

He took her hand and held it as he met her gaze. "It is the truth. The legend Mrs. O'Malley told ye isnae fiction. It is the truth, ye ken?"

She shook her head.

"Ye saw it—the creature," he insisted.

"I...I saw something." She leaned over to place the mug on the coffee table.

"Did ye think the man who threatened ye a figment of yer imagination also?"

"The man, if there was indeed a man, held something over my mouth and nose, chloroform maybe. Whatever it was, it made me drowsy. I could have seen my fairy godmother."

"Aye, but ye dinnae."

"What are you saying, Alan? What are you trying to tell me?" She pulled her hand away again.

She didn't want his touch to hamper her decision to see clearly. Shape shifters and monsters were for horror films and such. *Monsters are not real.*

"Ye ken weel enough what I'm tellin' ye. Ye saw me dive into the water and ye saw *me* rise out of it."

She chewed on her lower lip as his words echoed in her head. Her hand flew to her mouth as his words sunk in. "You're the Loch Ness Monster."

He nodded slowly, never taking his gaze off her.

She shook her head in denial. "Impossible. You're a man not a creature from the loch."

"Michaela." He reached for her but she scooted to the far end of the couch.

"Don't." Her hands clutched the blanket around her.

Alan stood in one fluid motion if only to put distance between them. Lithe and handsome, he stood tall before the fireplace, firelight dancing off the dark strands of his hair. Her gaze lingered on the pulsing tick at his jaw. The only indication of how he felt.

Elvis must have sensed his master's mood and whined at his feet. Alan leaned down on his haunches. His hand rubbed the area behind Elvis' ear. His soft Gaelic murmur soothed the dog.

She upset Alan, but what did he expect? He just confessed to being the Loch Ness Monster.

"Remember how I was injured last night?" His voice was steady, unnerving in the way he asked her.

"Yes, the cut on your left side." Funny, she didn't notice it this morning, but she'd been preoccupied with Alan's kisses.

His head lifted and his eyes burned bright. He stood and pulled off his shirt, tossing it to the side. His chest wide and smooth tapered down his washboard stomach with a trail of dark hair at his bellybutton and traveling down and disappearing below the rim on his jeans.

He lifted his arm and turned slightly to the side, allowing her to see for herself. Beautiful, nothing marring his smooth skin—no slash, no open wound, no scabbing or bruising—all of which she'd expected to see.

Her gaze flew to his. "I don't understand."

"Preternatural beings heal faster than humans. If a shape shifter hadnae slashed me, I would have healed as soon as I shifted."

She shook her head. "It doesn't prove anything. You weren't hurt as bad as I thought." But she knew in her heart that wasn't true. The angry slash on his side couldn't have healed over night.

His broad shoulders lifted in a shrug.

"Let's just say all you're telling me is true. You said the man who attacked me is a shifter. Is he the one who attacked you last night, too?"

He nodded.

"What can he change into?"

"Anythin'."

A chill ran down her spine and she felt the blood drain from her face. "He could change to look like you?"

"Nay. Humans are a complicated species. He might be able to contort his features for a few minutes, but he wouldnae be able to hold it. Animals are easier."

"As in he could be the Loch Ness Monster, too?"

He nodded.

Michaela was instantly sobered by the frightening possibility that Alan was telling her the truth. Alan was the Loch Ness Monster, the beast that had risen out of the water to save her.

He came to her rescue like an avenging angel. If all this was true, then... She glanced at the water bottle on the coffee table.

All her symptoms had vanished since she

arrived in Scotland. No, that wasn't entirely true. She felt better the day Alan had given her a sip of his own personal brand of water. He told her it was *well* water. Her gaze riveted to his again.

His ancient eyes beseeched her to believe him.

"The water you give me is from *the well,* isn't it."

"Aye."

"Will it cure me? Has it cured me?"

"I believe so. Maybe. Ye... smell different and I doonae sense the aura of death."

Her mouth fell open, but closed again with a gulp. He knew from the beginning she was dying. "I smelled like death?" Her voice caught in her throat in a horrified whisper.

"My senses are heightened and I've learned to distinguish subtle changes."

"Like death."

He sighed. "I know when someone is ill."

"Oh fantastic." She smelled like death. Rotting corpses came to mind, zombie-like creatures masquerading as humans. "How could you stand to be around me?" She pulled her legs close to her body, her hands hugging them close.

He took the steps that separated them and sat down next to her again. "Ye're thinkin' like a human."

She choked back a chuckle that didn't speak of humor. "I am a human."

"I know. It's just...smells arenae necessarily unpleasant to me. They are no' different than me knowin' the difference between red and green. Healthy is springs of summer and sunshine, death is the coolness before the embers of the fire go out."

She looked at him now, swiping away a tear with the back of her hand. Dammit, she wouldn't cry.

"Come here." He opened his arms to her. She hesitated a second before she went to him, sitting on his lap. He wrapped the blanket around her and held her tight. They sat there for a few minutes not saying anything. Her head rested against his chest and she could hear his heart beating in an even rhythm under her ear.

His skin felt firm and warm against her palms. His hand rubbed her back in a slow caress. She inhaled with a ragged breath. "I felt better the first time I drank the water." His hand stilled for a second before continuing to rub away her anxiety. "No more headaches. I don't feel lethargic and I have energy I hadn't had in awhile."

"That's a good sign then."

She nodded.

She glanced at the water bottle again. "What happens when I go home, Alan? Am I cured forever or only as long as I drink the water?" She tilted her head back to look him in the eyes, knowing she'd see the truth there.

"I doonae know. I have never given anyone the water in hopes of a cure. We were forbidden by the gods to interfere."

"Forbidden," she repeated the word. "Then why? Why would you give it to me?" She sat up, but didn't leave his lap.

He stared at her, caressing her features with his gaze. Her skin tingled as if he actually had touched her. The curse could be broken if he found his soul mate. Did he think she was his?

She shook her head at the thought. She didn't believe in soul mates, but then again she hadn't thought the Loch Ness Monster was real either. The sound of his voice drew her to look at him again.

"There's a bond between us, Michaela. I recognized it the first time I touched ye. I just dinnae know what it meant until later." His hand tucked a strand of hair behind her ear. "I've waited a lifetime to find ye."

"The first time I met you, you acted as if you hated me for intruding on your life."

"No, ye scared me is all."

"I scared you," she said, disbelievingly.

"When I touched ye, a electric current rushed through me as if it jolted me alive for the first time. I keep relationships simple while I'm earth bound. It complicates things. Break ups arenae somethin' I look forward to. If ye ken."

"Hmm." *How many had he experienced?*

"But with you I couldnae stop myself. It's as if ye dropped a bait I couldnae resist. I was caught. All ye had to do is reel me in."

"Nice analogy, fish-boy." She gave him a crooked smile. "Are you sure it's me you were looking for? Perhaps you only wanted to save me. You knew I was dying. You said so yourself." Hyatt had also alluded to the fact Alan liked to save damsels in distress.

He frowned. "That isnae it. I mean, aye I wanted to save ye, but it was for selfish reasons." He stared at her with smoldering intensity. "I dinnae want to lose ye."

This was all too much to take in at one time. She loved being with Alan, she wouldn't deny it, but he spoke of curses, magical waters and soul mates as if he were discussing the weather. He believed every word he spoke and a part of her wanted to believe it, too. "The curse would be broken once you found your soul mate. It isn't broken, Alan. You can still turn into the beast."

"I doonae know how this all works. Perhaps for the curse to be broken, ye have to believe ye found yer soul mate as weel. Do ye believe, Michaela? Do ye believe I could be yers and yers only?"

She opened her mouth and shut it again. She didn't know. How was she to know when she didn't believe in such a thing only moments before?

"Ye doonae believe it's possible." Pain showed plain in his eyes. The usual burning blue faded, paling, threatening to go out.

"I didn't say that," she said carefully.

"Yer hesitation is enough."

Her hand reached for his. "I don't know what to believe. Give me a moment to digest that you're the Loch Ness Monster." She frowned. The legend spoke of two sea creatures. "Is Hyatt..."

He nodded.

Her lips twitched.

"What is that gleam in yer eyes?"

"I was remembering our first conversation about the Loch Ness Monster. Hyatt suggested Nessie wasn't necessarily a girl."

Alan chuckled. "Aye, I can attest to that."

She laughed too, the tension leaving her. "If I'm to believe that I'm not having an episode and all this is true, where does the shape shifter fall into all this? Who is he? What does he want?"

"All good questions and I plan to find out." His brow furrowed as if something troubled him.

She could relate to that. A shifter tried to take her. He had come after them at the cottage. The shape shifter could look like the Loch Ness Monster. It all fell into place. The sighting at the castle, Alan's frantic behavior to find Hyatt because he believed his brother was the one on the loch that day. The photo she found on the Internet.

It had been Hyatt and Alan in that photo, looking as young and vibrant as they do now. Then she remembered something else. "Alan, did the shifter kill Kait?"

"Aye. I dinnae know for sure until I saw her body. The tearin' marks couldnae be from anythin' in the loch. For what he did to Kait, that alone I will hunt him down, but now..."

"Now?"

"I'll find him is all I mean."

She didn't believe that's what he intended to say. He was holding something back.

He looked at her sympathetically. "I'm sorry."

"Sorry?"

"He knows of ye as weel it seems."

She frowned. "What are you talking about?"

"He knows ye are important to me. That's why he went after ye. He's toyin' with me."

"If that's so then you must know this shifter."

"I'd have thought so, too, but I doonae know who he is. He has blended weel with the humans."

Her hand gripped his arm as she recalled her conversation at the library. "Alan, he's killed another."

His nostrils flared in anger. "Who?"

"Steve Corbin."

His dark brows dipped together into a frown. "Do ye mean the Yank we met at Fiddler's Luck?"

She nodded. "I ran into the two women who gave him the map at the bar, Nell and Ria."

He nodded. "I know who they are. Nell's mother works at the morgue."

"He didn't deserve to die like that." Michaela blinked back the horror. "Christ." She let out a long breath "They haven't announced it. The authorities are keeping it quiet so not to alarm the village."

A low growl rumbled from his chest almost sounding like a snarl. "We'll find him. He'll no' get away with this."

"You have fifteen years on land. How long have you been on land now?"

"Less than a year, aboot six months. Why?"

She tapped her chin then looked at him. "Six months and the shifter decided to strike now?"

"Unfortunately, just Hyatt and I bein' in the same town could set the shifter off. They can be territorial, but usually differences can be settled without bloodshed. This almost seems…"

She looked at him, seeing his expression as he thought about who could be responsible for the attacks.

The clock of Elvis, dressed in his jailhouse rock garb ticked loud on the wall, his hips swaying back and forth like a pendulum.

"Seems what?" she coaxed.

"Personal."

Priscilla meowed and stretched her bottom in the air before jumping from the couch, sashaying toward the kitchen. Elvis lifted his head with a doggy snort as if contemplating a chase.

"Doonae think aboot it," Alan warned.

Elvis whined in protest, but settled back down, keeping a wary eye for the cat's return.

"Alan?"

"Hmm?"

"Whom have you ticked off since you've resurfaced?"

Chapter Thirty-Four

"I've kept a low profile, but Hyatt..." Alan's words trail off as he thought about the fights Hyatt had instigated. Nothing stood out as a potential problem. Usually the hard feelings were eased with a dram of whiskey.

"Ethan doesn't seem to like you," Michaela offered.

Alan stiffened. "He has his reasons."

"Could he be the shape shifter?"

"Do ye believe he would be strong enough to grab ye the way the shifter did?" The thought of the shifter's hands on her angered him all over again.

"He could be faking his frailty, to fit in."

Alan stood to add another peat to the fire. "Ethan was a boy the last time I was here. No, he is no' the shifter."

"He remembers you, doesn't he? From before? He knows your secret."

He didn't meet her questioning gaze, but leaned against the mantel, staring into the flames. The heat warmed his face and body. There were many things he regretted doing in his life. There were things he wished he could change. How he handled his time with Ethan MacGregor was one of them.

"Alan, why doesn't he like you? What happened between you two?" Michaela's soft voice encouraged him to talk, to finally say what he kept bottled up inside.

"I doonae understand why Ethan loathes the sight of me." That much was true.

"I think you have an inkling," she said softly and

he finally looked at her. "Ethan told me about Mary *MacGregor*, his mother." She drew the last name out for emphasis. "He wanted me to find out what happened to her."

"Mary... I..." How could he explain?

"Who was she to you?" she asked.

He could lie, but the truth would come out eventually. He'd face her now with the fact and hope Michaela could accept his past transgressions as a life he led before her. "Mary MacGregor was my wife." Her look of betrayal made him hurry to explain. "It isnae what yer're thinkin'. It was a different time, fifty years ago. Mary was with child and unwed."

"Oh... I never thought... Ethan called ye *da*. Ethan isn't delusional. He really is your son." She lowered her gaze but she couldn't hide her emotions from him. No matter how ludicrous the feeling may seem to her, he knew she felt betrayed.

It didn't matter that she hadn't been born yet, that he had a different life—many lives before her, but the life that mattered now was the one he wanted with her. She had to believe that.

"No, Ethan isnae my son—no' by blood. Mary was pregnant with Ethan when we wed."

He had her attention again. Her moss green eyes touched a place deep inside of him. He never wanted to hurt her, but no matter his good intentions, his past would come back to haunt them and cause her heartache.

All he could do is remain honest with her and hopefully she'd accept all of him—for the good and the mistakes he'd made along the way. "Ethan's father left them with nay thoughts of returnin'. Mary would have been ruined. I wanted to protect her from ridicule and shame. She'd been good to me and to Hyatt, a true friend. When ye lived as long as I have, ye'd know those are tough to come by. I wanted Ethan no' to have the stigma of bein' a bastard. Ye ken?"

"So you married her and gave Ethan your name, but his last name is MacGregor."

He sighed. "I've lived a long time, luv. I've had many names."

Her ruddy brows drew together and she chewed on her lower lip. He had to give her credit for holding up so well with all she had learned in the last few hours.

"This is a lot to digest," she echoed his thoughts.

"Aye, it is." He nodded and came to sit by her again.

"Why would Ethan hate you for marrying his mother?"

"Perhaps because I left them. My time had come to an end. I had to return to the loch as the curse foretold. I couldnae stay even if I had wanted to. Fifteen years then to the depths of the loch to hibernate most of the time until fifty years have ticked by again. Ethan was almost a laddie of ten and he dinnae understand when I told him I had to go. I shouldnae have let him become so attached. I should have provided for him, but kept my distance."

She placed a hand on his. "You're a good man, Alan. You did your best and that was more than Ethan's real father had done."

He drew in a deep breath. "Ah weel, what good all my intentions were. I was already gone when Mary died, leavin' Ethan with no mum or da."

"I saw you with Mary."

He looked at her with a frown.

"In a photo." She gave him a ghost of a smile. "It struck me odd at the time that two men could look so much like you and your brother."

"Now ye know the truth."

"Yes." She nodded. "In the photo, you and Hyatt were in Fiddler's Luck, standing near the bar."

"I suppose there are other photos as well. Some I have in a cupboard." He nodded toward the hall where two large doors lined one portion of the wall.

"My mom and dad's house had storage in the hall, too, but my mom kept linens in hers," she said wistfully with a sigh. She refocused then and turned her gaze on him again. "Are there any other wives I should know about?" One brow arched half in jest and half in curiosity.

"Michaela, I willnae lie to ye. I'm verra auld and I dinnae always share a roof with Hyatt." He didn't fully answer her question, but listing all his past relationships wouldn't help matters. It was better left unsaid.

"I know firsthand you didn't live as a monk." Her gaze wavered over him with a thick beat of awareness, turning her eyes from moss to a dark forest green.

It was his turn to lift a brow. "And if ye keep eyein' me as if ye'll eat me up, I'll be showin' ye how unlike a monk I can be."

"You've already done that."

He chuckled. "I suppose I have." His thoughts turned back to Ethan, the boy with the easy smile. Ethan had looked up to him once. "I was Ethan's father for almost ten years." He defended himself, not really knowing why he felt the need to. "I dinnae realize it would give him a chance to hate me for it."

She placed her hand on his shoulder. "It's all right. It's not your fault he grew up bitter. He blamed you because there was no one else."

"Maybe. It wasnae always like that ye know. He trusted me. I tried to be a father to the laddie. I took him swimmin' and fishin'. I showed him how to make jellied eel."

"You abandoned them as far as Ethan was concerned and too young to understand why."

"Then his mother drowned, leavin' him

orphaned."

"Drowned?" The surprise in Michaela's voice had him looking at her. "I came across an article where it stated Ethan's mother fell overboard into the loch and her motorboat ran her over. They only found her torso, nothing else. Something about her name being stitched in the collar of her shirt is how they identified her."

His eyes narrowed as he took in this new information. "Mary made her clothes, a fine seamstress, too. Her finishin' touch was to stitch her name on the back collar. Where did ye read this?"

"At the library today."

He leaned forward and brushed his hand over his face.

"Alan?"

"Ethan accused me of killing his mother, but I knew his anger spoke. So I asked Mrs. O'Malley if she remembered what happened. She was once close with the family. She told me Mary had been ill. She took the boat out and must have fallen overboard. Mrs. O'Malley also believed Mary drowned, but she'd have been only a lassie when Mary died. She may no' have known all the details."

"In the article, it stated they found only her torso. It doesn't sound like a drowning to me. They assumed she hit the blades on her motorboat."

His gaze latched onto her. "Or the shifter killed her."

The color drained from Michaela's face, but she nodded obviously coming to the same conclusion. "That's why Ethan said you were dangerous. He really believed you had something to do with her death. Kait suffered the same fate his mother had."

"The coincidence is too much to be dismissed."

"The shifter could have been someone you knew fifty years ago. If Mary MacGregor died at his hands, then he knew her, too."

Alan inhaled deeply. "Many of the people I knew are already dead, but this bloke is a shape shifter. He wouldnae have aged a day, but I doonae recall a familiar face other than those that have aged half a century."

"God." She leaned over and poured more tea into her cup. She took a generous gulp. "Mary's death was almost fifty years ago. The shifter waited until you and Hyatt returned to kill again just to get back at both of you? That's one hell of a grudge and for what?"

"Shifters have long lives. Fifty years is nothin'." He could come up with no other explanation than the shifter waited for them. "Mary's the key then." He shook his head. "I cannae think of who would be so cruel as to harm her. Mary was as sweet as they come."

"Did you love Mary?" Her voice didn't waver, but her eyes were bright as she tried to hold back her emotions.

His sigh was long. "I loved Mary like family, but she wasnae my soul mate."

"As much as I like to believe in soul mates, you must see the truth for what it is. You said so yourself that for the spell to be broken you must find your soul mate. You're still chained to the loch, Alan. How could I be the one you seek to free you from the curse?"

Of course she had a valid point, but it didn't mean he wanted it voiced. "With ye, I felt the magic and doonae laugh." He pointed at her in warning, but he saw the corners of her mouth lift before she moistened her lips in a nervous manner, giving the best imitation of a stoic expression.

"I wasn't. Go on. What did you feel?"

"It's similar to the way I feel when I shift to the beastie. There's a ripple, a flash that vibrates deep inside like ripples in the water, expanding as it ebbs." His gaze met hers. "Ye dinnae feel it, too?"

She worried her lower lip. "I felt something, Alan." She placed her cup down and reached for him, caressing his cheek. "I'm afraid to believe it because if it is true, we won't have long together." Tears filled her eyes and she swiped them away with a sniffle. "You have to be wrong. I can't be your soul mate."

"I'm no' wrong." He brought her hand to his lips with a quick kiss. "As long as ye drink the water..." Would she be fine? He didn't really know. The water prolonged life, but it didn't actually cure ailments, but he held fast to the hope the water would be enough to give her years instead of months.

"Don't you see, Alan? If we're soul mates and the curse is broken, there will be no more water. You won't be the Loch Ness Monster anymore and there will be no trips to the well."

Fear coiled in his gut, knowing she spoke the truth. He took a deep breath against the panic. "Then we take what we can now. I'd trade eternal life to have one day with ye."

"Oh, Alan."

He drew her to him and folded his arms around her.

The blanket slipped down, his hand sliding over bare skin. The bulge in his pants painfully obvious that he wanted her, but after the ordeal she'd been through, he'd vowed to leave her alone.

Her lips pressed against the crook of his neck, hot and moist as her hand slid over his chest, teasing his nipples.

His voice was a hoarse whisper, but he didn't want to misread what she wanted. He had to know. "Michaela?"

Her lips skimmed the crook of his neck. "Do you expect Hyatt back soon?"

"No." At least he hoped Hyatt would stay away.

It didn't matter. He'd hear him coming up the walk in plenty of time to scoop her up and bring her to his room.

He parted her legs, feeling for the small nub. He flicked his thumb over the sensitive area. She was already wet with want, but he teased her anyway.

"You have way too many clothes on, Alan." Her voice had taken on a sultry edge.

He had been thinking the same thing and chuckled. "I can remedy that." Clothes left his body in a spray of scattered jeans and undergarments, leaving him as bare as she was. She returned to his lap, straddling him, taking him into her warmth. Her hips rotated in slow rhythm and he held onto her waist, guiding her. The need to be deep inside her consumed him.

Her gaze never left his, green to his blue. They were one with each other in perfect harmony as the tempo quickened. The first tremors began inside, moving along his manhood as wave after wave of pleasure coursed through him, washing over him with one final triumph.

Her breath came hot and labored and she leaned against his chest. His heart pounded as fast as hers did against his breastbone. He rubbed her back, warm and glistening with the afterglow of their lovemaking. *She's mine. I willnae give her up.* He wasn't sure if he meant it as a prayer or a challenge, but in the end it didn't matter.

His hand stilled as his ears picked up movement outside. He inhaled deeply, taking in the scents around him. Heather and lavender, female arousal, peat from the fireplace and…"Sheriff Comyn."

"What did you say?" Michaela asked in a dreamlike voice of a woman fully satisfied.

A knock at the door broke the calm. She lifted her head and looked at him.

"Rrrr…ruff." Elvis stood and barked with low

growls. Priscilla darted across the living room into the back rooms.

Another knock.

"It's Sheriff Comyn comin' to call," he told her. "Elvis sit."

Elvis didn't look like he wanted to obey. With a low whine, he circled and lay back down again with a grunt of annoyance.

"Were you expecting him?" she asked already leaving his embrace.

"No' that I'm aware of." He grabbed his jeans and slipped them on. "Yer clothes are in the dryer. I'll give ye a moment."

Alan waited until she rushed down the hall and out of sight before he headed for the front door, pulling on his T-shirt as he went.

The knock pounded again. "This is Sheriff Comyn."

Alan glanced out the window to find the sheriff flanked by Officer Jonas Wiley. This obviously wasn't a social call. He opened the door. "Sheriff." He nodded his head in greeting. "What brings ye to my place?"

"We need to speak to yer brother."

"Hyatt? What for?" He lifted his brow in surprise.

"Damon Nokes and his pals had an altercation wi' Hyatt."

It wasn't a question but Alan answered anyway. "Aye, Damon was the one to start it."

"So it's been said, but we need to speak wi' yer brother all the same."

"I wouldnae deny ye, but he isnae here at the moment."

A sound from the back room had the sheriff drawing his gun. Alan stepped back in surprise, his hands in the air. "What's goin' on?"

Just then Michaela walked out into the living

room fully dressed though her hair was still a little mussed. She froze once her gaze latched onto the sheriff's gun. "Alan?"

"Is Hyatt in the back room, Miss...Grant?" Sheriff Comyn asked.

"No? What's going on?"

The sheriff must have believed her for he lowered his gun and holstered it.

Alan lowered his hands. "That's what I'm wonderin'. Ye come to my house, sheriff and pull a gun on me. I think ye best tell me why ye need to see my brother."

"Troy Ackman's been murdered. His mother said he dinnae come home the other night. Come to find out Morton Rander and Damon Nokes dinnae either. The three were last seen wi' yer brother wantin' to beat them to a bloody pulp."

"I assure ye, the young men were all alive when Hyatt went home. And no blood was drawn."

Michaela had moved beside him now and she slipped a hand into his.

The sheriff nodded. "Still, I need a word with him. If ye see him, tell him I'm lookin' for him."

"Are ye arrestin' him?" his gaze landed on the holstered gun. Comyn wouldn't have used the gun unless he thought Hyatt dangerous.

"Troy wrote a note in the dirt. One word," Officer Wiley corrected. His gaze shifted to Michaela with a once over then he stared at Alan again.

"Aye, and what was that?" Alan inquired impatiently.

Wiley's thin lips curved. "He named his murderer. He scrawled the name Hyatt."

Chapter Thirty-Five

Alan walked Michaela back to the cottage to pack the rest of her belongings. With the shape shifter on the loose and intent on kidnapping Michaela, Alan feared her staying alone wasn't an option anymore. The shifter already killed three people, maybe more since Morton Rander and Damon Nokes were still missing. Thank goodness, convincing Michaela to stay at his place hadn't proved difficult.

Once he had her secured, he'd find Hyatt. They would face the sheriff together. The last thing he needed was for Hyatt to lose his temper and end up behind bars.

Hyatt liked to fight, maybe even went out looking for altercations, but he never lost control of the situation and outright injured a person to the point the bloke couldn't walk away. Unfortunately the authorities wouldn't see it that way. Hyatt's name had been scrawled in the dirt next to a murder victim.

"Alan?" Michaela stood in the archway of the bathroom staring at him, her eyes betraying her anxiety. She wore jeans and a blue, close fitting, cable-knit sweater that showed off her womanly curves.

She'd tied back her auburn hair in a ponytail. She looked so young, so worried and he felt a pang of remorse that he put her in this position. She had enough to think about with her fading health without worrying if a homicidal shape shifter wanted to end her precious life even sooner.

"Hyatt didn't do it." Michaela spoke, surprising him that the concern he noted hadn't been for her but for him.

"I know. The shifter is settin' us up for the fall."

"But why go to all the trouble? Why not just take you out? The killings are so senseless."

"He's made it personal. He's goin' after people I care aboot. Killin' Hyatt would be more difficult to manage, so he's done it another way. If Hyatt's blamed and locked up..." He ran his hands through his hair. "We need to be close to the water, Michaela. Even in our human state the water calls to us."

"Hyatt would die behind bars."

"Aye, an agonizin' death to be sure."

A knock at the door put them both on edge.

Not that he would think the shifter would come calling with a knock at the door, but so far he hadn't followed any sort of protocol. Alan placed a finger on his lips, indicating the need for silence. He looked through the peephole and frowned. A man stood there, a stranger if ever he saw one with an expensive suit and tie.

His sable colored hair was parted on the side and slicked back with some sort of product to keep it in place by the way the sheen caught the light. Could this be the shifter? He breathed in, hoping to catch a whiff of the man who stood there and if he had a preternatural scent.

Cologne and aftershave stung his nostril, along with some other products rubbed on the skin. Not a shifter's scent, but it didn't mean the shifter hadn't used some kind of chemical to mask his true self.

The man was average height, but well built with a studious look about him. Alan didn't remember him from the Village Green or from his past. Would the shifter actually have the audacity to show up here?

There could be only one way to find out.

Alan turned toward Michaela and pointed to the window and mouthed, "I'm goin' around to surprise our visitor, aye?"

Her eyes widened and she shook her head.

He didn't have time to argue with her. The shape shifter may have already sensed that he was here.

Chapter Thirty-Six

Michaela stared in disbelief at the open window Alan had exited through a second ago. What did Alan think he was doing? And what exactly was she supposed to do? Wait here and hope Alan returned? What if he didn't, then what?

The scuffle on the other side of the door had her heart pounding so hard she could feel the beat in her temples.

Someone slammed into the door with a grunt. Making her feet move, she looked out the peephole, hoping to see what was happening. "Oh dear God, no." She hastily flipped the lock and swung open the door.

Alan held the man in a chokehold against the wall of the cottage, the guy's eyes bulging in surprise at the assault and his hands gripping Alan's arm in an attempt to throw him off.

"Stop, Alan! I know him."

Both men shifted their gazes at the same time to stare at her.

"Ye know this bloke?" Alan's eyes narrowed with suspicion, still keeping his arm pressed against the man's neck.

"Yes. For God's sake, let him go. His name is Blake, my... A friend from back home."

Alan's arm fell away, but he didn't look happy about doing so.

Blake drew in a ragged breath, holding his neck. "What the hell, Michaela?" he choked out. "Who is this goon?"

Alan lifted his dark brows and waited for her to

explain.

Michaela stared at him for a moment then looked at Blake who wore a wounded expression. Maybe now wasn't the time to tell Blake about her involvement with Alan. "He's...a friend."

Alan snorted, making Blake turn to glare at him. "A friend with a violent streak."

"Ye were lurkin' around her place," Alan said without apology.

"Lurking..." Blake stuttered in exasperation. "I knocked at the door."

With blue skies and the wind a mild whisper, people were out and about, tourists and locals heading for the loch or for the hiking trails. The three of them were drawing unwanted attention with Alan scowling and Blake glaring back with a challenge.

"Uh...maybe we should take this inside." Michaela motioned toward the door. Both seemed reluctant as they eyed each other with the intent on having a second round.

Alan did have an animal side to him, the Loch Ness Monster lurked beneath the surface for Christ's sake, but Blake's attitude took her by surprise. Blake lived by a doctor's schedule—long hours and little sleep. His only physical routine had been the treadmill. Yet with his usually neat hair in disarray, his eyes narrowed and his fist clenched, she could imagine him in a brawl.

"Men," she muttered under her breath and turned, stalking back into the cottage. Either they followed or resumed beating each other senseless. At this point she didn't care which.

It only took a heartbeat before both men walked in. Alan closed the door behind him.

Michaela leveled her gaze on Blake. "What are you doing here?" His gaze wavered to Alan for a second before returning to her. He obviously had questions about Alan and why he had been in her room. Later. She'd asked the questions first.

"Well?" Her hands went to her hips in a stance to do battle. The men weren't the only ones who could hold their own. She bet Blake's sudden arrival had nothing to do with his change of heart concerning her wishes. His next words told her what she suspected.

"I came to take you home. Christ, Michaela do you realize how worried I've been? It's been all over the news—the murder. The news reported an American woman had been slain. You haven't answered your cell phone. What was I supposed to think?"

"One, I'm not the only American vacationing in Scotland, Blake, and the poor woman they found was a local. Two, my cell must be turned off." She wasn't about to tell him she'd been ignoring his call. "And three, I don't need to check in with you."

"Check in..." His voice held a note of surprise. "Is *he* the reason you've been too occupied to give a damn about those who care about you?" His head nodded in Alan's direction with a quick movement, his nostrils flaring in disgust.

"We aren't a couple anymore. The last I remember you told me you didn't want to wait around and watch me die."

He had the decency to flinch. "I wanted you to make the right decision."

"No, you wanted me to do as you commanded. This is my life, not yours." She pointed to her chest. "My life."

Blake studied her, the vein pulsing in his jaw. Still looking at her, but directing his question to Alan, he asked, "Did she tell you she's dying or did you just learn about it now? It could be anytime. She could be laughing...having sex," he said icily as if he already came to conclusion they'd slept together, "or

226

walking down the street."

"Oh, aye, I know." Alan's voice was steady, quiet but the warning rang in his tone.

Blake turned to meet Alan's gaze. "Then you know she needs to go home."

"Perhaps." Alan took a step forward, offering his hand. "I believe we werenae properly introduced. I'm Alan Maclachlin."

Blake blinked in surprise at Alan's change in attitude. He hesitated as if he suspected a trick of some kind. Alan didn't shy away, but waited for Blake to come to his own conclusions. Finally, Blake took the offer with a firm grip. "Dr. Blake Stuart."

Michaela rolled her eyes. Did Blake really think throwing his title of doctor in there would impress Alan?

Alan's lips twitched, but he managed to keep a straight face. "A doctor, ey. Is this a house call then?"

Blake drew back his hand with a huff. "Michaela needs medical care."

"I told you I'm fine," Michaela snapped.

Blake leveled his gaze on her with the professional doctor look he wore when giving a patient bad news. "You're not fine. The sooner you realize this—"

"I do realize," she interrupted, "but it sure in hell doesn't mean I want someone cutting my head open."

"If what ye say is true, Doctor...Stuart," Alan spoke, his Scottish flavored speech sounding more pronounced. "Should ye be excitin' the patient in such a manner?"

Blake closed his eyes in a deliberate blink before inhaling deeply. "No."

"Then I suggest ye back off a bit and let the lassie choose her destiny, ey? Since ye're here why no' join us for a dram of Scotland's finest whiskey.

Ye look like ye could use one."

Michaela thought Blake would refuse, but he nodded his head. "It's been a long day."

"Splendid." He opened the door. "Why doonae ye meet us a Fiddler's Luck. Do ye know where it is?"

"I saw it on my way here."

"Good, good. Then ye know yer way."

Blake's mouth opened in surprise, before he shut it again with an inhaled breath that made his nostrils flare. "Are you throwing me out?" His gaze locked onto Michaela, but when she remained silent, he turned and left in a huff.

"He shouldn't have flown here." Michaela shook her head. "What could he possibly be thinking?"

"Obviously, he cares aboot ye," Alan replied with unwelcomed frankness.

"Maybe...yes, I suppose."

"How does that make ye feel?"

"Feel?" Her brows drew together. "What do you mean?"

"Ye thought he only cared aboot fixin' ye, but he wouldnae of flown here for the opportunity of cuttin' ye open. He's in love with ye, if ye havenae figured it out for yerself."

Michaela frowned. His words were spoken as if he was curious, but something more was being asked here. Alan hummed with energy though he did well keeping it in check. Only the small tick at the side of his jaw—and his eyes—they always gave his feelings away. Lighter blue flames when pleased or amused, darker when aroused or when his temper flared. She didn't think he was aroused. "I'm not in love with him. If that's what you're asking me."

"Good to know. I have enough to worry aboot without worryin' my mate will run off with another bloke." Her harrumph had one of his dark brows tilting up.

"You don't own me either, Alan."

"I never claimed to own ye, but I want ye, Michaela Grant. Ye belong with me and ye know it as weel, but I'll leave it to ye to tell Blake."

"Tell him what exactly." She threw up her hands. "Tell him I'm in love with the Loch Ness Monster and by the way his brother is one, too. My medical condition is the least of my worries because a shape shifter who has a personal vendetta against my mate, is stalking me. So don't worry about me, Blake. Go home." She whirled away, tears stinging her eyes. Dammit, why was she crying?

Alan's arms slipped around her and she leaned back against him, taking in the warmth of his body.

"I'm sorry." His lips pressed against the top of her head. "I'm worried aboot ye, aboot us. I've only found ye and I doonae want to lose ye."

She turned in his arms to hold him, too. "I'm not going anywhere with Blake or anyone else for that matter. We'll find the shifter and put an end to all this."

"Aye."

"Alan?" She looked up at him so she met his eyes, wanting to gauge his response when she asked her question.

"Hmm."

"When you find the shifter, what do plan on doing with him?"

His hand gently caressed her hair, brushing a loose strand behind her ear. "He has to be eliminated, but ye already knew that, dinnae ye?"

She swallowed hard. "You're going to kill him, you mean."

"He's a preternatural bein' no' a human. He'll prey on other innocents and no law can keep him behind bars for long. He can shift into any creature, slitherin' out as a rat or a cockroach. Ye understand, aye? It's either us or him and I vote for us."

His finger lightly caressed her chin, tilting her

head before his lips descended upon hers, giving her a sweet kiss...a promise. "I willnae let anything happen to ye."

She believed him. He'd fight to his last breath to keep her safe. What he didn't realize, she wouldn't let him go without a fight either. She wanted him to have the best chance to beat the shifter, not that she didn't believe he couldn't hold his own, but why not have back up. "You need to find your brother."

"Aye." His lips pursed together, his eyes narrowing in thought.

"Do you know where he might be?"

"I have a inklin'. We had a disagreement on how to catch the shifter and he went off to brood. He's a hothead and does things half cocked."

"Out of curiosity, what did he have in mind?"

"He wanted to set a trap by tauntin' the bastard into facin' us. Now I'm beginnin' to believe perhaps it isnae such a bad idea."

"You'd have the upper hand if you drew him out to meet you."

"Oh aye, but this bugger is no' a fool. He'll smell a trap, I'd wager. He's thought this plan out and knows who he wants to target, leavin' victims that will lead the authorities to our door."

"We'll think of something to stop him." She left the warmth of his arms. "I'm going to go to the pub and meet Blake. You go find your brother and make sure he speaks to the sheriff before he's arrested for avoiding the authorities."

His mouth pressed together in a fine line and his brows drew together.

"I'll be fine with Blake," she reassured him.

"That's what I'm afraid of," he growled.

She leaned up and gave him a quick kiss. "I'm yours, Alan. You don't have to worry."

"And when this is all over, are ye goin' to stay with me?" His large hand encircled her waist and held her captive as his eyes searched hers with a hungry, predatory look.

He wanted her, all of her and wouldn't settle for anything less. Her desire to be with him couldn't be denied, but he wanted her to be his soul mate, to change his destiny. "What if you're wrong?"

His brows drew together then understanding lit his eyes. "I'm no' wrong, but ye doubt what we have. It doesnae matter. Share yer life with me, Michaela. A day or fifty years, I'm at yer service."

In his arms, she felt there could be a tomorrow. "You're notoriously charming and seductive, aren't you? If we live through this, then my answer is yes. Yes, I'll be with you no matter how long we have."

His lips claimed hers, sealing her pledge. Power radiated off him like heat of a furnace and the charge swept through her. Her heart pounded against his chest and she felt his heart sync with hers as if a link joined them, bonding them.

She tore her mouth away, breathless and a little unnerved. Meeting Alan's gaze told her he was still reeling from the kiss, too. "What was that?" Her hand touched her tingling lips then his chest with a light touch.

"Magic," his voice held a note of surprise.

Michaela frowned. Had something more profound joined them, bonded them? The tingling didn't stop at her lips but had spread through her body like an electrical current through her veins, bones, penetrating tissue and muscle. If Alan touched her, she was sure sparks would fly from her skin. "Alan?" The unsure sound of her voice drew his attention with his brows furrowing over the bridge of his nose.

"Are ye all right?"

"Uh... yes and no. Your kiss..."

"What is it?" He gripped her shoulder only to let her go. "Yer body is hummin'. I felt it beneath my fingertips."

"I know. What's going on?" She wasn't exactly scared, more curious by the sensation.

"Does it hurt?"

"Actually...it feels good. It's like power is shimmering through my veins." She shook her head. "That sounds crazy, doesn't it?"

"No' at all. When I shift the sensation is similar."

"When you shift?" To her dismay, her voice broke slightly. "Alan, am I going to shift into the beast?"

"I doonae think so."

"What do you mean you don't think so? Don't you know?"

His gaze wavered over her before he shook his head. "Ye willnae shift into the beast," he said with finality. "Ye arnae cursed, Michaela and I cannae give ye the curse with a kiss. It isnae a contagious disease. We dinnae share blood either. Nay, it must be the matin' link ye feel, bondin' ye to me."

"Heart and soul," she murmured with unease.

He took her in his arms, wrapping his warmth around her. "If it makes ye feel better, my heart and soul were already lost to ye the moment I saw ye."

She hugged him back and a sense of strength came to her. No matter what happened, she had a feeling they were stronger together.

Chapter Thirty-Seven

Michaela zipped up her windbreaker as she walked to the pub. The sun was warm, but the wind had picked up from an hour ago. Her thoughts lingered on the mind-blowing kiss she and Alan shared. *Magic* had been Alan's explanation for the connection that swept through them like an electrical current. Hell, why not. God knew she could use a little magic in her life.

Opening the door to the pub, it only took her a moment to locate Blake. Most wore casual clothing, but Blake wore an Armani suit and tie. He sat at a table looking uptight and uncomfortable with his glass of wine. She headed over to him and he turned to look at her. He rose from his seat and held out a chair. He at least had the decency to wait until she was seated before laying into her with his wrath.

"What the hell is going on with you, Michaela? Please explain why knocking on your door gives a guy the right to accost me? What was his name—Alan? Then after he nearly chokes me to death he politely tells me to get the hell out. Don't think I didn't hear the underlying threat beneath his gracious dismissal." He rubbed his brow in obvious frustration. "I've been sitting here wondering why I listened to him."

"Alan has been a good friend to me."

Blake harrumphed. "I'll just bet he has."

"What is that suppose to mean?"

"Isn't it obvious?" His tone took on a condescending flare of annoyance. "He must have come from your room. What did he do climb out the window? He attacks me and wants to know why I'm looking for you. Obviously, he's possessive of the tourists he decides to bed."

Her hand shot out with a resounding slap across his face before she even knew her intent. George, who stood at the bar, turned toward them, as did everyone seated near them.

"Is the gentlemen botherin' ye, Miss Grant?" George asked. He placed the glass down on the bar he'd been drying and wore a look that told her, given the word he'd leap over the bar to her rescue.

"No, I'm fine."

George nodded and resumed his work, but he kept a wary eye turned in their direction.

She looked at Blake and lowered her voice. "I'm sorry."

He rubbed his jaw but gave her a curt nod. "I suppose I deserved that."

"You did."

He took a deep breath and let it out again, straightening his tie in the process. "I know you believe this is your last vacation. I'm not judging you for wanting one last fling." He didn't quite keep the terseness out of his voice, but at least he tried.

She wondered where Blake was taking this.

"I'm not judging you," he said again, defensively. "I'm jealous. There, I said it." He sat back in his seat, his lips drawing into a grim line as if he didn't like the idea of being jealous at all.

"Blake—"

"No don't." He held up his hand. "I blew it. I know I did. I should have stood by you, but instead I let my stubbornness win out. Truthfully, I was scared of losing you. Well I did anyway, didn't I? Just not in the way I thought." His dark brown eyes focused on her. "Tell me one thing."

"What?"

"Is he worth spending your last days with?" His

gaze didn't waver, intent on seeing her reaction.

She didn't want to hurt him, but if she lied, he'd see the truth anyway. "Alan's everything to me."

He inhaled deeply again, his jaw tightening for a moment before his head nodded with acceptance. "Okay then."

"Blake, I'm touched you thought to come all this way to see that I was all right."

His expression changed again and he cleared his throat. "I was asked to come here. They want me to help with the investigation. I want you to know though I had already bought the ticket to come here—to see you."

"You don't have to explain, Blake." She covered his hand with her own.

"Yes, I did."

She frowned when she realized what he had said. "Why did the authorities call you in for the investigation?"

"I worked on a similar case when I did my residency near Lake Champlain. It was right before I transferred to Hoag."

She knew the lake. It bordered New York and Vermont. It was where she met Blake when she'd stayed with friends for the summer. "There was a Loch Ness Monster in Lake Champlain?"

He chuckled slightly. "No, the residents like to call him *Champ*."

"Really?"

"You aren't buying into all this nonsense about monsters rising from the depths and killing innocent people, are you? On my drive from the airport, I couldn't believe the nutcases out there hoping to capture a glimpse of the creature. It's complete madness on the A82. It's backed up from here to Inverness."

She lowered her voice so no one else could hear her. "There's more than meets the eye. There are monsters, Blake. Real ones."

"Yes, but they walk on two feet, they don't live below—" He paused mid-sentence and stared at her. "You believe there's something in the loch. Did you see something? If it is a monster, give me a clue to what the authorities should be looking for."

She hesitated for a moment and Blake jumped on it as an admission that she knew something.

"Come on, Michaela. If I'm dealing with some kind of creature, I need to know."

"You'll keep an open mind?"

Blake stared at her for a long measured moment. In the background, she heard the espresso machine hiss as George pressed the button to clear the steamer. The low murmur of voices could be heard and laughter floated in like a tease from the back room where a game of darts was in motion.

Finally, Blake nodded his head. "I'll keep an open mind, but be honest with me. Don't hold back."

"Okay." She leaned forward, leaning on the table with her forearms. "There's a shape shifter impersonating the Loch Ness Monster." The moment the truth left her mouth, she knew it had been a mistake.

Blake's eager expression to know more quickly changed to one of pity. He closed his eyes and let out a sigh. He never believed there was a monster. He'd been baiting her.

"You need to check yourself into a hospital. Now."

"I'm not hallucinating." She slid her chair back, scraping it across the hardwood floor as she stood.

"Really? You just told me the Loch Ness Monster is responsible for the killings."

"No, I said a shape shifter was impersonating the Loch Ness Monster. I'm not the only one who has seen him. A lot of people here in Drumnadrochit have witnessed the Loch Ness Monster's presence.

There are photos. Haven't you been listening to the news? Weren't you the one who just told me the A82 was backed up with people trying to catch a glimpse of the creature?" She threw up her hands. "Why am I wasting my time?" She whirled around intent on storming out of the pub, but escape wasn't so easily accomplished.

Blake came after her. His hand snaked out as she stepped outside, halting her. "Does Alan know you've seen this so-called monster?"

She yanked her arm free, her chin lifting in defiance. "He knows." Wouldn't Blake be shocked if she told him not only did Alan know about the Loch Ness Monster, he and his brother were the keepers of the loch. However, revealing that information wouldn't be in her best interest right now.

"He does know." His response confused her. It wasn't the words, but how his face turned a shade of red and his hands balled into fists. "That bastard." He stormed down the walkway only to whirl back on her. "Where the hell is he?"

"What's wrong with you?"

His mouth opened as if to issue a retort, but then his features softened. He took the steps that separated them and his hands cupped her face. "Dear Michaela, you don't realize the danger you're in."

"Blake—"

Shouts about Kait and Troy's murder drew their attention and people left their shops to gather around the town crier.

Blake dropped his hands and stared, too. "What's going on?" His hand snaked out to stop a man as he passed by.

"They caught the murderer," the man told him, continuing down the street to where the others were gathering.

"They did?" Michaela whispered under her

breath. That was impossible. The killer was a shifter and he wouldn't allow himself to be caught by the authorities.

Sheriff Comyn stood surrounded by a crowd who wanted to know if the news were true. Comyn's voice rose over the crowds' uproar of speculations. "We are makin' inquiries. There have been no official arrests. Now, move aside and go back to yer day."

"We saw you bring in Ethan MacGregor," a man with a dark beard shouted, shaking his cane.

"We're holdin' him for questionin'. Nothin' more."

Michaela pushed her way forward until she could meet the sheriff's gaze. "So is Hyatt off the hook?"

The sheriff didn't answer. Not a good sign.

"Sheriff?"

He looked at her. "We're still lookin' for Hyatt so if ye know where he is, ye mus' tell him to turn himself in."

Her blood ran cold. Did they find more evidence that implicated Hyatt and now Ethan, too?

"You see the sheriff is looking for a man not a monster." Blake stood beside her now.

She whirled on him. "He's wrong. Ethan is crotchety and bitter, but he's not a killer. His grandson is missing, too. He wouldn't harm him."

Once the crowd realized the announcement of the monster's capture proved premature, the people lost interest and returned to their business.

Blake didn't budge. "You'd be surprised what people do to their loved ones. By the way who's Hyatt?"

"Alan's brother."

"Of course. This just gets better and better. His brother is a suspect? Why am I not surprised?"

She shook her head in disgust. "I don't have time for this. Go home, Blake or go look at the evidence like you were sent here to do, but leave me alone." She turned to leave only to come up short when her gaze landed on Alan who stood a few feet away from them. His heated gaze made her shiver and it wasn't even directed at her. He took the steps separating them. Her hand touched his forearm, feeling the tense muscles beneath her fingertips. "Alan?"

"Is he botherin' ye?"

"Who? Blake? No, he's..." She looked over her shoulder at Blake, his gaze bordered on feral, too. She cleared her throat. "He's worried about me."

"Umm hmm. Ye doonae have to worry aboot her." His arm came protectively around her shoulders. "I'll make sure she's safe."

That seemed to rile Blake further. "Oh you will, will you? You take advantage of a woman who's ill. Feeding into her fantasies won't help her. She needs to be in a hospital."

"Michaela isnae yer concern now. Ye relinquished the privilege."

Blake's eyes narrowed. "How dare you."

"Oh, I dare." He let go of her and took a step toward Blake, but Michaela held him in check, grabbing his arm and pulling him back.

"Boys! Enough!" They both looked at her at least distracted for the moment from wanting to kill each other. "I can take care of myself."

Blake harrumphed while Alan gave a Scottish snort.

She rolled her eyes at their behavior, both alpha men wanting to prove they were in control of the situation. She inhaled deeply, a cleansing breath in hopes to remain calm. "I can take care of myself," she repeated. "I don't need you fighting over who is going to babysit me." Her gaze locked onto Blake. "I'm not hallucinating. I feel wonderful. No headaches and no blurred vision. So stop being my doctor and just be my friend. Can you do that for me?"

His shoulders relaxed and he gave her a stiff nod.

"And you." She looked at Alan. "Please try not to beat up Blake because he cares about my welfare. There's no need to feel threatened."

"Threatened?" He bristled at that, his burr rolling the r with flourish.

"Yes, threatened. I wish I had a mirror to show you how your eyes go dark and dangerous."

His mouth hung open for about a second before he closed it again. His brow relaxed as if aware of his threatening gaze and now tried to rectify it.

"Good." Having settled the potential brawl, they could concentrate on what they were going to do to find the shifter. "Did you find Hyatt? And did you hear they arrested Ethan?"

"No' yet on the first and aye, on the second. I was headin' to the sheriff's office when I came upon ye two."

"I'll go with you." She looked at Blake now. "Will I see you later?"

"I don't know." Sarcasm dripped, frosting the words. "Do you want to see me again?"

Blake's feelings were hurt. Their relationship may not have worked out, but she still cared about him. "Of course I do, Blake." The wind picked up, blowing her hair in her face. Her hand brushed the loose strands from her ponytail back and tucked them behind her ear. "We need your help to solve this case."

"What?" Both men spoke at once then glared at each other.

Her eyelids fluttered in frustration, but her thoughts of their childish behavior remained unvoiced. "Blake was called in to help with the investigation. Maybe there's a chance he could tell us something that could lead us to the shifter."

"Christ, Michaela." Blake ran his hand through his hair. "There's no shape shifter. Legends don't suddenly come alive and start attacking people."

"Ye'd be surprised," Alan mumbled under his breath but Blake heard him.

"You believe a monster lives in the loch? Dammit to hell. You've got a screw loose and I should have realized it with your macho superman stunt back at the cottage. Don't tell me. You own a cape and mask and plan on saving the day."

"I doonae have time for this." Alan tried to walk past, but Blake stepped in front of him, a deliberate move that could prove to be his downfall.

Michaela pushed her way between them. "Please, stop it." She motioned with an indiscreet nod toward the people staring at them. George stood in the archway of the pub with a watchful eye. Sheriff Comyn had turned to look at them, too. His leveled gaze pinned on Alan.

"Let's walk down by the loch," Alan suggested. "The sounds from the watercrafts and the trees will muffle our words. The breeze is in our favor, too."

Blake didn't look happy to follow Alan, but he stiffened his back and held his tongue.

Reaching the water bank, away from tourists, they had a bit of privacy. The smell of pine, moss and damp earth tickled Michaela's nostrils. Her gaze lingered on the waterfront. Loch Ness' dark waters shone with different shades of blue, some light and some dark almost black in appearance.

Steeped in mystery, the wind-swept surfaces hid what lurked beneath. Cold and forbidding it was where drowned victims were never found unless the menacing depths relinquished them.

A shiver ran down her spine. The shape shifter waited somewhere out there ready to claim its next victim, dragging them down to the icy depths.

"Could the man they arrested have killed those people?" Blake asked.

Alan addressed him, his expression grim and lines of worry creasing his brow. "No matter what ye heard, Ethan MacGregor is innocent."

Alan belonged to the loch and Michaela had seen him in his other form, sleek and powerful. She should fear him, but she didn't. Alan had the power to weave an enchantment like casting a magic spell, but there was no evil surrounding his gift. She'd witnessed his talent as he calmed animals and people. Could the shifter also manage the same feat?

No. She didn't believe the shifter could use his abilities for good. His cruelty showed in the way his victims had suffered. He wanted to hurt, wanted his victims to know terror before he killed them. Icy fear slid through her veins, chilling her blood. He'd come for her and he wouldn't stop at one attempt.

She shoved her hands into the pockets of her windbreaker and forced herself to focus on what Alan and Blake were discussing.

Blake had his arms folded across his chest. "Why should I believe you? Both of you." His arms came apart and he waved his hand at them in disgust. "Michaela thinks a shape shifter is responsible and you've hinted as much that you believe her. I look at facts, not at fantasies and legends."

"Fair enough," Alan said with a nod of his head. He looked at her then. "It's yer call luv, can we trust this bloke?" He pointed to Blake with his thumb.

She cherished Blake's friendship. He was always concerned for her welfare, always taking an extra step to keep her healthy. It hadn't been his fault that she didn't want the surgery. He didn't know what she'd been through and telling him hadn't been the same as living through it.

Their relationship had been comfortable at

most, not passionate and they both knew if time had been on their side, their relationship would have eventually ended on its own accord. They were never meant to be lovers, but friendship worked for them.

Blake appeared to be holding his breath, hoping she'd have faith in him. He needn't have worried. "You can trust him, Alan."

Her word was good enough and Alan nodded his head before addressing Blake once more. "Ye go and see yer doctor friends and decide for yerself if a man could have done such a savage act."

"Even if I do find the injuries suspicious, I can't share the information with you. You heard the sheriff. This is officially a murder investigation."

Michaela knew he was right. He couldn't do his job then report his findings to them. "Blake, you said you worked on a case similar to this one. Did they catch the guy?" She gave Alan a quick update. "In the States, there have been sightings of a creature with similar characteristics of the Loch Ness Monster."

"Interestin'," Alan murmured with curiosity.

They both looked at Blake who shook his head at them in disbelief. He believed they were delusional. For now, it couldn't be helped. "Well? Did you find the guy?" Michaela asked again.

Blake shook his head. "No," he said slowly, thinking his answer through. "They thought they had a suspect, but there wasn't enough evidence." He licked his lips and he didn't meet their gaze.

"What is it?" Michaela knew something was bothering him.

"The injuries inflicted looked more like the victim had been attacked by a great white, but evidence in the saliva around the wound came back with traces of human DNA, but nothing conclusive."

"Another shifter." Alan said more to himself.

"Can we dispense with the shape shifter

theory?" Blake snapped.

Alan ignored the request. "Later tonight, when the sun is near to set, I'll prove to ye monsters do exist, Dr. Stuart."

Blake's brows drew together. "Only for curiosity sake, I'll be there." Alan gave him directions to his home. "This ought to be good." With a nod to Michaela, he stormed back up the path, mumbling curses as he went.

Alan turned to look at her. "I hope ye're right aboot him."

"I am."

"Right aboot, whom?"

They both whirled around to find Hyatt strolling toward them, looking windblown with his long hair sticking up in places. His hands were stuffed in his pants' pockets. He hunched forward to ward off the blowing wind, his black long sleeved T-shirt flapping against his chest in aggravation.

"We must be in for a storm, aye?" His head tilted up to look at the dark clouds moving in angry formation.

In more ways than one, Michaela thought. She pulled the hood of her jacket up, carefully tucking her hair beneath it. They needed to find cover and soon. Alan and Hyatt hadn't even donned a jacket. Alan's sweater would be soaked in seconds and Hyatt's T-shirt plastered to his skin.

"Where have ye been?" Alan zeroed in on his brother with annoyance.

Hyatt's shoulders lifted in a nonchalant shrug. "What's it to ye?"

"What's it—" He threw up his hands. "The gods in heaven protect me. There's been another murder. Troy Ackman. The sheriff is thinkin' ye had somethin' to do with it."

Hyatt's eyes widened. "Me?" His hand tapped his chest in disbelief. "Why would he have a fool notion like that?"

"Oh maybe because ye tried to beat the livin' hell out of him the other night."

"He may have been a bit bruised, but I dinnae kill him. I left the wee bastard and his friends alive and breathin' as ye weel know."

Michaela looked at Alan, but he didn't meet her questioning gaze. Did he witness the fight or had he participated?

Large drops of water began dampening the earth around them, not a heavy rain, but the way the clouds had darkened it wouldn't be long before they'd all be soaked.

"Can we move this conversation to a dryer spot?" she shouted over the rustling of the trees as the wind teased and whipped around them. The rough waters of the loch rose and fell in angry white caps. She was glad they weren't out on *The Hound Dog* right now.

"We can move this conversation to the sheriff's office," Alan said.

"Are ye bloomin' insane?" Hyatt threw up his hands.

"Ye need to go there and give yer account of where ye've been or ye'll have a manhunt after ye."

Hyatt looked like he wanted to protest further.

"He's right," Michaela said, halting Hyatt from saying more. His gaze riveted to her. "Alan is right," she said again. "If you don't go in willingly, they'll assume you're guilty. They have no real proof you killed Troy."

"That's because I dinnae," he fumed.

Michaela nodded. "Yes, but Troy left a message—at least the sheriff is convinced he did."

"Message? What effin' message?" Hyatt looked to Alan then to her.

"Uh...just your name, apparently." Michaela cringed as Hyatt's face mottled with anger, turning dark red. "Oh, bloody fantastic."

"Come on," Michaela took his arm. "We'll go with you. Surely the sheriff can't believe you had anything to do with Troy's death. Troy didn't write your name. It's obvious the shifter did."

"Weel, ye and I know—Did ye just say shifter." His brows rose high on his forehead, his gaze riveting to Alan.

"It's a long story. I'll tell ye later. Just know Michaela knows aboot us."

"Is that so?" He looked at her then.

"Your secret is safe with me. I would *never be cruel to a heart that's true*." It took a second but Hyatt realized what she was telling him.

His eyes lit up and his lips spread into a grin. "Good to know."

Alan gave Michaela a look of *what was that all about*, but she just shrugged. His brow lifted, but he turned his attention on his brother. "Let's go." He took hold of Hyatt's arm intent on marching him to the sheriff's office himself.

Hyatt shook free. "I doonae need ye holdin' my hand. I can walk to my own hangin' if ye doonae mind." He brushed by him and headed up the walk.

Chapter Thirty-Eight

Michaela and Alan followed Hyatt into the sheriff's office. Ethan MacGregor sat on a long bench with his head resting in his hands, but he glanced up as they entered. His grief stricken gaze turned to fury when he caught sight of them. "Ye murderer!" His hand whipped out with a pointing finger.

Sheriff Comyn and Officer Jonas Wiley turned to stare at Ethan then their gazes shifted to the doorway.

Hyatt lifted his hands in surrender. "I dinnae kill anyone. I'm here because my brother said ye wanted to speak to me, Sheriff."

"Arrest him!" Ethan jumped to his feet. "He's the one and ye bloody weel know it." He threw himself at Hyatt, grabbing his shirt in his fists and shaking him. "Where's my grandson? Wha' did ye do to him?"

Sheriff Comyn moved quickly around his desk. "Ethan, unhand Hyatt. I will do the questionin'."

"I willnae let him ou' of here." Like always, Ethan's fuse was short and burning.

"Ye will unhand him now. If ye doonae listen, ye'll force me to arrest ye."

Ethan turned to look at the sheriff, his mouth hanging open in disbelief.

"Unhand him," the sheriff ordered again.

Officer Wiley looked ready to help out if the need arose. He'd moved around to the front of his desk. He only waited for the sheriff's word.

Ethan let Hyatt go with a shove as he took a step away with a grumble.

Sheriff Comyn relaxed his stance. "Now, sit

down, Ethan. Ye can ha' yer say in a moment." His gaze wavered to Michaela and to Alan. "Ye can both wait in here, bu' I'll remind ye no' to interrupt."

Alan nodded and led Michaela to the bench. Michaela could feel the tension radiating off Ethan—hot and explosive. One wrong word and he'd go through her to get to Alan. Probably not a wise move to sit between them, then again maybe it was the best place for her. She might be the only thing keeping Ethan in line.

The smell of stale coffee wafted in the air and her gaze found the source. The coffeemaker sat on a fold out table situated near the window. Feeling chilled from standing outside in the drizzle, something hot to warm her insides sounded good.

She'd even settle for stale coffee, but instinct told her it would be better not to move from the bench if she didn't want to provoke the sheriff's wrath.

Hyatt took a seat in front of the sheriff's desk. Sheriff Comyn moved his papers aside and opened a notebook, turning the pages until he found the spot he was looking for. He picked up his pencil and looked at Hyatt. "Did ye start a fight wi' Damon Nokes?"

"He did," Ethan spoke and the sheriff rewarded him with a glare. "Weel, he did," Ethan insisted.

"Do I need to lock ye in the back room to keep ye quiet?" the sheriff asked.

Ethan sat back on the bench with a huff, folding his arms across his chest.

"Good. Now keep yer mouth shut." Sheriff Comyn looked back to Hyatt.

"I fought with Damon, I willnae go and deny the fact, but I wasnae the one to start it. Damon called me out and I felt obliged to follow him outside."

"I see." The sheriff scribbled down the information in the notebook. "Did ye fight with Troy and Morton as weel?"

"They came after me. I should be the one makin' a complaint."

"Troy Ackman is dead," the sheriff reminded him.

"Sorry. Aye, I may have thrown a punch at them. Guess they dinnae like me knockin' their pal, Damon on his arse."

"Why ye..." Ethan jumped to his feet with his hands balled. The bench slid back despite Alan and Michaela's weight upon it.

"Sit down!" the sheriff pointed the pencil at him. "This is my last warnin' to ye, Ethan MacGregor."

Ethan sat down, murmuring obscenities under his breath. His eyes held a blaze of contempt as he tried to stare a hole in Hyatt's back.

The sheriff returned his gaze to Hyatt. "And did ye follow Damon, Troy or Morton home to finish the job ye started in front of Fiddler's Luck?"

"No, sir. I went home with Alan." He pointed his thumb over his shoulder toward the bench.

The sheriff glanced at Alan then back to Hyatt again. "Did anyone else see ye go wi' yer brother?"

"Oh aye." Hyatt grinned but didn't say anymore.

"Do ye mind tellin' me who saw ye?" the sheriff's voice held a note of impatience.

"Doonae mind if I do." He turned in his seat and pointed. "Ethan MacGregor. He stopped us on our way home to...hmm... To give us a piece of his mind."

"He's lyin'," Ethan shouted.

"Is he?" the sheriff questioned. "Ye mean to tell me ye dinnae run into Hyatt and Alan on their way home?"

"I... Weel... Aye," he stammered. "But that doesnae mean Hyatt dinnae come back later."

The sheriff closed his notebook and looked at Hyatt. "That'll be all for now, bu' doonae disappear in case I need to question ye further."

Hyatt stood. "To be sure. And Sheriff?"

"Aye?"

"I want to catch this man as much as ye do. No one hurts my friends and Kait was as good as they come. As for Troy... We dinnae see eye to eye, but the laddie was young and I would have never wished harm to befall him."

The sheriff nodded. "I'll keep tha' in mind, Hyatt."

Hyatt turned to go and Alan and Michaela also stood, but the sheriff's words halted them from leaving.

"Just remember to let the authorities handle this matter. Doonae play hero." His gaze drifted to Alan and then to Hyatt. "Do I make myself clear?"

"Oh aye, perfectly." Hyatt nodded.

Alan gave him a curt nod, too. Only Michaela knew Alan and Hyatt had no intentions of letting the authorities stand in their way of finding the murderer.

Ethan followed them outside into rain that was now falling heavier. His aged old face contorted in anger and frustration. He opened his mouth to say something, but closed it again when a voice from behind them broke the silence.

"I'd think twice before ye curse those who wish to help ye, Mr. MacGregor."

Michaela turned to see Mrs. O'Malley standing there with one hand on her hip, the other holding a large flowered umbrella. Her blue eyes narrowed with intent and her chin rose in determination to be heard.

"Ye need to mind yer own business, auld woman," Ethan snapped.

"You'd like that, wouldnae ye? But someone needs to stand up to ye." She covered the steps that separated them. She stood next to Michaela, offering her shelter under the umbrella.

Thankful for the reprieve of being soaked, she nodded her thanks and shoved her hands in her jacket pockets for warmth.

"Ye've always been a hard headed man with no sense," Mrs. O'Malley told Ethan with a shake of her head. Ethan snorted his protest but it didn't stop Mrs. O'Malley from continuing. "Ye're so blinded by hate, ye missed out on yer whole life."

He waved his hand at her. "Wha' are ye witterin' aboot? I had myself a good life."

"Would Marsella say the same?" Mrs. O'Malley must have hit a nerve.

Ethan straightened his back and inhaled deeply, his nostrils flaring in response. "Ye leave my wife ou' of this. God rest her soul." His hand hastily went to his head, chest and shoulders in a sign of the cross.

"She knew ye chose her out of spite."

"Ye're jus' jealous I chose her over ye."

"If that were the truth, I would have lived with yer choice, but I know the truth as did Marsella. Ye turned yer back on me because ye found out aboot my lineage."

Michaela looked to Mrs. O'Malley then to Ethan MacGregor. What lineage? Why would it matter who her parents were?

"I couldnae live with ye, knowin' ye were related to them." He pointed to Hyatt and Alan, confusing Michaela further.

Michaela looked at Alan for an explanation. His blue-eyed gaze touched her. More secrets. Would she ever know this man fully?

"She's a descendent of Gordana's lineage, our sister. Her children and their children's children for generations have kept the lands in the family. The one appointed waits for our return to make our transition on land easier."

"Gordana dinnae share her brother's fate," Mrs.

O'Malley explained.

Michaela remembered the story Mrs. O'Malley had told her. Alan and Hyatt took their sister's punishment in return that she could raise her son.

"Gordana wouldnae abandoned them, ye see," Mrs. O'Malley continued. "With each generation, we were taught, trained and expected to carry out our duties to keep the brothers safe from interference. We couldnae change their fate, but we could help by makin' their transition to land easier."

Michaela now understood how Mrs. O'Malley knew the legend, but why did she share it with her? Her instincts told her there had been a point to Mrs. O'Malley sending her to meet Alan and Hyatt.

The rain fell off the edges of the umbrella like tiny teardrops pooling at her feet. She turned her gaze to the old woman, meeting her blue eyes. They weren't the same shade as Alan's but deeper in color, grayer. "You sent me to them. Why?" She didn't have to explain what she meant. Mrs. O'Malley understood.

"Oh aye. Ye needed them and they needed ye."

"She's a witch," Ethan's statement was more an accusation.

"Doonae condemn what ye refuse to understand," Mrs. O'Malley snapped at him.

Michaela could see Ethan had met his match. Mrs. O'Malley would never let him get the best of her.

"Oh, I understand all too weel. Ye cast yer spell over me, but I ken wha' ye were aboot and broke free."

Mrs. O'Malley's laugh didn't speak of humor. "Still the fool, I see. After all these years, ye would have thought ye'd see yer folly, but hatred keeps ye ignorant. Alan and Hyatt arenae yer enemy. Help them and ye may still find yer grandson."

"Why should I believe a word of wha' ye say?"

Her sigh showed frustration, but her gaze met Ethan's. "I loved ye once, auld fool and deep down ye know what I say is true. Pull yer head out of yer arse and open yer eyes, aye? It's the only way ye may find yer grandson."

Mrs. O'Malley bid them good day then, leaving Ethan obviously moved by her words. His gaze followed her and his features softened as if he remembered what she once meant to him.

Without the protection of the umbrella, Michaela huddled deeper under her hood, hoping they weren't planning to stay out in the rain for much longer. Her windbreaker wouldn't hold back the rain from dampening her clothes.

Ethan turned his aged old eyes on Alan and Hyatt. His eyelids lowered in a deliberate blink and he inhaled deeply as if coming to his own conclusion. "If ye know a way of savin' my grandson, I beseech ye to try."

Alan gave him a curt nod. "We will do our best, Ethan."

Ethan nodded. He shoved his hands into his pockets and headed up the walk and away from them.

Michaela glanced at the police station. Officer Wiley stood in the doorway. His eyes narrowed and his lips turned down in a frown as he stared at them. How long had he stood there?

"We should probably get a move on," she looked at Alan, but gave a quick nod toward where Wiley watched them.

Alan's gaze shifted and nodded in agreement. "Aye," Alan reached for her arm, pulling her toward him. "Ye need to find cover for ye and wait out the rain."

Alan and Hyatt didn't look like the rain bothered them in the least. While the rain rolled off her hood and dampened her face and clothes, droplets hung on Hyatt and Alan's hair like tiny little crystals, pebbling away as if they were waterproof. "You're barely wet and I feel like a drowned rat."

Hyatt chuckled. "We weather just fine in the rain. We are from the water, are we no'?"

"Well that doesn't seem fair." A shiver ran through her and her shoulders lifted in response.

"Come on," Alan urged her forward. "We'll warm ye up with a good meal and a hot cup of tea."

Fiddler's Luck's business boomed when the weather turned damp. Tourists and locals alike came in for a dram of whiskey or a hot meal.

They took a booth in the back. Hyatt waved to George who stood behind the bar.

His thick hair was held back in a ponytail. His long sleeved shirt sported the logo for the bar. "Tad bit crowded today." He called back to Hyatt.

"When ye can manage, we'll have the special for the day and a spot of tea all around, too, if ye doonae mind."

"Be right up," George assured Hyatt.

Like the other walls in the pub, their booth sat below old photos of the pub in its early days. The one above their table was a shot taken outside in front of the pub. People lined the front steps. Some smiled for the camera while others wore a somber look.

Michaela shook free of her wet jacket. Alan took it from her and hung it on the coat rack against the wall with the other garments. She glanced back to the photo. Her gaze scanning those who stood in front of Fiddler's Luck forever captured as part of history. Business attire, and casual wear marked what these people did for a living. One man drew her attention. His stance, the way he smirked... something was familiar—

"Here ye go," the waitress delivered a hot pot of tea and three cups. Michaela forgot about the photo and smiled at the young woman with chestnut colored hair and soft brown eyes. With the tea poured, Michaela wrapped her hands around the porcelain for warmth. "Aah." She took a cautious sip and let the liquid warm her insides as well.

"Feelin' better?" Alan asked.

"Much, thank you. How much time do we have before we have to meet Blake?" The smell of food made her stomach growl, but the brothers were polite enough not to point it out.

"Four hours tops."

"Are ye sure aboot doin' this?" Hyatt asked. They'd filled Hyatt in on their conversation with Blake on their way to see the sheriff. "Ye witnessed the frantic behavior of the people out gawkin' at the loch. Do we really need to have one more hysterical cry that the monster is real? Exposin' yerself will only make it more difficult to keep wraps on this fiasco."

"So concerned, Hyatt. To think I've waited centuries for ye to grow up." Alan shook his head with a quirk of a smile tilting his lips.

Hyatt sat back in the booth with a huff of exasperation. "Even I know the situation is border linin' on a witch hunt or in this case a Nessie hunt. The loch is becomin' jammed with sonar buoys."

"You don't have to worry about Blake," Michaela reassured him.

Hyatt's brow lifted. "Ye may know the bloke, but it doesnae mean we should invite him over for a swim."

"For now we need him," Alan pointed out. "I need to see the bodies and Blake's the only way I'll have the chance."

"So long as we doonae join the bodies on the slab." Hyatt grumbled. He took his cup and drained the contents. "I need somethin' stronger."

Chapter Thirty-Nine

The sky had cleared and the wind died down to a soft breeze. The sun glowed orange and yellow against the sky, the only indication that the night claimed another day. Elvis sat on his haunches staring up at Priscilla preening her glossy black coat on the railing of *The Hound Dog*.

Alan's brows drew together as Blake headed down the pier to join them. Michaela caressed his arm and he turned to look at her. Her gentle touch soothed him. His brow relaxed and he gave her a quick smile.

"Well, I'm here," Blake announced, clearly not pleased to be in their company.

Without a word, Alan turned and strode to the edge of the pier.

"Where's he going?" Blake asked her.

"Just watch," she told him.

Without warning, Alan dove into the water, the whitecaps claiming him beneath the surface.

"What the hell." Blake took a step forward, but she restrained him.

"It's okay."

"Okay?" he sputtered. "You're both mad. I'm not going to—Holy...!"

Alan rose out of the water as the gray beast, a roar penetrated the night air with a vibrating rumble, giving a good imitation of thunder.

Blake stumbled back with shock, tripping over his feet, but somehow, still managing to stay upright. "Christ." He shook his head. "It's a trick."

"A trick, Blake? Come on. You wanted proof.

There's your proof. Not a hallucination unless aneurysms are contagious."

His eyes narrowed. "Real funny, Michaela."

"I wasn't trying to be."

Elvis barked and wagged his tail, racing to the end of the pier, wanting to play with the beastie. He knew who his master was in human form or not. Priscilla arched her back and yawned, obviously bored with the show as if she'd seen it a million times.

Alan leaned his head toward her and Blake tried to pull her back, but she resisted. "No, it's okay. Alan won't hurt me."

"I'm not so sure. Look at him."

"I am." She reached out to caress the side of the beast's face, smooth and wet. The skin felt like a seals' skin. His eyes turned to her, light blue depths she recognized as Alan's. Her heart beat faster in her chest, not because of fear but for love. It didn't matter what form Alan chose, her heart knew it was him.

"Okay, I believe," Blake blurted. "Now change back. Can the beast understand me?"

The Loch Ness Monster stared at Blake point blank. He snorted and water blasted out of his nostrils, spraying Blake from head to toe.

Michaela covered her mouth to stifle a laugh. "Oh, I'd say he does."

Blake glared through wet strands of hair. He brushed them aside with an irritated flick of his hand.

Alan shifted back to his human state, stepping onto the boardwalk dry and clothed in what he'd worn before jumping into the loch.

Blake shook his hands, water flinging off his fingertips like raindrops. "Any chance you can wave your wand or whatever it is you do to shift and dry me off, too?"

"Umm...no." Alan's shoulders lifted in a shrug. "Only works for me when I shift."

"Of course." Blake straightened his silk tie that was probably ruined.

"If ye have the mind to come back to the house, I'm sure I can find ye somethin' to borrow. Aye?"

Chapter Forty

"Almost got it," Hyatt mumbled under his breath as he used the tool to jimmy the lock. The click sounded off in his ears and his hand gripped the handle, sliding the glass door open. The room stood dark, only because the drapes were drawn, but Hyatt's vision proved perfect in dim or bright light.

The *Ockley House Hotel* rented out garden suites nestled in a forest of pine trees. There were two separate rooms per unit. The pretty blonde at the front desk gave him the information with only some mild flirting on his part. The garden suite where Blake was staying had both units rented out.

Hyatt had taken the wooded path, the suite coming into view around of bend of planted foliage and trees. Blake's room was the one on the right with the wild flowers beneath the window. Thank the gods the family in the other suite was loud and boisterous. It made breaking and entering so much easier.

His brother believed Michaela was his mate and trusted her with his life, but they both hadn't survived for centuries without being cautious. While Alan did his shifting act down at the pier, Hyatt volunteered to snoop around Blake's hotel room and find out more about the good doctor.

"Be a good laddie, Dr. Stuart and give me yer story."

A queen size bed sat in the center of the room with dark wood nightstands on both ends. A matching dresser with a mirror stood on the opposite wall, facing the bed. A tea table and two chairs were positioned near the shadowbox window where plush maroon cushions covered a bench. The early morning sun would give this room plenty of light and the bench an ideal place to sit back and read.

He investigated the dresser first since his gaze caught sight of papers and folders stacked at one end.

The aroma of stew and baked bread hit his nostrils from the suite next door, reminding him that he hadn't eaten supper. Through the walls, he could hear people conversing about their day on the loch. They had taken pictures and were going over them to see if they missed a sighting of the Loch Ness Monster.

Hyatt snorted. "No' likely. If ye dinnae see the beastie, ye dinnae capture it on yer camera," he muttered.

He focused on the task at hand and tuned out the tourists next door. His fingers rifled through the papers, most of them printouts of what had been in the news. His fingers froze when he caught sight of pictures of Kait or what was left of her. "Ah Kait, ye poor lassie."

There were pictures of the college student they met the other night and Troy Ackman, too. He closed the folder, not wanting to see anymore of the gruesome details.

He spotted a suitcase on the stand near the bathroom, which was situated across from the closet. Lifting the lid, he didn't find anything of interest. In the closet, three pairs of slacks hung on the rack, along with four dress shirts and one sweater. A pair of blue jeans and *Grateful Dead* T-shirt lay across the back of one of the chairs. He headed for the bathroom and his hand flipped the switch, lighting the room with a warm glow.

A red toothbrush stood in the glass cup with toothpaste next to it. An electric shaver in a brown pouch, aftershave and cologne lined the side of the sink. "A tidy bastard, arenae ye?"

He wouldn't call himself a slob, but he didn't go around making sure all his belongings were lined up in perfect formation. He flipped off the light in the bathroom before heading back into the main room.

His eyes landed on the wastebasket. In the good spy movies, the hero rummaged through the trash left behind. His hand gripped the edge and dumped the contents onto the bed. "A half eaten candy bar, napkins from Fiddler's Luck, three toothpicks and today's newspaper. Nothin' interestin' here."

As far as his investigation turned up, nothing appeared suspicious. Everything was too neat, too precise, as if Blake expected him to come calling. If that were the case, the doc would only leave out what he deemed innocent.

"But what of the things ye doonae want me to see?" His gaze scanned the room once more. "The drawers." He opened one at a time, finding them empty except for the nightstand by the bed.

Blake had his passport and his plane tickets there. He opened the paper folder securing the tickets and read the dates—arrival and departure. "So ye arrived in Scotland three days ago and ye plan on leavin' in a week. Hmm." He tapped his chin with the ticket. "Three days ago. Why did ye wait until today to seek out Michaela? Where have ye been hidin'?"

Chapter Forty-One

Michaela sat on the sofa holding Alan's hand as they waited for Blake to say something. Blake had showered before donning a clean pair of slacks and T-shirt that Alan had loaned him. The pants were a little long and bunched over his shoes. His hand rubbed his hair vigorously with a towel to dry his wet strands.

On the walk back to the house, Blake remained quiet as if he was in shock. Michaela couldn't blame him. A man changing into a sea creature and back again was a lot to take in all at once.

Blake finally looked up, his hair sticking up on end. "You don't know how much this galls me to say this, but I believe. Christ, the Loch Ness Monster is real." His gaze locked onto their clasped hands before riveting to Michaela, meeting her eyes. Questions obviously danced in his head.

Alan rose from his seat. "I believe we all could use a drink. I'll be right back." He headed for the kitchen.

"You could say that," Blake mumbled. He could have taken the seat across from Michaela on the black leather recliner, but with a slight hesitation he chose to sit next to her on the sofa. "Is that Elvis I hear?" He was referring to the music that Alan had selected, some of Elvis' mellower tunes, easy background noise.

"Yes. If you haven't noticed, he likes *the King*."

"Oh I've noticed. He has an Elvis bobble head on the bathroom sink, for Christ's sake."

Michaela smiled with a chuckle.

Blake draped the towel over the end of the sofa and leaned forward, resting his elbows on his thighs. "I thought you were with Alan to fill in the time...you know."

"Fill in the time before I died," she finished.

He shook his head. "No, I thought he was your one last fling, but now I realize the truth."

Her brows drew together. "What do you mean?"

"You're in love with the guy. You absolutely glow because of it."

Her lips twitched. "I do love him," she admitted. Her gaze took in Blake's messed up hair and without thinking she smoothed down the strands, making him look more like the Blake she knew. Her gaze locked with his. The realization of what she was doing hit her and her hand fell away. "Sorry."

He gave her a ghost of smile. "Me, too." His voice gave him away. His words meant more than sorry for now. "I'm sorry for everything. For how our relationship ended."

"Blake-"

"Don't say it." He shook his head and took a deep breath. "You said you felt better. He's good for you, Michaela. He makes you happy where I couldn't."

She reached for his hand and he returned the gesture, his fingers firmly clasping hers.

A low growl startled both of them. They turned to see Alan standing in the doorway with three beers, and a bottle of water and a scowl on his face. "I'll ask ye to unhand her now."

Blake released his hold, his face paling.

"Alan, really?" Michaela warned.

His shoulders relaxed at her tone and his face smoothed. "Sorry." He cleared his throat before taking a step toward them. He offered Blake a beer.

"Thanks," he said carefully.

He handed Michaela the water. "Ye should

drink this first. It's been a while."

"I feel fine, really."

"For me. To be safe." Worry etched his brow, making her realize she shouldn't take her good fortune for granted.

Blake took a swig of his beer before glancing at the two. "What gives with the water?"

"May I tell him?" Michaela asked, knowing it wasn't her right to reveal the secret without permission.

Alan nodded.

"Tell me what?"

"The water is from a well that is beneath the loch," she told him.

"In a cavern," Alan clarified.

"Of course it is." Blake's words were laced with resigned belief. "What's so special about it?"

"It gives eternal life," she told him and he choked on his beer.

"It does what?" He wiped his mouth with the back of his hand.

Michaela went on to explain. "I believe that's why I feel better. No more headaches. No more symptoms."

"You believe you're cured because of this water you've been drinking."

Michaela looked to Alan to explain.

"I doonae know. The water prolongs life, but I doonae know if it cures an existin' problem."

Blake placed his bottle down on the coffee table. "There's one way to find out. We could do an MRI and find out what's going on in your head."

Michaela's heart raced at the prospect of finding out if she had more than a few months to live, but a dark fear festered, convincing her she didn't want the truth confirmed if it wasn't what she wanted to hear. Her hopes would be dashed if they discovered the aneurysm was still there and the water only masked the symptoms.

Alan stood there waiting for her to say something.

She looked up at him, his gaze touching her, making her feel safe, protected and loved. It didn't matter to him one way or the other. She took a deep breath. "Yes, I want to know."

"I'll set it up," Blake said.

"And what aboot seein' the bodies. Are ye able to arrange it?" Alan pinned Blake down with his impressive blue-eyed stare.

"No, not through the normal channels, but I have the keys in the car. We can go tonight if you're up to it. No one will be there this late. We'll have the place to ourselves."

Chapter Forty-Two

They piled into Blake's rental car and drove to the morgue in nervous silence. Michaela and Alan stayed out of view while Blake went in first to make sure no one had stayed late. It took a few minutes but then Blake peeked outside and waved to them.

The temperature had dropped and the air hung damp and heavy. The sun had set a long time ago, but the summer sky never looked completely dark. Filtered light illuminated the heavens, making it look like an eerie fog hovered over them.

"How appropriate." Michaela muttered.

"What is?" Alan looked at her.

"The eerie sky is the perfect setting for a visit to the morgue."

His chuckle rumbled with humor. "Ye've seen too many horror flicks, aye?"

"Maybe." Her shoulder lifted in a shrug, but it didn't stop her from glancing over her shoulder to make sure no one followed them.

They entered the building, the tomb like silence adding to the ambiance of the evening. They followed Blake down the hall and to the back room where the dead slept for now. Double doors led to where the bodies were stored until burial or cremation. Blake motioned for them to follow him.

Stainless steel vaults lined the walls on two sides. Three housed the remains of the shifter's victims. Tiled floors, white washed walls and an autopsy table in the center with overhanging lights made up the rest of the room. The air gave off a pungent smell similar to rotting pickles. "I'll never get used to the smell of formaldehyde," she murmured.

Blake looked back at her with a nod. "Not exactly a fragrance to be bottled, is it?" His hand reached for the light switch, illuminating the room.

Michaela hung back for a moment, swallowing hard. No laughter, no murmuring of voices, no rustling of clothes—cold and still—as if time held its breath, denying life the substance to continue on. Trying to shrug off her morbid thoughts, she walked over to join Alan and Blake.

Blake stood in front of the third vault on the left. Undoing the latch, he slid the slab out. The body lay covered by a thin blue sheet. His gaze met Michaela's then Alan's. "Are you both ready?"

Michaela squeezed Alan's hand and nodded her head.

Alan gave a curt nod of his own.

Blake pulled the sheet back and Michaela couldn't quite hold back a gasp. Over the years, she'd seen plenty of dead bodies working at the hospital, but never one mutilated. Hideous bite marks ravaged the body. Nose, cheek and one eye were missing, but Kait's long blonde hair remained attached to the scalp.

"Do you recognize the bite wounds?" Blake asked.

"Animal no' human." Alan inhaled deeply, ignoring the smell of formaldehyde and death. He wanted another scent. A preternatural being had a signature scent unique to the species.

Werewolves were more earthy like fresh overturned dirt and plants. Vampires were iron based and a sea witches' scent was sea salt topped with a little charged oxygen. This preternatural being smelled liked crushed heather and peat.

Would he be able to smell these scents when the shifter took his human form? Possibly. Hopefully.

That's why he wanted to see the bodies. He needed a scent to track him. He nodded to Blake that he was finished. Blake went to the center of the room to open the other drawer.

The college student wasn't ravaged as severely as Kait had been. It was as if Kait's killing had been personal. Steve Corbin had been killed quickly, his death more of a statement. He most likely hadn't been the shifter's first choice as a victim. It was unfortunate for Steve that he'd crossed the shifter's path.

"I'll see the next one."

Blake nodded and opened the adjacent crypt, which held Troy Ackman. "This guy didn't die easily. He fought. There's defensive wounds on his forearms and legs as if he tried to kick and hit whatever attacked him."

"Oh God." Michaela covered her mouth. "How could anyone be so cruel?"

"No' anyone," Alan said. "The shape shifter has lost his hold on humanity. He likes the sport of the kill, craves it." He leaned in close, noticing the different sizes and tears of the bite marks left behind. The shifter had used different shapes to kill Troy. Played with him, torturing him until shock or loss of blood killed him. However, the same scent lingered on Troy as it did on the other two victims.

"Seen enough?" Blake asked.

"Aye."

"If you don't mind me asking, what did you expect to find here?" Blake slid the slab into the vault and closed the metal door, the latch catching with a click.

"The shifter's signature scent. If I cannae catch him in his beastly state, I'm hopin' to catch him in his human form. If he doesnae mask his scent in some way, it will be like a callin' card."

"And if you do find him, what then?"

"The authorities can't hold him," Michaela stated. "He has to be eliminated."

Alan nodded. "He's beyond savin'. If we let him go, he'll only go somewhere else and kill again."

"I'm assuming this shape shifter or whatever it is," Blake said, "won't combust into dust and disappear. You know like vampires do."

Alan at first didn't know what he meant, but then he realized he referred to the film and television version of vampires disappearing in a cloud of dust once killed. "No. For yer information, vampires doonae combust into dust either. It's a bloody mess when one is killed."

"Good to know. I'll keep that stored for future reference." He didn't try to hide the sarcasm. "What are you going to do with the body?" He shook his head. "I can't believe I just asked that, but by letting you in here, you've made me an accessory to whatever you have planned. I would like to know what that entails."

Alan gave him a wry smile. "The loch is deep. No one will find his body."

"They found Kait's," Michaela reminded him.

"Nay. The shifter wanted us to find her. He wanted us to find all of them."

"What's the motive for all this?" Blake waved his hands. "I mean why kill tourists and neighbors?"

"We knew the victims," Michaela said.

"Aye, Hyatt and I had contact with all three victims days before they were murdered and the shifter knew aboot it. He's made a statement that Drumnadrochit is his."

"Are you saying the shifter is making a territorial statement?" Blake leveled his gaze on Alan.

"It's exactly what it is."

"Good God. Animals claim their territory, fighting what they deem a threat," Blake's sarcasm bit through with his words. "If what you say is true, the shape shifter has embraced his animal side to a lethal degree."

"He's warnin' the competition," Alan said grimly. "He doesnae want us here. He's decided the loch is his and is strikin' people we know to get his point across."

Michaela's gaze wavered to the second vault they looked at. "Steve Corbin was just a tourist, passing through."

"Aye, but he shared a drink with us at Fiddler's Luck and was right friendly with all of us."

"Then the shifter could go after Michaela," Blake stated what they already knew.

Alan's back stiffened and a low growl rumbled in his chest as he remembered the shifter's attempt to kidnap her.

"What the hell was that noise?" Blake's eyes narrowed as he stared at Alan in disbelief.

Michaela placed a hand on Alan's forearm. "It's okay."

"What's okay?" Blake demanded.

"The shifter went after me, but—"

"Christ, Michaela." Blake ran his hand through his hair. "You say it like it's no big deal. Didn't you just witness what the shifter can do to you if given the chance?"

"I'll protect her," Alan defended.

"Really? Do you plan on sticking by her every second of the day?"

Alan didn't care for the way Blake questioned his ability to protect Michaela, but he did have a valid point. The shape shifter watched them. He'd wait for the right opportunity to strike. "She's no' stayin' at the cottage by herself. She'll stay by my side." Not exactly a strong argument for her safety.

Blake's gaze shifted to Michaela. "You need to take the first flight out of here until this is finished."

"No, I don't. I won't go home." She held on tighter to Alan's arm. "Besides I can't leave."

"Why not?" Blake's voice rose in disbelief.

"The sheriff told me I couldn't. If I leave, I'll be arrested."

Blake opened his mouth to protest further, but stopped when a distinct opening and closing of a door could be heard from the other room. Lights flared bright through the frosted window on the swinging doors, warning them that someone had joined them.

Blake swore under his breath.

Chapter Forty-Three

The doors flew open to the back room and Sheriff Comyn barged in. The sheriff stood large and menacing with his dark red hair glimmering like fire.

"Wha' are ye doin' here?" Comyn demanded, his Scottish brogue thick and with dropped letters, his hand on the hilt of his gun.

Blake's hand flew to his chest in mock surprise. His heart thudded against his ribcage portraying his worry, but thank God no one could hear it. "Sheriff, you startled me. I didn't think anyone would be here tonight."

"Ye dinnae answer my question." Comyn didn't relax his stance.

Before he could answer him, a noise from the other room silenced them both. Comyn drew his gun. Still keeping his eye on Blake, he stood behind the door.

Another police officer strode in and jumped back at the sight of Comyn's drawn gun.

"Sheriff?" The officer raised his hands.

"Wiley, wha' the hell are ye doin' here?" He holstered his gun.

"The silent alarm went off and I came by to investigate. What are ye doin' here?"

"The same thing apparently." They both turned to eye Blake.

Wiley's speech was more refined, a Scottish dialect easier to understand, if one wasn't accustomed to the accent. He was smaller in stature, his hair a dark brown, but his eyes narrowed, giving

Blake the impression the officer would be just as lethal as the sheriff if provoked.

"Ye better start talkin' and fast," the sheriff warned.

"I'm sorry, I should have introduced myself. I'm Dr. Blake Stuart. I'm one of the examiners on the case." He withdrew his identification and handed it to the sheriff.

"Oh aye," Wiley nodded, relaxing his shoulders, his grim expression softening. "I gave ye the list earlier today, Sheriff of who was workin' on the case. I recall Dr. Miller mentionin' a Yank would be joinin' her team."

The sheriff removed his hand from his gun, but it didn't mean he wouldn't be tempted to use it if he saw the need. His gaze took in the room with suspicion. "Are ye workin' here alone tonight?" His eyes narrowed in on him again.

It probably didn't help that he was wearing casual attire that didn't quite fit him. Alan was taller and broader in the shoulders. He should have donned a lab coat before the sheriff charged in so he at least looked somewhat professional. He resisted the urge to pull at his collar. The constriction at his throat had nothing to do with the fit of his T-shirt. He cleared his throat in an attempt to keep his voice from revealing his apprehension. "I was just finishing up. You know how paperwork can be."

The sheriff didn't look like he actually believed Blake, but there was no evidence to prove differently. "The silent alarm went off and when I drove by I saw the lights. Ye have to be careful when ye disarm the alarm." He handed Blake back his credentials.

Blake frowned. This room didn't have windows facing the parking lot and they were careful not to leave any lights on as they came in. Come to think of it, he'd locked the door behind them. Did the sheriff possess a key due to the investigation?

"Ye really should lock the door when ye come in alone," Wiley offered his advice, too.

"I thought I did," Blake told him honestly.

"The lock can be tricky." Sheriff Comyn said. "Tends to stick a wee bit. If ye're all right here, we'll leave ye to yer work then."

"Sure, I'm fine. I'll walk you out and lock the door. My heart couldn't take another surprise visit," he joked to lighten the mood. The sheriff didn't crack a smile, but Wiley chuckled behind his fist.

Blake opened the door for Comyn and Wiley. He hovered in the doorway and waited until the sheriff and the officer pulled out of the parking lot. Once he was sure they were gone, he let out the breath he'd been holding. "Too close." He secured the door and hurried back to the autopsy room.

He unlatched the bottom vault and slid out the drawer. Alan and Michaela lay huddle together on the cold slab, their eyes wide with worry. "They're gone," he told them.

Alan's long legs swung over the edge with ease. On his feet, he offered his hand to Michaela to help her up. "Ye're hand is like ice." He drew her near, folding his arms around her to warm her. She put her hands beneath his jacket.

"I don't like it." Blake shook his head, drawing their attention with frowns lining their faces. "It's not you two." He waved his hand at them. "The police showing up here. The sheriff claimed the front door was open. I know it wasn't. I distinctively remember turning off the alarm and I know I turned the latch to lock the door before we headed back here."

Alan nodded. "I was thinkin' along the same lines. Either the sheriff is lyin' and has a key or someone followed us here to find out what we were doin'."

"But how would the alarm be tripped?" Michaela's eyebrows furrowed as she let out a breath in frustration. She moved away from Alan, assuring him she was fine. "What if someone was already here? Maybe it wasn't someone following us, but someone who was already here checking out the bodies. Maybe we arrived before he could make his exit."

"Did anythin' look out of place?" Alan questioned Blake. "Would ye notice if someone tampered with the bodies?"

"I'm not sure, but I wasn't looking for tampering." Blake strode past Alan and opened Kait's drawer first. He grabbed gloves from the back counter, looking for signs that something was missing or that someone had tampered with the remains.

It wasn't like they could do anymore damage to the poor woman with the way she'd been ravaged. If not for the long strands of hair and few noticeable body parts, it proved difficult to believe the body was once a vibrant woman with her whole life ahead of her. "Nothing."

He closed the door, going to the tourist's vault next. It was the same as the other—nothing. One more. He pulled out Troy's drawer. He was ready to dismiss there'd been any tampering when something white and thin trapped between Troys' fingers caught his eyes. "I think I found something."

He turned the hand over to reveal a folded piece of paper shoved between the middle and forefinger. He pulled it out and unfolded it. Cold dread whitened Michaela's face as he read the words. "I'll win," He handed the paper to Alan.

"He knew," Michaela rubbed her hand over her mouth. "The shape shifter knew we'd come here."

Chapter Forty-Four

Blake dropped them off at the house and headed back to his hotel with the promise to keep them informed about any new developments in the case.

Alan watched Michaela pace the living room as she fought off the nervous energy. She finally stopped in front of the fireplace, staring up at the blue-velvet Elvis portrait. Alan was glad it survived the time with no ill effects, not because the portrait was a fine piece of art, but because it had been a gift from Ethan.

He'd been only five or six at the time. Despite the seriousness of the evening, his lips curved at the memory of the boy presenting it to him with wide eyes and a big grin.

"We don't know who the shifter is," Michaela's voice brought him out of his reverie. "You only have a scent. How in the world are you going to find him? Are you going to go door to door to sniff the culprit out?"

"No," he said slowly. "I know it isnae much to go on, but it's all we have right now."

She turned to look at him. God, she was beautiful, standing there with the firelight haloing her reddish locks. Every part of him wanted to protect her, lock her away so the shape shifter couldn't find her. The other part of him wanted to make love to her and forget the troubles that awaited them outside the front door.

However, reality forced him to take a stand. Hiding wouldn't save them, only prolong the final confrontation.

"Do you have any idea at all who it could be? Any inkling?"

He shook his head. "Come here." He opened his arms to her and she came willingly into his embrace.

As the front door open, Alan looked up.

"Are ye decent?" Hyatt announced as he walked into the living room followed by Elvis trotting behind him and Priscilla darting toward the kitchen.

It was a good thing they were. Michaela moved away from Alan, folding her arms across her chest.

Alan met his brother's gaze. Hyatt gave a slight nod. Good, he managed to snoop around Blake's room without incident.

"Did ye go by the pub?" Alan asked, wondering if his brother had found out anything of importance on his first night out as a sleuth.

"Oh aye. I sat there, sharin' a pint or two with Damon's girlfriend. She cried and sniffled most of the time. She dinnae go home with him the night he disappeared. She left hours before closin'."

"It's as I figured. Damon and his pals were the last to leave."

Hyatt nodded. "The usual blokes were there tonight. After I left, I watched the place from afar to see if anyone looked suspicious or appeared to want to follow someone home." He shook his head. "No' a soul looked even a wee bit dubious. They were rightly bladdered, but that goes without sayin'. As soon as George locked up for the night, I headed back here." Hyatt plopped himself down on the sofa, kicking his feet up and resting them on the coffee table. "And was yer night as eventful as mine?"

"No' overly helpful. I have the shifter's scent, but ye know how easy that will be to find. Oh and the shifter decided to leave us a message with one of the dead."

Hyatt frowned, his brows narrowing over the bridge of his nose. "How did he know ye'd end up at the morgue?"

Alan shrugged. "A guess possibly."

"Or he's watching us," Michaela's expression filled with uneasy worry as she chewed on her bottom lip.

Alan didn't blame her. The shifter had come after her and there was a good possibility, he'd try it again.

"What did the bastard have to tell us?" Hyatt rubbed his nose with the back of his hand.

"He believes he'll win." Alan told him.

"Is that so. No' bloody likely if I have a say aboot it."

Michaela sat down on the other end of the sofa. Priscilla decided her lap looked comfortable and after a proper kneading, settled down to sleep. Michaela yawned, stifling the effect behind her hand. "Sorry, I'm a little tired, too." Her hand stroked the cat with light caresses.

She needed sleep unlike Hyatt and himself. They could get by with only few hours, but humans required at least six to eight hours to rejuvenate. "Why doonae go to bed. It's late."

"I think I'll take you up on that." She moved and Priscilla jumped from her lap. At the archway she turned back to look at him. "Will you be long?" She may be tired, but her gaze spoke of other things on her mind.

His lips curved. "No' too long."

She gave a quick nod and disappeared down the hall.

Hyatt rose from the couch and headed for the kitchen. Alan followed intent on hearing his brother's findings in Blake's hotel room.

Chapter Forty-Five

The kitchen still had the scent of spiced apples, smoked haddock and chappit tatties. A smile slid into place when Alan remembered Michaela's surprise when she found out chappit tatties were nothing more than mashed potatoes.

"What has ye grinnin' like a fool?" Hyatt smirked at him. "It wouldnae have anythin' to do with the lassie waitn' in yer bedroom, now would it?"

Alan sobered. "She means the world to me."

"Aye, I know." He sighed with resignation as he opened the cupboard above the counter for a teacup.

"So what did ye find out aboot Michaela's doctor friend?"

"Nothin' short of the man havin' a stick up his arse. Not an item out of place, mind ye." Hyatt walked over to the stove intent on heating the water in the teapot.

"I could have told ye that without ye breakin' into his room." Tea sounded good. He opened the cupboard for the mug he used for tea. He didn't like the frilly teacups that held no more than a few sips.

Hyatt harrumphed. "Oh aye, but ye wouldnae know the good doc's been here in Scotland for three days." He turned to look at his brother with a leveled look. "Doonae ye find it odd, he dinnae contact Michaela sooner?"

"Three days." Alan rubbed his chin, feeling the rough stubble. He'd shave before he joined Michaela in bed tonight. "He could have flown in and taken his time to come here." *But Blake had seemed anxious to be with Michaela. Why would he wait to be reunited?*

The teapot whistled and Hyatt removed the pot. Taking the teabag from the box, he threw one to Alan before dropping one into his cup. They only used the premade bags when it was late and didn't plan on indulging in more than one cup.

Hyatt did the honors of pouring the water. "I thought the same, but I checked with the front desk at the hotel to be sure. He checked in three days ago."

Alan could read into it if he wanted to. Blake Stuart wasn't at the top of his list as a best friend. The man still harbored feelings for Michaela, too. That alone rankled him, but he couldn't accuse him of being the shape shifter without proof.

"Do you think he's the one we're lookin' for?"

Alan lifted his shoulder in a shrug. "I doonae know. Maybe, but if he's the one, he'd need a more private place than the garden suites for his killin'. I think the personnel would frown upon screamin' and blood soaked sheets. Besides, I dinnae detect the shifter's scent on him."

"As ye said, he could have masked it easily enough. Especially if he suspected ye would be lookin' for it. And it wouldnae take much to find a secluded place in Drumnadrochit."

"He'd have to know the area. It would be a lot to learn in few day's time."

"Aye, but no' impossible."

Alan nodded and sipped his tea. It went down warm and smooth, a perfect blend of spices. "Let's find out little more aboot the doctor, shall we? He claimed he worked on another case similar to this one in the States."

Hyatt lifted his brows. "In the States?"

"We know of other sightin's in Ireland, too. Why not in the states as weel? Scotland cannae be the only one who had a *well* designed by the gods, aye?"

Hyatt rolled his eyes. "Where is this place? We can look it up on the Internet and go from there."

"Exactly what I was thinkin'. I do love this century and its conveniences."

They took their cups and headed to the study with Elvis and Priscilla following close behind. Alan sat behind the desk and Hyatt leaned over him to view the monitor. Priscilla situated herself at the end of the desk and proceeded to lick her paws, while Elvis circled three times before settling down at Alan's feet.

Alan typed in Lake Champlain. The famous photo taken by *Sandi Mansi* in 1977 appeared on the screen.

"Looks like a cousin," Hyatt snickered.

"Sightin's have been noted back to the Abenaqi Indians and *Samuel de Champlain* in 1609 noted his own sightin' of a twenty foot serpent with a horse-shape head." He calculated the feet into meters. "Could be a relation to us. The size is close."

"But what does this have to do with Blake Stuart?"

Alan typed in the Blake's name in association with the aquatic beast. An article from a local newspaper stated the doctor's involvement as being the expert pathologist. "A woman and three men were found mutilated. The killin's were pinned to a man named Howard Benson Hawkins, but the bodies mysteriously disappeared before the man was brought to trial."

"What happened to Hawkins?" Hyatt asked.

Alan scrolled down, skimming the article. "Committed suicide."

"Rather convenient."

"Oh aye. The shape shifter had to clean up any loose ends." Alan turned to look at his brother as he speculated what the shifter would do. "The woman." Alan looked at the screen again. "What if the woman were the shifter's mate? And he retaliated against the men for killin' her."

"Maybe, but why would the shifter relocate here?"

Alan looked at Hyatt again. "If Blake's our shape shifter, he's here because of Michaela. He met her while workin' in Lake Champlain. If he's the shifter, he may have set his eyes on her to start over."

"And ye stole his intended mate." Hyatt nodded. "He's makin' an example of ye then."

Alan pursed his lips together. He discussed the possibility with Michaela that the shifter was from his past. If that were true, this scenario didn't mesh. As much as he'd like to pin the deaths on Blake, he didn't have enough evidence. "I doonae know. We need to tread lightly here and make sure we have all the facts. Blake could be the shape shifter or his bein' here could be purely what he claims. We cannae react without more proof."

"We know the shifter is after Michaela. I say we use her for bait."

Alan felt anger burn his flesh in a rush of adrenaline. "We will no' put Michaela in danger."

Hyatt wisely took a step back. "We'll be there to capture him. We wouldnae let him take her."

"I willnae take a chance with her life. We'll think of another way."

"Why doonae we ask Michaela," Hyatt pushed.

"No, I say." Alan slammed his fist on the desk. Elvis whined at his feet, but he ignored him. "I want her protected. I'll no' let the bastard touch her. He came too close in takin' her today. I'll no' allow it again. We think of another way. Do you hear me, Hyatt?"

Hyatt gave a slow nod, but the tick at his jaw indicated he wasn't pleased in complying.

Alan rose from his seat. "I'm goin' to bed. Ye

should do the same."

"In a wee bit." He slid into the seat Alan vacated. "I want to do more research on my own."

Elvis looked up as if debating if he wanted to follow Alan, but Hyatt reached down and patted his head. "Good, laddie. Stay with me. Alan needs some time alone with his bonny lassie."

Elvis thumped his tail, before lying back down. Priscilla perched herself on the desk, straining her neck to check out the computer screen.

Alan left his brother to tend to the pets and he headed for his room and to Michaela.

He closed the bedroom door behind him with a soft click. Leaving his clothes on the floor to deal with in the morning, he slipped beneath the sheets. Michaela instinctively sought his warmth. He cradled her near, spooning against her. She adjusted her curves to fit the hard plane of his body, her round sweet behind pressed against his groin.

Sweet heavens, he wanted her, needed to feel her flesh against his without the hindering clothes, but he didn't want to wake her. It'd been a long day for her physically and mentally. She accepted his true self. Even claimed the beastie was beautiful.

Ach, she needs her eyes checked. He suppressed a chuckle. *Fearsome, hideously large, powerful, aye... No' beautiful, my luv.* He pressed his lips against the top of her head, the scent of her hair a pleasant aroma of lavender, heather and sunshine filled his senses. *"Tha gao agam ort."* He did love her, all of her, his sweet bonny lassie.

"Mmm..." She stirred in his arms, turning to face him. Her eyelids fluttered open and her heated gaze met his. Her lips parted, proving too much of a temptation to ignore. He captured her mouth, gently sucking her lower lip. His hand slid under her T-shirt, feeling her soft skin. She moaned in pleasure and he sealed his lips over hers, taking possession of her mouth.

Fully awake now, she responded in kind, kissing him back. Her hands slid beneath the covers, her hands claiming him in a warm caress and igniting the hunger to take her.

Her lips dragged to the corner of his mouth. "I want you." Her voice was thick and husky with need.

He wanted her, too. Now and forever.

His hands made short work of removing the hindering clothes. Naked, her body hummed beneath his touch. His fingers dipped into her womanly heat with a caress and used her own dampness to stroke her. Her arousal blended with her other scents, a fragrance meant for him and him only.

Her hand grasped his forearm. "Now, Alan." Her gaze flickered to his and his heart picked up a beat.

He moved above her, fitting himself snugly between the vee of her thighs and sheathing himself in one swift move. Her gasp, a sigh of pleasure slid across his senses.

She wrapped her legs around him, bringing him deeper inside of her. Spurned by need, he moved faster, her passion equaling his own. Her heels dug into his back and her hands gripped his shoulders. Sweat glistened her brow and the sweet scent of her skin drove him to possess her with each sensuous thrust. "I love ye, Michaela."

"I love you, too." The words fell from her lips with heartfelt truth. Her hands gripped him tighter as her body took flight and he followed close behind, sharing the rapture.

He dropped a feather light kiss on her forehead and rolled to the side, bringing her with him and cradling her against his chest. He loved the feel of her lustrous strands, sliding through his fingers like a cascade of silk. *I love you.* Her words lingered in his mind. He'd known she did, but to hear the words left an imprint on his heart.

Chapter Forty-Six

While Alan headed for the kitchen to prepare breakfast, Michaela sat in the small room meant to be a study with its two bookcases cluttered with novels and other books of interests. The rugged décor included paintings of hunting lodges and landscapes of the Scottish moors. One framed window with shutters pulled back allowed natural light to seep in with a warm glow.

She turned her attention back to the computer screen and concentrated on searching for the article about Mary McGregor. Alan wanted to read it and see if anything stood out as a clue to finding the shifter. It was a long shot, but worth a try. "There it is." Her finger clicked the mouse and bookmarked the link.

Priscilla jumped onto the desk with a meow.

"Well, hello to you, too." She ran her hand down the length of her sleek black coat. Priscilla answered her with a motorboat purr. It was strange to contemplate that Alan was both the Loch Ness Monster and a man. As the beast, he could devour a little kitty as a snack, but he didn't. He held onto his human side and had pets and owned a house.

Alan had lived centuries, had a life—no, countless lives before he met her. The earliest sightings of the creature dated back as early as the sixth century. Of course it was only reasonable to believe some of the sightings weren't Hyatt and Alan, but simply the way the sun hit the water or the wake of the waves rolling and giving the appearance that a creature had surfaced.

"Alan is an old being, Priscilla," she said to the cat.

Priscilla stared at her with her gold-green eyes and meowed in agreement.

Alan had seen so many changes, the land, the people, wars and bloodshed. *I've had many names*, he told her. He'd seen Urquhart Castle in its splendor. "The tale about Deidre of the Sorrows," she murmured. She realized he wasn't sharing a legend with her, but a story he knew first hand. *Warrior. Husband. Lover.* "He's been all three. He became the man that time demanded."

"Awright?" Hyatt knocked on the open door before entering the room.

She turned in her seat to greet him. "I'm doing fine. You're back from your walk already?" Elvis pushed his way in, his tail wagging. He obviously enjoyed his outing. He nudged her hand, demanding a little attention. She chuckled as she scratched behind his ears.

"He fancies ye. Ye know that, dooncha?"

"I'm fond of Elvis, too."

"Elvis...oh aye him as weel." He cleared his throat. "I mean my brother."

She looked at him, his blue-green eyes studying her, waiting for her to declare her feelings. She should be annoyed at his prying, but found she wasn't in the least.

Hyatt and Alan were close, not just brothers but friends as well. They knew they could count on each other *time* and *time* again. Hyatt didn't want her to hurt his brother. She could respect that. "Alan is special to me, too." She smiled and his lips curved in response.

His gaze wavered to the computer screen. "Doonae believe all they say aboot the sightin's. Some are greatly exaggerated."

"I'm sure some stories are, but what of the

others?" she teased.

His rich chuckle rumbled from his chest. "Oh weel, I'll leave it to ye to weed out the true tales. If ye're ready, Alan sent me in here to escort his lady to the kitchen." He gave her a quick bow and she smiled at his gallantry.

"Good, I'm starving." She pushed back the chair and stood. "Hyatt, may I ask you something?"

"Oh aye."

"This house holds all of Alan's interests. What about you?" She craned her neck to look at him. Alan was tall, but Hyatt stood a few inches taller than his brother did.

He glanced at her with a shrug. "Alan has always embraced his human side, wantin' to hold onto it as long as possible. I learned early on to let it go, no' to become attached."

She shook her head. "I'm sorry."

"For what? I love the water and doonae fret aboot returnin' to it. There is always another adventure waitin' for me in the next life. A clean slate, too."

Michaela refrained from saying she thought the life lonely, but perhaps distancing himself made it easier to say goodbye when he had to leave.

In the kitchen, Michaela took a seat. The table was made of pressboard. The white lamented top had silver and gold flecks sprinkled throughout the finish. She reached for the mug Alan placed in front of her. The freshly brewed coffee lavished with cream and sugar tasted heavenly. For a moment, she closed her eyes, letting the morning rays, seeping through the large open window, warm her.

Alan finally sat down by the window and Hyatt across from her to enjoy breakfast and discuss the shifter and the possibility of who he may be.

It proved obvious the shifter watched their every move. Michaela put her mug down. "We need to make a list. If we're going with the theory that the shifter is targeting people you both knew, Steven Corbin was only with us one night, the night Kait went missing."

"Fiddler's Luck was near to full," Hyatt sighed. "It'll take some time."

Alan nodded and rose to find a pen and paper. "The lassies at the bar were Nell Miller and Ria Clark. They gave Steven Corbin the map. The Browns and the McLearys were there, too." Alan scribbled the names down.

"Ethan MacGregor, Sheriff Comyn and an officer were there. Kait had a word with him. Looked like they didn't like each other much." Michaela tapped her chin, trying to remember everyone she saw.

"Officer Jonas Wiley." Hyatt pointed to the paper. "Kait and Wiley dated, but dinnae last long. Did ye write Wiley's name down?"

Alan brushed his brother's hand away. "It's there."

"Don't forget the bartender." Michaela picked up a potato scone and nibbled on it. The aroma of eggs and sausage lingered in the air, tempting her with the thoughts of dishing out seconds.

"George Fallon," Hyatt said and Alan wrote the bartender's name down below the other names on the paper.

The list grew longer, but it didn't mean they'd remembered everyone who frequented the pub that night.

Alan studied the list with a frown. "We can count out the lassies. We know the shape shifter is male." Alan made a line through the women's names.

"Is there anyone on the list that is new to the village?" Michaela asked. "You two reinvent yourselves every time you come back on land. If the shifter lived in the village when you did, he'd have to create a new identity, too."

Alan nodded. "There are new family names, but it doesnae mean they're shifters." He dug into his blood pudding and Michaela wrinkled her nose. The dish didn't appeal to her in the least, but Hyatt and Alan both devoured the blood sausage with gusto, licking their lips in the process.

"You've been topside for six months. It has to be someone fairly new or why wouldn't he attack sooner?"

Hyatt and Alan exchanged a quick look.

"Out with it." She leveled her gaze on both brothers.

Hyatt dug into another sausage, leaving Alan with the honor of answering her.

"Well?" she waited.

"We need to add Blake to the list."

"Blake? What for?"

"He's new here," Alan insisted.

"Why would he kill Kait or anyone else for that matter? Besides he wasn't at the pub that night."

Again the two looked at each other as if they shared a secret.

"He wasn't at the pub," she insisted.

"We're no' sure that's true," Hyatt reached for a scone and slathered it with butter. "He's been here for a few days or so his airplane ticket proved."

Michaela narrowed her eyes, suspicion creeping up on her like a foul specter. "And how do you know this?"

"Does it matter?" Alan lifted one broad shoulder in a shrug.

"Yes, it matters." Then it dawned on her how Hyatt knew. "You spied on him." Her gaze leveled accusingly on Hyatt. "That's why you weren't there when Alan revealed the beast to Blake. You broke into Blake's hotel room, didn't you?"

Hyatt cringed with a shrug. "Seemed a good idea

at the time."

She slid the chair back, the legs scraping across the floor. "You had no right."

"People have been murdered. We had the right." Alan kept his voice low and even, but there was no mistaking the anger simmering beneath the surface of his calm. His gaze held hers. "Michaela—"

"Don't." Her hand waved an accusing flip in his direction. "Don't use your calming powers on me, buster." Her chin lifted in defiance and she folded her arms across her chest. "I've known Blake for a long time. I'd know if his hobby included murdering people."

"Really, ye have the gift, then?" His voice turned deep, rough and edged with a warning. "Ye missed yer callin'. Ye shouldnae waste yer time bein' a nurse practitioner. Ye should join the police department and pick the criminals from a lineup."

Her arms flew apart and her hands fisted. "Why you pompous—"

Alan didn't let her finish, butting in with intent to be heard. "Murders seem to happen where Blake lives. The records arenae hard to find since he's always involved with the investigation."

"He's a forensic pathologist for God's sake. It's not uncommon for another county or country for that matter to call him in to look at a case."

"He's in love with ye," Hyatt pointed out.

She turned her anger on Hyatt. "He's not in love with me. He loves me, yes and there is a difference, if you think you're going to argue with me. Either way, it doesn't make him a murderer."

"Fine, a suspect then," both Alan and Hyatt said at the same time.

Michaela snatched the paper and pen from Alan.

"What are ye doin'?" Alan shifted in his seat.

"I'm writing your names down as well. Hyatt you fought with one of the murdered victims; flirted with Kait and offered Steven a drink. Alan was supposed to meet Kait at the pier. Who's to say you didn't. As for love, didn't you tell me you loved me last night?" She glared at Alan, daring him to say otherwise.

Hyatt cleared his throat behind his fist and looked away, obviously feeling uncomfortable with where the conversation had gone.

"Oh aye," Alan's voice rose. "But I dinnae try to drown ye, now did I?"

"How should I know? I saw a beast and masked man. I didn't see you at all." She slammed the pen down and leaned on the table to meet his glower head on.

"We'll look at the other suspects first, aye?" Hyatt looked to Michaela then to his brother with intent of defusing the situation.

Alan closed his eyes and inhaled. "Fine." He met her gaze again, but she could tell he hadn't let it go.

"Blake isn't the shape shifter." She wanted to hear him say it.

Alan's nose flared, but he finally gave in with a stiff nod. "If ye say so, he isnae the shape shifter."

Michaela didn't believe he'd truly dismissed Blake, but now he would focus on the other suspects. "How about we look at your old photos. I recognized you two from one. Maybe the shifter will be someone from your past." It was a long shot at best, but it couldn't hurt to check.

Alan pushed away from the table and headed to the hall where he kept the photo albums in the cabinets below the towels and blankets. Michaela took the opportunity to top off everyone's coffee cup with a warm up.

Alan returned with an armload and plopped them on the table. "We need to take care of the mass hysteria on the lake, too." He looked to his brother. "Too many are after blood and someone is bound to end up hurt. We doonae want easy pickin's for the shape shifter."

Hyatt's grim expression mirrored Alan's. "We could maybe lead the mass of would-be hunters farther down the loch and away from Drumnadrochit. Maybe another sightin' is in order." He leaned against the table as he rose to his feet. "I'll see what I can manage." He turned to go, but Alan halted him.

"Hyatt?"

His brother looked back over his shoulder.

"Doonae get caught, aye? Draw notice but doonae show off."

"Do ye think me an eejit?"

"I dinnae say ye were, but extra precaution is warranted now. The shape shifter isnae the only one after blood. There may be a hothead determined to take Nessie down himself."

Hyatt rolled his eyes. "I'll be careful." With that he turned on his heels and headed out the door.

Elvis trotted into the kitchen and Priscilla perked her ears and chirruped from her bed in the corner of the kitchen. Alan tossed Elvis the last piece of blood sausage from his plate.

Michaela turned the pages of the photo albums with interest. She was seeing a life Alan had lived before she'd been born. The hairstyles and the clothes spoke of another era and Alan had been a part of all of it. She hummed a few bars then sang one of Elvis' songs. "Is it this one, *Come on Everybody*?"

Alan looked at her with raised brows.

"Your favorite Elvis song. Come on Everybody." It felt good to lighten the moment.

His lips curved. "No, but keep tryin' ye're bound to figure it out."

"Just like we'll find the shifter."

"We'll find him. Of that I am certain."

Michaela looked back at the photos and Alan moved behind her to peer over her shoulder.

"This one here is of Mrs. O'Malley. Though she went by Shona Watson then."

Michaela looked at the little girl with long brown hair held back by a black velvet hair band. "Mrs. O'Malley. She's so young here." She looked up at him.

"While I havenae changed in fifty years." He read her thoughts.

"Yes." The photos were of his life, a witness to his past, but he'd lived through other centuries with no photographs to mark his existence.

Her hand touched a photo of Alan sitting next to a pretty dark haired woman, smiling as he looked at her. The little boy seated next to them must be Ethan. He was leaning against Alan and she could see it in the young boy's eyes how he cared for him. "You look happy. You were a family."

Alan sighed. "I cannae change my past. I had friends and lovers before I met ye." His hand caressed her cheek and she tilted her head to look at him. "Please believe me. My heart will never belong to another as long as I draw breath."

Michaela knew what his pledge meant. His life could be eternal as far as they both knew. Her hand brushed his forearm sprinkled with sun-bronzed hair. "That's an awfully long time."

"I mean it." His gaslight blue eyes burned like an eternal flame, never wavering. He did mean it.

"I believe you."

His gaze softened in relief. Alan was a powerful being capable of magnificent feats and yet he feared she might reject him. This made him vulnerable, more human. "Kiss me, Alan."

His mouth quirked into a half smile and his eyes glinted mischievously as he leaned down to obey her command.

Chapter Forty-Seven

Hyatt headed through the wooded area of pine, larch and spruce, away from the house. He chose the western shore to enter the water, wading in with his clothes on. When he shifted back to his human form they'd be dry. He didn't know how the magic worked and he hadn't been inclined to dwell on it.

The magic rolled over him, vibrating the water and scaring the three-spine sticklebacks. The bony fish only swam in the shallow areas of the loch, but now they scattered in all direction as if sensing the beast within him crying for release.

He dove under the water as the tingling ripples of current slid over his frame, transforming his bones and flesh to the gray-slicked beast. Deeper and deeper he dove into the black depths, the Arctic charr, trout and other fish staying clear, fearing he'd make them his next meal. Today, they were safe from him at least.

Divers feared being lost in the loch's murky depths, where peat particles hampered vision, but the water was his home.

He swam past the Urquhart Castle where it sat above him as a testament of how much time had gone by. Once a grand castle filled with knights and ladies, it now was a ruin with only ghosts for company.

There were only a few boats stationed there with a crew on the lookout for Nessie. This would be the perfect spot.

He swam to the surface with a splash to draw attention. Shouts and screams, told him he'd been spotted. He let them capture a few photos before he led them on a merry chase away from Drumnadrochit. Good enough. One stroke, two then he dove beneath the surface and away from the flashing camera lights.

His long and sure strokes took him to the underground cavern, located deeper than any modern instruments could detect. Eels lingered in the crevices of the rock, but even they knew to stay hidden from the beastie.

The cavern's darkness hid nothing from his preternatural eyes. Roughen walls and items of long ago stacked on the rock floor. *Pirate treasure*, Alan had called it.

The thought of the shape shifter threatening their world had his blood boiling again. *Damn wanker. We should take action soon and no' wait for the bloody bastard to make his next move.* Of course it would help if they knew what the shifter looked like in his human form.

His large beastly body rose heavy out of the water, but not awkward onto the cavern floor. His structure could move with ease in or out of the water.

He stared at the well, standing as it did centuries before, when only land surrounded the stone structure. Cursed to protect it, at first he'd resented the responsibility, but as centuries melted into the next, his resentment had eased to acceptance, then finally to duty. He endured his fate and didn't look for a soul mate. He didn't want to give this up. *"Nay, no bonny lassie would sway him, soul mate or no'."*

Alan had grown to love this life too, but there was always a part of him that clung to the human side of their existence. The house held possessions of the human world, the world Alan mourned when he had to leave it. Hyatt refused to become attached to his time on land.

Alan protected Michaela Grant and would with his life. Hyatt couldn't deny there was something special about the lassie. She made Alan smile and he hadn't seen the likes of his brother's grin in a long time. Perhaps she was his soul mate after all.

Would the gods lift Alan's curse? If they did, what would happen to Michaela? If the waters hadn't cured her, she would die soon.

He'd still have access to the well. Fifteen years on land then fifty years the beast. For a while he would be able to bring the water to the surface, but when the beast took over, there would be no way to manage it. He couldn't shift. Druid Daly made sure the curse kept them chained to the loch as a punishment. If Alan hadn't bargained with Druid Daly for a loophole to end the curse, their human side would have been forfeited.

Fifteen years was a long time for a human and perhaps a new medical procedure would be developed by then. No matter what the consequences were, he knew Alan would choose to be with Michaela as long as he could.

To love so deeply seemed like a fantasy to him.

He stared down at the water lapping at the edge of the cavern floor. It was difficult to believe he was fathoms deep when his gaze looked at the inky black water that spread out like a pond beneath the air-filled cavern.

Michaela's health was the least of their problems when the shifter threatened them all. He needed to be eliminated before he killed someone else. If anything, he would personally avenge Kait's death. She'd been a good friend.

How will we stop him? He thought. *A trap surely, but we doonae know who the bugger is.*

They couldn't monitor all the shores of the loch, but it seemed the shifter's hunting ground was on the western shore. Alan could take the areas around Urquhart Castle and Invermoriston and he'd scour the shores between Abriachan and Drumnadrochit. Still a lot of area to cover and they could miss him. He sighed which sounded more like and wheezing snort in his beastie state.

He rolled into the water with barely a splash, leaving his sanctuary behind.

Once on shore, he shifted back to his human form, dry and clothed. There were perks to being a preternatural being. This was one of them.

He took long strides through the wooded area.

Snap...

The sudden noise pricked his ears and he halted his steps to listen. Silence greeted him, as if the birds and animals had scurried away to hide.

There was a muffled sound to the right of him. Human, he thought. His brows furrowed. No one came out this way since there was no designated path. Perhaps a hiker became lost or... not. His lips curved up at the corners. Being out of the way of the normal path would provide privacy as well.

"Ah, lovers no doubt out for a afternoon shag." Even as he said this, a prickling in the back of his mind told him this wasn't the case. His smile fell away. The muffles weren't sighs of rapture, but urgent...panic stricken. With caution, he headed in the direction of the noise. The muffled sound turned to an eerie moaning.

A movement up ahead slowed his steps until he peered through the foliage. His brows rose up in surprise. "What in the hell?"

Morton Rander was tied and bound with the rope wrapped around the tree trunk. The silver duct tape plastered to his mouth encircled the tree trunk too, preventing him from moving his head in any direction. Morton eyes were wide with fear as he struggled, making incoherent noises behind the gag.

The poor bugger looked like hell with his red spiked hair greasy from not being washed. Tear stains streaked a trail down his cheeks.

The shifter just left him out here. What for? In hopes he'd perish from the elements?

"Hold on." Hyatt strode over to the spruce, hoping the rope wasn't knotted too tight. A quick look told him he could work the knots loose.

Morton's stifled cries became more frantic.

He looked at him. "For gods' sake, stop yer blubberin'. I said—" Then realization dawned on him. Morton's cries weren't for sympathy, he was warning him. He whirled around to meet the threat, but it was too late.

A flash of silver glinted in the sun as it struck his side, spearing him like a pig. He gasped in shock and horror, his hands grabbing his side as blood seeped from the wound. His mind shouted for him to shift, heal himself, but the injury slowed his reaction.

The assailant raised his hand and slammed the hilt of the sword across his skull. As blackness took over his last thoughts, he cursed at the injustice of it all. He knew who the shape shifter was and he couldn't do a bloody thing about it.

Chapter Forty-Eight

Michaela didn't like the idea of having a bodyguard at all times, but the alternative proved worse. She couldn't fend off a shape shifter and she didn't want to become the next victim.

She followed Alan into Fiddler's Luck where a crowd was already buzzing with talk about the new sighting. Hyatt hadn't returned yet, but it appeared he'd pulled off the ruse.

Blake called before they left the house and met them at the pub. Alan hid his feelings well to the rest of world, but Michaela noticed the slight frowning of his lips and the clenched teeth that caused the side of his temple to pulse in agitation. He didn't like Blake. Worse, he didn't trust him.

Blake looked tired, worn out with dark shadows beneath his eyes. He pulled out a chair and took a seat. "I'll only take up a few minutes of your time. I'm beat. I'm going to head back to the hotel for a hot shower before I hit the bed." His gaze traveled the room with a suspicious eye as if making sure no one would hear what he wanted to tell them.

The noise level was at a minimum. Strong smells of alcohol and cooked meat wafted in the air. The fire burned low in the fireplace, keeping the room at a comfortable temperature. Ethan MacGregor, Nell Miller and Ria Clark sat at the bar talking to the bartender, George Fallon.

Three families sat in a booth near the fireplace. Officer Jonas Wiley, dressed in his uniform, rose from his seat in the back corner booth and sauntered over to the bar. He placed his dark checkered hat down and stood next to Ethan.

The two women glanced at each other. They said something to Wiley before grabbing their drinks and heading to a table.

Obviously satisfied that no one sat close enough to eavesdrop, Blake leaned forward, resting his arms on the tabletop. "We finished the autopsies." He paused and inhaled deeply.

"Weel?" Alan encouraged him to get to the point.

"The wounds weren't postmortem. The shape shifter." The word stuck in his throat. "He...*it* tortured the victims, bit and slashed them up while they were still breathing."

Michaela sat back in her seat. "Christ."

"He must have some medical background to know where to cut while no' lettin' the victims die too soon, aye?" Alan asked.

Michaela narrowed her eyes, annoyed by his insinuation. His question seemed innocent enough, but she knew the reasoning behind it. No matter what Blake said, he would still be a suspect in Alan's mind.

"I thought as much, too. It would take knowing how to avoid major arteries so the person didn't bleed out."

"I see."

Blake took the bait without realizing Alan had led him into a trap, but Alan's clipped response sent out warning signals. Blake stared at him, his lips pressing together.

"The shifter gets his jollies from inflictin' pain," Alan continued, his unnerving gaze locked with Blake's.

"It would appear so." Blake sat forward not intimidated by Alan's rude behavior. "I thought you wanted an update."

"Oh aye, I did."

"Then what's your problem?" He pushed the

chair back and stood.

Michaela decided to intervene. She reached for Blake's hand. She could feel Alan's eyes on her, burning a path down her arm to where her hand rested. She gave Blake's hand a quick squeeze of affection anyway. "Thank you, Blake for sharing the information with us." Michaela didn't see how it would help them. They already knew the shifter didn't value human life.

"Stay safe, Michaela." Blake tempted fate further and leaned down and kissed her cheek.

Fury rose off Alan like an electrical vibration, but she didn't face him until Blake walked out the door.

"What was that all about?" He wasn't the only one who was pissed.

His shoulder lifted in a nonchalant shrug. "I only asked a few harmless questions."

"There is nothing harmless about you."

"Bugger that. I only spoke the truth. Blake agreed with the observation. The shifter has medical trainin'."

"Or he's a sick bastard who Googled or bought books to perfect his hobby involving torturing humans."

It was obvious by the way his jaw pulsed that he wanted to say more, but he clenched his teeth to hold back the retort.

She inhaled deeply. "Pick and choose your fights wisely," she muttered.

"What does that mean?"

"My mother always told me to pick my fights wisely." Her gaze met his. "I don't want to fight with you."

His posture relaxed and his hand touched her shoulder in a caress. "I doonae want to fight with ye either. I question everyone...and I mean everyone. I doonae want to miss a clue that will help me find the shifter. Yer life…everyone's life here in Drumnadrochit is in danger."

"I doonae care wha' ye do!" Ethan's loud clamoring drew their attention toward the bar.

Officer Wiley grabbed his arm.

"Let go." Ethan glared in unbridled defiance.

"Ethan, ye either go with me quietly or I'll be forced to handcuff ye."

"Go with him, Ethan," George encouraged. "Sleep it off and ye'll have a spot on the stool come tomorrow, aye?"

Ethan hesitated but then gave in with a harrumph. "Wait." He yanked free from Wiley's hold. His hand reached for his mug. Raising it to his lips, he downed the contents in one gulp. He slammed the mug down and wiped his face with the back of his hand. "Now I'll go." He teetered on his feet, but Officer Wiley steadied him.

"No more investigatin' either," he told him as he led him to the door. "Ye leave that to the authorities."

"Doonae know why I should. Ye havenae found my grandson."

"We're workin' on it."

Their voices faded away as they turned the corner of the pub. Michaela looked at Alan who stared at the empty doorway. His fingers rubbed the rough stubble on his chin.

"What's wrong?"

He turned to look at her. "Ethan's been askin' questions. George usually puts up with a lot from the auld man. Why encourage Wiley to haul him away?"

"We couldn't hear everything. Ethan can be…"

"…abrupt," Alan finished.

"Yes." She glanced at her watch and realized the morning had slipped into the afternoon. "Shouldn't Hyatt be back by now?"

Alan's brows furrowed, thinking the same thing. "Aye."

"He couldn't be...I mean he'd be careful not to be caught."

"Harrumph," the Scottish snort followed. "If he'd been caught, Fiddler's Luck would be buzzin' with the news. Let's take *The Hound Dog* out for a quick look for ourselves."

Chapter Forty-Nine

The farther Alan maneuvered the boat from land, the more the wind slashed and shoved to be noticed. Alan didn't need a jacket, but he knew Michaela did. She zipped her windbreaker to her chin then shoved her hands into her pockets. She wore a turtleneck sweater and jeans. Clothing covered her, but Alan would bet her skin had goose bumps. "There's a blanket down below if ye want it," he called over the wind.

She brushed her hair behind her ear and smiled. "Thank goodness." She sighed in relief and headed down below. A few minutes later she emerged with a plaid blanket draped around her like a cape.

He glanced at her with a smile. "Better, aye?"

"Much."

He maneuvered *The Hound Dog* a distance away from the other watercrafts on the loch and shut the engines down.

"What exactly do you plan on doing?" she asked.

"I'm goin' down below to the cavern. Just for a look."

"You don't really think Hyatt would stay down there this long, do you?"

Alan lifted a shoulder and brushed his windblown hair back away from his eyes. "I can imagine him lingerin' for a wee bit, but no. I just want to see if he's been there. Gives a startin' point." He thought he hid his worry, but obviously not well enough. He leaned forward and kissed the top of her head. "I'll no' be long, I promise." His hands gripped the side of the boat before swinging over the edge and diving into the water.

His body shifted with ease. He looked up to see Michaela leaning over the railing, looking for him. The water made the Hound Dog sway up and down over the swells. He was too deep for her vision to detect his movements in the peat-laden waters. "Be careful," her whisper reached him. Oh, he'd be careful. He didn't know what waited for him below the depths. Hyatt hadn't returned and he didn't know if the shifter had anything to do with it.

Fish scattered as he dove deeper and deeper. He missed his swim this morning and relished in the way the water rushed over his body in waves. As he neared the cave, the eels scurried back inside their hidey-holes; their eyes glowed, watching his every move.

In the pool area of the cave, he lingered below the surface of the water to survey what awaited him. Nothing looked disturbed. No one lurked in the shadows and Hyatt wasn't there either. He surfaced and rose out of the water, shifting as he did so. His hand touched the well, checking to see that the lid remained sealed. The treasures lining the walls remained untouched.

He inhaled deeply. The shifter hadn't been here, but his brother had, his scent still strong in the air. "Where did ye go, Hyatt?" Hopefully, they'd passed him in their search and he now waited at Fiddler's Luck for them.

His gaze lingered over the mementos his brother and he had collected over the centuries. There was one item in particular he looked for as he rearranged the cups, bottles and jewelry.

Nothing rusted or changed color in this room, keeping the items preserved as new. His hand closed over the bronze cuff he crafted centuries before. The spiral curves were delicately intertwined and would sit light on Michaela's wrist. He pocketed the bracelet. Not wanting to leave Michaela alone any longer up top, he shifted and dove below the water.

Coming near the surface, his ears picked up male voices. He swam below *The Hound Dog* to find Sheriff Comyn's official police watercraft beside his boat. Smaller in structure, it sat lower than *The Hound Dog*.

"Where are Alan and Hyatt?" the sheriff asked.

Officer Wiley leaned over the boat. For a second, Alan thought the officer spied him, but he knew that was impossible. The skin of the beastie blended with the dark water and he floated too deep for him to detect any movement. Wiley shifted his gaze back to Michaela. "Do ye need any help? Ye look a bit nervous."

Alan didn't need Sheriff Comyn and Officer Wiley nosing around. He dived under his boat again, coming up on the other side where the sheriff and the officer wouldn't be able to see him. He reached for the ladder and shifted, his grip tightening as he did so. He pulled himself over the railing. Michaela had seen him. He pressed his finger to his lips, not to let on he was behind her. Then he pointed for her to move to the left, hoping she'd block his movements as he dove below deck.

With ease, Michaela shifted her position, stretching her arms to the side and pretending to adjust her blanket around her. *Smart lassie. It was a perfect cover.*

"I'm fine, really. I'm not sure where Hyatt is, but Alan is down below. Do you want me to get him?"

"Get me for what?" Alan popped his head up.

She turned to smile at him. "Alan, the sheriff was concerned we were floating adrift."

Alan came fully up on deck, wiping his hand on a greasy towel. "Good day, Sheriff. Officer Wiley. I believe I've fixed the problem. *The Hound Dog* should start right up."

"Good." The sheriff nodded. He removed his hat and brushed back his hair before placing the hat back on his head. "We've had another sightin' I doonae want anyone stranded on the loch."

"We understand," Alan told him. "We were headin' back anyway. Michaela's a bit chilled."

"See tha' ye do then." The sheriff moved to the front of his boat, while Wiley took a seat in the back. Wiley tipped his hat at them before the sheriff turned the watercraft around.

Michaela let out a breath and sagged against him. "I didn't know what to say when they pulled up beside us. I couldn't tell them I drove the boat out here by myself."

"Ye did fine. I doonae think they suspected anythin'." His hands encircled her, bringing her close, his fingers messaging the tight muscles of her back.

His gaze followed the sheriff's watercraft, growing smaller by the seconds. When they searched the Internet earlier, they discovered a grandfather of Sheriff Comyn lived here years ago—a red head, too.

Family genes sure, but what if Comyn came back to the village and reinvented himself as the grandson and in truth they were one in the same? Michaela had the right idea. He knew all about creating a new identity and so would the shifter.

"Ah, that feels wonderful," Michaela sighed with pleasure finally relaxing under his fingertips. "Was there any sign of Hyatt in the cave?"

"He was there, but he left a while ago."

When she turned to look at him with raised brows, he clarified how he knew of Hyatt's visit with a tap of his nose. "His scent."

She nodded with understanding.

"We'll bring *The Hound Dog* back to the dock and have a look at the house. If he's no' there, we'll check out Fiddler's Luck again."

She looked up at him. "I've been thinking about what Mrs. O'Malley told me. You know about your sister's descendents welcoming you and your brother when you return to land. Does Mrs. O'Malley have children?"

"This is what ye were thinkin' aboot while I was down below?"

Her eyes met his, a deep green, shadowed with worry. "Well, if she didn't have children, who will meet you the next time around?"

He sighed with a smile. "I'm hopin' I willnae have to worry over much aboot it."

"Because you believe the curse will be broken, but what about Hyatt?"

His thoughts had dwelled on his brother, too. "Mrs. O'Malley has three children. Her two daughters live in Edinburgh and her son lives in London. No matter what happens, ye need no' worry aboot us." He leaned forward and kissed the tip of her nose. "I have somethin' for ye."

"You do?" She stepped away to look up at him. "Please tell me you didn't wrap up an eel dinner to go," she teased, her laughter music to his ears.

"No." His hand slid into his pocket. "I brought ye a trinket." He held up the bronze cuff for her to see.

Her hand flew to her chest, her face lighting up brighter than a sunrise. "Oh my, Alan it's beautiful."

"I was hopin' ye'd like it." He took her hand and placed the cuff around her wrist.

Her fingers traced the spiral etchings. "Where did you come across this on your journey below? Don't tell me there's a market of mere-folk selling their wares."

"Ye do have an imagination, luv. I have a few items in the cave for safe keepin'. I made the wee bracelet a long time ago, but I never had anyone to give it to."

Her gaze met his. Her moss colored eyes

misting. "I love it. Thank you." She threw herself at him, hugging him before her lips sought his.

His hands went around her in a hug, loving her more each time he did so.

"We should head back. Maybe see if we can have a word with Ethan."

She left his embrace, her brows arched in question. "Do you really think he knows something?"

"There's one way to find out."

Chapter Fifty

There was no sign of Hyatt back at the house or Fiddler's Luck. "Hyatt can take care of himself," Alan claimed, but Michaela didn't miss the subtle signs he was worried. His gaze swept the pub as if he hoped his brother would materialize from the shadows. They may be preternatural beings and more difficult to kill, but they weren't invincible.

They left the warmth of the pub and made their way to the sheriff's office. "Where are Damon Nokes' parents?"

He glanced at her but didn't miss a stride. "They died in a car accident when Damon was no more than four or five. Mrs. O'Malley told me." He shrugged. "Ethan only had one daughter."

"Damon is all he has then."

"Aye." He held open the door for her and she entered the office.

Officer Wiley looked up from his desk, surprise lighting his features. "May I help ye?" He stood, his gaze flickering to her before centering on Alan.

"When will Sheriff Comyn be back? We'd liked to have a word with Ethan MacGregor," Alan told him.

Alan stood a good four inches taller than Wiley with broad shoulders and muscled limbs. Wiley was short in comparison but wiry strength could be deceiving. Michaela had a hunch Wiley could hold his own in a fight. His stance looked military with his feet apart and his arms crossed over his chest.

"He dinnae say when he was returnin'."

"Would ye mind then?" Alan thought it wouldn't hurt to ask.

"Ethan's a might bladdered at the moment. Doonae know how much sense ye'll get out of him."

"Oh aye, but he's that way much of the time." Alan smiled but the grin didn't reach his eyes.

Officer Wiley debated for a few heartbeats, but then nodded his consent. "I suppose it would do no harm, but doonae rattle him into a tizzy."

"Of course no'."

Officer Wiley stood aside with a wave of his hand. "Take the door there. He's in the second cell. Says it's roomier and no' as drafty."

"Thank ye."

The older man looked defeated sitting on the cot with his head resting in his hands.

"Ethan?" Alan kept his voice controlled.

The older man lifted his head, squinting his eyes in their direction. "Wha' do ye want?" his bitterness spilled into his words as well as his frown.

"We want to help ye."

"Oh ye helped me all right. My grandson is missin' and the sheriff and tha' no good Jonas Wiley are all bu' convinced I did somethin' to my own flesh and blood."

"We know you didn't." Michaela stepped forward. "It's a shape shifter. We know this, but we don't know who he is."

His chuckle held no warmth. "A shape shifter ye say. Oh, aye. I know this first hand." His gaze wavered to Alan. "He's standin' right beside ye."

"You know Alan had nothing to do with this. He wouldn't harm your grandson."

"Even so..."

"We want to find the bastard." Alan wrapped his fingers around the bars, his knuckles turning white with his fierce grip. "He killed Kait and Troy. He also took another young man's life, a tourist. He willnae stop. We both know this."

"And now he has Damon." Ethan's voice broke.

It was the first time his rant didn't condemn Alan.

"We'll find him," Alan said with determination.

"Can you tell us anything that might help?" Michaela moved closer, standing next to Alan now.

"Alan and Hyatt are the only shape shifters I know of. It's no' like they leave a callin' card, ye ken?" He scratched his chin. The beard stubble sounded like fine sandpaper being rubbed against wood. "I was in Fiddler's Luck and the next thing I know I'm bein' hauled out like a common criminal."

"What were you doing? Anything out of the ordinary?" Michaela questioned. Maybe Ethan pissed off the shifter and he wanted him out of the way.

"Now wha' would I be doin' in a pub, I ask ye?" He shook his head. "I had myself a drink of course and askin' everyone standin' at the bar if they'd seen my grandson the night he disappeared. Two of the lassies spoke up—Nell and Ria. Damon was there with his friends, but George claimed they dinnae stay long that night. They skedaddled out of there when Damon fought with his girlfriend. Only he made up with her and she left before him the night he disappeared. She's the one tha' went home early, no' the laddies. I already questioned her before I headed to Fiddler's Luck." He snorted with disgust. "George cannae keep the days straight no more than his grandda could. Ye'd think he was sippin' a bit of the whiskey behind the bar."

"His grandda?" Alan asked casually.

"Oh aye. Looks jus' like him. Ran the pub until...weel, I doonae rightly know when he left. Pete Townsend owned it for a spell, but he up and disappeared wi'out notice some three years back and George took over. Seemed fittin' since it was his grandda's place before him."

"Hmm..." Alan looked at Michaela with a nod.

"Thank ye, Ethan."

They were about to leave when Alan turned back with another question. "Did yer mum have any men callers after I...left?"

"Wha' is it to ye?" His response was curt, delivered in a cool tone.

"The shifter's been here a long time. I read the reports aboot yer mum's death."

This caught Ethan's attention. His eyes leveled on Alan. "Is tha' so?"

"It's possible whoever took yer grandson knew yer mother, too." He was only guessing but it didn't hurt to ask.

Ethan frowned as he thought back. "She had someone sweet on her after ye left. Only met him once. He dinnae stay long after they found her." His nostrils flared as he remembered his mother's death. He rubbed his hands over his face.

"I'm sorry aboot yer mum. I did care for her. Cared for ye, too. Still do."

Ethan gave him a curt nod. "If tha' is so then find Damon."

"I'll do my best. Ye have my word."

Alan waited until they were outside the office and walking toward the loch, away from anyone overhearing their conversation. "I dinnae know aboot George's grandda ownin' Fiddler's Luck. If we're goin' with the theory the shape shifter wanted Ethan to stop askin' questions then George is high on the list of suspects." He frowned with a long tired sigh. "The sheriff comes in a close second on the list. The Comyn family lived here at one time. Sheriff Comyn speaks of a family, but no one has seen them other than the pictures on his desk."

"Could be all part of his story to live here again." She brushed a lose tendril of hair behind her ear. The air smelled of peat and moss the closer they came to the water.

Alan nodded. "We've narrowed it down to two maybe..." he trailed off but Michaela knew he meant to say three.

"You can't be serious," she snapped, stilling her steps. Alan turned to look at her with raised brow. "Cross Blake off your list? He isn't from here."

"Why does the shape shifter have to be from here? Blake was an actin' physician on a similar case in the States. Maybe he was actually the creature, a shape shifter coverin' his tracks. With all that's goin' on here, how can I totally dismiss the idea?"

She threw up her hands in frustration, but tried to keep her voice level. "Even if Blake is a shifter—and I tell you he's not—why would Blake want to terrorize Drumnadrochit?"

Alan lifted one brow. "Ye truly doonae understand, do ye?"

"Enlighten me." She placed her hands on her hips.

"Ye are the reason, Michaela. He's in love with ye." He held up his hands when she tried to argue. "He's in love with ye," he repeated. "He wants ye to be his, but ye have chosen no' to be. Shape shifters are jealous creatures when they've decided on their mate."

"I suppose that goes for you, too." Sarcasm dripped from her words, but she didn't care.

"Oh aye. I would do anythin' to keep ye safe."

"There's the difference, Alan. You would keep me safe. You wouldn't go around killing innocent people."

"I wouldnae let someone take ye from me."

"Even if I wanted to go?"

He hesitated. He wanted her, this much she knew. He told her he wanted her to be with him always. "If ye wanted to go, I wouldnae stop ye." His voice lowered with emotion.

"Thus the difference. The shape shifter is

selfish. He only cares for himself. Blake isn't like that. He wouldn't kill others to keep me at his side. He's a good man, Alan. He goes out of his way to help people. If anything, he's guilty of caring too much."

His fingers slid through his hair in frustration. "Maybe what ye say is true and I only feel threatened that another man vies for yer affection." He pulled her toward him. "I'll check out George Fallon first. Do a little questionin' of my own. Will ye stay with Mrs. O'Malley while I do my sleuthin'?"

She wondered what his sleuthing would entail, but thought it wise not to ask. "Sure, Mrs. O'Malley makes a fine pot of tea."

"Good." His fingers lightly touched her chin, tilting her head so she met his gaze. "Ye do know I love ye, Michaela."

"I know." She gave him a ghost of a smile.

Chapter Fifty-One

Hyatt rolled to his side and grimaced. "What the bloody hell?" Bloody was right. His hand came in contact with his side where the damn shifter had stabbed him with a sword of all things. "Effin' bastard!" Who carried a sword in this day and age?

"A sociopathic shape shifter," he answered his own question. He sat up, leaning against a tree trunk. He blinked, hoping to clear his vision. A quick survey told him the shifter left him on the wooded path where he fell, but Morton Rander was no longer tied to the tree. Hopefully Rander wasn't another of the shifter's victims as of yet.

Judging by the fading light, he'd been out here for a while. Long enough for Alan to become suspicious and wonder why he hadn't returned.

The birds fluttered overhead and something scurried beneath the brush, disappearing from site. He needed to shift and find Hyatt. He closed his eyes in concentration but nothing happened.

"Gawd blimey," the oath flew from his mouth. His hands gingerly lifted his shirt to inspect the damage. The red skin puckered away from the wound as if in an angry attempt to escape touching the open area.

"Silver." If silver were embedded in the wound, he wouldn't be able to shift. If he couldn't shift, he'd eventually bleed out. He tried to rise to his feet but fell back hard, hitting his head against the tree trunk.

"Damn it all to hell!" His skull didn't hurt half as much as his side did. The pain radiated through his system like a jolt of electricity, making his vision blur. The wound wasn't life threatening yet, but he had to staunch the bleeding. With slow movements, he removed his shirt, grimacing and biting his lower lip with the effort.

He made an attempt to dab the wound with his shirt, hoping for a better idea of how deep the gash was and if he could see the silver that weakened him. The jagged cut was deep, but no vital organs had been punctured and he could assume no arteries were nicked either since he wasn't dead.

He tore his shirt in half. Placing part of the material over the wound, he took the rest of the shirt and tied it around him as tight as he could stand, hoping the pressure would slow the bleeding.

"I'm a damn eejit, letting the bastard have the jump on me," he mumbled under his breath. If he gave into the pain, it would be over. He had to move. Dragging his arse to a standing position took considerable effort. How in the hell did humans deal with pain? He realized it had been too long for him to remember.

If the shape shifter had Morton Rander, he most likely had Damon, too. Were they already dead? If not, they would be soon.

A low moan, faint and drawn out reached his ears. Then he realized the sound had come from him. He blinked back the pain and concentrated on moving his feet. "Bullocks." He slid down to a sitting position again. Beaded droplets of sweat slid down his face and into his eyes.

"Doonae pass out. Buck up." Giving himself a pep talk seemed to help. He blinked back the pain, ready to try and move again, but halted his efforts when his ears picked up movement to the right of him. The shape shifter? Was he back to finish the job? "Not bloody likely, mate." He tried to rise to his feet again.

"Rrruff."

"Elvis?" He slumped back down in relief.

The German Shepherd, a large blur of black and brown fur leapt out of the brush and took a giant leap toward him. Hyatt braced himself for the impact, but the air was knocked out of him anyway. Curses flew from his mouth, but he'd never been so happy to see the mutt.

Elvis whined and his thick tongue slobbered his face.

"It's all right." His hand slid down Elvis' coat, trying to sooth him. "Elvis, be a good dog now and see if ye cannae bring Alan back to me, aye?"

The dog sat back on his haunches and tilted his head to the side.

"Bring back Alan." He glanced down at his side where the blood had oozed through his shirt and was spreading. He looked at Elvis again, hoping the dog understood the urgency of his plea. "Alan. I need Alan. Go. Go get him and come back directly. I doonae know how long I can hold on."

"Ruff Ruff." Two short barks then Elvis took off at a run, leaving Hyatt alone once more.

All he had to do now is survive until help arrived—if—it arrived. "Doonae be an eejit, MacLachlin. Ye've been in worse scrapes and managed to come out of it on the right side."

Chapter Fifty-Two

Michaela stood on Mrs. O'Malley's porch, hoping Alan didn't notice how anxious she was for him to leave. He hesitated at the end of the walk, looking back at her, his intense blue eyes narrowing. *Dammit, he was suspicious. Smile and wave.*

After a moment, he returned the gesture. "I willnae be too long."

"Try not to be," she called after him.

As soon as his tall figure disappeared from sight, she bounded down the porch steps and took off at a jog in the opposite direction to find Blake.

The hotel had a main building with rooms, but they also offered private accommodations, too. Blake had booked a room in one of the garden suites situated in the back wooded area of the hotel.

She entered the lobby and headed straight out the back doors where the lit path led to the suites. Pine trees were on both sides of the path, closely planted and making up most of the landscape. As the evening approached, the light faded in the cloudy sky. The whorl of braches rustled in the wind, like whispering entities warning her to turn back. She shivered with unease. There was no reason to be apprehensive, she told herself with little effect, but she couldn't go back now.

Alan suspected three people of being the shifter. George Fallon, Sheriff Comyn and Blake.

Alan may have made up his mind that Blake was the shifter, but she couldn't wrap her mind around it. It would make him a cold-blooded killer. For God's sake, she dated Blake for months and

never felt anything but affection from him. When he
found out about her condition, he searched for the
best surgeon.

Hyatt claimed Blake arrived here a few days
ago. He'd seen the tickets and had talked to someone
at the hotel, but it was easily explained. Blake had
an aunt living in Foyers. He could have visited his
aunt first before coming to see her.

She'd prove his innocence…somehow. As Blake's
cottage came into view, a movement caught her eye.
A large dark shape crouched low to the ground. Her
steps faltered to a stop and she edged toward the
shadows, instinct cautioning her to assess the
situation.

Careful not to make a sound, she edged a little
closer. There were two figures not one. Fear raced
through her, turning her blood to ice. By the size and
shape, the crouched figure was a man, leaning over a
figure sprawled on the ground. Had the shifter lain
in wait and attacked Blake?

Without thought to her safety, she ran forward
before she realized her folly. The shifter had the
advantage in height and supernatural strength. One
swipe of his hand and she'd be out of commission.
Possibly dead on impact.

She didn't care. If it wasn't Blake, someone lay
unconscious, defenseless and at the mercy of a killer.
She couldn't turn her back.

The man's head lifted at the sound of her steps
and his eyes met hers. Her feet came to an abrupt
stop as if time froze her into place. A scream clawed
up her throat only to choke her into silence. It
couldn't be true.

Blake stood with the bloody knife still clasped in
his hand. Her gaze shifted to the mound of some
poor unsuspecting victim, a woman. Shock fused
with anger overrode her fear for the moment. "I
trusted you!"

His eyes grew larger and rounder. "Michaela." He stood, taking a step toward her.

"Stay where you are." She held out her hand and took a step back.

"Michaela listen. We need to talk."

Talk? What was there to talk about? He was the freaking shape shifter. Tears stung her eyes, but she forced them back as she edged farther away from him.

"Don't go, please." His dark eyes pleaded with her, but the bloody knife in his hand made her decision.

Run. Get the hell out of here! The thoughts screamed in her head and her feet obeyed with swift movements, whirling around and sprinting away.

"Michaela stop." The thud of footsteps behind her told her he wouldn't let her go. She ran through the brush, trampling right then going left in hopes of throwing Blake off her trail. A strangled laugh escaped her lips of how ludicrous that sounded. He was a shifter. He could track her scent with ease, but still she didn't slow down. Stopping meant giving up.

How could she be so stupid? "Blake." His name slid out like a curse. "The damn shape shifter is Blake." Her heart thudded in her head and her breath came hard and labored. She defended the bastard and told Alan to look at someone else for his monster. This was her fault. He listened to her and now another person died because she refused to recognize the truth.

The main building of the hotel loomed ahead, bright lights leading the way. Blake wouldn't attack her in the hotel lobby where witnesses could identify him. She grabbed for the door handle, but a hand clasped over hers, stopping her from finding sanctuary. She yanked her hand away and whirled on him with fist raised.

He took hold of her wrist. "Whoa, hold on there!"

Her vision cleared and she realized it was Officer Jonas Wiley.

Not Blake.

Not the shape shifter.

Not the killer.

She let out a breath of air she'd been holding in a sigh of relief. "Thank God."

"I dinnae mean to startle ye. Ye act like the hounds of hell were at yer feet." He chuckled not realizing the danger they were both in.

The shifter...Blake wouldn't stop. He'd taken down three strong men at one time without any trouble. A woman and one man should be easy to handle.

But Officer Wiley carried a gun. Her gaze landed on Wiley's holster. Surely a bullet would stop Blake or at the very least slow him down, but he wouldn't die easily. Even wounded, Blake could kill them both.

"We have to go inside. Now!" She glanced behind her expecting to see Blake hurling toward them.

"Why?" His brows rose high on his forehead.

Good question. She couldn't tell him about Blake without sounding insane.

She had to find Alan. Only he could take care of the shifter. Telling Wiley a shifter pursued her would only insure his death. He'd think she was being foolish and would feel honor bound to show her there was nothing to fear.

"I... I'm suppose to meet Alan and I'm late." Lame excuse, but her mind couldn't think of a better one on such short notice. Wiley's hand tightened on her wrist and she let out a yelp of surprise. "What are you doing?"

Wiley's eyes glowed unnaturally bright and his mouth slid into a smile of triumph.

Her heart fell in her chest, stopped and

restarted as fear caused her adrenaline to speed up. "Your eyes..." she swallowed hard. No human had eyes that glowed like his did. "You were there at the pub." Her mind went over the clues. He sat at a table and watched all of them—his key players.

"Oh aye, I was there," he answered already knowing she was piecing all the evidence together.

"You knew Kait. You dated her."

His brow lifted in surprise before his eyes narrowed.

He'd seen Steven Corbin share a drink with them—with Kait. Was his deranged killing spree about jealousy then? She'd sensed the unease between Officer Wiley and Kait. He wanted Kait, but she spurned his attention with her blatant affection toward Alan.

Shape shifters are territorial. Alan had told her. Kait's death had been vicious—personal. "Kait spurned you."

"Taught her a lesson, too." The arrogant bastard's smile widened.

She blinked and shook her head. His grin triggered a memory of a black and white photo framed on the pub's wall. One of the men in the photo had looked familiar, but his clothing and the way he wore his hair threw her off.

Instead of the officer's uniform, he'd been dressed in slacks and a dress shirt. His hair slicked back and parted on the side, but his smile had been the same—snakelike and smug.

"You're the shape shifter." Her voice came out in a hoarse whisper. She knew it, but to say the words out loud made her stomach knot with dread. Blake was innocent, but being captured by the shifter put a damper on the discovery.

"How perceptive, Miss Grant. But then again ye'd recognize our kind since ye've latched onto a shifter of yer own." He closed his eyes and inhaled

323

deeply. "Oh aye, ye mated with Alan MacLachlin, bounded yer soul to his." His dark framed eyelids snapped opened. "I had a mate once, too."

"Kait?"

"Kait?" He chuckled. "Weel she wasnae hard on the eyes by no means. The woman could turn a few heads with her silky long hair cascadin' down her back. The hair was good for pullin', too, if ye know what I mean." He winked as if they shared an inside joke. "And her fine round arse. Mmm hmm. Mighty fine." His chuckle sent a chill down her spine, his breath hot on her cheek where she could feel and hear his words.

"Perhaps the little fool could have been my mate, but her affections were focused elsewhere. She knew my secret. Saw me shift. Oh, no' as the Loch Ness Monster, but as a wolf. She called me a freak. Isnae that a corker? I'm a freak, but she wanted the MacLachlin brothers between her thighs weel enough. Guess yer Alan dinnae realize Kait had a thing for preternatural beings. Some humans have that genetic gene and are drawn to us. Perhaps there's a shifter in their lineage." His shoulder lifted in a shrug. "It's only a theory."

Keep him talking. The longer he gloated the more time it allowed for Alan to realize she wasn't visiting Mrs. O'Malley. Would he look here? He'd look for Blake since he suspected him as being the shifter. "Why did you kill Kait?" she asked.

"I had to eliminate her. She knew my secret and the bitch wouldnae keep her trap shut. If she'd agreed to be my mate things would have ended differently. It's the MacLachlins' fault she's dead. This is my territory. Mine! They waltz in wantin' to lay claim. I've been here forty-nine years and countin'."

Forty-nine years. After Alan and Hyatt took to the loch for fifty. He didn't know their secret, the curse that bound them to the loch. "You said you had a mate. What happened?"

His composure slipped as if no one had ever asked him. "She..." His thoughts must have drifted to his mate for his features softened in remembrance of her. "I couldnae save her." His tormented voice told her he had truly loved the woman.

She might have felt sorry for him if he hadn't gone on a killing spree to exact his revenge. Sociopathic behavior obviously wasn't just a human trait. She glanced at the glass doors only a few strides away. The sun lay hidden behind dark clouds, allowing her to see inside the hotel, but she knew the people inside couldn't see her. The lobby's lights would reflect back from the glass, blinding them to what went on outside.

A couple stood at the hotel desk conversing with one of the employees. Three college-aged men had entered the lobby from the front entrance. If she could manage to just get inside, maybe Wiley would let her go. He may be able to subdue her, but he wouldn't be able to take care of six witnesses without exposing his true nature.

Even as she spun the escape in her head, she knew the plan sucked, but she had to try something or she'd end up dead like the others he took hostage.

A silent prayer and a glimmer of hope had her taking her chance. Her body went limp, pulling Wiley forward and throwing him off balance as she hit the ground. His grip loosened... slipped. That's when she rolled and sprung to her feet like a jackrabbit, lunging for the door.

Her finger brushed the handle, but she was yanked back by her hair. She slammed against his chest and he twisted her arm behind her back, causing pain to shoot up her arm. Wiley's breath felt hot against her ear, searing a path down her neck with impending doom.

"Doonae move or I'll snap yer neck like a twig."
He pushed her arm higher and she yelped. "Do ye
hear me?"

"Yes. I hear you." She forced the words out,
gritting her teeth. "Please, just let me go."

"Oh, ye cannae leave, I've waited too long to play
with ye. Now move."

They only took a step when his hand clamped
tight over her mouth and he dragged her back into
the shrubbery surrounding the hotel. "Doonae
struggle."

Like she could with her arm pinned against her
back. Any move and she feared he'd break it. She
didn't understand the need to hide until her gaze
caught sight of Blake. He sprinted into view,
stopping then whirling around, scanning the path
he'd taken through the wooded area across from
them.

He was looking for her, his features frantic in
his search to find her. The bloodstains glinted harsh
in the light, but now she knew Blake didn't murder
the woman. He must have come upon her and had
tried to help her.

"Do ye know him weel?"

The sinister way Wiley asked the question,
made her blood run cold.

"Dr. Stuart is a smart one with his skills down
at the morgue. Askin' questions, nosin' around
where he shouldnae. Nell Miller came to see him
here at the hotel."

Her mind raced. Nell? Nell from the library, the
young woman who gave Steve Corbin the map?

"Nell knew aboot my house nestled in the woods,
not far from where Steve Corbin hiked. The land's
been in the family a long time now." He leaned in
close. His breath was hot on her ear.

"Nell's mum works at the morgue and gave Nell
a job answerin' the phones. The lassie has been

hankerin' after Dr. Stuart since he arrived. She fancied herself keen on the man and decided to impress him with what she discovered. Be glad she dinnae have the chance to reveal what she knew to yer friend there or he'd be dead already."

He nibbled on Michaela's ear, making her pull away. He chuckled low, unperturbed at her reluctance to accept his advances. "I doonae know, maybe I shall kill Dr. Stuart anyway."

Her foot came down hard on his foot. His grip tightened on her arm and the breath went out of her with a squeal of pain muffled against his hand.

Blake turned again, looking in their direction, but she didn't think he could see them.

Wiley's breath against her cheek and ear felt hot and foul. "Doonae call to him unless ye want to see me gut him from neck to groin. Ye know I will."

Tears stung her eyes, but she remained still. She wouldn't let him kill Blake. She'd die first.

Dread slammed into her as the truth of her unsaid words sunk in. She probably would die first.

Chapter Fifty-Three

Mrs. O'Malley informed Alan that Michaela never showed up for a spot of tea. "Of course she dinnae. She had another agenda."

Standing at the bottom of Mrs. O'Malley's steps, with his hands on his hips, Alan wondered where he should look first for her.

Hyatt was missing and now Michaela. He swore under his breath. He should have waited until she was safely inside Mrs. O'Malley's door. "No, I leave her to her own accord and she goes as she pleases."

George Fallon wasn't a shape shifter. This he was certain. His scent was all wrong and if that wasn't enough proof, the man had thrown his back out completely. His movements were labored and sweat glistened his brow with each step he took. Definitely human, meaning the shifter still roamed free and Michaela had put herself in danger by not staying at Mrs. O'Malley's. Anger fled to be replaced by fear.

"Where did ye go, Michaela?" Realization dawned on him as he remembered his last conversation with her. "Blake." She didn't want to believe he could be the shifter and she would want to prove it. "Bloody hell," the curse flew from his lips in frustration. He knew where Michaela had gone and prayed her assumptions about Blake's innocence were spot on.

As he neared the hotel, his steps took him around back to the garden suites, away from tourists. If Blake turned out to be the shape shifter there was no telling what he'd have to do.

On his next inhale the strong scent of pine vanished to be replaced by a whiff of blood. Not animal, but human blood with the odor too strong to be a minor injury.

He kept to the shadows and not the lighted path that led to the suites. His gaze landed on the heap of dark clothing in front of Blake's door. The small frame indicated a woman, making his thoughts leap to conclusions. "No." Frantic, his feet flew over the rocks, brush and the lights on the path.

His heart pulsed in his head like a loud hammer bent on damage. "Please..." The rest of the prayer lodged in his throat, but he clung to the sliver of hope that the still form wasn't Michaela. He slid to a halt, sinking to his knees with a sick feeling in his gut. Too much blood pooled around the head, the hair hidden beneath a knitted cap.

His hand gripped the shoulder and rolled the body to the side. "Oh God." His breath came out in a rush. The sightless eyes stared back at him, horror and surprised stamped into her expression. His hand wavered over the face before he lowered her lids, closing her eyes forever. He recognized her from the Fiddler's Luck, the dark hair lassie—Nell Miller.

The rustle of brush to the left of him had him on his feet and ready for a fight. His gaze latched onto the figure standing on the pathway. *Blake.* "Where is Michaela?" his voice came out in a growl. He wanted to pounce and kill the bastard, but first he had to know if he had taken Michaela.

Blake shook his head. The worried lines on his brows looked frozen in place. "I don't know."

"Ye lyin' bastard!" If he wouldn't tell him willingly, he beat it out of him. He lunged at Blake, bringing him down hard. His fist plowed into his face, wanting blood.

"I don't know." Blake managed a few punches of his own while struggling to get away from him.

Another punch and a kick to his stomach knocked the breath out of him and Blake wiggled free.

Not for long, Alan thought, squelching the pain and leaping to his feet, too. They circled each other, both ready to do another round.

Alan didn't want to chat, but Blake seemed determined to do so anyway. "Michaela came upon me. I was trying to help Nell. I didn't kill her." His eyes wavered to where the body lay like a heap of black clothing with crimson splatters for coloring.

"I saw yer handy work," Alan seethed. "Did ye really think ye could fix her? Did ye bring a large enough band aid with ye?"

"You think I did that?" The incredulous look of disbelief clouded his features before his brows drew together in anger.

Either Blake's acting could win awards or he was innocent. "Dinnae ye?"

"No." He lifted his hands caked with dry blood. "But it seems Michaela thought I did, too. She ran away from me. I tried to catch up to her...explain, but her trail ended as if she disappeared into thin air."

"Explain to her? Why dooncha explain it to me then."

"I left you and Michaela at Fiddler's Luck and came back to my room to shower and—"

"I can do without the recap of what ye planned to do. Just get to the part where ye slit the woman's throat, aye?"

Blake's face turned dark with anger, rising from his neck to his cheeks. "If Nell still had a heartbeat I might have been..." His mouth closed as if he felt he said too much.

"A quick slice with a sharp blade opened her carotid artery. She was dead in minutes. Ye couldnae do a thing to help her."

"I could have." His gaze met his unwavering

with conviction.

"Is that so. Are ye some super doc I doonae know aboot then?"

"I'm a healer."

Alan stood silent. He no longer fisted his hands, but he still kept his guard up. "And what does that mean?"

"I can heal what I can see, but only if the patient's heart hasn't stopped."

"Ye could have saved her if her…"

"…heart hadn't stopped. Yes."

His words sunk in and took shape. Blake was a healer, a human with preternatural abilities. Alan shook his head. This was a trick. "If what ye say is true, why couldnae ye save Michaela?" His accusation came through with the tone of his voice, making Blake flinch in response.

His eyelids lowered and opened in a deliberate blink, guilt lay evident in the brown depths. He took a deep breath and released it. "I could save her, if she'd agree to an operation. I must see the damage to repair it."

Blake held the power to save her and yet he did not. Damn the man. "Ye should have forced her to have the operation then."

Blake's laugh came out harsh, his gaze locked onto to Alan, pinning him like he was a wee bug. "Really?" His voice lowered with control, but the underlying anger lingered beneath waiting to be unleashed. "Maybe you aren't aware of this, but it's frowned upon in the States to drug someone and perform surgery on them when they haven't consented to do so. Michaela is a stubborn woman, if you didn't know. Nothing I said budged her. I thought if she wouldn't do the operation for herself perhaps I could persuade her another way, but threatening to leave her had no effect." His gaze was filled with contempt. "She didn't love me enough. It didn't matter to her if I remained in her life or not."

"If ye dinnae have yer head up yer arse, ye might have seen it was never aboot ye."

Blake opened his mouth with what Alan was sure could only be a lethal retort, but voices approaching stopped him cold.

Children's laughter and grownups' deeper rumbles followed. They were heading down the path and would be upon them in a matter of few seconds. Most likely it was the family staying in the room next to Blake's.

They couldn't be seen with the body. They'd be forced to wait for the authorities. If Blake wasn't the shape shifter and George wasn't either, his bet was on the sheriff. They couldn't afford to be hauled in for questioning.

His first priority was to find Michaela.

Alan looked at Blake. "Go. Now!" he hissed. "And for the gods' sake, doonae let anyone see ye. Ye're covered in Nell's blood."

Blake looked down to inspect his clothing and seemed shocked at the discovery of blood staining his pant legs. He glanced at Alan again. Blake nodded but paused when he saw him take a step toward Nell. "What are doing?"

He glanced back at him with impatience. "I cannae leave Nell here. Doonae worry aboot me. I'll take care of her."

"The morgue," Blake blurted.

"What?"

"We could hide her body there for now."

Alan hated to admit the idea was a sound one. He nodded in agreement. "We'll go through the wooded patches."

Alan gave him a quick nod before leaning down and scooping Nell into his arms.

Chapter Fifty-Four

Alan clicked the metal door in place, sealing Nell's body from sight. In the light, Blake's skin had turned to a pale version of his normal tanned appearance. His gaze fixed on the vault. His Adam's apple bobbed up and down in a slow manner as if swallowing became difficult to master.

"She was only twenty-two," Blake choked out.

"Her death will be avenged."

Blake looked at him now. His brows furrowing together as his eyes narrowed. "It won't bring her back. It won't bring any of them back."

"No, but we'll make sure no one else suffers at the shifter's hands." His worry turned toward Michaela and his brother, his stomach knotting with apprehension. Where were they? "Let's go."

Hyatt hadn't returned since this morning and Michaela disappeared at the hotel. What if her disappearance had nothing to do with her hiding from Blake?

His long strides took him through sterile rooms and to the main office of the morgue. Blake followed close behind. The sun had set and a filmy layer of white frothed the moon, making it appear hidden in a fog-laden field of blue. The breeze scented the air with pine, heather and burning peat fires, but it didn't mask the spilled blood on their clothing.

Blake locked the door to the building and they headed to the car. "I don't know how I'm going to explain the blood stains in the trunk of the rental."

"Ye'll report it stolen." Most of the blood had been spent at the scene, but a black light would pinpoint the residue in the vehicle.

"Hmm." His disgruntled response told Alan the idea didn't sit well with him, but they had more important issues to worry about for now.

They drove in silence to the house. The lights from the street reflected off their blood stained hands, which were now dry and caked, tightening the skin in response. With the car parked, they walked down the path, the night too quiet and the house bathed in darkness against the spruce and pine trees.

"It doesn't look like anyone's there."

Alan nodded. Where was his brother? Where did Michaela go? At the side of the house, he turned on the water faucet and washed his hands.

Blake followed suit before wiping his hands on his pants to dry them. He then retrieved his mobile from his pocket.

"Who are ye callin'?" Alan frowned.

"Michaela."

"Really? Do ye think she'll pick up once yer caller ID blinks on her screen? She believes ye are the shifter."

He slipped the mobile back in his pocket. "Do you know where to look for her then? Where she might hide?"

"Maybe she backtracked back to Mrs. O'Malley's place. I'll ring her straight away to find out." He hoped that's where she fled to for safety. He jogged up the steps to the house and slipped the key in the lock, turning the knob as he went. The house was bathed in darkness and he flipped the switch, illuminating the room.

As Blake stepped inside, Alan turned to close the door, but stilled his actions when he heard the sharp rapid barks coming closer. He strolled back onto the porch as Elvis bounded out of the woods.

"What's wrong?" Blake joined him.

"It's Elvis."

The German Shepherd slid to a stop at the foot of the steps and barked in repetition of three cycles then ran forward a few feet then back again to repeat the process.

Alan strode down down the porch steps. "Do ye want me to follow ye?"

Elvis lifted his snout with one sharp bark for his answer.

Alan started to follow only to have Blake halt him with his words. "You're going to go out there with a dog?"

His incredulous remark caused his back muscles to tense in response. He turned to look at him. "Elvis needs me to follow him. He wouldnae be so insistent."

Blake shook his head and his voice did nothing to hide his disbelief or the fact he thought him an eejit. "Did you ever stop to think you might be heading into a trap by following your mutt?"

"Ye doonae understand the ways of shifters and I have no time to explain it. Go inside and shower if ye like. Ye can borrow clothes from my room. I'll be back as soon as I can."

Without another word or a backward glance to see if Blake followed his instructions, he kept up with Elvis, letting him lead the way.

Trees and brush were the only witness to their urgent pace. They were away from the populated areas and frequent hiking trails. Elvis didn't slow down, knowing Alan could keep up with him. The trees were closer together here, blocking most of the light filtering in from the sky. The dense fog didn't help matters even with the summer sky not darkening completely.

Once Elvis stopped and sniffed the ground as if making sure he still had the scent. "Where are ye leadin' me, Elvis?"

"Rrruff." Elvis quick bark of impatience told him not to ask questions. His four legs took off again with determination.

It didn't take Alan long to realize they were heading toward the path he and Hyatt used often to enter the loch.

Elvis slid to a stop. "Rrrrfff rrruff rruuff." He circled, and whined before he plopped down.

Alan slowed his stride as his gaze took in the heap Elvis had rested his head upon. "Bloody hell." Realization hit him and he ran forward, dropping to his knees, his hands gripping his brother's shoulder. "Hyatt?"

Hyatt's eyelids fluttered open. "It's aboot time ye showed up." He grinned then grimaced, clutching his side.

"What happened?" Alan's hand grasped his blood soaked shirt tied around his waist, lifting it to reveal a gaping wound. "Why havenae ye shifted and healed yerself?"

Hyatt's laughed turned into a cough. "The shape shifter imbedded a silver sword into my gut, leaving a piece of it behind, ye eejit."

A light flashed from the wooded path behind him, shining on the tree trunk. Alan whipped around to meet the adversary. His shoulders relaxed when his gaze caught sight of Blake coming toward them. "I thought I told ye to change out of those bloody garments."

"It looks like it's a good thing I didn't." He knelt down next to Hyatt.

Alan didn't see the point in arguing. Blake was here. Perhaps his medical expertise would come in handy. "He has silver embedded in him," he told Blake. "It must be pure silver if he cannae shift and expel it."

"I thought only werewolves were plagued by silver."

"All preternatural bein's are allergic to silver based items, but pure silver will eventually kill us if it reaches the bloodstream."

Blake leaned forward with the torch, shining it on the wound. "Definitely a nasty slash. Here hold the light so I can work." He handed the torch to Alan before he placed his hands on the wound, separating the flesh.

Hyatt gripped Blake's forearm. "What the hell are ye doin', ye damn wanker?"

"If silver kills you, I thought I'd see about removing the offensive object. Now pipe down and unhand me. I need to concentrate."

"Concentrate? Alan?" His voice turned to a whine then a curse as Blake dug his finger into the wound.

"Hold on brother," Alan said. "Blake's a healer."

"The effin' healer better hurry then," he cried and gripped Alan's arm with a crushing force. Then just as suddenly, he let go as his body went limp.

"Hyatt?" His brother had lost consciousness, his head lolling to the side.

"I almost have it." Blake's hands were drenched in his brother's blood.

"He's lost too much blood. He willnae be able to shift." Alan stared at his brother. His skin was already a ghastly pale shade.

"Give me a second," Blake grumbled, still diligently looking for the silver fragment that caused the damage. "Got it." Blake held up the offending silver tip of the blade. He threw it aside and placed his hand on the open wound, the blood oozing in a steady stream down Hyatt's side.

"Now what are ye doin'?"

"Saving your brother," he grumbled with impatience. His fingers pressed onto the wound and a low hum vibrated from his lips.

Alan sat back, the tension leaving him as he

realized Blake was too cocksure of himself not to know what he was doing. With his gift, the man could save many lives, but he chose to be a forensic pathologist. Curiosity got the better of him. "Why do ye work with death if ye can heal?"

"And how would you propose I explain the lack of needing instruments in surgery?" He swore under his breath.

Alan snorted. "Humans are ignorant when it comes to magic and so they perish because of it."

Light illuminated Blake's hands and Alan could feel the warmth of the glow from where he kneeled. He watched enthralled as the bleeding stopped and the wound began to close. "I'll be damned."

"We might all be, but at least Hyatt's journey to perdition will have to wait for now." The wound puckered then sealed, leaving only a slight scar. "I can feel his body rejuvenating. Fascinating. A human would need a blood transfusion."

Hyatt shot from full sleep to wakefulness, sitting up straight with a gasp. His hands were fisted and readied for battle. "Where am I?"

Alan placed a reassuring hand on his shoulder. "It's all right. Ye're on the mend."

Hyatt looked down at his side, feeling the area for proof. "I suppose I owe ye one, doc." Hyatt nodded toward Blake with gratitude. "I thought this was it for—" His hand clasped Alan's arm. "I know who the shape shifter is. It's Jonas Wiley, the wee bastard."

"Wiley, are you sure?" Blake's startled response had both Hyatt and Alan staring at him. "I ran into him in the hotel lobby," Blake explained. "Before I found Nell. He told me there'd been a disturbance and he was called in to take care of it. Joked about it like the call had been a prank. He must have just come from killing Nell."

"Nell?" Hyatt asked. "What aboot Morton Rander?"

Blake's brows drew together in confusion.

It took them a few minutes to sort through the stories that had led them here.

"If Michaela's no' at the hotel and no' here..." Dread hit Alan causing all sounds other than his beating heart to cease. Terror was a new sensation for him, but he was powerless to stop it from taking form.

"Wiley's taken Michaela."

Chapter Fifty-Five

Wiley opened the door to his house and pushed Michaela inside. She stumbled and fell, hitting hard on the wood floor.

Click.

The sound of the bolt sliding home made her heart pound against her ribcage. She was trapped in Wiley's lair, far from the Village Green where someone might hear her screams.

She closed her eyes and breathed in slowly. Trapped, but not dead. *Yet.*

For the moment she stayed where she fell, her gaze taking in the layout of her prison. The living room was sparse with tan chairs and a striped couch facing the overly large fireplace.

To the right of her, she assumed led to the kitchen and the hall in front of her probably was where the bathroom and bedrooms were located. It was only a house and it had windows and doors. She could find a way to escape.

Wiley stepped around her and walked over to the fireplace, picking up a photograph from the mantel. "Mary MacGregor."

"What?" She stared at him, frowning in confusion.

"I wanted to change her, share my shifter blood, but her body couldnae take the change." Wiley pinned his gaze on her. "Do ye know who she called for when the fever racked her body?"

Michaela could take a wild guess and be right, but she felt silence would prove safer at this point. Wiley seemed bent on telling her anyway.

"When Mary fell ill, she revealed many secrets, told me aboot the beasties in the loch. I investigated her claims to be sure they werenae tales from her fevered brain. They were all true. Then it all became clear. I knew why Mary rejected our bond. Her heart pined for another shifter. The effin' bastard married her, but dinnae mate her properly to change her."

"What are you talking about?" But she did know and fought to keep the fear out of her voice.

Wiley chuckled. "Oh aye. Ye dinnae think I knew aboot Alan MacLachlin, though he was MacGregor then. I know who he is: man, legend and beastie. I've waited for his return and now I'll have my revenge."

"By killing innocent people?" Wiley blamed Alan for Mary dying when it was he who caused her death. His blood not Alan's.

"Alan will suffer for what he did. What he left unfinished. He claimed a human, but dinnae mark her. She pined for him and tricked me into changin' her in hopes she could go to her lover beneath the loch's depths. Mary should have been mine."

He tapped his chest. "He dinnae love her. I did." He swiped his hand at his eyes in an angry attempt to stop the tears that sprung to his eyes. "She should have loved me."

"Mary's death was an accident. Alan didn't kill her." It was a mistake to try and reason with Wiley who was beyond thinking logically. He threw down the photo and lunged, grabbing her arm and dragging her to her feet.

His hands were around her neck, preventing her from drawing in air. She clawed at his arm in a useless attempt to stop him. This was it. Death would claim her like all his other victims. Her eyelids fluttered and blackness clouded her mind. Her hand slipped away and all attempts of escape ceased to matter.

Chapter Fifty-Six

Michaela's eyes fluttered open and it took a moment for her to remember what happened. When she did, she sat up with a start. Big mistake. Her world tilted on its axis, making her want to vomit. Her hand went to her throat where the flesh felt tender and bruised.

"Take a deep breath and let it out slowly."

Her gaze riveted toward the voice. Her vision cleared, focused. Not one but two young men sat huddled together, both marred with cuts and slashes on their arms and faces. Her brows furrowed in confusion. Where the hell was she?

"I'm Damon Nokes and this is Morton Rander." He pointed with a quick jerk of his thumb to the battered young man next to him.

Damon and Morton. She remembered the two were friends and Damon was Ethan's grandson. Then she recalled their other friend. Troy hadn't been so lucky. She did her best to swallow back her fear.

"Michaela Grant," she croaked out her name. Her hand brushed over her face with a quick intake of breath. She looked around her, taking in the room.

Ceiling, floors and walls were covered in a thick plastic, giving the room a gray dismal appearance. There were no windows and no furniture, but in one corner there stood a sink and primitive looking stainless steel toilet.

"Do you know where we are?" she asked.

Morton snorted and chuckled as he rocked back

and forth, his arms wrapped around him. "Hell, dooncha ye think?"

Damon ignored his friend's response. "I think we're off one of the hikin' trails."

"Yes." She nodded. "Wiley mentioned a cabin his family once owned."

"What good is knowin'?" Morton sobbed. "He's goin' to gut us like he did Troy and Hyatt Maclachlin."

Her head snapped up. "Hyatt? What are you talking about?"

"Doonae pay attention to his blatherin', aye?" Damon nudged Morton, throwing him a steely look to keep quiet.

"Listen, you don't have to protect me. I know what Wiley is capable of doing. I've seen his handiwork." She looked at Morton. "How did he manage to capture Hyatt?"

"He dinnae capture him. Hyatt came upon us in the forest. Wiley heard him approachin' and hid. I couldnae warn Hyatt." He shook his head. "Wiley gagged and bound me, tyin' me to a tree like a some kind of catch." His haunted gaze met hers, telling her he witnessed what happened next.

She swallowed the lump forming in her throat. "Of course you couldn't have warned him. It wasn't your fault. Tell me what Wiley did."

Morton licked his cracked lips. "Wiley waited in the shadows to get a jump on him." His body shuddered as he recalled the horror. "Hyatt tried to help me, but the wanker stabbed him with a sword."

That's why Hyatt hadn't showed up back at the house. He was hurt or possibly dead. She shook her head, refusing to believe it. Hyatt was a shifter. They didn't die so easily. She wrapped her arms around her suddenly feeling cold.

Wiley hadn't killed Damon or Morton. Hell, he hadn't killed her and he could have snapped her

343

neck with ease. Was there a purpose? Did he plan on luring Alan here to trap him?

"He's goin' to kill us." Morton murmured, his thread to sanity slipping away an inch more.

Michaela wanted to comfort him, give him some hope, but words of encouragement weren't forthcoming.

She turned her head at the sound of a click, like a bolt being slid open. Morton and Damon jumped at the sound of it, their hands raised in a defensive manner. Morton whimpered softly.

She stood as Wiley entered the room with his snakelike grin plastered to his face. "So ye're up and aboot, are ye?"

She didn't answer him, fearing her voice would give away her fear.

He shut the door behind him and crossed the room to her. She lifted her chin and glared at him, but her attempt at bravery was shot down with his low chuckle.

His hand snaked out and grabbed her, pulling her against his chest, his foul breath on her face. Damon stood and made an effort to come to her aid, but Wiley turned his gaze on him. "Stand still or I'll kill her then ye and it willnae be pretty."

Damon hesitated, looking at her then to Wiley. She appreciated the gesture, but his attempts to save her would only hasten his death. "It's okay, Damon. Stay where you are."

"Oh that's so sweet." Wiley's other hand grabbed her hair and yanked her head to the side. She squelched the cry of pain by clenching her teeth. His tongue slid across her bruised neck in a slow lick. "Mmmm... oh aye, ye are sweet." With a roar, he struck, his teeth sinking into her flesh. This time there was no holding back. The scream broke through her lips.

Damon came at them, but Wiley sensed him and

met the attack, slamming his fist into his face. Damon flew back, losing consciousness before he hit the floor.

Still gripping her hair, Wiley raised his other hand and tore at his wrist, causing blood to pool. He thrust his hand at her mouth. Her attempts to escape were useless. He proved too strong.

The metallic taste of his blood slipped past her lips making her choke in protest, but still the blood slid down her throat. Finally he shoved her away, tossing her to the ground.

A sob escaped her as she spat, trying to rid the sickening taste of blood from her mouth, but no matter her attempts, she knew she'd swallowed a good amount. She sat down, wiping her mouth with the back of her hand. With a shakey hand, her fingers pressed against the wound, hoping to stay the blood flow dripping down her neck and onto her shirt.

Wiley's chest heaved in and out as he stared down at her, his eyes glowing with an unnatural gleam.

"Alan may have mated with ye, bondin' with ye with his touch. It's an old custom, transferrin' the magic through the skin, but I shared my blood. It's more brutal, but direct. Some humans cannae take the pure transfer, but without it, ye would remain human."

Panic filled her. What had he done to her?

"Ye'll either survive the blood exchange and become a shifter or ye'll die." He lifted his shoulder in a shrug of indifference. "If ye live, ye'll be bonded to me then. My mate."

"Never," she choked.

He chuckled. "We'll see. Ye may change yer mind once Alan is dead."

345

Chapter Fifty-Seven

Alan knew without a doubt where Wiley would take Michaela. He also realized now why Nell had been murdered. Her death hadn't been random. Wiley stalked her and killed her. Blake said himself he'd questioned the lassie about the hiking trail she'd mapped out for Steven Corbin. Nell must have remembered where Wiley's homestead stood, nestled in the wooded pines and spruce trees.

Blake and Hyatt followed behind. They left Elvis locked up in the house for the dog's own safety, his barks of protests echoing as they headed back into the forest.

They didn't bother hiding the fact they were coming. Wiley expected it and would be waiting.

Jonas Wiley signed his own death warrant when he killed the first time, but if he harmed Michaela in anyway, he'd make him suffer before ending his miserable life.

The single story cabin came into view. The cabin sported a fresh coat of green paint and the wood framing looked intact. Over growth of vines and foliage lined the pathway, not from neglect but for camouflage. It kept the dwelling hidden from curious hikers unless they stumbled upon it by accident.

They didn't have to knock on the front door. Wiley opened the door and stepped out onto the porch with Michaela in front of him like a shield. Her mouth was bound with a dirty rag, tied at the back of her head. Her hands were behind her back, probably constricted as well by the way she struggled against Wiley's grip.

The scent of her blood hit his nostrils as his gaze took in her disheveled appearance. A ragged gash, rough and raw on her bruised neck made him clench his fists and take a step forward. Hyatt placed a sturdy hand on his shoulder, forcing him to gain control.

Wiley must have sensed his fury. His lips curved and his eyes glowed with a golden hue. "Oh goody, visitors. Isn't that nice, Michaela."

"It's over, Wiley." Alan faced him, while Blake circled left and Hyatt went right. "Give me Michaela and we'll settle this the shifter's way, aye?"

Wiley's chuckle told him he thought he had the upper hand. He was wrong. Tonight it would end.

Wiley tilted his head to the side, stretching the tendons in his neck with a loud popping noise. "Do ye think I will fight ye and yer clan of would-be-followers?" He motioned to Blake and Hyatt. "Hyatt, I underestimated ye. I thought ye'd bleed out with the amount of silver I left in ye."

"Seems it wasnae my time to go, aye?"

"Hmm, fair enough. We'll see if yer so lucky the next time we go at it."

Michaela tried to talk through the gag, but her words were strangled, muffled by the cloth. She shook her head, her eyes large and frantic to communicate with him. Wiley jerked her back.

"Let Michaela go," Alan warned again.

"If I agree to fight. It's with ye only." Wiley slid the back of his hand down Michaela's face and she shut her eyes. Her nostrils flared with a sharp inhaled breath as his hand swept down the ragged gash on her neck. "She tasted like aged old brandy. No wonder ye wanted her for yerself." His gaze locked with Alan's. "She tasted my blood as weel."

"Ye effin' bastard." Every muscle in his body tightened, only by pure will did he stay put. He needed to draw him away from Michaela.

Wiley threw back his head and laughed. "Is that all ye have to say."

"Come down here and ye'll see what I have to say."

"We'll fight for her, aye?"

"How aboot I just kill ye instead." Alan held his ground but it was difficult when Michaela's eyes pooled with tears and he could hear the rapid beat of her heart. Buhbum bump, buh bump, the rhythm sped up, terror was the conductor.

"A fight to the finish then. Understand if I doonae believe ye aboot fightin' fair." He looked to Blake. "Human, tie up Hyatt with these." He tossed Blake the handcuffs. "They're made of silver. He willnae be able to break free or shift while we fight."

"Why would I agree to yer conditions?" Hyatt glared and his hands fisted.

"Because if ye doonae agree, I'll break sweet Michaela's neck." Quick as lightning, he held her head between his hands.

"Stop!" Hyatt yelled, stilling Wiley's attempts to go through with his threat. "I'll do it." His hands opened in surrender. He looked at Alan. "Kill the bastard." His gaze shifted to Blake with a nod. "Cuff me, doc."

Blake's features darkened but he walked over to Hyatt who placed his hands behind his back. "Sorry, man."

"I doonae mind cuffs now and again, but with ye I'll pass in the future if ye doonae mind."

Blake smiled at his attempt at humor in this dire situation "You can bet on it." Before he cuffed him, he turned to face Wiley. "Where's the key?"

Wiley hesitated. Then with a shrug, he dug his hand into his pocket and threw the key at Blake's feet. Blake picked it up. He checked to make sure the key truly unlocked the cuffs before he slipped the key into his pocket.

Wiley laughed. "Ye arenae as dumb as ye look human." His lips curved in a smile. "Though a key willnae matter in the end," he prophesized.

The silver cuffs hissed, burning Hyatt's flesh as Blake locked them in place. Hyatt fell to his knees. The silver weakened him immediately, making shifting impossible.

Wiley's finger slid down Michaela's face and she grimaced, leaning away. "Now Blake," Wiley said. "Come take Michaela so I may fight our friend, Alan."

Michaela kept shaking her head frantically as Blake strode toward them.

A whisper of unease settled over Alan, but before he could warn Blake, the flash of steel glinted with intent. "Blake stop!"

Blake turned to look at him and Wiley took the advantaged and let the knife fly from his grip. Blake stumbled back, a look of surprise on his face as his hand held the hilt of the knife lodged in his chest. He fell backward onto the ground.

"That was too easy. An eejit after all." Wiley sighed.

"Ye damn bloody bastard!" Alan shouted as he dashed forward to Blake's side. Keeping one eye on Wiley, he knelt down to look at the doctor, inspecting the damage. It wasn't good.

The blade missed his heart, but must have hit a lung. Blake's face took on the color of gray over white, but his gaze was still direct, shock hadn't taken hold completely. His hand gripped his forearm with more strength than seemed possible. "Just take him down, Alan. Save Michaela." His body convulsed and he coughed up blood.

Alan swallowed back the lump in his throat and gave Blake a quick nod. He looked up, his eyes meeting Wiley's. "Oh aye, let's fight the preternatural way." Alan stood, his fist clenched at his side. "But first, let Michaela go."

Wiley lifted his shoulders in a nonchalant shrug. He shoved Michaela at him, making her stumble forward with no way to steady her fall with her hands tied behind her. Alan catapulted forward and caught her. He lowered the gag and she took a large gulp of air.

He leaned close, shifting her position away from Wiley. "Doonae let on I release ye," he whispered. He sliced the rope holding her.

"You have to go, Alan. Take your brother and save yourself." She kept her hands behind her, going with the ruse. "Don't you see he's thought this through? He bit me. The odds of me surviving the change aren't good. That's why Mary died. She didn't take the boat out on the loch and drown. That was a cover-up. Wiley bit her. I'm dead no matter what happens." Apprehension for his safety shone bright in her eyes, darkening the lovely green to almost black.

Wiley clapped his hands. "So noble. I do love a woman who will sacrifice herself for the one she loves. That's why I've decided to take her as mine—of course after I kill ye."

Alan's gaze locked onto Michaela's. "Ye willnae die," he commanded her. He let the black rage lance through his blood, readying his body for the final battle.

Michaela must have sensed the change in him. "Oh God, no. Don't." Michaela's frantic plea pierced his heart, but he had to do this. He kissed Michaela quickly, ignoring her desperate pleas for him to stop.

Wiley's thin lips curved like a snake ready to strike. "I was hopin' ye would say that." His body contorted, reshaped, shifting into a rugged more primitive version of the Loch Ness Monster.

Chapter Fifty-Eight

Wiley was a cheap version of the regal beast Alan and Hyatt portrayed, but just as lethal. Michaela thought.

Alan let out a primal roar, shifting to meet the challenge.

Shifters fought to the death when a territory was threatened or their mate was in danger. Alan explained the moral code and this would be no different. Michaela wanted to turn away, but she stood frozen in her place unable to tear her gaze away from the horrible scene before her.

Ripping and tearing of flesh showered the ground with blood. The screams were a ferocious reminder of what these beasts could do. *Run.* The voice inside her head kept telling her, but she couldn't leave. Her hands loose she rubbed her raw skin where the ropes had burned her tender flesh.

Her gaze riveted to Blake, his skin ashen against the blood pooled around him. She knew in her heart there was no hope of saving him. The blade must have hit something vital and help was too far away.

She knelt down beside him, tears stinging her eyes. "I'm so sorry, Blake," she sobbed with regret, knowing she had no time to mourn him. She needed the key to free Hyatt. Her hand slid into his pant pocket in desperation.

Grasping it in her hand, she ran toward Hyatt who lay on his side. Sweat poured down his face. His skin burned and blistered where the silver cuffs rubbed his wrist.

"I have the key, Hyatt. Hold on." Her hands shook but she managed to slip the key in and release the lock. She grabbed the cuffs and hurled them away before helping Hyatt sit up. "Can you help Alan?"

He nodded. "Give me a moment."

The sky darkened overhead, clouds covering the moon. A low rumble shook the ground and lightning flashed. Michaela looked up expecting rain to pour from the sky, but there was nothing. *Yet.*

Hyatt stood now, his strength returning. "Move back," he warned her and shifted as a flash of light lit the sky again.

Alan and Hyatt, beautiful and deadly, stalked Wiley, whose primitive beastly form didn't compare. Wiley backed up toward the loch. He'd lost a lot of blood and Michaela wondered if that was why he hadn't shifted to another beast and escaped. He couldn't. He was trapped.

Before Wiley could reach the safety of the water both brothers lunged. Hyatt, the darker and larger of the primal beasts went for his side and Alan lighter in color attacked, his sharp teeth sinking into Wiley's neck.

Wiley let out a final cry, the blood filling his throat and drowning out the sound. Alan shook his head, tearing flesh before he released Wiley. He fell to the ground with a thud, his large reptile head bouncing on the dirt before settling with a final rasp of air. The golden hued eyes blazed bright then dimmed with death.

Thunder roared overhead and lightning struck the ground between Michaela and the horrible death scene in front of her. She stumbled back. Smoke swirled where the bolt hit, forming a shape. Michaela blinked hard, believing her mind was playing tricks on her, but the figure remained, solidifying into a man wearing a long gray robe.

Magic of the Loch

Chapter Fifty-Nine

Both, Alan and Hyatt shifted to their human forms as Druid Daly appeared once more to do the gods' bidding. The druid's blue eyes narrowed when he caught site of the fallen shape shifter. He took in the scene assessing his own understanding of what played out before his gaze leveled on Alan and Hyatt once again.

"Ye've done what the gods have asked of ye, protectin' the well." He glanced at Blake, who lay still now, the blood haloing his body like a dark shadow. "The human helped, too. I am sorry his life was forfeited." His gaze traveled to Michaela who had moved to stand beside Alan. "Ye have found yer soul mate at last, I see."

Alan slipped his arm around Michaela, drawing her near. "Aye, but I'm still the creature."

Druid Daly nodded. "Ah, but ye doonae have the curse of bein' sentenced to the loch for fifty years. Ye are free of its confines. Ye may return to the waters at will."

Alan was pleased with this; he would have missed the depths of the loch. The water was as much a part of him as his human side was a part of the land. "Michaela was bitten by the shifter." He glanced at the angry raw wound still oozing. "Will the waters cure her?"

"The well water doesnae heal. It prolongs life only. Did ye share the shifter's blood?" he directed the question to Michaela.

She nodded. "He forced me."

"Pity. Shifter blood doesnae blend weel with

353

human blood." Druid Daly gave her an apologetic shrug. "It changes the blood, makin' it more like the shifters. It's no' as pure, but a human may take on the shifter's abilities. However, some doonae survive the transformation. It is brutal and the human form is fragile in comparison to a shifter's sturdy structure."

He tilted his head as he regarded Michaela with a critical eye. "Yer spirit is strong. If ye're healthy, ye'll survive the shift."

"How long..." Alan's voice faltered, a hoarse whisper of despair. He cleared his throat. "How long before the transformation?"

"No more than one cycle of the moon."

Alan's arm tightened around Michaela as if he could keep her safe if he held her close. He'd face pain, terror, even death for her, but this path he couldn't take. Her spirit may be strong, but she wasn't healthy. He knew in his heart she wouldn't survive. The aneurysm would burst before she completed the transformation and shifted.

Druid Daly's furtive look vanished when his gaze locked with his. The druid already knew her life was limited. "I was sent from the gods to grant one wish. I can heal her," he offered.

Alan opened his mouth to say do it already, but Druid Daly held up his hand.

"I give ye a choice. Think on it weel because it will only be offered once."

Alan nodded.

"Ye can free yer brother from the curse, heal Michaela, allowin' the transformation to be a success or..." He looked at Blake with a nod of his head. "Or I can heal yer fallen friend, who sacrificed his life for ye and yer soul mate."

Alan closed his eyes. He had a choice, a choice to condemn two of the three.

Hyatt stepped forward. "Save Michaela, Alan."

He met his brother's gaze, his friend through many lives. He'd stood by him, had his back and now he laid his life at his feet.

As if Hyatt could read his mind, his brother's mouth curved into a smirk. "My life isnae in danger and who knows perhaps I will find my own soul mate. Hell, if ye can find one, I'm sure I can as weel."

"And if ye doonae find her?"

His shoulder's lifted in a shrug. "I love the water, Alan. I never thought to return to the land. I'll be fine."

Alan turned his attention on Michaela.

She slipped from his embrace and glanced at Hyatt with a sweet smile. "Thank you. I'll never forget your sacrifice." Her gaze met Alan's again. "I must also refuse. Do not use your wish on me."

"What? Michaela, ye must agree." Hyatt took a step forward, but Alan waved him back.

"No, let her speak."

"Please, you have to save Blake," Tears fell from her eyes, but she didn't wipe them away. "You can't let him die. You told me you'd be with me until my time ran out. Let's take what we have, but don't let Blake suffer for it."

Thunder rumbled overhead as if the heavens were tired of the talk.

"Ye must make yer decision soon," Druid Daly warned.

"Save Blake," Michaela pleaded, taking his hand. "Please. I couldn't live knowing we let him die when we could have saved him."

Alan looked at her, her green eyes the soft color of moss. Her lips trembled as she reached up to touch his face with tentative fingers. "Please."

She was his heart, and soul. *His mate.* He leaned down and kissed her lips, a gentle kiss filled with promises. "If the choice is to save Blake, ye will agree to have the operation. Ye must repair the aneurysm before the shift. No waitin'." He'd have her word first.

Her hands fell to her side, her lips pursing together, but she gave him a curt nod of agreement. "I'll contact my doctor—"

"No," he interrupted. "Blake will handle the arrangements. Here, in Scotland. Tomorrow."

He hated how her eyes clouded with betrayal. She left Blake because of his insistence and now he demanded her to do his bidding as well.

"Trust me, Michaela," he said softly. His fingers tucked a lock of her hair behind her ear.

Her gaze softened then and she swallowed hard, wiping away the tears. "If the operation fails, you better be willing to wipe away the drool from my mouth."

"I'll take care of ye always, forever, but doonae worry, luv." He rested his forehead against hers, drawing her near. "I know everythin' will be all right."

Tears welled in her eyes again, but she nodded.

Alan released her and stepped forward to face Druid Daly. "Ye will promise me that Blake will be as he was before."

"Fair enough," Druid Daly agreed, a gleam in his eye indicating he was pleased with his choice.

"Then do it."

Michaela had moved beside him and he drew her close. Hyatt came to stand on his other side.

The druid took steps toward Blake. He circled his body, while chanting words of a language long dead and forgotten. He raised his staff high and called to the heavens.

Thunder rumbled the earth beneath their feet and lightning lit the sky as bright as day before a bolt struck the staff's bulbous tip, illuminating it with energy.

Druid Daly brought the tip of the staff down on

Blake. A blue glow covered his body, lifting it off the ground, the electrical current alive and sparking around him like a shield.

Minutes passed before the light diminished. Druid Daly lowered his staff until Blake's body rested on the ground once more. The druid turned to look at the three of them. "It is done. He will awaken soon."

"And what shall we do with the shifter's body?" Alan asked. "Humans will accept many things, but to blame a shifter for the deaths willnae go over so weel."

Druid Daly sighed and glanced at the creature. "The gods have already seen to it. Sheriff Comyn stumbled upon evidence connectin' Wiley to the murders. He is already on his way."

He slammed the staff into the dirt and an explosion of light blinded them, causing them to turn away. Then as quickly as the light appeared, it vanished along with Druid Daly. The clouds and threatening storm settled, leaving the night undisturbed except for the siren blaring in the distance.

Alan glanced to where the shifter's body had fallen. He was relieved to see the gods had returned the shifter to his human form of Jonas Wiley.

The sheriff would be here soon. They had their murderer and the village of Drumnadrochit would mourn the victims, but in time they would heal.

Blake bolted up right with a quick intake of breath. He stared at them with a look of utter confusion. "What the hell happened?"

Michaela left Alan's embrace and ran over to him, throwing her arms around him, nearly toppling him over in the process. "You're all right. You're safe."

"I…" Blake was at a loss for words as his arms encircled Michaela. He looked over her shoulder at

Alan.

"Are ye all right, healer?" Alan asked.

Michaela let go of Blake and turned to look at him. "Healer?" When he didn't answer she looked back to Blake again who seemed at loss for words.

"Let's go back to the house," Alan offered. "Let Blake regain his bearin's and then he'll explain."

Michaela didn't want to wait. He could see it in the way she glared at him, but she stood and didn't press for answers.

"I nearly forgot." Michaela's eyes widened and she turned toward the house. "Damon and Morton are locked inside."

"Morton is still alive." Relief laced Hyatt's words. "I thought for sure he dinnae make it."

"Ethan will be pleased to have his grandson back, too." Michaela nodded. "He was brave. He tried to stop Wiley from hurting me."

Hyatt and Alan exchanged a look of amazement. "Will wonders never cease," Hyatt proclaimed. "The eejit may have hope of becomin' a man after all." Hyatt turned toward Blake. "Ye could probably use a brandy or two, am I right?"

Blake looked dazed. He lifted his blood stained shirt and stared at his chest, unmarred and whole again. "I'll take the whole bottle if you don't mind."

Hyatt chuckled. "And here I thought ye were a tight arse Yank." Offering his hand, he pulled him to his feet and slapped him on the back.

Blake's gaze riveted to Hyatt, his eyes narrowing, but then the tension left him and he laughed, too.

Michaela turned her smile to Alan. "Thank you." She mouthed and blew him a kiss.

The heavens, but she was beautiful. She thanked him, but his motives to save Blake were purely selfish. With one word from him, Druid Daly could have saved Michaela.

Her face lit up like sunshine as she grinned at Blake, a smile that spoke of friendship. Yes, he could have saved Michaela with just one word, but the guilt of Blake's death would have killed her in the end.

He had already made his choice before her plea. Blake had the power to heal and with Michaela's promise to have the operation, she would survive.

Her body would change and shift with no ill effects. They all won this way. His gaze shifted uneasily to his brother. Their gazes locked. No, not all of them won, but somehow he knew Hyatt would be all right.

Epilogue

Six Months Later

Michaela felt like she'd been reborn. Perhaps in a sense she had. So much had happened in a short time. Falling in love, being threatened by a sociopathic shifter and getting married. She stared down at her wedding band, a platinum Celtic design that represented everlasting love.

Blake didn't turn out to be the shifter, but he was a healer. His magic touch fixed her, healed her in a way no surgeon could.

Jonas Wiley with all his evil intent actually did her a favor when he bit her. He was a trueborn shifter and his blood strengthened her, changed her DNA. She'd never have to worry about an aneurysm again. Her artery walls would never weaken and bulge with the threat of bursting.

She could shift shapes at will. It was a weird dreamlike experience, but she supposed in time she would get use to it. She would age like a shifter, giving her a long life with her husband, *her mate.* Funny, she never thought she'd like the possessive ring to that phrase.

Alan's lips came down on hers with a kiss. "What are ye thinkin', my bonny lassie?"

"How much I love you."

He stood behind her then and wrapped his arms around her. She leaned back against his broad chest, enjoying the warmth he radiated.

"Would ye look at how grand it is?" Alan sighed with wonder. A large white-columned mansion stood before them in majestic elegance with two large lions perched on both sides of the portico. It consisted of twenty-three rooms, including eight bedrooms and bathrooms. Or so the brochure boasted.

"Are you excited about seeing Graceland?" She turned in his arms.

"Oh aye." He glanced down at her. "Arenae ye?"

"I'm thrilled to be with you." She gave him a quick hug before taking his hand and lacing her fingers though his. They started up the walk, the sun beating down on them, the air humid, but neither of them noticed. "So what is your favorite Elvis song? No more guessing. I want to know."

His smile broadened to a grin. He hummed a few bars before he sang the words. A few tourists turned to look at him as his baritone voice echoed in the King's style.

Then she recognized the song: "*I want you, I need you, I love you.*" And didn't those words say it all. She tugged on his arm, halting their steps. She met his blue eyes the color of a gaslight flame, blazing with love for her. "I want you, too. I need you always."

"I love ye with all my heart, Michaela." He leaned down and brushed his full, sexy lips back and forth over hers. Man, beast, her mate. He shared the magic of the loch with her.

"I love you," she murmured and threw her arms around him. Graceland loomed larger than life with its beckoning gates, but for the moment it could wait.

A word about the author...

Karen Michelle Nutt resides in California with her husband, three fascinating children, and a houseful of demanding pets. Jack, her Chihuahua/Yorkshire terrier, is her writing buddy and sits long hours with her at the computer.

Whether your reading fancy is paranormal, historical, or time travel, all her stories capture the rich array of emotions that accompany the most fabulous human phenomena—falling in love.

Visit the author at:

http://www.kmnbooks.com

Stop by her blog for Monday interviews, chats, and contests at:

http://kmnbooks.blogspot.com